THE SECRET LIFE OF JOHN TAYOR

Willowbank Farm

Neil Elson

Elson books

In loving memory of my dear mother who would often ask, "Have you finished that book yet?" Well Mum, I finally did it! Rest in peace.

CONTENTS

INTRODUCTION

With the bank breathing down his neck John Taylor (farmer) needs cash and he needs it now. He's determined not to see his way of life slip through his fingers and his beloved farm end up as some rich mans second home.

With the help of his long suffering wife and his country snob of a mother, who frankly couldn't possibly have her comfortable life in the countryside disrupted by the the trivial inconvenience of lack of money, John embarks on an idea so radical that no self respecting farmer would ever contemplate. Yet this risky, taboo venture may just be the solution, but no one could envisage the inevitable consequences, forcing his life and those around him into a tangled web of unexpected passions and secrets, with a sprinkling of mild adult themes upon a bed of humour.

Thought provoking, with hints of giggles throughout to full on chuckles and outright laughter, this first book in the series delves into the lives of the inhabitants of sleepy Willowbank Farm.

Prologue

It was strange, if that was the right word, to look upon her after all these years, to think back to lost beauty. But for John her attraction had never wavered. Lucy was different, she had captured his heart from the very beginning. He sighed, it seemed so long ago now, yet here they were, alone again, tucked away from view, hidden within the peace and serenity of the old weathered barn.

He looked on, his eyes tracing the curves of her body. Lucy was older now, her hair, what little she had, showed signs of neglect. Matted, unkempt, as it sprouted from the top of her head. Her figure portrayed her age-somewhat bony with slightly protruding hips. Yet she seemed willing, that much he was certain of as he found himself running his fingers around her entrance. Something he wouldn't necessarily complain about, but on this occasion the whole experience was altogether rather off-putting as her offensive odour steadily drifted up through his inflamed nostrils forcing his eyes to well up. Tears of discomfort trickled down his face as his hand ventured further, exploring the inner workings of the older female anatomy.

In truth he found little pleasure in what he was about to do – but needs must and with the rearrangement of his body he forced himself to go on.

"There, there, girl, steady on."

His words seemed of little comfort as Lucy turned her head and let out a barn-shuddering bellow, a sound so strong it immediately dislodged a gathering of chattering sparrows who had been watching from above. They scattered, flapping their wings in a state of confusion, narrowly avoiding colliding with large oak beams before finally deciding to return to their exact same spots.

John reluctantly found himself feeling his way along a rotting length of placenta, as every withdrawal brought a constant supply of foul-smelling blood-stained mucous, the likes of which no human being should ever be subjected to, but he had to go on. Lucy's health depended upon it. He tried to look away, sheltering his face from the worst of the onslaught and noted the sparrows had wisely decided enough was enough as the pungent smell rose up, infecting their simple brains and telling them that it was perhaps a good time to leave.

He was aware of the fact that Lucy's internal body heat had been slowly cooking this unwanted outer casing in which her calf had happily grown, but for reasons unknown had conveniently left it behind when entering the world some days before. This in itself wasn't an unusual occurrence but it was something that needed attention.

A sudden wave of nausea ran through John's weary body as the red-stained fluid clung to the hairs of his chest; his whole arm was now inside Lucy's bony frame as he explored a partially open cervix. He gently ran his fingers around the opening, encouraging it to enlarge. Time stood still, how long he was unsure but eventually his confidence was enough for him to gently pull the dying tissue from its slumbering state, allowing the length of afterbirth to slowly squeeze towards freedom.

Lucy sensed the time was right to rid herself of this embarrassing stench, and with an overpowering urge gave one almighty push, forcing a pus-filled ball the size of John's fist to hurtle past his hand and up along his arm before hitting his chest. With little time to react it ricocheted off his body and fell to the barn floor like a floundering squid.

"That's better, aye girl." he said with relief as he drew his arm back and forth, bringing the last dregs of placenta from the murky depths of her body.

Lucy stood, tail half-cocked, showing off her most private parts that now resembled the over-inflated inner tube of a wheelbarrow, her entrance quivering in the welcome breeze as John opened the barn door allowing much-needed fresh air to enter the stale interior. With one almighty toss of her head the old cow sent the metal bars of her restraints rattling in their sockets, demanding she be let loose. John muttered words of comfort and then gave her a quick rub between the ears to show there were no hard feelings before letting her go.

He stood to one side and watched the rather bandy-legged old girl walk to freedom, briefly glancing back at her master as if to say, don't you ever do that to me again! Then, as if to protest against her supposed ill treatment, she let rip, channelling a rather loud unladylike amount of built-up gas which echoed around the building, her nose leading the way as if she were royalty and it was quite the done thing to fart in someone's face without apologising. She waddled off in search of her long departed companions. John made his way over to the doorway and leant up against the frame, his body desperately trying to dislodge the discomfort that seemed to lie deep down within his lungs.

Lucy had gone, virtually out of sight having broken into a steady trot forcing her to occasionally backfire as if she were a badly tuned motorbike, but she didn't seem to care. Her only concern was her waiting grass.

John wiped the sweat from his forehead, welcoming the cool early spring breeze that whipped up around the buildings as he gazed upon the place he adored. A farm he proudly worked alongside Mother Nature – her long gentle arms wrapping around the land that he loved. He sighed, for his meeting with the bank later that day would almost certainly confirm his financial fears. Yes, he knew how things were, he wasn't a fool. Of course the farm had been in tight situations in the past – his grandfather and his father would, if they were still alive, certainly confess to that – but this felt different. It wasn't just the weather any more and God knows that was up the creek. Global warming, they said. No, as a farmer you adapted to those sorts of things, even though they were frustrating at times, but at least you did have control of your decision making. It was the things you had little or no way of altering that hurt the most.

His mind drifted to ever-changing government

policies, world markets and then, he almost raised a weak smile, even the cost of a new pair of wellies! He clenched his fists in frustration – bureaucratic paperwork, you can damn that to hell! Could they not understand all he wanted to do was farm, but that, apparently, wasn't enough any more. It didn't seem important that he cared passionately about the land, his animals, the wildlife and their habitats, anything in fact that walked, crawled or flew upon his little patch of paradise. Things were changing. People's attitude towards men like him who were seen to be doing the right thing had gathered pace, but would this be enough to help him?

He went to walk away and felt his upper body crackle in protest at being subjected to the increasing warmth of the sun, her rays baking the blood-stained slime to his exposed skin. "Great!" he grumbled, then shook his head in utter annoyance and cursed under his breath as he headed towards the farmhouse. This wasn't how it should be, he thought, but then he was just one man against the rest of the world.

Chapter 1

The peace and tranquillity of the countryside cracked under the ever demanding voice of John's mother hollering across the lawn. "A little towards the barn! No, not that barn, you oaf – the big one. Yes, that's better, now a bit to the left. No, that's right. George, really, what I have to put up with! Now where's he gone? George! George!" Her voice squealed like a dog caught by an electric fence as he finally reappeared from behind a large bush. "What have you been doing?"

The old gardener fumbled with the zipper on his pants. "Oh dear Lord, could you not wait until your designated break?"

"Bloody woman."

"I can read your lips, George, my eyesight isn't that bad yet. Now a tiny bit to the right. Perfect! Plant, George!" Sylvia had just turned her head back to the comfort of the recliner when John wandered over.

"Good morning, Mother."

"Is it! How can one enjoy such a pleasant day when surrounded by incompetent staff?"

"And how is George this morning?"

"Don't go there, John, I'm in no mood."

"Wrong time of the month?"

"Don't be so crude, do I look like I still suffer from

the growing pains of womanhood? Permanently bad-tempered, you should know that, so let's cut the crap and get on to why you're here, or have you just come to see if I'm dead yet so you can claim your inheritance, what little is left?"

"You *are* in a bad mood."

His mother glared at him. "It could get worse – I could decide to leave everything to the Cats Society."

"You don't like cats, Mother."

"That's beside the point. So what did you come round for?"

"Just to remind you that the fête meeting is forthcoming, one week to be precise. The vicar and our dear old Miss Goodman will be there."

"Good grief, is she still alive?"

"You know she is."

"The woman's a complete arse, why she can't get a proper hearing aid I will never know. It's like trying to communicate with the local council; you can talk until you're blue in the face with that lot and still get nowhere."

"I'd have agree with you there, Mother, but she does have a heart of gold."

"Really? How she ever gets anything organised I'll never know, and I suppose we'll have to put up with the same old things as usual."

"It's a small village fête, Mother, not a grand country

show."

"Precisely. Same old things."

"If you must know, the vicar's even persuaded a number of Sisters from Saint Catherine's to come and accompany him on the banjo."

"Lord help us. Is that the best he can do?"

"It's a fête, Mother."

"So you keep saying. Perhaps the Sisters could be persuaded to do the cancan, that should liven things up a little, might even persuade me to come."

"You're already here, Mother."

"More's the pity. I can't understand why it always needs to be held here every year – surely the vicar could have it at the vicarage for a change?"

"Tradition, Mother, it's been held here since the war. Grandfather was kind enough to offer the use of the gardens all those years ago and we should continue in his good name."

"Poppycock! You know why he offered the gardens, don't you?"

"Yes, of course, because he was a pillar of society. The landed gentry, that's what they did in those days, show willing to the people of the parish."

"Load of old tosh, dear. It was because he was the only one who still had a lawn. Every other poor blighter had been made to dig for victory, even the cricket pitch went down to vegetables." She tapped the side of her nose. "Your grandfather knew the right people, slid them the odd steak or brace of pheasant. He was a canny old rodent, your grandfather. I could tell a tale or two about his crooked deals, even had a mistress down on the coast. Didn't know that, did you? Good grief, what is he doing now?"

"Who?"

"George, that's who." She waved a finger in the direction of the vegetable plot. "I do believe the man's lost his marbles."

John turned to see George, his trousers around his ankles, sitting on freshly dug soil.

"Move out the way, I can't see properly. Dear God, he's half naked. Heavens above, do something, John. If the women of the WI should happen to come calling I'll be the laughing stock of the village." With a wave of a stiff hand John was ushered out onto the lawn. "Well, what are you waiting for? The man's clearly gone mad."

"Yes, Mother."

"George?" John stood a short distance away, not wishing to view the ancient remains of an elderly gentleman's long-lost manhood, but was surprised to see a rather impressive soiled lump basking in the sunlight.

"Ah, sir, 'tis you. Did proper give me a fright, you did."

"Apologies, George."

"Be no need for that, sir, 'tis your garden after all."

"Quite right, George." The old man said nothing more, his whole concentration now seemingly channelling towards the job in hand. "George?"

"Yes, sir?"

"This may seem like a silly question, but what on earth are you up to?"

"Ah, be something I'd be wanting to try out for a while now."

John waited for the man to finish his sentence but after a few moments of silence realised he was done. "And?" he prompted.

"What be that, sir?"

"What have you been keen to do?"

"Ah, yes, be an old Victorian method, sir."

"Victorian?"

"Yes, sir. For testing the soil, sir."

George shuffled his position as he tried to rearrange his rapidly numbing buttocks. "They were clever buggers, them there Victorian farmers. Used to pull their trousers down in the middle of the field and sit on the bare earth testing the temperature, sir. If it be warm enough, they could start planting the crops. Me missus gave me a book for Christmas, *Farm and Gardens the Victorian Way*, real good read it be."

"And?"

George now looked puzzled by John's question. "And

what, sir?"

"Is the soil warm enough?"

The old man thought about this. "Don't rightly know, sir, having never done it before."

"There's a problem, George, for as far as I can see you actually have no way of telling one way or the other, having never spoken to a Victorian farmer or taken any advice on the matter." John was met by a thought-provoking silence.

"Umm, could be right there, sir. Hadn't thought of that."

"Perhaps we should buy you a thermometer, much less revealing for all concerned, don't you think?"

"Ah, maybe right, sir. Trouble being I be stuck, me buttocks be proper wedged well and truly, sir, and I don't like to say but me old toggles be a bit chilly too, like frozen Brussels sprouts they be. Kind of you if you'd give me a hand?"

John couldn't see any other way out so found himself reluctantly holding out his hand while trying to avert his eyes away from George's lower half. With one almighty pull the old man's bottom suddenly popped out of its possible early grave. John's mother watched on from a distance as George waddled back and forth along the carrots, his backside swaying to the rhythm of a flapping set of rather impressive crown jewels.

"Don't worry yourself, sir, be me legs, see, not much feeling. I'll be all right in a jiffy." His attempt at pulling his trousers up saw him overbalance and head at speed towards the potting shed. "Be all right, sir. Madam."

Samantha appeared from around the corner just in time to catch the full benefit of what George had to offer. "George," she replied with a wave, unable to hide a smile as he disappeared out of sight.

Sam stopped by her husband. "Who said the countryside was boring!"

"Sorry about that, George is trying out a new method of soil testing."

"Really?" Sam could hardly restrain herself.

"Yes, but I'm afraid it needs improvements."

"John!"

His name shot through the air like an arrow. "Damn, my mother. I forgot about her."

Sam gazed over to the occupied sun lounger. "Perhaps I could go and see her."

"If you could, I've got the bank stuff to sort out."

"How wonderful to see you Samantha," said Sylvia as she approached.

"Sylvia."

"I must apologise for my gardener's unacceptable behaviour, can't imagine what's got into him. Most embarrassing."

"Apparently he was testing the soil," she replied.

"What, with his backside? The man's a complete idiot,

next he'll be using his dingly dangle as a dibber."

Sam just couldn't help herself as her laughter took hold. "Dingly dangle dibber!"

The older woman peered at her, straight-faced. "And pray tell me what else does one call it?"

"Well, quite a lot actually."

"Is that so? I fear most would be far too vulgar for general chitchat. Such an inconvenience of a man's body I've always found, my dear. Charlie, God rest his soul, would insist on trying to stick it in the most inappropriate places, but a good sharp slap with a ruler put paid to that sort of thing, I can tell you." She leant forward eyeing the garden for listening ears. "Word of warning, my dear – these country men can be such crude individuals at times. I blame it on all the fresh air, but enough of that I feel quite parched after being compelled to view half-naked relics roaming around my garden, won't you come in for tea?"

Chapter 2

"What time's your appointment?" Samantha stood at the kitchen sink, hands submerged in a bowl of soapsuds as her irate husband pushed back his chair and grumbled under his breath.

"Two!"

She reluctantly turned around, wiped her hands on a towel resting across the back of a chair and stared at him with a feeling of dread. There he was, surrounded by a sea of past farm accounts, screwed up receipts and unpaid bills. The poor man's eyes seemed to be attempting to make sense of it all, yet his glazed look reminded her of a rabbit sat in the middle of the road with a juggernaut bearing down.

"You'd better get on, it doesn't hurt to be slightly early."

"I suppose so." He seemed to wait for some sort of reassurance, perhaps a fragment of support towards life in general. His body language and that facial expression warned Sam he was almost certainly itching for some sort of debate, an argument, something to match his mood. She wisely decided to say nothing.

Realising his wife wasn't going to bite, John gathered up the surrounding paperwork and unashamedly stuffed it all into a tatty carrier bag. Ignoring her, he turned and left the room. His spirits lifted by the warming sun upon his cheeks the moment he stepped out of the back entrance of their imposing six-bedroom farmhouse. He walked into the small courtyard, its smooth cobblestones worn down by past inhabitants, John's ancestors, many of whom had carved a good and respectable living from the surrounding acres. Now it was his turn to work those same fields, his turn to carry on the family legacy. He owed it not just to their memory but to his own boy, Luke. His heart went out to those farming families who had children who were not remotely interested in taking on their farms.

He'd been plunged headfirst into farm ownership at the tender age of nineteen. There were those who said he would crash and burn, waiting patiently like vultures to swoop in and pick on his bones, but he'd shown them, by Christ he'd shown them, and prospered – but not without the help of two good women. He pictured Sam and his beloved mother … yes, he owed them so much. He was barely halfway across the courtyard when his thoughts were interrupted by a familiar face.

"Ah, Mr Taylor? I say, John."

Damn. He could do nothing but walk towards the ever helpful Miss Goodman, almost certainly a direct descendant of a wiry old weasel. Tall in stature, a pointed noise that cried out for a set of whiskers and a body curved through old age, yet a woman with a heart of gold. But on this occasion she was an unwanted distraction to his quest to arrive at the bank on time.

With unusually small pigeon steps and waving a

white sheet of paper in her hand the old bird made a beeline for him, leaving little options for escape. John couldn't help muttering a few unpleasant words under his breath before smiling politely and raising his hand in a gesture of unwilling good humour.

"Miss Goodman, how nice to see you. Are you well?" he said, attempting to hide his frustration.

"Very good to see you, Mr Taylor, and I'm quite fine if you have a mind to ask."

He *had* asked, but clearly she hadn't heard, and without giving him a chance to make his apologies she careered into her day's mission.

"Now, Mr Taylor, village fête, we really do need to discuss a number of items before the meeting."

John watched as she tapped the side of her head then fumbled with her sheet of paper indicating her reluctance to move from the spot until she had some answers.

"I know you're a busy man, you farmers are always on the go, but it's only a short time away, can't emphasise enough the urgency, Mr Taylor." She tapped the side of her head once again. "Can't leave things to the last minute now, can we?"

John saw his chance as she paused briefly. "I don't like to be impolite Miss Goodman, but I am rather busy at the moment, you see ..."

He was cut short by the old dear turning her head to one side and tapping continuously as if she had a stray insect crawling around in her ear.

"Sorry, Mr Taylor. Hearing aid, wretched thing, keeps cutting out on me. Jolly inconvenient."

John attempted to raise his voice to a level she could hopefully hear. "I said I'm rather busy at the moment, meeting in town, two o'clock." He pointed to his watch for emphasis.

"Really? Two already? How time flies." She again proceeded to fumble with her earpiece, now hitting the device with some force.

John shook his head in annoyance. "No. I have to be in town by two o'clock – it's not two yet."

The words were clearly not registering. "Never mind." His attention drifted out across the main yard, noting at first the sound of growling dogs. Slightly concerned, he watched for possible movement and wasn't disappointed when confronted by the sight of Kim, the farm's black and white geriatric collie slowly emerging from behind the old cart shed. Her head was crouched low to the ground, her arse stuck skyward, as she inched her way backward before stopping to take a well-earned break to reposition her grip on the contents wedged in her jaw.

Miss Goodman had somehow managed to reinstate the working functions of her hearing aid and was now prattling on, seemly able to talk continuously without the need to pause between sentences. John nodded every so often, but in truth had become more interested in what was happening behind her back.

"I thought Jennifer Rickey and that ghastly husband

of hers could man the book stall, frankly he's not much good for anything else. Between you and me I really don't like the way his eyes meet in the middle of his face, far too close for my liking. My dear mother always used to say you can tell a man's intentions by the way his eyes look and I'm afraid his don't pass the test. The man can't be trusted, books will do him just fine and Mr Holdsworth has promised to bring his ferrets along again. Lord, let's hope he keeps them under control this time, we certainly don't want a repeat of last year – poor Mrs Woodley, we had to buy her a new pair of stockings you know, and I'm sorry to say she won't be coming again, I believe the memories are still far too painful."

John vaguely noticed Miss Goodman effortlessly run into mindless details, but with great relief he seemed to have mastered the art of nodding at appropriate times while taking little or no interest in what she was saying. Kim could now be seen forcefully yanking at a length of material that stretched out like a highly tensioned rope a good two metres long. It hovered, smeared in cow muck with a fine covering of yard dust while her tail lashed from side to side, showing determination towards the job in hand. Then, from the shadows, the nose of a Jack Russell slowly appeared, eagerly determined in his quest for farm superiority but on this occasion failing to hold ground against the power of a much larger, experienced dog. The smaller canine's unproven techniques found him continually being pulled through the dry dirt but still happy to play tug-of-war with the discarded placenta of a freshly calved bony old cow.

John glanced across in amusement while Miss Goodman paused momentarily, totally unaware of the spectacle presenting itself only ten or so metres behind her. Luckily for all involved, her temperamental hearing device presented only limited coverage at the best of times, ensuring total silence from a two-metre radius. However, now the situation had become a rather more complicated affair as the two dogs appeared to have reached a common ground, blocking the only way out with a length of rotting material clearly stretched to its limits and waiting for the inevitable consequences brought on by such tension. Few could argue the dogs' determination, but it seemed a lack of common sense was also to play its hand as without warning they parted company with such speed it sent an overconfident terrier somersaulting through the air, closely followed by a length of stench intent on inflicting serious pain and discomfort to anyone or anything that had the misfortune to come into contact with it. Kim, however, had played this game before, and anticipating the final tear she could be seen rocking safely back upon her rear end thus securing an ample amount of chewing material to keep her occupied for days. Unlike John's newly acquired young terrier he'd affectionately named 'Pup' (for reasons his wife couldn't understand), who'd caught the full force of his share, ricocheting off his right ear while being showered with a mucous-filled object the size of a tennis ball.

Miss Goodman had now developed problems of her own, her head once more propped to one side as she battled against a growing high-pitched sound radiating from her ear piece.

John studied the old woman's actions with concern as she gave it one almighty swipe with the side of her hand, forcing it to crackle and spit in protest while its malfunctioning airwaves scanned the surrounding area, finally picking up a stray signal from a passing tractor radio. Her whole body shook in utter horror through the onslaught of mind-destroying heavy metal music, the likes of which no one of her considerable age should ever be subjected to. Her eyelids flickered against her now damaged nerve endings as the solid beat continued to blast away at full force. Protesting violently, her only option was to rip the offending article from her ear before the wailing decibels of Black Sabbath had her falling to the ground. With shaking fingers she latched on to the piece of man-made rubbish and threw it in the air where it landed upon the hardened cobblestones, buzzing like some demented pollen-induced bee.

"Wretched thing," she announced. "Such a ghastly contraption!"

John could hear the faint sound of Ozzy Osbourne's cry for help, just before a surprisingly strong elderly foot stamped on it in sheer anger, laying the poor rock star to rest amongst the muck of passing soiled wellington boots.

"Another day, Mr Taylor, can't hear a thing."

She turned just as the last piece of rotting afterbirth seemed to drag itself out of sight. "Another day ..."

Her voice trailed off as she shuffled across the yard, muttering about man's engineering incapabilities before finally arriving at her olive green Morris Minor. She forcefully opened the door, jumped in, and rammed it into gear before speeding off up the driveway as if her life depended on it.

John found himself all alone, the two dogs nowhere to be seen, almost certainly holed up in a quiet corner chewing their prizes. A quick glance at his watch confirmed his fears – he was running late. With little time to think, he raced over to the cart shed and unbolted two massive oak doors. As the light flooded in he rested his eyes upon a vehicle no self-respecting police force would ever tolerate travelling upon their roads, but there she was, the farm's relic of a Land Rover. There she stood in all her glory, with the willingness of a Ferrari, yet the body of a chain smoker.

He jumped in, turned the key and counted up to nine, ten and start. At first she struggled in her attempt to turn over, labouring with every pull in an attempt to fire into life. The inner workings of her antiquated motor rattled the pistons, somehow persuaded them to gallantly supply that all-important injection of nicotine fuel into her blocked arteries, allowing just enough of a fix to kick-start her into action. Drawing on the first fag of the day, her whole body spluttered and coughed, inhaling self-imposed jet black smoke that chuffed out of her rear end. John slammed the old girl into reverse and waited for the wearing cogs to connect as a grinding loud clunk saw her exit at speed. John desperately tried to see through a cracked rear window – its sliding function lost years past by the overwhelming competition of sprouting grass and moss that now blighted its runners.

Emerging out of the smoke he persuaded the oil-immersed dinosaur to trundle across the gravel and eventually onto the main driveway. He sat rocking back and forth in rhythm with the clanking sounds of the engine while the mist slowly cleared from the cab, allowing the last flecks of soot to settle on the vacant seats beside him. With bloodshot eyes and some annoyance he spotted two rather concerned farm dogs.

"Damn it!" he cursed.

Still some distance away, they both sat watching and waiting – there was no way Kim was going to miss out on a jolly trip in the Land Rover.

"Damn and blast!"

John weighed up his options; he knew Kim wouldn't give in without a fight. Where the Land Rover went, she went. It was her God-given right as head dog, but the thought of taking two barking canines to a town environment filled him with concern.

Kim channelled her sights along her pointed nose, fixing her razor-sharp vision straight at the rocking vehicle and inspecting its every move as her master perched himself on the edge of his seat. He gripped the oversized steering wheel, almost suffocated by an air of bloody minded determination that swept through the cab like a winter breeze. But there they were, blocking his way out, sitting patiently scanning

THE SECRET LIFE OF JOHN TAYLOR

possible exit routes of which there were three.

Pup was placed on a less than favoured route. Unable to keep the required concentration, he began rolling around on his back attempting to rid himself of the unwanted smell of an exploded puss ball, only occasionally glancing up to see if the enemy was on its way. Careful not to attract attention, John surreptitiously looked in the direction of the open grass lawn, but Kim was already two steps ahead, glancing sideways at the same patch of green turf calculating the time, distance and speed required to out-flank a tired, clapped-out old farm vehicle. Pup was now licking his balls, only too pleased to have something meaningful to do while awaiting further instructions.

Selecting first gear, John enabled four badly worn tyres to gently roll across the gravel. Kim sat firm, the tip of her tail twitching with alertness as she watched the Land Rover inch ever nearer. Pup sensed an air of tension flow over his dampened testicles as he lay with his legs apart, collecting much-needed warmth from the drying sun. Selecting second, John rattled his way forward, choosing the relatively safe conditions of the driveway. Slowly picking up speed he concentrated all his thoughts upon his chosen route, his normal exit temporarily out of the question and too obvious, too easy for an ambush. Kim rolled her tongue along the outside of her lips, her ageing body tensioned like a coiled spring ready to pounce at any moment.

John made his decision. Right or wrong he would go out wide, head for the third and rarely used exit, push past the smooth free-wheeling ley of cut lawns and out into the rough, hoping to catch the dogs by surprise. Conditions were unpredictable; speed would be compromised given the undulating ground, but Kim's attack would also be hampered. Any hesitation at this point would certainly allow the dogs to gain an advantage, but he had to stay focused – once he left the easy going of the gravel it would be every man (or dog) for themselves.

The pressure was now showing – a quick glance in the lopsided mirror revealed beads of sweat dotted precariously upon his forehead. He wiped them away, for he dared not be hampered by them trickling into his eyes. Kim quickly reassessed the proceedings unfolding in front of her, watching intensely for any slight change in direction, waiting for that inevitable surge of power to tell her for certain her master was on the attack. Then without warning her mind suddenly clicked like a third sense as she heard the foot of a desperate man slam down on a peddle demanding it to connect with the floor. Smoke punched its way out of every crack and crevice, black tar like oil pouring from the sagging exhaust as the Land Rover veered off to the left.

Kim broke ranks, signalling Pup to attack, ordering the inexperienced Jack Russell to chase at will. She took to the striped lawn, picking up speed. John peered through the open side window as his transport coughed and spluttered its way across the grass before hitting the rough with a sudden unexpected jolt. Failing to grip, the rear end slid, and like an industrial lawnmower she forced her way through the high grass, thrashing hardened grass heads against the radiator mesh.

A quick check in the mirror revealed the two dogs chasing for all their worth, Kim's arthritic hips surprisingly showing no signs of hindrance as she forged on, tongue flapping against her open jaw. Pup sensibly followed the tyre marks but the shredded grass stalks still played havoc with his private parts. A split-second decision saw the Land Rover change its mind and fall back onto the mowed lawns. John couldn't help let out an early victory chuckle – his plan had worked! Did they really think he would risk running through an opening that hadn't been used for a good twenty years or more?

Kim was flagging, stumbling over the long grass, but Pup was nowhere to be seen; perhaps he'd become entangled in the matted grass? John picked up speed. Of course he felt sorry for his old friend, yet with such growing confidence his ego had got the better of him. The main gate was now in sight – with good judgement he would be out onto the open lane in no time. Kim would stop; she'd been taught to respect the farm's boundaries and would never cross without instruction. One final glance in the mirror confirmed his victory – Kim wasn't going to make it, her legs had almost buckled beneath her ageing frame. It wouldn't hurt her to be left behind just this once. Without thinking he looked towards the main entrance just in time to see a rather worried, shaking Jack Russell sitting in the gateway doing as he was told, but wondering if it may not be such a good idea. His ears pricked up upon hearing the squeal of badly maintained brakes thundering towards him as the Land Rover slid to a shuddering halt only feet from his now contracted testicles.

Moments later John felt a skull-crushing thud to the rear. His heart flipped, raising his fear for a willing old companion. Jumping out, with guilt threatening to engulf his whole presence, he ran to the back. Expecting the worst he found Kim desperately trying to hang on to the closed tailgate, her front paws struggling to cling on to something, anything in a pathetic attempt to try and control a pair of legs jostling for some kind of grip.

John saw there was little energy left as she slowly started to slide to the ground. Once she would have jumped clean into the back, but not now – old age and arthritis had put paid to that. He urged his hands forwards, placing them gently beneath Kim's back end, taking the weight that now threatened to wipe out any self-respect she might have and lowered her to the ground. There was no sign of resentment, no bitterness, and no anger of any sort, just her warm joyful eyes peering back at him. She was exhausted but still glowed with total devotion towards their unbroken friendship, a bond that had lasted almost fourteen years. Such betrayal by one man could only be forgiven by such a devoted dog. Pup had a lot to learn; perhaps he would never quite get there but that was fine. John let the tailgate down and with overwhelming guilt lifted his friend into the back, placed his hands either side of her head and gave her a good rub. The response was uncontrollable excitement – how could he ever break that trust?

"Sorry girl." He leant forward to give her a kiss, a token of his acknowledgement to her unbelievable love, but quickly drew back as the overpowering smell upon her breath of rotting placenta stung the inner workings of his eyes.

"Whoa, another time, aye girl?"

Chapter 3

The bank stood like some impregnable German fortress, its vast tasteless exterior fronted by two imposing marble pillars. John's father had used the bank's facilities well, securing finance to tide the farm over until the season's fortunes changed in his favour, bringing with it a windfall of much-needed cash to repay the bank to everyone's satisfaction. In this John was no different, having used these same methods of business since his untimely inheritance of the farm. Mr Harold Pottenger, the bank's long-standing manager had served them both well through the good times, but most importantly through the bad times. He had guided a young John Taylor into safe and trusted directions, securing finance when needed, but cautioning against borrowing when appropriate. His help in these matters had been invaluable and so it was that John now entered the vast expanse that housed the very heart of this large bank with the hope of a satisfactory outcome to his problem.

His appointment was scheduled for two o'clock. Given his hold-ups, he had made reasonable time and now found himself with a good ten minutes or so to spare. Making his way over to the 'Enquiries' counter, the enormity of his meeting began to play heavily on his mind. Up until now he had been too busy to worry about its possible implications, but if a satisfactory solution could not be found … No, he wouldn't think like that. He tried to dislodge a solid lump in his throat, but only managed to aggravate a sinking gut-ache brought on by the thought of the unknown, the 'what if'. He rang the bell for assistance.

"Good morning, sir." A happy smile glowed from behind the glass. "Oh, silly me, it's the afternoon already. Shall we start again? My mind is all of a flutter today. Time just flies by when you're enjoying yourself." The young man behind the counter shuffled a pile of papers then knocked their ends down upon his desk, forcing them into some sort of orderly manner. "There we are. Now, how can I be of assistance?"

John peered through the glass. "I have an appointment to see the bank manager. My name is Mr Taylor. Two o'clock."

"Ah, let me see, sir." The young man tapped his keyboard and then looked up to focus on the bright screen. "Mr Taylor … Taylor."

John watched on as he ran his sights slowly down the list of named appointments.

"Ah, yes, Mr Taylor, two o'clock, to see Mr Nesbit."

John immediately looked rather puzzled. "No, Mr Pottenger, Harold Pottenger."

The young man shook his head, clearly knowing something John didn't. "I'm afraid Mr Pottenger has been taken ill. Mr Nesbit has stepped in for the time being." He could now see John's concern. "Oh dear, they clearly didn't inform you. Apologies for that."

This wasn't good news. John really needed to see his old friend Harold, not a complete stranger. Discussing your private affairs was hard enough, but to someone you had never met before was quite another matter entirely. John moved his head slightly closer to the glass. "Umm ..."

"Yes, sir?"

"Do you mind me asking, just out of interest, you understand, what's this Mr Nesbit like?"

The young man thought awhile before answering, then quickly looked around to ensure no one was listening. He eased himself towards the front of his seat, meeting John face to face. "Well, I'm not one to gossip, you understand, and this may just be rumours, and you know you should never believe what other people say, but ..." he paused for a second or two, glancing around once again, "but, I believe, from what I've heard, he may be a little ..." his head shot from side to side as he nervously played with his pen. "Let's say a bit full of himself, yes, that's the word, a little ..." Another bank employee walked past, forcing him to fumble with his papers. "I've said too much, Mr Taylor. Very unprofessional of me."

John could see he wanted to say more, but chose not to push the subject any further. He was just about to thank him for his assistance when he saw the young man's lips curiously move as he whispered, "Three times, Mr Taylor," with a nod of his head.

John looked a little confused. "Three what?" he asked.

Lowering his voice even further, the young man leant right up against the glass. "Divorced, Mr Taylor, three times. Just rumour you understand, but that's what they're saying. Well, says it all, doesn't it." His lips tightened as if he'd just tasted pure lemon juice, before quickly pulling himself away. "I mustn't say any more." Then he promptly sat upright in his chair, pulling his composure back to an efficient-looking bank employee busying himself with the unnecessary task of tidying of his desk. He eventually looked up again. "But don't you worry yourself, Mr Taylor, you'll be just dandy." Raising a rather limp hand he added, "Please take a seat and I'll call you when he's ready."

John was just about to say he'd prefer to wait until Harold Pottenger was over his sickness and abandon his quest to seek much-needed finance, but then thought better of it. He wasn't sure how long Harold would be away. His own needs were becoming more important than that of an elderly bank manager's health. That was wrong, he thought, and cursed himself for being so unsympathetic, but he needed cash and the sooner the better. That's all there was to it. Yes, he could last a while longer yet but there were bills that would need seeing to over the next three or four months and as it stood he would have trouble paying them. So if he had to deal with a complete stranger, then so be it. He wasn't happy about it but as he saw it he had little choice.

Reluctantly he moved away, thanking the nice young man and somewhat pleased they were separated by a wall of glass as he was sure he was that way minded. Not that that had anything to do with anything – it was just he hadn't met too many of his kind before. He saw very few people on the farm as it was, so casually bumping into a ... one of those men roaming about the countryside would be pretty remote. Not that they weren't allowed to have access to the countryside, he didn't mean it like that, but then he really wasn't sure what he meant. His mind wandered back in time … come to think of it, he *had* come across a vet that had tendencies in that direction and would insist on bringing his extremely young playmate along on his visits. But that was quite a few years ago now.

His thoughts were interrupted by a tap on the glass. He turned to see the nice young man waving his rather off-putting drooped hand in his direction.

"He's running a bit late, Mr Taylor. I'll call you."

John raised his hand in acknowledgement, making a conscious effort to show his true red-blooded male determination towards this simple gesture. He scanned the foyer and opted to make his way across to a row of uninspiring grey upholstered chairs. Two seats along and beavering away with a set of knitting needles sat a wrinkly specimen from the older generation, busy producing what looked like a baby's jumper. John smiled politely.

"Good afternoon."

"Yes, it is." She almost spat the words out, far too consumed in her stitches to have the courtesy to look up and make eye contact.

John turned away, contemplating the comments of the nice young man. The last thing he needed right now was the Grim Reaper of a bank manager breathing down his neck. He looked at the old woman again, who seemed to be attacking her project with a single-minded determination as the needles rattled their way along the rows at an alarming speed. He averted his gaze to scan the vast open room, and soon found himself people-watching to pass the time away. This always fascinated him – he would find himself wondering what they might do for a living, where they had just come from, where they were going after their dealings with the bank. Mindless things, nothing nosy or perverted, just curiosity really.

He watched as the queue built up. There were the normal labourers, perhaps on a late lunch break, dressed down in their working clothes, coated in a mix of mud and cement powder. A woman with an unruly child that seemed intent on disobeying every order given, sprawled across the highly polished floor screaming its head off. And of course the normal sprinkling of pensioners, sadly reduced in size by the unforgiving hand of old age, some bent over to such an extent that it made communicating to a cashier almost impossible. Then there was the occasional scantily dressed young lady, just like the one walking in at that very moment.

John immediately found himself drifting into an awkward stare typical of men his age when confronted by such a perfectly formed female body, his eyes unknowingly locked in on his intended subject where they refused to budge. God! There she was, showing off everything but her PIN number. He studied her whole form of unblemished, silky smooth skin. That sensuous flowing light brown hair, waistline highlighted by frayed cut-off jeans that stretched across the contours of the most erotic arse John had ever seen. Why were those curves sending him to a place where he ought not to be?

He shuffled uneasily in his chair, noticing the old woman giving him a wary look of disapproval. He would ignore her – she couldn't give him a civil reply earlier. His eyes wandered back to the girl he had suddenly fallen in love with. She'd reached the back of the queue and seemed happy to wait her turn while being silently undressed by every red-blooded male in the building except for the nice young man who seemed more content in eyeing up tough workmen in hard hats and hobnailed boots.

She'd become a pleasant diversion, drawing John's thoughts away from what possibly lay ahead. He returned his gaze to her time and time again, watching her as she slowly made her way towards the front of the queue, finally taking her turn as the flashing light of cashier two beckoned her to the counter. He watched as she worked her way through various envelopes, the cashier politely opening each one in turn, counting out the money within and registering the amount. Nothing unusual about that, John thought, his eyes now running up her slender legs. The cashier handed back the empty envelopes and wished her a good day as she smiled and moved her lips before preparing to receive her next customer.

The young lady flexed her buttocks to the delight of all the men waiting their turn, and with her transaction completed, turned and started to walk away. John quickly averted his eyes, lowering his head in an attempt to disguise the fact that he, like many others, had been staring at her since she appeared. Focusing directly on the floor in front of him, he listened to the sharp sound of stilettos making their way across the tiles. He'd made a decision; he would wait until she'd passed, give her a few seconds to make her way towards the door, then sneak one last glimpse at this utterly divine creature, for he was sure that once she made her way out into the street he would sadly never see her again.

He heard the click clack of her heels draw ever nearer, its rhythmic beat competing against his thumping heart. Not long now – his mind was racing. Not long before he could watch those curves of her buttocks move in that manner, that only girls of her calibre knew how to do. He waited, but suddenly realised something was wrong. Surely she should have passed by now, surely he hadn't missed her. He couldn't have. How? She must have gone another way. His heart sank.

"Mr Taylor? It *is* you, isn't it?"

John felt his whole body stiffen – surely it couldn't be her. He lifted his head a fraction, a pair of bright red stilettos coming into view directly in front of him.

"John Taylor? Willowbank Farm?"

My God, she's actually talking to me! She said my name. My *name*. Hang on, how does she know who I am? He was now confused as he slowly lifted his head, allowing his vision to travel its way up her naked legs. Legs that ran effortlessly into those tantalisingly tight frayed jeans. His head was so close he could almost smell her female presence. She stood, legs slightly apart, allowing the light to highlight every last detail of her lower body, leaving a love-sick man to willingly fill in the missing bits. One hand on her hip, the other clutching a bright green handbag, she welcomed John to her world of seductive greetings, with her warm friendly smile meaning so much more to a slightly greying middle-aged man.

"John Taylor, it *is* you, I knew it."

John could hardly swallow as he attempted to speak. "Yes," was all he could say.

"Tony," she announced.

His head tilted to one side, somewhat puzzled at what he had just heard. "No, I'm sorry, I'm afraid …"

The young lady sensed he was having trouble remembering her. "Antonia Chapman, we used to live next door to you. Well, not exactly next door – the other side of the hill."

John still looked vague.

"Mum and Dad, Joyce and Ted."

Finally, the penny dropped. "Of course, yes, I'm sorry, I didn't recognise you. You've …" He stared at her perfect body for longer than was necessary. "You've changed so much. Blimey, the last time I saw you, you were knee-high to a grasshopper." He shook his head in disbelief. "God, you've developed. I mean, you've grown so … big. I mean … Sorry, I didn't mean that the way it came out." He wanted to just crawl into a hole and bury himself.

"It's fine, Mr Taylor, really."

He could feel the blood rushing to his cheeks. "Sorry." He had to move on, and quickly. "Anyway, it's been years, how are you?"

"I'm fine, thank you."

"And Mum and Dad, how are they?" He found it hard to have a sensible conversation with a girl who was clearly not wearing a bra, her ample young bosoms showing their delight at being constantly stared at as they pushed against the tight cotton of her shirt.

"They're good. Dad's taken early retirement and Mum's doing lots of charity work."

"Excellent." His uncontrollable imagination had now started to undo the buttons of her shirt. "So, what are you doing with yourself?" John really had to sort himself out.

"I'm in Public Relations. I mostly work from home, self-employed."

He could feel his breathing becoming more erratic as his imaginary fingers traced along the curves of her upper body. He tried to sound enthused but his mind was slowly drowning in his overzealous thoughts and the fact that he hadn't a clue what 'Public Relations' involved.

"And how's Samantha and Luke?"

Somehow he managed to drag himself back into the real world. "Yes, good thanks. Sam's fine, still got her cooking, scrubbing the floors, emptying the bed pan, you know how it is – nothing much changes really.

And yes of course, Luke, I almost forgot, you two played together all the time. Right little mischiefs, according to Sam." In truth, Antonia was a complete stranger to John. He'd seen her about the farm but she was just a child and he'd met her mum and dad a few times, but he couldn't say he was pally with them. Sam knew them far more than he did. "So yes, he's great," he continued. "Just taken himself off travelling. I think two years at agricultural college was enough study for him. Heading off to America, then Australia."

"Whoa, that sounds fun. I knew he always wanted to go farming, we were forever playing with his toy tractors."

John smiled. "Yes, he's a good lad. We miss him already and he's only been gone a few months."

"Do say I've asked after him, and of course Samantha. Perhaps I might try and pop in one day."

John could think of nothing better than to see this gorgeous girl again, for that's what she was. Just a girl dressed up as a woman. "We'd both love to see you, any time, we're always around, don't go out much."

Tony smiled politely. "That's a date. Anyway, I must be getting back to work."

John nodded back. "Really nice to see you."

"And you."

He watched her walk away, his eyes transfixed on her whole body. This was a girl who had it all and wasn't afraid to show it off. He teetered on the edge of his seat just to get that last glimpse, only to be attacked by a short sharp grunt of disapproval as the old woman latched onto his gaze, her needles forcefully attacking her knitting in a fit of uncontrollable frenzy. He tried to look away as sparks flew from her fingertips throwing a stitch. In sheer anger she turned her vengeance towards a man she now thought of as Satan himself.

"You should be ashamed of yourself. A man of your age, practically drooling over a young hussy like that. See the way she flaunted herself, and in public. Shameful, that's what it is. Shameful. She knew what she was doing. I curse the both of you, and may your souls burn in Hell!" Her knitting needles twisted and jerked as she spoke.

John sat speechless, as passers-by turned their heads and walked on, giving him the chance to come to the conclusion the old woman was, perhaps, one of those poor unfortunate souls for whom sex had been an unfortunate chore of life. An act of male pleasure that must be endured for the sake of producing children. Nothing more. God forbid there be any suggestion towards personal fulfilment. Of course he was condemning her without a scrap of evidence, but on this occasion and with such a public outburst he felt quite within his rights to think of her as a wrinkly, wart-infested, frigid old bat who should mind her own business.

"Mr Taylor?"

John turned and found the 'nice young man' from the counter standing next to him.

"Mr Taylor, Mr Nesbit will see you now. If you'd like to follow me."

It was a blessed relief to do as he was told, as he could sense the old woman's temper reaching boiling point. He needed to get away, for he was sure her next move would involve pain inflicted by a set of pointed knitting needles put into places he'd rather not think about.

As he followed the man across the open foyer, he tried to avoid the curious looks from the waiting room, embarrassed that they assumed he'd upset a lovely little old lady sitting quietly producing a quaint toddler's outfit.

The nice young man pulled back slightly. "Good luck."

John knew it was supposed to be a calming remark, but unfortunately it had the opposite effect, setting his nerves on edge and reminding him of the enormity of the task ahead. As they reached the manager's door, the nice young man knocked three times then waited. Moments later a muffled acceptance to enter was heard. He opened the door and announced their presence.

"Mr Taylor to see you, sir."

A middle-aged man pulled his eyes away from his desk and peered at the two standing in his doorway. "Ah, yes. Thank you ... um ..."

"Daniel, sir."

"Daniel. Right." He waved his hand in a dismissive

manner, signalling Daniel to leave, as if he were an inconvenience to his daily workload.

Daniel raised an eyebrow as he turned and caught John's attention, leaving him standing like some naughty schoolboy waiting for the headmaster to acknowledge his presence.

"Mr Taylor. Please take a seat."

John quickly scanned the room, as a sudden realisation hit him fair and square between the eyes. Harold Pottenger wasn't coming back. It was as if his good friend had never existed. The room smelt of fresh paint while weird, twisted triffid-like plants sprouted from every convenient space. This wasn't Harold's doing. He peered down at the grey gold-flecked carpet that dominated the whole floor area. Not at all to Harold's taste. John had known the man long enough to know his likes and dislikes – this was clearly the work of a man who'd been divorced three times. It was as if the devil himself had arrived in a white transit van and completely wiped out Harold's whole lifeworks and carted it away, towed it up the motorway in the dead of night only to be sold at some dodgy car boot sale up north somewhere – no questions asked.

John was brought back to earth by Mr Nesbit sniffing loudly while shutting off his left nostril, allowing a maximum amount of air to be forcefully injected up his right one, supposedly dislodging some sort of blockage that had occurred during the last appointment. He leant back in his seat and studied the man in front of him.

"Now, Mr Taylor, what can we, the Bank, do you for you today?" He threw his arms wide open, as if inviting some imaginary panel of overpaid businessmen and women to join in on their meeting.

Wanker! John now realised he was in deep trouble. He'd come to the conclusion very early on in their appointment that Mr Nesbit was, in fact, a complete prat. Perhaps he was judging the man unfairly, not giving him enough of a chance to prove his worth, but John liked to think he could recognise a good person when he saw one – and Mr Nesbit wasn't one. But what the hell, he'd made the effort to come here, so he'd give it to him straight. He was always told by his father never to beat around the bush when doing business. Just get right to the point then everyone knew where they stood. He could feel a small lump develop in his throat, but chose to ignore it. He needed money and this man had a lot of it.

"I'd like a small rise in my overdraft." There, it was said.

"Okay." Mr Nesbit didn't seem too concerned by John's request. Perhaps he wasn't such a dickhead after all. "For how long and by how much?" Mr Nesbit's hands dropped to the desk, his manner a little more serious.

Things had suddenly changed. The atmosphere felt clinical, more business-like. John peered at him with wavering determination. "Six months, and let's say ... what ... another twenty thousand?" He was probably pushing his luck but he could always drop that figure if need be and still have enough. He sat patiently in his chair and waited, watching Mr Nesbit's mouth twitch from side to side, followed by an agonising period of silence as the bank manager studied a number of typed-out figures on a piece of paper that just happened to have John's name printed on the top.

The silence was finally broken by a large drawn-out sigh, accompanied by a huff, then a grunt while the air rushed out of his hairy overgrown nostrils. "You have a cash flow projection plan I assume, Mr Taylor?"

Oh dear! John felt sweat forming on his forehead and his hands became clammy. He had lots of things in his carrier bag, but a cash flow projection plan wasn't one of them. "Well, no, but I do have the farm accounts, admittedly from twelve months ago, and up-to-date bills and receipts. It's all here." He went to retrieve his bag, but was stopped by the raise of a hand.

"That won't be necessary, Mr Taylor." A concerned look fell upon John's offerings. "Hmm, there I was thinking you had just done your weekly supermarket shop. No, Mr Taylor, I have all the information I need, thank you."

John pulled at his collar. "I'm afraid I only did a cash flow when requested. Harold never really believed in them. He knew our farm as well as we did and dealt on a trust arrangement. It always seemed to work fine for me and my late father."

Mr Nesbit could almost be seen picking himself up off the floor. "Trust." His voice seemed to crackle with fear as he spoke. "Trust, Mr Taylor, is a rather old-fashioned word. No, we – and I talk for the bank here

– we can't possibly work on the goodwill of people like yourself. I'm sorry if I'm sounding a little blunt, but no, Mr Taylor, we can't possibly work on that basis. I would have to see a cash flow, although even then I doubt if it would convince me to lend any more money. You see I took the liberty of studying your past projections in some detail and I fear nothing seems to resemble your present financial situation, and I have to say Mr Pottenger has been more than generous with the bank's money. Far more than I could ever hope to be. Bank's policy, Mr Taylor." He paused. "In fact, we at Grimms Bank would be only too delighted to see a reduction on the money owed to us. Yes, delighted."

Mr Nesbit had just reinforced John's earlier assumption that indeed he was an arrogant, smug, pompous twat and that was putting it politely. John pushed his carrier bag to one side with the heel of his foot. "So I take it that's a 'no' then?"

Nesbit didn't even hesitate with his reply. "I'm afraid so, bank's policy, as I've already said."

John was about to get up and leave – he could see no point in prolonging the discomfort he felt in the pit of his stomach.

"Er, look, Mr Taylor, I understand this is not the outcome you were hoping for, but you have to look at it from the bank's point of view. Yes, the value of your farm significantly outweighs the amount you presently have outstanding, but it just isn't sustainable to keep lending you money that you clearly can't repay. Frankly Mr. Taylor it doesn't look good for the bank if we have to resort to other means of recovering our money."

An air of silence fell over the room. Finally the bank had come out and said it. It hit John in the chest, temporarily winding him – the realisation had suddenly come home. He felt sick just thinking about it. His farm was his life, his livelihood, his inheritance, and here he now sat drowning in the reality that he could possibility lose some, or all of it.

Mr Nesbit broke ranks and shattered John's thoughts with a suggestion that took him into another world. "Sell a few cows, that should release the pressure for a while. Less cows, less costs, money in the bank. Win-win situation."

John couldn't believe what this buffoon had just suggested. "Are you mad?" His voice showed his utter annoyance towards the proposal. "Let's get this right: you're asking me to sell my only real assets? These are dairy cows, dairy cows produce milk. Yes. With me so far? Milk gets sold, money comes in. Now, I wasn't the brightest kid in school but correct me if I'm wrong – less cows means less money. So you tell me the logic of selling the only things that bring in an income. Well?" John could feel his whole body heat up to near boiling point.

"Mr Taylor, Mr Taylor, I understand your frustration, believe me I do, but the fact is, the bank, and that's yours and mine, have come to the conclusion that farming, be it dairy, beef, arable or sheep cannot and should not expect to be treated any differently than any other business or trade. It cannot be seen as a special case. We have to be totally convinced the figures add up and I'm afraid yours don't. You can't keep borrowing against the value of your farm."

He started to rock back and forth in his chair while juggling his pen between his long bony fingers, a line of thought developing. "This is what I'll do. I'm prepared to give you six months at your present level of borrowing. Six months for you to come up with some sort of solution to your problem. No action will be taken by the bank until that time has lapsed. It's the best I can do. I'm sorry if it's not what you expected, but as I've already said, 'bank policy'."

Six months. John knew that if Harold had been sitting opposite him right now a solution would have been worked out, temporary finance would have almost certainly been forthcoming and an honest down-to-earth appraisal of the farm's state of affairs would have been discussed. But not this man, not this Mr Prickliness. Bank's policy his arse. He was just a puppet – no more than that. That was the trouble with everyone today, no one had the authority to make a decision any more, run with their gut instinct. Everything had to be passed on to someone else, someone who only dealt in black and white figures, not real people's lives.

He felt the sweat form under his armpits. He was angry all right, damn angry. Six months was nothing in farming, plenty long enough to lose money but little time to make any. He could feel his head swirling around the room, but he'd had enough. Rising from his seat, he begrudgingly shook Mr Nesbit's hand and walked out.

The old woman was still knitting in her chair. John briefly glanced her way. Why was she still here? Perhaps she had no intentions of doing any bank transactions; perhaps it was just a warm, comfortable place to spend the day, but surely that's what libraries were for. She gave John a forceful glare, but he really didn't care much about her attitude. To be fair, he didn't much care about anything.

"Ah, Mr Taylor? Yoo hoo," called Daniel with a wave of his limp hand. He walked over to John, glancing around to see if anyone was listening. "Well?" he asked, eyes lit up with curiosity as he waited for a reply, which John was sure wasn't 'bank policy' – openly discussing customers' private matters in the middle of the foyer – but by now he couldn't give a monkey's and had lost all sense of reasoning.

"You're right."

"I knew it, didn't I say, Mr Taylor? Three times, says it all!"

"Yes, it does Daniel."

Chapter 4

Kim and Pup had gradually been getting more excited the nearer they approached the farm. It never ceased to amaze John how dogs could sense the approach of their home.

The drive back had been a total blur, so many thoughts swirling around in an ever-decreasing circle, finally ending up at a point of total confusion. Foolishly perhaps, he kept telling himself there was nothing to be concerned about; it had all been one big hilarious joke played out by the bank, and the money the farm needed would appear – no questions asked. For a while he'd actually convinced himself so. That was until he came face to face with the reality of bricks and mortar.

Of course he could go on as normal. Why not? He and Sam could just join so many others as they buried their heads in the sand hoping that next year would be the best that farming had ever seen. He felt a half-hearted rumble of hope pushing its way up from the pit of his stomach, then vanish before it even had a chance to make an appearance. Damn them all! No, he couldn't be fooled that easily. Dangerous thoughts of that nature could and would only compound the inevitable misery suffered by the foolhardy. He swallowed hard, trying to force down the reality of the real world, before it had a chance to blow his mind. The reality that he could very well lose a large part of his life.

John slowly pulled the old chain smoker gently into the barn allowing her to wheeze a sigh of relief.

Exercise wasn't something she was particularly fond of. Her now aching nuts and bolts needed rest, only too willing to have an afternoon nap as her engine fell silent.

He swung open his door and solemnly made his way to the rear of the vehicle, only to be met by one teenage delinquent and an over-eighties lap dancer with a dodgy hip, both exploding with sheer jubilation. He couldn't help but smile; if only life were that simple, that uncomplicated. He ran his hand over Kim's head and immediately felt an air of emotion wave over him. "You've got the life, eh girl?" His eyes rested upon Pup. "And as for you, mad as a hatter. That's what you are. I reckon Sam could be right, you're an untrainable mongrel." Pup was almost wetting himself as he rolled on his back, inviting John to give his stomach a rub. The attention was met with a squeal of excitement before John placed his arms around his ever-devoted Collie and lifted her to the floor. Kim looked on for guidance as if sensing her master's mood – she wouldn't leave him until instructed. "Go on, off you go." She hesitated, knowing full well there was something wrong, her head tilting to one side as if to say, 'I'm here, don't shut me out.' Their eyes met, John's glazed over with emotion, hers a deep sultry pull of the heart, but both minds working simultaneously as if each of them knew what the other was thinking.

"I'll be all right." No other words were needed. John knew she understood. "Go on, be off with you." Reluctantly she wandered off across the track, stopping briefly to see if her master was still there.

"Go on." He waved his hand in defiance of her reluctance to obey orders, but finally she accepted his wishes, turned and headed for the barn.

Pup couldn't give a damn and had disappeared from sight, almost certainly in search of his chewing piece of afterbirth, leaving John to wipe the moisture from his eyes and focus on his time alone with a degree of pride. The farm he so loved, nestled peacefully among the scattering of mature trees, of past wisdom. Shade in the summer, windbreaks from the north-westerlies during the colder months. He sighed as his mind drifted back in time to imagine his grandfather planting these same trees, their thick overhanging branches now swaying in a light spring breeze and yet for all its beauty, the land, the buildings, his home sagged under the ever-bearing weight of modern life. John picked up a twig and gently snapped it in two, his mind racing in all directions, unsure of the way forward. What was he to do?

His thoughts were broken by Sam's voice drifting across the yard, a voice that immediately put him at ease; just knowing she was there ran a warm feeling through his body. He didn't have to face this alone. Gazing around, he spotted her in the distance, standing in the doorway of the farmhouse. There suddenly seemed to be a need to be with her, if only to moan of things he had little control over. She would lend an ear, he was sure, listen to his woes, nod politely when necessary, disagree at times, that's how she was. That's how he was. It was a marriage that had settled over time into a steady acceptance into each other's ways. Yes, they'd had their shouting matches,

THE SECRET LIFE OF JOHN TAYLOR

life wasn't perfect, but on the whole they rubbed along reasonably well. Yet he always felt there was something missing – as if she was holding back a part of herself that wasn't allowed to be touched, in mind or in body. The physical side of their relationship had him aching at times, yearning for the intimate side of this woman to show through her hardened shell. To love and hold as if she really wanted him, but it hadn't been like that. It had never been like that.

He made his way towards her, longing for open arms, a smiling face, a light kiss upon the lips, but all he got was a worried frown as she picked up on his restless state. If only she knew.

"How was it?" She spoke in a matter-of-fact tone that did nothing to help his mood.

"Not too well. It seems poor old Harold has been taken ill and has been replaced by a prat of a manager, a Mr Nesbit."

Sam's first concerns were towards their long-standing friend and his health. "We need to find out how Harold is. Send him a get well card. It's the least we can do – he's been a good friend to the family."

John was consumed by a sudden sharp stab of guilt. He'd been so wrapped up in his own troubles he'd not spared a thought for the man who had been such a big part of his life.

"Yes, we must. You're right, he's been a good friend."

"So I take it I can't book the world cruise just yet then?" said Sam light-heartedly. John smiled at her humour.

"No, best not. I'll take you to the abattoir next time I go, how's that?"

"Oh, that bad?"

"'Fraid so." He paused a moment, preparing himself to deliver the news.

Sam could see what was coming and braced herself.

"You know what he said? Do you?"

"Who?"

"The new bank manager, of course. He sat there in his fancy well-fitted suit and told me to sell some cows!" John's arms shot up in disgust. "Sell some bloody cows! Who does he think he is, trying to tell a farmer how to run his own business? God, he made me angry. All I want to do is scream when I picture that smug face of his."

Sam saw her husband hadn't quite finished, so thought it best to just keep quiet and listen.

"At least if you're going to tell someone he can't have any more money you should have the decency to respect their intelligence. I could've rung his bloody neck!" Without realising it, his anger had been temporally subdued by the warm gentle touch of Sam's hand.

"Come on. I'll make you a nice cup of tea. I really think you need to calm down, otherwise you'll be upsetting those cows this afternoon." She turned and led him down the back passage. "Tea, with a home-made caramel slice – that should dampen down the flames."

They sat at the kitchen table. Sam paused to hear all the grisly details, if only so John could get it off his chest and move on. "So, do you have any clue how Harold is?" She placed a second slice onto John's plate. One slice a day is all you would be allowed usually, but given the circumstances she felt she would overlook such details.

"No, they just said he was off ill, but it's pretty obvious he's not coming back. Nesbit's had the whole office completely done over. New carpets, lick of paint, some hideous lighting and what looks like the Brazilian rainforest sprouting from all the corners."

Sam looked mildly concerned. "That's definitely not Harold's style."

"No, like I said, he's almost certainly not coming back."

Sam rested her arm on the table and gently tapped her fingers on the woodwork. "So, this Mr Nesbit isn't going to lend us any more money then?"

John shook his head. "No. Not only that, can you believe 'the bank would be delighted to see a reduction in our present overdraft'. That's when he suggested selling the cows. I reckon they're starting to get cold feet. The way farming's going, someone's decided it's time to try and recover some of their money before the whole agricultural sector in this country goes under."

"You could be right."

"I know I'm right. Nesbit seems to think it's in both the bank's and our best interests to reduce the borrowings. He says Harold's been far too lenient over the years and new bank policy would never allow such lending." Sitting back in his chair he took a small bite of caramel to steady his nerves, allowing Sam to slowly digest every last scrap of information her husband had forced upon her. John sat silently savouring the smooth sugary texture of his slice of heaven, its thin chocolaty coating tantalising the taste buds before the overwhelming sweet sensation of that unmistakable flavour that only caramel could deliver, pushed him into another world.

Sam waited, hoping the sugar rush would numb his brain just enough to allow her to announce her risky reply. "He's probably right, you know. Nesbit, I mean." She quickly withdrew her arm from the table, just in case he took offence, for in that brief moment she knew she had sided with the enemy, but in a way she felt relieved that someone had, finally, brought her husband down to earth. She'd worried in silence over the amount of money they were owing the bank, but John loved his cows and the farm they grazed, so she had kept quiet, desperately hoping things would get better.

John took another bite as he gazed at his wife, trying to think of a pleasant reply to her outright treachery. But she was right of course. Trust a woman to bring in some sort of rationale to the proceedings.

"Yes, of course, he's right."

Sam looked bemused. "So why are you blabbering on?"

"'Cause it makes me feel better, all right? Anyway, the

man's still a prat." John ran his hand through his hair, scratching his scalp, trying to relieve the constant throbbing in his brain. "Six months. That's all he's given us. Six months to come up with some sort of plan. You know as well as I do, nothing is going to change in that time. It'll more than likely get worse. I've got bills to pay."

Sam rose from her chair, collected both cups and walked to the sink. Turning her back to the farm's problems she gazed out to the wonders of the garden. "So what are we going to do then?" She could hear a deep low groan snake its way across the room.

"I'm not sure. I need to go milking. I think better when I'm with the cows; no offence."

Sam felt her lips move into a slight grin but said nothing. At least he hadn't lost all his sense of humour. She heard him get up from his chair and start to make his way out of the room. She turned and gave him an encouraging look of support. "We'll think of something."

John tried to smile. "Yes, of course we will, but I know one thing is for sure – we can't start anything new. That all costs money and could take years to get off the ground." He shook his head in despair. "I don't know what to do. I really don't."

Chapter 5

The afternoon milking was a sombre affair, although the sun was pleasantly warm on the face, the levels of grass acceptable and the cows content. John just couldn't find anything to be cheerful about. His mind had been constantly bombarded by so many conflicting thoughts that he struggled to concentrate on milking. He found himself vaguely listening to the background noise of the radio, its antiquated weather-beaten exterior of faded mahogany Art Deco design shuddering through the constant vibration of trivial nonsense. He hoped the light-hearted banter of the presenters would help distract him from the troubles he now faced.

Not long into the afternoon he'd been presented with a subject he knew little about as the station broadcast a programme exploring the pros and cons of the sex trade, piquing his interest. Why such a topic needed to be aired on a Tuesday afternoon was beyond John, but the presenter handled this potentially explosive debate with the utmost care and professionalism expected from such a well-known broadcaster.

John had found himself being force-fed a wealth of impartially informed knowledge and information, exploring in depth this taboo subject and willingly being introduced to faceless females, young and not so young, for whom this trade was providing a steady and at times well-earned living. Interview after interview spoke of the values of such a profession, but one in which we are led to believe is blighted by scandalous reports of forced labour and the like. And of course this unforgivable side of the trade had, without question, been explored in depth and at times through heated opposition, but it had been noted that the station condemned such activities vigorously.

While it wasn't a subject John would have gone to the local library and spent valuable time searching out a book on, surprisingly he had found himself warming to the content. Not simply because he was a man, but because it just happened to be an interesting topic, a pleasant diversion from his burdened mind, something to nibble away at as the afternoon progressed. It was simply another sack-load of useful knowledge that he'd quietly store away in his subconscious mind to possibly be browsed upon at a dinner party, or more likely, the local pub. Certainly not something that had the capability to alter the whole of his future life.

A solution to the farm's financial problems had, unfortunately, not been forthcoming during the course of the milking, or so John had thought. Answers to most problems, they say, are quite often staring you in the face, meaning most people try far too hard in their search in finding that solution and in doing so miss the obvious. John, through no fault of his own, had fallen into that trap, bogging his weary mind down with ideas that frankly had little or no chance of ever seeing the light of day. His overriding worry of watching his family's inheritance slip into some rich man's second home in the country had clouded his vision, sending him into a downward spiral of emotions.

He came away from milking more frustrated than when he'd started. Nothing – or so he thought – had the capability to produce an income without a large amount of investment poured into it in the first place. Money he clearly didn't have. There lay the dilemma.

It was late evening by the time John made his way into the kitchen having completed his last check around the farm buildings and surrounding fields. His short walk with the dogs had, as always, been his escapism from the trials of modern life. Just man and dogs alone with nature as daylight gradually lost her grip to a slowly darkening sky. A calming time to relax the mind before enabling the body to rest between the clean sheets of the marital bed.

He was met by the dependable sound of the grandfather clock as it struck ten. Sam had already made her way to bed, almost certainly wrapped up in the pages of another large novel. Her recent tendency towards vampires had started to worry him somewhat, having experienced a certain degree of biting during one of their rare lovemaking sessions, but being the ever practical thinking man that he was, John had wisely taken steps to see off any such behaviour in the future. His investment in heavy-grade pyjamas had allowed him to rest his head upon the pillow without the fear of being munched upon during the hours of darkness. The choice of such thick material had baffled his wife who questioned the need for such winter clothing during the spring, but John stood his ground. Soft talk didn't fool him. Let his guard down for even one night and he was sure she'd be at him and drawing blood before he knew it. At least with his snugly fitted boxers for added protection, he felt he had made the right decision. Sweat admittedly would form in restricted places, but at least he would be safe.

It was his responsibility to put the house to sleep, simultaneously switching off the lights as he made his way towards the bedroom. As he reached the top of the stairs there was only one light left to put out, but for some unknown reason he lingered longer than usual. His thoughts were interrupted by a murmuring, a distant voice, desperately trying to communicate with him. But what was it saying?

John gazed along the narrow landing, the worn carpet telling of many passed occupants, their tired limbs dragging weighted feet to their much-needed place of rest; but it wasn't their lives that had caught John's imagination. Still he gazed, not knowing what he was looking at, but feeling there was something. He tilted his head as that voice rang in his ears. It was nothing. He was tired, that's all, but now it was almost screaming at him, making him look for the obvious, whatever that was. But as far as he could see there was nothing out of the ordinary, nothing had changed, and yet he was drawn towards the evenly spaced doors that led into all six bedrooms.

They were doors, nothing more, but he soon realised it was what lay behind them that had gripped the way he was now thinking, as he slowly found himself building an idea that frankly shocked him just considering it. Something so ridiculous that even to his own ears it sounded bizarre, mad, ludicrous even, to invite people into his home, their space. However did such a thought enter his head? Surely no self-respecting farmer would ever entertain such a plan, but the more he thought about it, the more he was convinced it could actually work. My God! Should he even allow himself a slight pat on the back? A congratulations for finally coming up with a solution to their money problems? Yes, he thought, his heartbeat quickening, he was embarrassed to believe he could.

The mind was now arguing the pro and cons while his legs carried him along the landing, passing each door in turn. There were six in total, all of which were a fairly similar size, his and Sam's being the biggest. Luke's needed to stay unoccupied, awaiting his return in the future. So that left four empty unused spaces. It had always rested uneasily upon John's conscience that it was just the three of them rattling about in such a large house, but what else could he do? It came with the farm. Like it or not it was their home, until, like many before him, you would have to step aside for the next generation.

Admittedly the extra bedrooms did become useful when friends and relations came to visit. Most of them now chose to stay away or only visit when passing through, knowing full well from past experience that if they lingered for any length of time farm work would eventually be placed upon their idle shoulders. Quietly John had to admit this discouragement was part of a master plan. A softly-softly approach, filtering out those unwanted guests that felt it their God given right to stay over and keep him up into the early hours talking about nothing in particular, yet would happily lie in the next morning while he had to get up early for milking. This was not to say all persons were warned off – occasionally there would be those whom John would happily engage in meaningful banter and didn't mind feeling crap at five o'clock the next morning. Alas those occasions had become few and far between, so it always seemed such a waste to have so many rooms gathering dust. Not that Sam allowed that to happen, in use or not. Every room would have to be ready, just in case.

His tired legs pushed him further along the landing. The long stretch of corridor was showered in darkened shadows, the only brightness coming from their bedroom as it drew him in like a moth to a shining light. Its encroaching glow seemed to play with his thoughts – thoughts that were now churning away at a plan and desperately trying to mould it into some sort of sensible suggestion. One that he could present to his wife.

By the time he'd arrived at their door he was brimming with excitement, keen to offload his wondrous idea to a willing devoted partner, someone he hoped would be eager to participate in any rescue plan he may have come up with. Sadly though, Sam was absorbed in the pages of yet another book, her interest towards anything he had to say overruled by the captivating words on the page. John now felt alone as every last drop of enthusiasm slowly dripped away. Perhaps this wasn't the right time. He would sleep on it. He was old enough and wise enough to realise that things would always seem different in the morning.

The cover of his wife's book caught his eye – an

attractive blonde female sinking her blood-stained fangs deep into the neck of some unsuspecting male lover as he lay half-naked upon silk sheets. Immediately John felt his body tense, sending the blood pounding in his veins. Without a second thought he threw his clothes off in all directions and shot his trusty boxers up his exposed legs, wrapping themselves tightly around his private parts. Standing well clear of the edge of the bed he frantically untangled his discarded, heavy-duty, industrial grade pyjamas while watching for any sudden movement from the woman who could spring on him at any moment. With some relief he finally managed to wrap the thick layer of cotton around his exposed body, while nervously watching on.

Sam's hand suddenly made a movement, causing him to jump backwards. Only a turn of another page. He breathed a sigh of relief. He had to stay alert – it could have been much worse, more sinister. She was playing a mind game, that's what it was, lulling him into a false sense of security. These blood-sucking females were clever thinkers, crafty planners. They pretended not to take any notice of what was going on around them, yet they were like creatures on the Devil's payroll, only really coming alive as darkness fell, their life, their whole well-being depending on the taste of their next victim.

Sam gazed up at her frantic-looking husband, a man with eyes that seemed to be fighting the bright headlights of life. She gave in to a weak concerned smile but inwardly shook her head. Oh dear, she thought, another night of sleeping next to a giant hot water bottle. What had got into him lately? She watched the buttons of his pyjamas jostling against fumbling fingers. A garment that wouldn't look out of place wrapped around someone on a ski slope. She shook her head and returned to her book. Whatever was wrong with him, he'd have to sort it out himself. She had far more interesting things to do with her time than to try and fathom out the way a man's brain works.

Seizing his moment, John slipped between the covers, laying his head upon the pillow before quickly pulling the collar of his rather stiff nightwear up around his neck. His eyes were now far too heavy to worry about the 'what ifs'. Yes, he felt uneasy, for sure, but sleep had started to drag him under, as he slowly drifted off.

*

Next morning, milking passed without incident, allowing plenty of time to mull over his proposition to try to sketch out the finer details before he presented it to Sam over the course of breakfast. With such a radical idea it had to be pitch-perfect. Her reaction, he was sure, would be one of shock at first, but he was convinced that once the dust had settled and the evidence placed before her she would see, as he had now come to believe, that as mad as this venture was, or could be, it did have possibilities.

He entered the back door with an upbeat feeling of confidence, the smell of fried food filling the cracks of doubt that threatened to ambush his mind. He could hear Sam moving various objects around in the kitchen and immediately his body slumped into a quivering wreck. Damn, he'd lost it again! What seemed like a wonderful, flawless idea when he'd put it to his cows at six o'clock this morning now didn't seem so convincing.

He anxiously made his way into the kitchen and was met by a spitting frying pan, a toaster ejecting its payload of lightly browned bread, and a neatly laid table. Plates were warming on the Aga, butter and marmalade jostled for their right to have centre spot on the oak table, and the whole room seemed to be in an organised calm of femininity.

"Ah, just in time." Sam's voice broke through the familiar sights and sounds that presented themselves to John.

How did she ever do it? he thought. The breakfast was never overcooked, never burnt and timed to perfection whatever time of the morning he seemed to come in for it. She placed two plates on the table and began arranging the finely cooked food in the exact same order and presentation as every other morning.

"How's the morning been?" she asked, turning to place the empty frying pan to one side.

"All good. Dear old Jezebel's calved, she had it just as I got out there. Lovely speckle-faced heifer."

"Oh, that's great, another daughter to carry on the line. How many heifer calves has she had now? Must be at least ten, surely."

John was relieved that Sam sounded so at ease with life. He would push the conversation on a little longer before saying anything about his plans. "I'm not sure, I'd have to look it up." John had to keep making small talk, get the feel of her general mood. You never quite knew with women. Now cows, they were much more predictable – still female though, so even they could be fickle at times.

He wondered if he should just jump straight in with his proposition while they were happily eating their breakfast. Or would it be better to carry on making polite conversation and then gradually test out the water by dropping an odd remark concerning the nature of his idea? He knew he only had one stab at this. Get it wrong and all his planning would have been a waste of time, but get it right and it may just help to ease their financial burdens. In no way would it completely eliminate their problems – far from it. But it would be a step in the right direction.

After much thought he decided to play it safe, wait a little longer. Why ruin a perfectly good breakfast? Showing his cowardly nature he cut another bite-sized pieced of apple and venison sausage and stuffed it into his mouth. After a short spell of general chitchat, interspersed with periods of silence, John felt reasonably confident he could take advantage of Sam's friendly mood.

"I've come up with an idea." He swallowed the last of his breakfast while he waited for a reply. The silence seemed to stretch out longer than he had anticipated. He was just about to open his mouth when Sam looked him straight in the eye.

"Well? Don't just sit there like a stuffed turkey. What

sort of idea?" She sounded a fraction annoyed that she'd had to prompt him into explaining, but at least she'd replied.

John's mouth felt dry. "Well, it's like this." He could see his neatly prepared speech stretch out across the room, the words desperately trying to stick together to form a sensible sentence but failing miserably. "Right." He cleared his throat. "Our problem, as I see it, is that we need more money."

"Yes, we already know that."

Damn it! John had to push on, be more positive, stop fluffing around at the edges. "Okay," he said, "so, as far as I can see, and given the present milk price, the cows are only just breaking even and that's without us taking any sort of wage out of the business." He stopped to take a breath and felt a slight quiver creeping into his voice the nearer he got to his final announcement.

Sam sat looking at him expectantly, wishing he'd get to the point.

John forced himself to continue. "The problem is, everything I think up requires money, so ..." He filled his lungs to capacity, then prepared the words that were resting on the tip of his tongue into some sort of convincing announcement. "I've come up with an idea." As soon as he'd said it he realised he had just come full circle and could hear a little voice in the back of his head, laughing at his incompetence.

Sam's vague interest was clearly slipping away by the second, her head now resting to one side, waiting, almost willing him to say something she didn't already know.

"This idea ..." Keep going, John. Ignore those doubting roars of laughter. "This idea ..." Damn! He'd just repeated himself again. Get a grip, man, lay it out on the table, for better or for worse. "Could bring us," he carried on, "over time, much-needed cash, without costing a fortune to set up." He watched as his wife finally took more interest, but still chose to look none too convinced with what she had been presented with so far.

"Go on."

John could hear his heart pounding in his chest. He just had to come out and say it. He took a deep breath and announced, "Prostitution!"

Like a bolt of lightning, fear shot through his body, a numbness in his head that threatened to swallow every last laughing voice in his mind, forcing them to run for cover, for he knew, if this didn't go down well, they would be back, louder than ever. He was sure he was going to be sick, as he could feel that last piece of sausage doing a U-turn.

Sam sat frozen to her chair, looking at him with a slightly glazed expression which then quickly turned into uncontrollable laughter. "Prostitution! Is that your great idea?" Her voice roared with utter amusement. John could only nod, choosing to say nothing as she continued to laugh almost to the point of crying.

"What's so funny?"

Sam briefly came up for air. "Well, be serious John. I know you mean well, but look at you.   You're over fifty, thinning on top, and what you do have is starting to turn grey. And even after a shower you still smell of cow shit. You've got a protruding belly and your hands are as rough as sandpaper." Her laughter only slackened for a moment before she carried on. "Who on earth's going to pay good money to jump into bed with that!"

John didn't change his expression as he stared at his now tearful wife. "Thank you very much for that, and I hate to spoil your obvious amusement, but it wasn't me I was thinking of!"

The room suddenly fell silent as if someone had just dropped dead. Sam's face drained of any humour, indicating her refusal to accept what she thought John was suggesting. "You're not seriously thinking *I* go on the game are you? Christ John! I love this farm but there's a limit. How dare you suggest I go with other men just so you can carry on milking your cows! I'm your wife, for God's sake! How dare you!" she shouted, fists clenched in anger.

John could see this wasn't going quite to plan. He really needed to take control, and fast, or he could end up sleeping in the barn with the dogs. "I don't mean *you*! What do you take me for? No, what I'm suggesting is that we get someone in. Someone who knows about these sorts of things. An experienced female. It's perfect, can't you see? We provide the room, with meals included and then share the earnings. We've got four empty bedrooms, two have only just been decorated. Think about it. Hardly any cost to us, and what's more we won't have to do any of the work ourselves, which would leave me free to carry on farming and you to do … whatever you do."

The look of shock slowly fell from Sam's face, but John wasn't sure whether that was a good thing or not. "It'll only be for a while, just until the milk price goes up. Then hopefully we'll be fine." He realised he had said enough, probably should have gone about it a little more gently, but it was said now and it was in the lap of the gods as to how Sam would react next. He could see her mind churning over the basic information she had been given.

"You do realise what you're proposing, John? To turn this house, our *home*, into some sort of farm brothel! *Brothel*, John! Do you understand that? A place of ill repute! A whorehouse!"

John wasn't too convinced by the tone of her voice. "I take it you don't like the idea?"

"I never said that! I was just pointing out some facts, that's all." A glimmer of hope crept across the room.

"So, you do like the idea then?"

"I never said that either."

"Oh."

Chapter 6

Sam had said nothing more, choosing instead to finish the last remnants of her breakfast. John could see she was thinking, mulling everything over, churning it around in her mind. That's what she did. That's how she worked, how she always worked. Sam was the thinker, the planner, the organiser of their partnership. He was the doer – just get it done and sort out any problems as they arose. Both worked in their own individual ways, but Sam normally came out on top. Yet John was quietly confident that his idea had met with at least a certain degree of curiosity. No objects, up until now, had been thrown, and no harsh words had been spoken, so it seemed right and proper that he should feel optimistic.

Worryingly though, her interest in polishing off the last of her food had taken priority, forcing away any actual communication between them and leaving John longing for some sort of direction. But he had learnt that his wife had a certain structure to follow when dealing with various situations and more importantly, he had learnt when to keep his mouth shut.

"You do know what you're suggesting is almost certainly illegal?"

John just nodded. He hadn't looked into that side of things, possibly because he had chosen to ignore the reality of the real world. To him it was a minor detail and one of no concern. After all, he was only trying to do something to help the survival of the farm, so it had to be the right thing to do. Didn't it?

Sam fell silent, drawing all her concentration to a slice of toast, only the crispy sound of its bite-sized pieces could be heard. John was relieved to see she was about to make a speech, only to be interrupted by the sound of the back door opening.

"It's only me!" John's mother marched down the passageway in her usual, solid, dependable manner. Her arrival wasn't entirely unexpected given she lived in the same building, only separated by a single brick wall at the far end of the main house. Not long after her husband's untimely death, Sylvia had insisted she move out of the main house and make room for the new guardian of the farm. John had converted the old out-house into living accommodation. Not grand by any means, but cosy enough for a single person and secretly his mother had gladly taken to it, only too pleased to vacate a draughty, cold country residence that looked from the outside to be picture-perfect, but in fact chilled the very soul from your body come winter time.

Sylvia stood in her place at the kitchen doorway, immediately sensing there was something wrong. "What's worrying you, dear?" She turned briefly towards Sam. "Good morning, Samantha. How are you today?"

"I'm fine, Sylvia, and you?"

"Oh, you know. Old age and all that it entails, but on the whole I can't grumble."

"Tea?" Sam asked as she walked over to the Aga.

"Yes please, dear. You know how I like it." Sylvia turned back round, eyeing her son with suspicion. "Now John, are you going to tell me what's wrong? And don't tell me there isn't anything – you never could hide anything from me, nothing's changed there. You were quite a predictable little boy, I seem to remember. I always knew when you were up to mischief, so tell your mother all about it." She pulled a chair from under the table and sat down, resting her arms in a matter-of-fact way across her chest as she waited for a reply.

John looked altogether uneasy as he thought about what to tell his mother. "Well, I'm afraid the meeting with the bank yesterday didn't go too well." He could see Sam choosing to keep well out of it as she placed a weak milky tea on the table.

"Just as you like it, Sylvia, a quick dip of the tea bag, lots of milk and one sugar." She stood back and waited for her mother-in-law's usual remark.

"Must keep the dairy industry going, my dear." There it was! The tea itself looked, and probably tasted disgusting, but that's how she liked it, so who was anyone to argue?

Sylvia sat contemplating John's last comment. "That's certainly not like Harold to be so uncooperative. Leave it with me, dear, I'll see him tomorrow."

"Mother." John tried to explain the situation but found his words immediately cut short.

"Let's say about two o'clock. You'll make me an

appointment, won't you, dear?"

"Mother!" He tried to raise his voice in an attempt to show some authority but soon realised she wasn't listening to him.

"I can't make it any sooner. WI meeting in the morning."

"Mother, please."

Finally she registered his pleading tone. "Oh, what is it, dear?"

"Harold isn't there and I'm pretty sure he's not coming back. They told me he was ill, but by the look of his office, I'd be pretty surprised if he returned. We have a new manager, a Mr Nesbit."

"Really! That's quite out of order. If what you say is true, I find the whole thing utterly preposterous. I must go this instant and seek out this Mr Cesspit! How dare they change managers without consulting me. Do they not realise how long the Taylors have banked with them? No John, I insist that you arrange for me to go."

"It's Nesbit, Mother, and I'd rather you didn't go. No, I *insist* you don't go. You'll only make things worse."

Sylvia glared at her son. "Really, dear, if you didn't remind me so much of your father, that comment would have almost certainly insulted my intelligence. Your dear late father could be quite forceful at times."

He and Sam watched as Sylvia's eyes glazed over, her whole stubborn existence drifting off to another place, a place of past memories. John raised an eyebrow, for it was clear to see where his mother's mind had gone and he didn't much enjoy the unwanted visions of his parents' private life flashing before his eyes. A shake of the head reluctantly brought Sylvia back to the land of the living.

"So be it, it's your decision." She sounded disappointed but it seemed there was nothing she could do. "You must do what's best, John."

"I'm sorry, Mother, but it's all been sorted, or trying to be sorted."

"At least you can tell me how bad things are. This is, after all, my home as well as yours. The farm has been through rough times before, you know, and I'm sure this present difficulty won't be the last."

John briefly looked towards Sam, hoping for some sort of support, but he was promptly sidelined by his mother's overpowering demand for an immediate answer to her question.

"Well John? I'm waiting."

There was nothing for it. John just had to come out with it, start from the beginning, as his mother had rightly said he could never keep anything from her, so he certainly wasn't going to try now. "It's like this, Mother. The truth is the cows haven't been making any money for at least two years or more, and like a fool I've been borrowing just to stand still, hoping that things would get better, but it seems we're just too small. The costs are running away from us, we're being squeezed from all directions and as much as

I dislike the man, our Mr Nesbit is right, we can't keep on borrowing against the farm. We could end up losing everything."

His mother just sat, taking an occasional sip of her milky tea, always prepared to challenge anyone who dared to comment on its appearance and only too willing to point out her overriding support towards the small family-run dairy farms, of which there were sadly less and less. John half expected her to launch into a lecture over the past financial history of Willowbank Farm and how her husband, John's father, had somehow managed to drag it through many such hardships and in doing so had left it in a fit and sound state for John to carry on, but to his surprise she chose to sit in silence, contemplating her next words.

He waited out of respect for the older woman to say something. His mother was a hard woman, there was no doubting that, but she also had a more sensitive side to her nature. He hoped she could see he wasn't fooling about; he had tried to set a tone in his voice that portrayed the seriousness of the situation.

"I'm sorry, dear, but never give up. Your dear father would have already thought of something to get the farm back on its legs. You're so much like him, I'm sure you'll come up with a solution."

"You have, haven't you, John!" Sam stood with her arms wrapped around her ample breasts, taking great delight in landing John in an awkward position, unashamedly prompting him into revealing his amazing, wonderful idea.

"There you go then. Problem solved." Sylvia looked not only pleased, but relieved to hear things were already in hand. She couldn't have her comfortable life in the countryside disrupted by the trivial inconvenience of lack of money. She was, after all, an upstanding peer of the village community and had worked hard to gain such status. It just wouldn't do to be associated with the destitute of society. She shuddered at the thought. "That's the ticket, dear, fighting spirit and all that." She paused. "Am I allowed to know of this life-saving idea of yours? Something I can help out with, I hope? I do like a challenge in life, you know, keeps the old heart pounding – don't mind doing my bit!"

"Yes, John. Tell your mother your plans. I'm dying to hear more. Why don't you tell her what you told me earlier?" Sam just couldn't help herself; she knew this was a serious matter but watching her husband squirm in his chair was so much more fun.

John took a sideways glance at his beloved wife and inwardly groaned as their eyes met, warning her to back off. He raised his hand to his face and nervously brushed his fingers across his stubble. A deadly hush fell upon the room as the two women waited for him to say
something.

"It's like this, Mother. I've been looking at all those empty bedrooms. It's always bothered me, a large house such as this and only the two of us rattling around in it now Luke's away."

"Excellent idea." His mother's look of delight took

John totally by surprise.

"What?"

"B & B, dear, I think it's a wonderful idea. I believe there's good money to be made in such things and times have changed. Such activities would surely now look favourable amongst the influential members of our society. We do, after all, have a standing in the village and I'm quite certain this would have been frowned upon in the past. Seen by many as lowering our standards, opening one's house to the common man, but many of the ancestral homes do just that. Samantha and I can work together. I'm not averse to handling a sausage or two in the morning."

John suddenly had visions of elderly couples clutching their National Trust cards tightly in their wrinkled hands while being ushered up to their respective waiting rooms with a view.

"No, Mother, it's not quite a B & B I had in mind."

Her initial excitement slowly melted away as she waited for John to explain.

"No. Not a B & B," John continued. "I was thinking more in line with hiring out the rooms – well, just one to start with. Then if things went well we might think about using the others, but only one for the moment. Nothing definite."

Sylvia clearly didn't have the foggiest idea what was going on. "You're talking riddles, John. Do come to the point, dear boy. I'm a busy woman and I can't sit here listening to you blabbering on about nothing in particular. So you're going to rent the rooms out? Is that it?"

"Kind of."

"Really, John, I haven't got time for this." She went to rise but was stopped by her son's raised hand.

"Please, Mother, let me explain. It's just not that easy to know how to." He found himself muffling his way through his next words, somehow thinking if he spoke behind his hand everything would sound that much better.

"I'm sorry, dear, you're really going to have to speak up."

"I want to hire out just one room. To a female." He could see his mother was going to say something. "Wait – before you speak, the reason why I only want to let it out to a woman is so she can run her business from it."

Sylvia, understandably, had now lost the plot completely, imagining dedicated WI members frantically knitting garments or crocheting into the early hours just to pay the weekly rent. Her idyllic scene of elderly ladies making polite conversation over a cup of tea while partaking in the delights of home-made cakes so keeping the cottage industry movement going was about to be well and truly shattered. John knew he had to bring his mother down gently. She was a strong-willed person but this had the capability to shake her. Realising he had reached a point of no return, it was time to lay it all on the table.

THE SECRET LIFE OF JOHN TAYLOR

He snatched one last intake of air and took a final shot of trying to explain the situation. "These women, or *woman*," he went on to explain, "would be earning their money from entertaining men." He nervously paused for a moment, then reluctantly carried on. "For sex, Mother, that's the simplest way I can put it."

Sylvia's teacup jolted, spilling half of her tea across the table. Sam's eyes quickly met John's as Sylvia went unusually silent. She gazed into her cup and ran her finger around the brim, before finally acknowledging their presence.

"Well, dear, I can honestly say this is one idea your father would never have thought up. You do realise what you're proposing is, I believe, illegal, and please put me right if I have it wrong, but you are suggesting running this illegal enterprise from a house that just happens to be in a village where I know for a fact you can't even blame a fart on your own dog without someone calling in the authorities. Do you not think that people might become suspicious of strange men coming and going, and what of these women's dress sense? This is the countryside, John, not London Soho. Scantily turned out young ladies strutting their wares around a working farm? Really, John, I think not! Lord only knows what it would do to poor George; it's hard enough getting reliable gardeners as it is without trying to kill the one we have. One glance at a half-naked young girl and I'm sure his pacemaker would never cope."

John raised his cup to his mouth, took a couple of sips then gently placed it back down on the table. "Not such a good idea, as far as you're concerned then?"

"John! Dear boy. Free-range chickens – now that I could have understood. A couple of hundred, I see as no problem, perfectly acceptable. Even alpacas, but God only knows why people would want to keep those – bog brushes on legs, ghastly creatures! Still, I could have accepted it, but this! Just think of my standing in the village should this ever get out. I would never be able to hold my head up in public again."

John said nothing, just waited for his mother to come in for the final kill. She looked subdued, still clearly against John's proposal, but also appreciating the severity of the farm's position, for she knew to come up with such a radical idea could only indicate the utter determination of her son to keep the farm afloat at any cost.

She looked him straight in the eye. "I don't suppose we're eligible for any diversification grants for this idea?"

"No, Mother, it's all hush-hush. The less people that know about it the better."

Sylvia leant across the table and placed her hand in her son's. "It was a joke, dear, you take life far too seriously." A half-hearted smile crossed her face. "Your father may not have approved but he always stood by one thing – the farm must come first; without it we are nothing." The thought of having to be forced to live amongst average men and women frankly didn't appeal to Sylvia one little bit. She squeezed John's hand tightly. "You must do what you think best, dear. I, of course, will do what I can to help, but fear that may be very little considering the subject matter, however the offer is there." Her voice clearly still showed signs of reluctance to accept what John was proposing, but he was in charge now. Pulling herself up from the chair she gently rested her hand upon his shoulder, silently reinforcing her faith towards an idea she had grave reservations about.

"I will, of course, visit you from time to time. I'm sure the prisons are not as bad as they say they are." John's face paled. "Another joke, dear. I bid you farewell Samantha and good luck, as I believe we are all going to need it!" She smiled politely and headed for the door.

"Goodbye, Sylvia," Sam replied. "And try not to worry too much, I'm sure whatever John decides to do, it will benefit us all."

"I do hope so dear. The thought of living my final years in shame and humiliation amongst the peasants of this land brings me out in a cold sweat. John." She nodded farewell to her son.

"Mother," he replied, as she marched back down the passageway.

A brief moment of calm settled on the room as they both heard the back door slam shut. Sam pushed against the back of her chair, lifting the front legs off the floor. "Well, that went well!"

"I suppose it could have been worse." John took another sip of his tea. "It was only to be expected; it is, after all, a ridiculous idea, thought up by a sad farmer who doesn't know his own mind." He glanced at his wife. "And you, what are your thoughts on this? You never did have a chance to say whether you liked the idea or not?"

"As mad as it seems, I actually quite like the idea – the thought of having another woman around the house is quite appealing. It's risky admittedly, but hey, life's not worth living if you're not prepared to take the odd risk now and again, and let's face it, we *are* in farming. Biggest gamble of them all."

John felt a glimmer of hope wash across the room. Sam had taken him by surprise, offered him support when he desperately needed it. "Thanks." There was little more he needed to say.

Chapter 7

It was all very well coming up with an idea, one that involved nurturing a willing female for the sole purpose of participating in sexual activities for profit, but where on earth would such a woman come from? John, by the sheer nature of his work, knew little of the trade he was about to embark on. Prostitution was as far removed from his daily life as you could possibly get, apart from a rumour that pointed a finger at a woman whose daughter spent a short time at the nearby secondary school that Luke had attended. A lady who played the game amongst the elite of society, were the gossips to be believed. Sam, although willing, also had no useful indication as to the whereabouts of such a lady, and why should she?

Quite clearly such an operation would be far beyond John's simple DIY farm set-up. He needed to stay level-headed. Nevertheless, what he could provide in terms of discreet off-street accommodation led him to believe his sights should be set slightly above those women who were tempted to advertise their wares upon the walls of men's public lavatories. Curb crawling had already been ruled out as a recruiting method. Not simply because of the obvious possible involvement with the police, but through its impracticability when applying farm vehicles to a back street situation.

John realised very early on that discretion needed to be his number one priority. So the old farm Land Rover had quickly been ruled out on most accounts with one off-side front light completely missing, brake lights occasionally working, passenger door permanently disabled and only having two speeds, neither of which involved crawling. He had leaned heavily in favour of the farm's family hatchback, but had soon been shouted down by Sam's ever practical approach, pointing out the inconvenience of losing the only real motorised comfort Willowbank had should it be impounded. The tractor posed serious concerns simply because of its inability to blend into a town environment, with only one thing going for it and that was its lack of identification in the shape of a missing number plate, but like the Land Rover, lack of suitable lighting seriously limited it when night driving was concerned. Sam had again pointed out the inconvenience of having the only operational tractor on the farm being seized by the law, and so John was sent away to rethink his approach.

"You could always try the internet." Sam's voice drifted across to him just as they had sat down in the front room. "You can find virtually anything on the web." She was met by a half-hearted grin to her suggestion. "What's so funny about that?" she asked.

John looked up from his armchair. "Nice idea, Sam, but really? I can't believe we're going to find local girls willing to fill our position on the internet. It's good for a lot of things, I grant you, but women for sex?" He shook his head, indicating the stupidity of such a suggestion.

"You're so naive, John, you really need to get out more. Anyway, you won't know until you try, will you?" An air of frustration began to creep into Sam's voice as she felt her cheeks blush, for she had ventured onto a number of risky sites in the past. Purely by accident she had convinced herself, of men and women performing acts of wanton lust. No, perhaps lust wasn't quite the right word. Something stirred within as she replayed in her mind scenes of tangled naked bodies performing sexual deeds. Shamefully she knew she had lingered longer than was appropriate. She was a married woman after all.

She swiftly moved across to the computer, its solid frame staring back at her. It was something neither of them readily used but it did work – to a fashion. Admittedly slow, but it was fine as long as you had time on your hands – something that was lacking in the Taylor household, so for the most part it lay idle, gently gathering dust.

She pressed the 'on' button and hesitated, her fingers hovering over the keyboard.

"What do you think we should type in?" He shrugged his shoulders. "Beats me! You're the one who seems to know about these things."

She didn't quite understand what he meant. "I don't. I know just as much as you. I just said it's worth a try, that's all."

"Okay. You don't have to get snappy about it. All I meant was you know how to work the wretched thing better than I do."

Sam said nothing more as she turned back and faced the waiting screen. Her fingers quickly pressed a number of letters and then waited. John seemed preoccupied, preferring to listen to the news on the TV. As the screen lit up Sam was confronted by a list of sites. "Well, that's interesting," she said over her shoulder, sounding surprised at what she had found.

The tone of her voice had immediately caught John's attention. "Found something?" It was only too plain to see he was more curious than he let on.

"Maybe. You better come and have a look."

"Oh, I suppose. If I must." Clearly he was trying to act cool about the whole thing, not wanting to show his eagerness.

Men, Sam thought, inwardly grinning, they really are so transparent.

John pulled himself out of his chair and made his way to Sam's side, still trying to show a reluctance to what was now staring him in the face. Peering over her shoulder, his eyes scanned an array of sites all seemingly competing for the business of seduction in its various forms. "Blimey, look at them all!"

Sam immediately sensed a surge of enthusiasm from her husband as he almost pushed her off the chair.

"Do you mind?" She wedged her shoulder firmly against John's body as he leant over her, pointing to one site in particular entitled 'Horny women for sex in your area'. The title, he had to admit, was a little crude, but very much to the point.

"That one. Try that one," he said eagerly.

"All right, calm down." His finger was almost touching

the screen. "John, please, now just wait." With a single press of the mouse the whole room suddenly transformed into a colourful advertising paradise of glossy willing females showing off their wares in an attempt to lure the unexpected, brainless male to part with their hard-earned money. Sam's expression took on a concerned look. "They're chat lines. You do realise that?"

An inexperienced man stood digesting the information his wife had just given him. Sam could see he was having trouble understanding. "You know? Sex over the phone?"

"Really?"

"Yes, really. So naive." She shook her head while browsing down the images as the visions of scantily dressed women assaulted her mind. "Here's one, looks quite nice. Shame about the tattoos, but she's got a friendly face."

John wasn't taking much notice of their faces, his eyes now glued to their exposed flesh. Sam tutted before reaching for a pen and paper. "Pay attention, John. This is not for pleasure, remember?" Ignoring her last comment he became oblivious to the outside world and stood in a state of numbness, transfixed by seemingly wonderful, generous, giving young ladies of reputable nature. By the time Sam had gone through the whole site she'd managed to find three possibles – two, supposedly from Castletown and the third from Manstead, some forty miles away. "Go on then." Sam looked at John who was still drooling over his angels from heaven.

He half pulled himself away from the screen. "Go on what?"

"Go and phone them, that's what. If you want this idea of yours to ever get off the ground, we need an experienced woman. Now go. See if any of them are interested."

Suddenly, reality hit John in the chest. This was no longer some fancy flippant idea that would never be acted upon. This was real and now. A deep sickening feeling rumbled in his gut threatening to churn up a wheelbarrow load of fear before casting a veil of doubt over the whole venture. He shook his head, indicating his reluctance to follow orders. "I can't."

"What do you mean you can't?"

He raised a finger and pointed it at his wife. "Okay Miss Know All, you tell me what I'm supposed to say, aye? Oh hello, my name's John and by the way, before we go any further, did I mention I was looking for a prostitute, very much like yourself, to come and work on a shared profit arrangement, but don't worry, we'll throw in board and lodging for free. Interested?"

Sam turned and faced the sarcasm with a look of sheer frustration. "They're not prostitutes for a start. Well, some may be. They're only chat lines, sex over the phone. It's a lot different from actually having real sex, and you can take that grin off your face."

John's hands went up in defence. "Okay, you've made your point. So if they're not prostitutes, why waste time ringing them?"

"Because we have to start somewhere. If they are, as they say they are and live locally, at least they might know someone. It's got to be worth a go. Let's face it, you've got nothing to lose by having a quick chat, and remember this is business. If there's any hanky-panky to be had in this house you can keep it for our bedroom, not over the phone, do you hear me? And don't stay on there too long, these phone lines cost a fortune." Such was Sam's efficiency, a piece of paper had already been written on, providing only the necessary information. Names, telephone numbers, place of residence and a blank space for John to write details that may be of use.

"Go on then, I've got cooking to get on with." Sam's forceful tone nudged John into the hallway, his enthusiasm still not quite at the level he thought appropriate for a man embarking on such a radical venture. With nerves that were sending his fingertips tingling with fear he gently sat himself down beside the telephone, placed the paper out flat and studied the first number belonging to a 'Lucy'. Immediately he found himself visualising a bony old cow standing waiting at the other end of the line. Coincidental perhaps, but he just couldn't quite get rid of the image of the old girl he had violated the other day. He quickly shut his eyes, trying to banish the scene that now confronted him. Surely she wouldn't be that old. Raising the phone to his ear, the number somehow found its way from his fingertips to a ringing tone, supposedly somewhere in Castletown, but as the seconds slipped by, John's willingness to terminate the connection grew stronger, believing that perhaps dear old Lucy had in fact wandered out into the field and was now munching happily with her mates and had no intention of answering his call. Convincing himself it was time to end his first attempt and move on, the phone had left his ear for only a split second when a woman's voice rattled down the line.

"Hello?"

Immediately John could detect a gravelly, hard edge to her voice. Perhaps she was his Lucy? He now realised he needed to say something. "Ah, yes. Hello?"

A little surprised at someone actually answering his call, John paused momentarily, giving Lucy the opportunity to reply. "Sorry. Just a minute." Her voice trailed off into a jumble of background noise involving what sounded like a blaring television and a barking dog.

John heard what he assumed was Lucy shouting, firstly at whoever was viewing the television then directly at the dog: "Will you turn that bloody thing off!" This polite request was met by the sound becoming noticeably louder. "You little turd, you did that on purpose." This last comment was followed by a short, sharp, ear-piercing scream that rattled its way down the phone line. John's first reaction was to put the phone down and call it a day, but something persuaded him to eavesdrop on the ever-changing developments of his first attempt at securing a reputable lady of the night. Lucy clearly wasn't what he had in mind but he just couldn't help himself. The dog had now become extremely excited by the unfolding events as John heard Lucy take her anger out on her next victim. "Oh, for God's sake, that bloody dog's crapped all over the kitchen floor again! Turn that wretched TV down or I'll beat the crap out of you. Where's that damn mongrel gone?"

John had heard enough, slowly putting the phone down when he heard the poor dog's harrowing cry in the background, obviously receiving a beating.

Sam, hearing the termination of the call, popped her head from out of the kitchen. "Any good?" She looked hopeful for a split second, then saw John's expression.

"Ah, no. I don't think she's really going to be suitable."

"Oh, right. Did you explain our situation?"

John shook his head. "We didn't quite get around to discussing that. She had to go. Important things to do."

Sam looked puzzled but tried to remain upbeat. "There's always the next one. You see? It wasn't that bad, was it?" She smiled encouragingly before disappearing back into the kitchen.

John wondered if she'd have said that if she'd been the dog. After his first failed attempt he found his enthusiasm even more lacking, his hand now hesitating over the phone while he fought to regain his composure. He wondered what the hell he was doing. How on earth had he persuaded himself that this was an idea worth pursuing? He sighed heavily, trying to clear his mind, allowing the blood to seep back into his brain. Finally he picked up the receiver, and plucking up a stray bit of courage dialled the number for Josie, half expecting a lengthy wait. He was surprised to be greeted by an almost instant, "Hello." It sounded like a young child. "Who's this?" she asked, in a slow, precise manner. The question was met with silence as it took John a second or two to figure out the conflicting messages that were now racing through his mind. The child had thrown him off guard.

"Hi, is Josie there please?" If the young girl announced she was Josie, he was hanging up straight away!

"No." There was relief on John's end of the line. The girl spoke matter-of-factly, clearly accustomed to answering the phone and possibly relaying messages to a third party. "She's in bed." Silence followed.

"Oh, is she not very well?" John's naivety had shown itself again.

"No silly, she's with a man." She paused again, before adding, "He's black."

This announcement took John by surprise. "Right. Not to worry. Maybe I'll try again some other time. Well, it was nice talking to you." He could see little point in continuing the conversation, but before he had chance to put the phone down …

"Do you know Tommy Pratley?" the young voice continued on.

"No. No I don't. Can't say I do."

"He's in my class and he's got a cat."

"Really? That's nice."

"Yes, and Mother says he hangs like a donkey."

"What, the cat?"

"No silly, the black man. He comes every Wednesday."

John thought about this for a while. "But it's Friday."

"Yes, and sometimes Friday. Do you know Sally Stubbs?"

"I'm afraid I don't. Any rate, I really must go. It's been nice talking to you."

"She's our teacher."

"Is she?" John struggled to hide his frustration. "I really must ..."

"She hasn't got a cat, but she is having a baby and she's really fat. Do you have a cat?"

John gripped the side of his chair, forcing himself not to slam the phone down. "No, I don't have a cat." God help us, he thought, if she knew he had sixty-five dairy cows. Common sense told him to say as little as possible and hopefully this little girl would tire over her obsession with cats.

"Shall I go get Mummy?"

"No. I think it's best if I go now."

"Okay. Bye." The phone immediately went dead, leaving John holding a disconnected line. He felt slightly unnerved, but mostly confused and somewhat deflated by yet another failed attempt. Could he go through with this? His will to live had somehow been stretched to its limit and the thought of navigating his way through yet another phone call filled him with a heightened state of fear. He glanced up along the empty hallway waiting for Sam to appear with some joyful comment, but there was no sign of her. He'd had enough – he was way out of his depth. He knew nothing at all about the trade he was entering into and it showed. Who in their right mind would ring up random strangers and try to persuade them to come and work for them? He was starting to question his own sanity as he pulled himself off his seat and made his way to the kitchen.

Sam stood in front of the sink, her hands submerged in a mass of white soapy foam as she cleaned remnants of Cottage Pie from their supper plates. She looked up to see her husband standing in the doorway, his expression revealing a man with a broken soul. She could have sympathised with him, shown him comfort in his hour of need, but she didn't. "Well?" She dried her hands with a towel and looked at him expectantly.

John looked up and with a shake of his head found his wife's frown burning into his eyes. Any positive thoughts towards 'Mandy', the next woman on the list, had long since disappeared, replaced with a solid, down-to-earth realisation that he had unwillingly joined the ranks of the new breed of bank manager and was in fact, a complete twat.

Not one to be defeated, Sam's positive attitude towards life shot across the room. "Third time lucky, aye?" Her unwavering tone ran through John's tired body like a razor-sharp arrow, leaving little evidence of entry but causing untold damage deep within. "Come on. It can't be that bad." Trying not to make things worse than they were, her lips broke into a gentle smile.

John's head slumped upon his shoulders. "It was a stupid idea," he protested, holding out the piece of paper with every intention of screwing it up and going to bed.

"Don't you dare."

John hesitated for a moment. "I'm not going to make any more of a fool of myself than I have already."

Sam clearly had other intentions as she threw back his negativity, forcing him to deal with the job in hand. To shape up and be a man. From that point on he knew he had no option but to turn around and unwillingly make his way back into the hallway. Of course he could have put up a fight, but where would that have got him? Hungry probably. He was spineless and he knew it. He now had an even bigger challenge. The telephone. A man-made instrument he had come to hate, loathe even. No, fear. It was as simple as that. The sheer thought of picking it up made his stomach churn. For heaven's sake, he was a dairy farmer, sometimes he wondered about his own mental state. How on earth had he convinced himself that this was his only option? His beloved farm, that's what. He sighed as he rang the next set of numbers on his list. Sam had allowed him space to carry on – at least she was enthusiastic about the idea. Alone with his thoughts he waited for someone to answer the call.

"Mandy speaking."

John's heart flipped to attention as he heard a pleasant female voice on the other end of the line. A voice so smooth and calming it could so easily belong to the pretty, well-spoken girl-next-door type. His heart pounded hard and fast. The expectations of communicating with a woman whose job it was to talk sex prevented him from any normal speech as he left a stagnant pause hanging in the air.

Mandy finally broke through the silence that prevented them from holding a meaningful conversation. Her experience of dealing with men who found it difficult to communicate with the opposite sex suddenly became apparent as her smooth, velvet-enriched voice immediately hypnotised John. "Don't be shy. Now why don't you tell me your name?" She spoke slow and precise, sending a gentle warming wave across John's entire body, his mind capturing a scene of crystal clear water trickling over smooth pebbles. He swallowed hard and deep before answering.

"John."

"That's better. Now John, shall I let you into a little secret?" She left a deliberate short pause before continuing. "John's my favourite name. I think it's such a strong name. Are you a strong man, John?"

"I … suppose I am, being a farmer."

"Oh John, I've always loved the rugged, outdoor type of man."

He could feel his throat tighten. "Have you?"

"I have, John." He sat dumbstruck, totally drawn in by Mandy's lust for money as she manipulated every twist and turn of their conversation, prolonging each word, extracting every last penny from her unsuspecting customer. "Talking to you, John, makes me feel so hot. Oh, I'm so hot. I think I need to take some clothes off to cool down. To feel the cool breeze caressing me. Would you like to help me take them off, John?"

Words stumbled as he felt himself harden with every word she spoke, his mind willingly visualising her request. "Are you still there, John?"

"Yes, yes. I'm here."

"You're a good boy, John. Now I think I might take off this warm, woollen top. I'm so hot and sweaty. It's bound to cool me down." There was a distinct lack of any sound while Mandy supposedly removed the mysterious garment over her head. John's bewitched mind could only hear and imagine what he wanted it to see – a beautiful blond female undressing before his very eyes, her flowing unkempt hair cascading in a free fall of tangled curls. "That's better. Would you like me to take my blouse off now, John?"

"Yes, and take it off fast, rip the buttons off if you have to, just get it off."

"My, my, John. You are getting forceful, aren't you?" Mandy knew her stuff, she had John exactly where she wanted him. All she had to do was play the game and like a typical man, he would believe anything. Men are such fools.

He'd been swallowed in so far only his wellington boots could be seen sticking out. Mandy smoothly ran into overdrive, throwing in the odd grunt and heavy panting as her imaginary blouse flowed across her body then fell helplessly to the floor.

"Would you like to know something, John? Come closer. We don't want anyone else to overhear what I'm about to tell you."

"What is it, Mandy? For Christ's sake, tell me."

She grinned to herself, for she knew she had him. Her low whispering voice told John he should brace himself. "I'm not wearing a bra, John."

Dear God! The thumping between his legs raised to alert levels, instinctively allowing him to visualise her topless body. Groaning inwardly he moistened his lips.

"Naughty me, John," her voice drifted down the line, "I completely forgot to put one on this morning."

"What else are you wearing?" John now took full control. Mandy was his to do what he wanted with.

"Tight jeans, John. Very tight. So tight they're rubbing my ..." Mandy left a deliberate blank space to arouse John's imagination and waited for the inevitable reply.

"Rubbing your what?"

There it was, worked every time! She almost laughed out loud at his stupidity while she sat on the sofa watching the muted television screen. "Now, that would be telling, wouldn't it?"

"Take them off." John almost cried with pain.

"But John, I'm not wearing anything underneath."

"Damn it girl! Take them off and fast."

"But you'll see everything John."

"I want to, I need to. Take them off." He wanted to scream down the phone, but even in his state of erotic emotion he was aware of Sam being only a short distance away.

Amazingly, and without much effort, Mandy had somehow managed to remove a pair of jeans that were supposedly so tight it would have taken a four-wheel tractor to pull them off. Her moaning now became noticeably louder, brought on by the contents of a rapidly cooling chicken and leek pot noodle as she balanced the carton in one hand while placing the phone down to change the channel on the TV. She tried to hold back a giggle as Lee Evans suddenly appeared, strutting his wares across the stage halfway through a sketch that Mandy knew all too well but one that never failed to make her laugh. She now had to turn up the heat. The pot noodles needed to be eaten – cold food wasn't an option, but she had timed everything to perfection.

 She heard John's heavy breathing over her moaning as she ran a finger around the inside rim of the pot to corral a stray noodle.

"Shall we play together, John?" She watched as Lee

Evans ran through his sketches one after the other. He was so good, her favorite comedian, and as much as she wanted the money, her eagerness to put on the sound was growing by the minute. She sighed to herself before groaning heavily once again, something that came easy to her now she had a mouthful of food. She moaned and groaned through the entire pot until that last solitary noodle rocked her into an explosive fake orgasmic climax. Mandy ran her finger around moistened lips, wiping away any remnants of her much-needed meal. "Oh, that was so good. You are a naughty boy, John, making me do that. I don't know what came over me."

John was almost at the point of no return when Sam suddenly appeared. Concerned by her husband's time-keeping, she stopped at the end of the hallway pointing to an imaginary watch, indicating the length of time he'd spent on an expensive phone line. Her presence made John suddenly rearrange his seating position, causing untold discomfort as his hardened state jammed itself into a confined space. Raising his hand, Sam's concerns were acknowledged.

Mandy, unaware of a third party, continued her performance to perfection, now in the full throes of yet another fake climax. John reluctantly found himself thrust back into the real world whereby he simply dropped the phone as if it were red hot, leaving Mandy to complete her West End performance to an empty theatre.

"Any good?" Sam's voice punctured John's dull mind.

"Umm, nice girl, but no, I don't think so. Something

about her."

Sam frowned. "You were on there long enough. Did you get any information from her?"

John shook his head for fear that if he said anything he would surely give the game away.

"I was sure you were onto something given you were on the line for so long." Her concern was met by a blank expression. It was now her turn to shake her head. "Never mind." She turned and headed back into the kitchen, the smell of half-cooked cakes drawing her towards the oven. A quick glance through the glass door reassured her everything was going along just fine. More than she could say for that useless man she found herself married to.

Chapter 8

The following days were uneventful. Miss Goodman had once again tried to attempt an unauthorised meeting concerning the village fête. Milkings had come and gone and George, the elderly gardener, had refused to go to the doctor after another temporary malfunction relating to his otherwise smoothly running pacemaker. The dogs spent much of their days trying to escape the slowly increasing temperatures, happy to rest amongst the straw while the mad world flew past the farm gate.

A lack of communication between the interested parties concerning John's rescue plan was beginning to worry him somewhat. Sam hadn't spoken on the subject, nor mentioned his failed attempts at securing even one possible lead towards recruiting a lady of ill repute. Sam much preferred to call them working girls. Like Sylvia, she disliked the word prostitute – somehow it didn't seem to sit well with her. As for John's mother, she seemed more concerned with the greenfly attacking her roses than the possible demise of their home. So John had been left alone, muttering to himself while he did what he loved – extracting milk from animals that hadn't a clue about the worries surrounding them. So life went on.

It was now Friday morning and John was having breakfast with Sam. She politely enquired about the milking. Nothing out of the ordinary had happened, so that ended that conversation. Silence followed while the old teapot dribbled, as usual leaving a small puddle of freshly made brew next to each mug.

Sam looked up, set a piece of paper in front of him, then continued eating as if nothing had happened, content in splitting her organic free-range egg so that its yolk was ready to dunk a bite-sized piece of sausage. John peered down at the neatly written note, words he immediately recognised as not being in Sam's hand.

"What's this?"

"It's three names of women who might be interested in coming to work on the farm." She placed another piece of food onto her fork, rather pleased with her announcement.

"What, prostitutes?"

"If you like to call them that, then yes. I prefer 'working girls', but whatever you call them, you're interviewing them over the weekend."

"I am?"

"Yes. The first one's arriving tomorrow at ten. Their details are next to their names."

John creased his face in surprise. "But where? How did you …?"

"Your mother."

"My mother!" He found himself forcing his food back into his mouth before it had a chance to be spat across the table.

Sam tapped the side of her nose with her finger. "Your

mother knows a lot of people."

"Yes, I realise that, but knowing these sorts of women is a lot different to rubbing shoulders with the general inhabitants of the village."

"I don't know anything about that. She wouldn't say how she came about the information, but just said the WI has its fingers in many pies. Just be thankful she's on your side in this."

"Yes, I am. Very grateful. But *Mother*?"

"Anyway, you can thank her later. For now, you need to get yourself sorted before tomorrow. I rang them yesterday explaining what we're about and what we're looking for. All three seemed really interested. It was quite easy really. What you were up to the other night I really don't know. Oh, and before I forget, you're paying their travelling expenses. I thought it was only fair, as expecting them to come out to the back of beyond is a bit much to ask."

"We're not that remote."

"No, maybe not to you, but to town girls anything past the city boundary is another world."

John was still shocked at where the information had come from. "I still can't believe it. Mother's hardly said a word since I told her of my plans, and then suddenly this."

"As I said, be grateful, and you probably know as much as I do, so let's say no more. The first one's coming by train – I told her you would pick her up from the station. Ten o' clock tomorrow, don't forget – I know what you're like. Didn't think you'd want to pay for a taxi. The second one has her own transport – you'll have to work out petrol money for her, and the third one is using the bus. You'll need to pick her up just outside the village, Granmore Lane – you know the stop, just outside the Blackmore place."

John studied the details of the women. "Oak Bridge? I thought we were looking for local girls? Oak Bridge has to be fifty or sixty miles away. How much is this lot going to cost me?"

Sam frowned, trying her hardest not to comment on John's ungrateful attitude. "Whatever it takes." Her unbroken stare warned him, in no uncertain terms, to drop the subject and be grateful for his mother's kind help.

"Sorry, only this is a little unexpected, that's all, but gratefully received. Thank you."

"Don't thank *me*, it was your mother's doing."

"I'll speak to her later."

"Yes, make sure you do."

He reached over the table and gently patted Sam's hand, hoping this small gesture would reinforce the help he'd received. Interviewing wasn't something John had ever needed to do. The farm, under his command, had never generated sufficient profits to warrant even suggesting hiring more help. George had always been on the farm. His father had taken him on long before John's time, first starting work on the land, then progressing to milking the cows.

Eventually, like so many older workers, he had ended up being retired to the garden, only too willing to give up the physical toll of day-to-day farming to be able to potter about the lawn and vegetable patch until such time as life finally tells him that enough is enough. Mother had taken on the responsibility of employing him, although at times she found his ways almost intolerable, but secretly John was sure she found his company a great comfort as the two unwillingly headed into old age. She would never admit it to anyone, however.

John could have accepted interviewing someone for a farm position given his knowledge of all things agricultural, but interviewing ladies for the sole purpose of extracting money from men in exchange for sexual services frankly scared the living daylights out of him and he'd already convinced himself he would surely make a complete pig's ear of it. What on earth do you ask such women? His own sex life wasn't great and with no experience whatsoever to what went on behind a prostitute's door he felt hopelessly out of his depth. He found himself fretting over such things as wages, work conditions, health and safety (whatever that entailed), additional equipment. Yes he had a workshop of sorts, but he wasn't a builder or a handyman. Would they expect things to be bolted to the walls? Were the bedrooms structurally sound for such things? That was his problem, he didn't know about these things.

Saturday morning dawned and somehow the cows had managed to milk themselves, metaphorically speaking. John moved amongst them in body only, his mind wandering constantly between fact and fiction, stirring the muddy silt that lay deep within a normally level-headed brain. He wasn't a natural forward thinker – that was Sam's department. He just dealt with problems as they arose. Working out a solution beforehand so eliminating the many stresses of life wasn't how he worked. He had, of course, armed himself with fragments of poorly strung together questions to ask the first young woman, but after two hours of watching cows wandering in and out of the milking parlour he still had no clue what he was doing.

Selbourne Railway Station required a twenty-minute drive through narrow awkward back lanes that would test even the best of drivers, but for all its difficulties its beauty never ceased to stir his innermost feelings and he was glad to be away from the farm's problems if only for a short while. Too many days, weeks, months had passed since he'd had an excuse to venture this way, to explore the wonders of the open countryside that surrounded his contented life. He headed towards a normally deserted railway station, its uninspiring gathering of wooden huts praying for the attention of some official person with a paintbrush to lick them into order, but alas no one seemed to care. John wondered what anyone from the city would think of such a place. Possibly their first reaction would be to just stay seated and move on, for the only good thing going for it was the warmth of a near-perfect day and the fresh clean air that drifted across the rolling hills.

He'd arrived early, parking the Land Rover beside the

only two other vehicles that sat waiting patiently for their owners' return. The stillness of the day was shattered by two overexcited dogs jostling amongst themselves in the back, growling occasionally, but mostly acting out playful banter while revelling in the sudden unexpected change in their normal mundane routine. John casually glanced at his watch. He wasn't one for sitting about even though he knew he was early and had only just arrived. He kept telling himself he should enjoy the moment, allow this time to settle his nerves, but as every minute passed his solitude was making things worse. It wasn't normal sitting around and doing nothing; there were always things that needed to be done. Time to himself was a luxury that took a lot of getting used to, and anticipating the arrival of a train wasn't helping. Navigating his hands around the steering wheel, his fingers found themselves tapping some unrecognisable tune that buzzed around in his head.

Ten minutes ticked painfully by as he peered up a deserted track that ran perfectly straight as far as the eye could see. The heat haze of the increasing warmth of the day rose from the ground, distorting the welcome sight of a tired, grimy diesel locomotive as it pulled towards the station, finally grinding to a shuddering halt alongside the waiting platform.

John rapped his hands nervously against the steering wheel, preparing himself for the job in hand. "Well, this is it." He swung the Land Rover door open causing the dogs to go mental. "Stay!" John's stern order did nothing to quieten them down, but stay they did, allowing John to watch the train slowly pull away.

He quickly made his way to the platform and was met by the sight of a lonely figure in the distance. John drew nearer, his nerves dancing within. This now seemed so real, so definite, so frightening, he almost felt like throwing up. Here was a human being. A living person. Not some figment of his imagination – a real live woman. What would she be like? Would she like him? Would he like her? Was she pretty? Ugly? He hadn't considered that. Hell, she could be as ugly as a baboon's backside. The hairs on the back of his neck tingled with uncertainly, for he had only been given the briefest of details. A sudden thought ran through his mind – was this, in fact, his potential candidate? She could be anyone. Perhaps she had decided not to come, been taken ill, or missed the train even. This woman might just have, coincidentally, got off at this stop and make her way to one of the waiting cars and drive off. Control yourself, John, you're overthinking things again. Keep calm, deep breaths, there's only one way to find out.

He glanced along the platform. Definitely a woman, at least that was a start. Long brown hair, nice figure and, surprisingly, a pleasant face as far as he could see. She stood looking slightly uneasy as her only means of transport slowly disappeared around a distant bend. She then turned to face John as he slowly walked towards her, past the tired wooden huts that represented Selbourne Station.

"Hello, Susan?" The young lady nodded much to John's relief, allowing them both to stand and study each other for a moment. Smiles formed on their faces.

"Hi, Mr Taylor? Nice to meet you." A welcoming hand reached out leaving John no option but to touch the warm flesh of a surprisingly attractive, well-manicured young female. Her voice portrayed calm intelligence, something he wasn't expecting, but then he wasn't really sure what he was expecting.

He couldn't think of anything to say; after all it wasn't as if she were an old relation whom he hadn't seen in years, someone weighed down by family history, ties from which he could draw upon and hold a meaningful conversation. He had to remember she was a prostitute, someone who made a living from selling her body.

"Good journey?" It sounded lame, but it was a start.

"Yes, thank you." There followed a short pause while each of them contemplated what to say next. Susan briefly looked around. "It's lovely here, Mr Taylor."

"Please, John."

"John. It's strange to think I live only an hour away, yet my world is so different. I rarely get out of the city."

She spoke, looked, and even smelt like quality. A pleasant young lady who had captured John's heart and seemed perfectly normal. Why that surprised him he wasn't sure.

"Here, let me help you with your bag."

Susan hesitated. "It's only a handbag, Mr Taylor – sorry, John. There's no need, really."

"No, of course not. A handbag. Silly. Any rate, we'd

best be off, if you'd like to follow me. I'm afraid it's only the farm Land Rover, so apologies before we get to her. The old girl means well but seldom delivers."

"I'm sure she'll be fine."

"Nice words, but you haven't seen her yet." John could feel the strain slowly melting away as he warmed to a young lady he was sure he could get to like. He almost felt like whistling to himself. Perhaps this venture of his wasn't such a bad idea after all. "Well, here she is."

Susan's face took on a polite look of surprise.

"I did warn you."

"I'm sorry, I didn't mean to be rude."

"No offence taken."

"Door's jammed," explained John as Susan went to open the passenger door. "You'll have to get in through the driver's side. It's a little awkward, so word of advice, when you get in, make sure to spread your legs over the gear stick." John was almost tempted to make a crude joke but thought better of it. He hadn't known her long enough for such low-grade country humour. "Don't worry about the dogs, they're perfectly harmless, all noise and no bite."

Susan was met by two faces peering through the back window of the cab, their constant barking giving way to increasing excitement towards someone new. Her eyes then fell upon a shambolic mess that lay scattered across the seats – objects that meant nothing to a town girl but clearly had some sort of function here in the countryside. She tried to ignore an unpleasant smell that caught her nostrils as she picked her way across the seats. She wondered if this odour was something she'd have to get used to if offered the opportunity.

"What are their names?" She squinted through the dirt that partially covered the dividing rear windows, the dogs' slug-infested saliva smearing what little vision she had of the two hyper creatures.

"Kim's the collie and Pup's the madcap terrier."

"They're funny," Susan replied.

"Yes, well, that's one way of describing them. Loopy, if you ask me."

"I'm sure they're lovely." John gave her a quick glance. It was hard to believe this pleasant, well-spoken young lady entertained men, and possibly women for all he knew, for money. He had only been with her for a very short time, but already he felt comfortable in her presence. But then perhaps that's how she worked. Maybe it was part of her act, luring men into a false sense of security, talking of nothing in particular and letting them believe they were the only one she cared about. Perhaps that's what most men really craved – to be wanted, and sex was just a bonus.

His mind had wandered yet again, overthinking the situation. He pulled himself into the driver's seat as Susan settled herself down. The Land Rover roared into action and was persuaded into reverse, jolting backwards kangaroo fashion. John watched with amusement from the corner of his eye as his passenger gripped both sides of her seat.

Susan looked concerned. "It is road legal, isn't it?"

"Er, kind of. I'm afraid Sam, my wife, has taken the car, otherwise I would have picked you up in that."

"Right." Susan smiled politely. It was a false expression as she started to wonder what she'd let herself in for. They roared out of the car park already touching twenty-five, but once on the open road her concerns soon settled when she realised that the vehicle's full potential could only reach thirty tops.

John was concentrating on the increasing bends in the road when he realised they hadn't exchanged a single word for a good ten minutes. "Everything all right?" He took his eyes off the road for a split second to see her staring out the side window.

"Fine. Why?" She pulled her gaze away from the outside world and looked in John's direction.

"If you don't mind me saying, you seem a little preoccupied. Nothing wrong, I hope?"

"It's beautiful, John."

"What is?"

"The countryside, it's just so perfect and there's so much green. I didn't realise you could get that many shades of the same colour."

"You're right, it's an amazing place. I see it every day and still never get tired of it, and it's constantly changing, that's what makes it so special. Each season has its own way of showing everything off." He paused for a moment. "I'm afraid it's only humans who mess it up."

Susan studied the man next to her. "You clearly speak with passion."

John took a while to answer, calculating his next words. "Passion. Yes, I suppose I do. I can't deny it, I love this place. She can be hard at times, but always gives you something in return for your labour. Unfortunately not much money though."

Susan looked back out across the patchwork of fields and rambling hedgerows. "I never get out of the city. It's a bit like a prison at times, but with no walls. Don't get me wrong, it's not that I dislike it, but I've always felt that there's something more, something …" She stopped mid-sentence. The air drained from her lungs, still transfixed by a landscape that had somehow hypnotised her.

John waited, allowing her to come back in her own time, for he could detect a pinch of sadness in her voice which only made his job of picking his final choice that much harder. He was certain everyone would have their own personal story to tell, but it was pointless worrying over what might be. "Early days yet," he heard himself say. "Nearly there." John proudly pointed to a group of cows happily grazing beside a small woodland, its weighted canopy of dark green leaves shading a determined flow of water as it snaked its way through rolling countryside. "They're mine. The rest can't be far away."

"You've got cows?"

Her surprised reaction sent a warm feeling of

satisfaction through John's body. He liked her, and in the short time they'd been in each other's company he'd felt something stir within him. Not just because she was young and attractive, although that helped. It was more than that. She was just a pleasant person to be around. He suddenly realised he needed her to be impressed with what she saw. He needed her to want to stay, live in the same house as him. The thought of sharing his days, weeks, months alongside someone like her sent a tingle of excitement through his veins.

"Yep, sixty-five in total." He pointed once more. "You can just see the farm over there." A set of red brick barns weighed down by weather-beaten terracotta tiles slowly appeared, nestled within a scattering of mature trees, their various shapes and colours set in a scene of peaceful calm.

"It looks so idyllic."

John was again pleased with the tone of her voice, but equally surprised at her reaction towards something he found so normal. They were, after all, just farm buildings, and having grown up in these surroundings, he found it hard to appreciate the feelings Susan was experiencing.

He wondered if she might not be so complimentary come wintertime, when the stark darkened land was highlighted against a sub-zero hoar frost, a landscape crying out for warmth. Yet John was sure she would fall for the scattering of enchanting colours that March could bring. Of sheltered ditches persuading perfectly formed primrose heads to shine within the ever increasing light, of the sight of bluebells nestling amongst the woodland floor while Mother Nature alone commands the chill of the winter nights into longer spring days. These were the things that tugged at the heart.

John suddenly realised he was daydreaming again, but in reality he secretly hoped Susan would be given the chance to react towards those changes as he did, to marvel at the simple things in life.

Travelling along the narrow lanes he guided the young lady through various field names. Names that had been handed down through the generations: Brooks Bottom, Dale End, Oakley, only too pleased to have someone who seemed genuinely interested in what he called his world.

Chapter 9

"Here we are then." John announced their arrival through a chaotic chorus of howling dogs.

The two nutty canines, sensing their release, jostled for position as the Land Rover pulled in through the open gate, its tired body eating up the gravel before grinding to a halt just beside the garden path.

"Remember," John announced with a rather cheeky grin, "be sure to part your legs before you get out." His wandering eyes just couldn't help run down the length of Susan's semi exposed legs, hoping she would sense the humour in his warning.

She smiled politely, accepting of his somewhat boyish behaviour and waited patiently as John jumped out, unable to take his eyes off her slender legs as she positioned them over the gear stick.

"Be careful now." He almost chuckled as he spoke.

So like a man, Susan thought. Well if that's what he wanted, she could play along. With her dress gathered as high as she dared without causing the man a heart attack, she lifted her legs either side of the gear stick and gave a performance that almost took his breath away, lingering far longer than was totally necessary, and clearly sending his mind to a place it should never be.

He cleared his throat. "Need any help?"

She shook her head. "Thanks, but no."

"Right. Handbag?"

"I'm fine."

The sight of her emerging almost brought tears to his eyes, her skirt riding up slightly higher than was normally expected within a farm environment as she manoeuvred her way out of the vehicle. Kim and Pup wrangled amongst themselves, eager for the tailgate to go down allowing them the freedom every country dog should expect. Once lowered, a virile Jack Russell leapt to the ground, leaving John to lower Kim gracefully. They jostled amongst a shower of gravel while Susan watched with amusement. As they fought for their right to welcome the new arrival she gave a wide smile, just as the dust-covered creatures jumped up for attention.

"Here, get down!" John reprimanded each one in turn, sending both scurrying off towards the garden. "Sorry about that."

"Come and meet the wife." John led the way through immaculately kept lawns and around to the front of the house hardly noticing if his charge was following. The long garden path allowed Susan to admire her surroundings before finally arriving at John's side. Sam appeared in the doorway. "Susan, this is Samantha, Sam for short."

The older woman held out her hand, eyeing the young lady from top to bottom. First impressions were very much to her liking. "We spoke on the phone."

"Yes, Mrs Taylor, nice to meet you." Their eyes

met, causing both to hide an unexpected flurry of schoolgirl giggles.

John, being a man, never noticed.

"Please call me Sam, you'll make me sound like a headmistress."

Their visitor felt an unexpected warmth rise to her cheeks. "It's nice to put a face to the voice," Susan replied. They held hands a little longer than was expected for a first meeting, then slowly parted.

"Come along in. I'm sure you'd love a cup of tea, or is it coffee with you younger people?"

"Coffee would be great." Susan's attention drifted briefly as they walked along a hallway the size of her one-bedroom flat. She couldn't help but look, to invade her hosts' privacy, sneaking the odd glance into rooms you could play five-a-side football in and still have space to swing the odd scabby cat. "You have an amazing house, Sam."

"Thank you, but looks can be deceiving, believe you me. You wait until winter." She suddenly realised she'd almost expected Susan to accept the job on offer. "I mean, it can get pretty cold here during the winter months."

"How many of you live here, if you don't mind me asking?"

"Not at all. Just the two of us now. Luke, our son, has gone off travelling, but there's John's mother – she has her own small place in an outbuilding joined to the far end of the house."

Susan looked a little shocked. "You stick your mother-in-law outside in the shed?"

Sam couldn't help herself. "Oh yes, like the dogs she gets fed twice a day. Has plenty of straw to sleep on, but no need to worry, you won't see much of her unless you're out wandering under a full moon!" Seeing the shock on Susan's face she added "I'm only joking, she has a lovely little converted flat, all mod cons – it's a lot warmer than this place, I can tell you. I know it seems a bit excessive, such a big house and only the two of us, but it comes with the farm so we don't have a lot of options. Right, coffee. John, tea for you?"

"Please."

"Don't mind me, I'll make the drinks if you to want to discuss business." She moved away, smiling light-heartedly.

John wasn't looking forward to this part, but it was, after all, his idea and why Susan was here, but it didn't help his unease concerning the thorny subject of this young woman's profession. "Okay, right, Susan, it's like this ..." He coughed, desperately trying to dislodge the fear that lay within his stomach. "I ... that is, we, yes we ..."

"Mr Taylor. John. May I ...?" Susan interrupted him, causing Sam to turn around. "I think what you're trying to say, John, is that you need the assistance of a prostitute."

He looked a little uneasy but gladly accepted

her observation. "Well, not me personally, you understand."

Sam felt completely within her rights to caution her husband's last comment. "John, try and keep it business-like."

"Sorry, carry on, Susan."

"Thank you, John. I'm not ashamed of what I do, and nor should you be. Whatever word anyone chooses to describe my profession, that's what I am, a prostitute."

His face took on the colour of beetroot. "I apologise. It's just, as you can see, we are rather new to this sort of thing."

"Yes, I can see that," Susan replied. "Would it be better for all concerned if I told you how I see it and then you can tell me if I am going wrong?"

John nodded, gladly accepting the suggestion. "Thank you. I think that's a great idea."

She pulled her chair in, casually resting her arm on the table. "So, as far as I can make out by the limited information Sam gave me over the phone, you, the owners wish to 'employ' in some shape or form the services of a 'professional lady', shall we call her?" When both Sam and John nodded Susan carried on. "For the sole purpose of generating additional income over and above the normal expected revenue generally obtained from a farm of your size. I am to believe said activity would be advanced by the uptake and occupancy of a number of vacant rooms from which normal activity has now ceased, thus changing their use from domestic to business. This would be seen as advantageous to the overall profit of the farm in general, notwithstanding any additional costs that may occur over time in respect to such activities. Am I right?" Silence fell upon the room. "You may respond." Susan raised her mug and swallowed a mouthful of coffee.

John glanced over in Sam's direction as he scratched his head in bewilderment. "I think that's what we mean."

Sam just nodded in agreement. "Where on earth did you learn how to talk like that?

"I'm sorry, I can get a little carried away sometimes. You see, I previously trained to be a lawyer. London. Old habits die hard."

"Blimey, and now you're a prostitute."

"John ..." Sam shot him a stern look.

"No, it's perfectly all right, Sam. It's funny how life turns out sometimes, isn't it?"

"Hilarious."

"John! Please!"

"Just saying."

A discreet glance from Susan reassured Sam she was fine with her husband's last comment.

"Well, now everyone's clear as to what we're trying to do, shall we take a look at the bedrooms?" He rose, led the way along the hallway and up the stairs, stopping outside the first door, giving Susan the opportunity to peer down the sheer length of the landing stretching out before her. Like a child in a sweet shop she clutched her handbag in anticipation of what lay ahead, watching with a racing heart as John gently turned the brass door knob. The thought of living and working in such an environment was almost too much to take in.

The door swung open and Susan's excitement slowly drained from her face. John, of course, hadn't noticed, far too busy proudly announcing their first inspection, but Sam had observed far more than her husband and could see this wasn't going to end well.

John straightened his back, feeling quite proud at what lay before them. "We've got the choice of four rooms – all on this floor, two on each side. They're very much the same size except one, that's a little smaller and slightly oddly shaped, but I'm sure we'll find something to suit. Oh, and of course, they all have different views to look out over. Two across the gardens and the others look out over the front, the fields and woodland beyond. So this is number one." He rubbed his hands, anticipating a good response.

It was a rather out-dated layout. Bold floral wallpaper roared at her as she stood speechless, as if the ghastly triffids would jump out and bite her head off. It was a well-proportioned room, but not to her taste, although for the sake of her hosts she needed to at least give it a chance. As she walked to the window her head began to spin unexpectedly, the uneven floor playing havoc with her brain, making it difficult to picture this room as a suitable place for seduction.

Any views from the window were hidden by a rampant but otherwise impressive woody plant about to come into flower – she was certain if the window was opened the plant would take her by the throat and drag her to certain death.

"It's a wisteria," explained Sam, noticing Susan's look of bewilderment.

"Nice." The word sounded hollow. Even John had cottoned on to Susan's disappointment.

"You don't like it, do you?"

"I'm sorry, it's not that I dislike the room. It's fine. It's just …" She hesitated. "It's just, it hasn't got that *something*. The window's not in the right place. The floor I could probably get used to, but I hate to think what my clients would say when they get thrown towards the outer walls. And the light …" she shook her head, "it's all wrong somehow. Just little things, you understand. I know it sounds like I'm being rather fickle but this is not just about having sex, as many people think it is. There's much more to it than that. You see it's my job to create an illusion, somewhere my clients can feel relaxed. Many of them are insecure, stressed, even lonely. I have to work within their boundaries but also create a seductive sense of calm." She quickly glanced around the room. "Certainly not one that involves scary, bright, devilish sunflowers."

John pulled himself in. "Right. I suppose if you put it like that then it's onto the next room." He gave Sam a worrying glance as he left. "Let's try opposite, you may get a different perspective overlooking the gardens – it's more peaceful, a bit of Swan Shy perhaps."

"Feng shui, John. If you're going to be sarcastic do try and get it right." Sam's apologetic look assured Susan things would get better, she just needed to give them a chance. "Sorry, Susan, men! I'm afraid what little brains they do have are hidden beneath their underpants."

Susan grinned. The short walk across the landing led them into an almost identical room in size and shape, but thankfully plain neutral colours adorned all four walls, the pastel shades blending perfectly against the backdrop of well-kept sweeping lawns and mature shrubs. Scattered trees enclosed the view perfectly between small glass panels. Susan quietly studied the room and with some relief walked upon a level floor of varnished timber before stopping momentarily to gaze out across the gardens. "Maybe ..." she sighed. Her face showed signs of doubt yet optimism towards possible future improvements.

John didn't bother waiting for a lengthy rejection, leading the way to his third offering. With little confidence he announced it was almost identical to the last one, having used the same paint to try and cut the overall cost of both rooms. His heart sank as he noticed the window shaded by a large oak tree, its dark green foliage hanging on twisted bark, threatening to enter the room.

"No." Susan shook her head and promptly walked out.

Not surprised, John shrugged his shoulders as he

silently screamed in frustration, pleading for some sort of guidance. "Right, okay. Last one." By now his confidence in securing Susan's perfect love nest had taken one hell of a battering, so without question his final attempt would, he was sure, receive a miserable shrug of disapproval.

The door swung open allowing all three to walk into an oddly shaped room, exposed beams jutting out this way and that, precisely held together by large wooden pegs. The floor was level, but barely covered by a badly worn carpet that did nothing to disguise the cracks between the floorboards that snaked across the room. There were more windows in this room, but they were clearly in need of a paint job, chipped and flaked. But none of that seemed to matter when Susan laid eyes on the four-poster bed in the centre of the room.

Susan admired the craftsmanship of solid timber, her eyes dancing upon the woven patchwork of delicate cloth that spoke of elegance and demanded respect by all those present. "My God!" Her voice was filled with sheer admiration as she walked in a trance, running her hand gently over the intricate carvings etched into its surface. John's eyes met his wife's as a glimmer of hope dared to show itself ...

"Do you like it?" he asked.

"It's amazing."

He seized the moment and went over to its grand structure. "They say it's as old as the house. But if you want it I'm afraid you're going to have to take the room as well, because apart from knocking it apart there's no way it's coming out, and I can assure you it's not made by IKEA!"

"I'll take it. Just look at it – it's every working girl's dream, a real four-poster." Her hands tested the all-important mattress. "Oh dear, paying customers won't like that!"

Sam could see Susan wasn't going to be persuaded to take up their offer purely because of a lumpy four-poster mattress; she would have to give her a little more. "We'll get a new mattress and George can paint the windows. And of course, you'll need a new carpet – these floorboards won't do it, but the rest will be up to you."

"Hang on." John perked up. "Don't I get a say in this? Things cost money, you know."

"Ignore my husband, Susan, he knows nothing of a woman's needs."

"But ..."

"No, John."

"Deal."

"What?" His face took on a look of sheer confusion, allowing Susan to seize the moment before he had a chance to say another word.

"Excellent."

Sam looked over at her husband who was desperately trying to calculate how much all this was going to cost him. "Unfortunately we can't give you a definite decision until John has interviewed the others, but we'll let you know as soon as possible."

"I understand."

The kettle was gently simmering on the Aga plate as the three of them made their way into the kitchen.

"I'll make us another drink, shall I?" Sam made her way across the room but seized the opportunity to delve deeper into Susan's private life. "You say you trained to be a lawyer? Sounds very exciting."

Susan pulled back a chair and sat down. "I'm not sure you can call it exciting. Interesting, yes, but there's a lot of mundane work involved. I did enjoy it, although I felt there was always something not quite right, something missing.

"A bit like our bedrooms."

"John."

"No, Sam, John's right, I'm a bit of a perfectionist. For me it's all about doing the best you can do. I'm certainly not saying everything I do is perfect – far from it, but as long as I've tried I'm happy. I'm sure I would've made a good lawyer, but it just wasn't to be and when your heart isn't in it, you start to question everything."

Sam busied herself making the drinks and talking as she went. "In what way?"

The young woman got comfortable, seemingly happy to continue. "It takes years to train as a lawyer and it isn't cheap. Tuition fees, accommodation, the list goes on. A lot of students fall by the wayside through no fault of their own and I'm afraid I don't have a rich mummy or daddy to support my studies like some, but I managed to get a waitress job. At least then I could afford to eat. The rest of the money – what little was left – went into paying the student loan, but as time went on the debt became bigger and my enthusiasm towards what I was doing hit rock bottom. That's when a friend of mine suggested I try her line of work. Nothing too serious to start with, a bit of lap dancing, that sort of thing, but one thing led to another and I found myself entertaining men back at the flat."

By now John was starting to feel slightly uncomfortable. This was something women talked about in private over a glass of wine, a light lunch, not over a mug of rapidly cooling coffee in his kitchen. Yes, they needed to know about the person who might share their house, but was all this personal stuff necessary?

Susan dampened her lips with another mouthful of coffee and continued. "So that's how it all started. Compared to waiting on tables it was a no-brainer. Yes, it was a little strange at the start. I cried, but like anything the more you do it the easier it gets, and my friend taught me how to handle men properly. You wouldn't believe how you can twist them around your finger if you know the right way to do it." She deliberately glanced at John and smiled, making his cheeks glow with embarrassment. "So I ended up quitting my studies and here I am. Not much of a life's history, but it's early days yet."

"I see." Sam could see the girl was sincere and it was

good that she was being honest – that went a long way in her book. "Anything else you want to ask, John?"

"Yes. Money. I know it's not the nicest thing to talk about, but I've spent some time getting up-to-date information on wages."

"John!"

"No, hear me out."

Susan wondered what was coming next. John carried on regardless of the looks he was receiving. "Of course this can only be taken as a rough guide," he continued. "As you are not officially a farmworker but as far as I can make out, working on the agricultural guidelines, it states a basic hourly rate of £8.70 per hour, but given you would be overseeing people ... er, clients, I believe we should be looking at a craftsman rate which would bring it up to £9.10 per hour. I'm still a little concerned that this may be a tad on the low side by the time we've both had our share, so I know I might be pushing our luck but what would you say to £15 per hour, board and lodgings included?"

Sam sat staring at her husband in disbelief. What on earth was he thinking? She watched Susan preparing her reply. This is going to be interesting, she thought.

"So what do you think?" John asked.

"You're joking, aren't you?"

"Well, er, no."

It was all Susan could do to stop herself falling off her chair in utter amusement at the man's naivety. Sam's head rested in her hands, wishing a hole would appear so she could jump into it.

"A little high, maybe?" He could detect hostility towards his suggestion – why, he didn't quite know. He was rather pleased with his overall presentation, but as the seconds ticked by he began to realise a favourable response may not be forthcoming.

"I'm sorry, John." Susan shook her head at the man in front of her and wondered about his total lack of knowledge towards a profession that had been in existence for thousands of years. "I don't charge by the hour. I charge by the job, and believe me, it's a lot more than £15 an hour."

"Oh. Right."

Sam shuffled uneasily in her chair. "I should apologise, Susan. Sometimes I wonder about my husband."

John still didn't really understand what he'd done wrong.

"No, it's fine. I'm the one who should be apologising. My reaction could've been better, this is your home after all, and I should respect that, but it's probably best, if I'm offered the opportunity, that I set my own charges. I'm sure you won't be disappointed."

John sat like a naughty little child forced into a corner and made to wear a silly pointed hat with 'twat' written on it. "I suppose that sounds okay." His bottom lip threatened to hit the table as he ran his finger around the rim of his empty mug.

Sam finally took pity, leant forward and ruffled his

hair. "Come on, cheer up, at least it's all sorted." A quick glance up at the wall-mounted clock told her that Susan needed to be off if she was going to stand any chance of catching the train. "You'd better take Susan back to the station, John, time's getting on."

They all rose, Susan offering her hand to the older woman, a woman she hoped she would see more of. "It's been lovely meeting you, Sam."

"And you, Susan. As I mentioned before, we've got others to interview but we'll let you know by Monday, assuming of course you're still interested?"

"Oh yes, very much, it's so lovely here."

Relief flooded Sam's face. She liked this young woman; she liked her a lot. "Well that's just fine then."

Chapter 10

"Don't forget you've only got half an hour before your next interview," Sam called out through the kitchen window as she saw John making his way across the garden.

Seemingly showing a distinct lack of acknowledgement towards her prompting, she saw him conveniently disappear out of sight, closely followed by two excited dogs.

The pigs had got out and were roaming the orchard. Not a concern, but John had to make sure Nell Gwyn and her ten piglets were obeying the boundary laws and had the decency to graze unsupervised for at least the next couple of hours while he attended to his second appointment. Thankfully, Nell was merrily scratching her dry flaky hide against the warty growth of a neglected apple tree. Now disfigured after years of being left to their own devices, these once productive bearers of fruit were merely rubbing posts for a rather grumpy Gloucestershire Old Spot sow.

John stood admiring the scene of unbroken simplicity. The calm of the overgrown orchard presented something that tugged at his existence in life, persuading him that the world should just pack its bags and leave him in peace.

He continued to watch and then counted each piglet as they popped up every so often from their rooting in the long grass. He'd successfully reached nine, but with little sign of number ten his concerns grew. He recounted, convinced his numerical skills had let him down, but no, there were still only nine. "Great! Just what I need!" John mumbled.

Kim glanced up, immediately understanding his frustration. Pup, on the other hand, had wandered off and was now more intent in finding a fresh pile of pig dung to roll in.

A quick glance at his watch revealed he had only fifteen minutes remaining, although he was relieved he hadn't needed to go and pick up his next interviewee. This did nothing to curb his annoyance at having to spend valuable time out of his busy day talking to someone he frankly had already written off. Susan was the one, he was sure of that, so why bother continuing on?

Sam had insisted though. "Susan may decide not to take up the offer," she had said, "leaving us with less choice."

It made sense, of course it did, but that didn't help his present mood. A quick sweep through the rest of the orchard just in case number ten had taken the opportunity to have a wee wander regrettably revealed nothing more than a long-lost sledgehammer, a bucket of rusty nails half submerged in rainwater and John's old cap he'd lost weeks ago. But no piglet.

He could now hear Sam's voice summonsing him back to the house. "Damn it!" he cursed under his breath before reluctantly making his way back, abandoning his quest to find the little pig wig. He was sure wherever it was it would probably find its own way back.

He reluctantly wandered across the yard, showing little enthusiasm towards any further involvement concerning the opposite sex. Miss Rose Katts had been asked to arrive at approximately ... he looked down at his watch ... now!

Then, just as he lifted his head, a distant throaty roar with the energy of an armoured tank echoed its way across the tranquillity of sleepy fields. John could almost predict each bend as the unknown vehicle navigated its way along narrow back lanes leading to the entrance of Willowbank Farm, the sound of its full throttle suggesting it was tackling the long drawn-out climb up the last hill.

He stood and listened as the noise drew nearer. Moments later, a motorbike fearlessly roared through the gate, the rider attempting to stay upright with the complement of a side car to counterbalance its lean. As the bike approached, John took in the rider's tightly stretched black leathers that did nothing to hide a stocky body that he supposed must belong to a female. The Triumph motorcycle screeched to an abrupt halt, worryingly close to his feet. The rider paused for a moment before twiddling various switches, thus rendering the bike harmless. Shielded by a full tinted face guard, she swung one leg over an impressively large fuel tank and slid to the ground, her oversize boots making contact with the driveway with a loud thud as both hands grasped either side of the helmet to reveal a hardened face. A face that showed strength and determination, but little beauty. Short cropped hair did little to convince John that he was in fact in the presence of a lady.

"Mr Taylor? Rose Katts." She pulled a solid dependable hand out of the gloves and waited, hovering in mid-air to receive a welcome handshake.

John nervously offered his hand and immediately felt immense pain through his finger joints and up his right arm as her grasp slowly took hold. Simple words were now impossible to pronounce as his eyes glistened in the sun, threatening tears to trickle down his cheeks. Finally, he managed a squeaky "Hello" that somehow forced its way through gritted teeth.

"Nice place, Mr Taylor, very nice. Got any woodland?"

"Sorry?" Her abrupt question took John by surprise. "Woodland?" he queried, head slightly tilted to one side in confusion.

"Trees, Mr Taylor."

"Just a bit, yes."

"Like how much of a bit?"

"About a hundred acres or so." This was bizarre. He was sure he was the one that was supposed to be asking the questions.

"Excellent. Good feel about the place, Mr Taylor."

"I'm glad you're impressed."

"Very impressed, Mr Taylor." Rose said nothing more as she glanced about her surroundings. With an unconvincing wave of his hand John indicated his intention to move towards the house. Heaven only knows what Sam will think of this one, he thought. Lowering his head he started to move, his mind growing with uncertainty. She certainly was different.

The walk along the garden path set his teeth on edge as the screech of heated leather protested loudly against a military stride complete with swaying arms. He really didn't know what to make of this one.

The kitchen showed no signs of relief. Sam politely greeted Rose into her home but deep down John could see she had been taken by surprise too. "Tea or coffee?"

"Coffee, strong, no milk."

"Please, take a seat." Sam briefly caught John's attention as she turned to make the drinks, raising her eyebrows in silent concern.

"No objections if I remove these wretched leathers?" Rose's voice betrayed someone used to authority; although the request was a simple one it still had an edge of sharpness to it. Something that instantly sent the senses tingling with unease.

Without shame she stripped before their eyes, slowly peeling her outer shell away to reveal a stocky figure that bulged through over-toned biceps. The thin cotton undershirt struggled to contain rippling muscles, the likes of which Sam couldn't understand a woman wanting to show off. Her coarse features appeared to drown her virtually invisible breasts, only recognisable by two harden nipples, supposedly aroused by tensioned leather constantly rubbing across their tips. Thankfully, for now at least, they were concealed by the pure white cotton.

Placing the hot drinks on the table, Sam's face ventured far too close to a woman that she worryingly realised was rather masculine. This unexpected close encounter had her averting her eyes. "Sugar?"

Glad for something else to focus on, she pointed to the floral china bowl in the centre of the table. To Sam and John's utter astonishment, their guest steadied her mug and unashamedly proceeded to shuffle a total of eight and a half spoonfuls of sweetened crystals into her cup. The sight of eight heavily laden spoons travelling back and forth was in itself a brutal act of madness, but the extra half seemed to totally overbalance any sensible logic.

Regaining his thoughts, John brushed himself down before attempting to verbally tackle this woman of stern character.

"Rose ..."

"Please call me 'Tick', can't stand Rose, never could." She pointed both hands towards herself. "Do I look like a Rose?"

There was temptation on John's part, and possibly Sam's, to elaborate further concerning Rose's own observation of herself, but they both momentarily glanced at each other – a warning to each of them to stay silent.

"Mother loved her garden, you see, hence Rose. Mind you, not as bad as my sister – she ended up as a

Marigold and Lord only knows if my parents had had a boy." A brief silence followed then Rose continued. "Now, am I right in thinking you are after a prostitute? Most requests from couples I can handle, but I believe yours is more of a business venture? Had brief details, but I must warn you, your plans as I see it are of a rather sticky nature as far as the law is concerned."

John immediately acknowledged Tick's concerns. "Yes, I've been told that a number of times."

"And you're fine with this?"

There was a nod of agreement from John.

"That's just fine then. So long as we're all clear as to where we are. It wouldn't be right talking out of place. One thing you get taught in the army is to cut the crap. Instructions should be clear and precise. People's lives depend on it."

"How long were you in the army for?" The enquiry stiffened Tick's back, showing a pride towards her former professional career.

"Twenty years."

"Very impressive."

She gave a distinct regimental pose before taking another large swig of her sugar fix, leaving both John and Sam still trying to come to terms with a world they clearly knew nothing or very little about. It was quite obvious that both he and Sam were being slowly dragged from their comfortable existence within the countryside into this unknown world of seduction.

John returned his thoughts back to the job in hand, for here was a woman he, and almost certainly Sam, found to be totally unacceptable for their needs and through no fault of her own, had been found wanting compared to Susan. The young lady had set standards to a high level, a woman who had immediately captured John's attention the moment she walked into his life. A woman of obvious good looks, even her finicky decision-making could be overlooked. But Tick? Whichever way you viewed her, she just seemed to walk along a totally different path. Without question, her ability to do the job, John was certain, wouldn't come into it. But fit in?

He felt his head wanting to shake – no, he just couldn't see it. His mind now gladly flipped back to Susan. He could see the attraction she would throw on the average red-blooded male. After all, he had been captured by her charm, her whole presence, her sweet smell. The smell that still lingered in his mind, urging him to undress her as she stood before him, her naked body tempting his hands to brush over her vibrant skin. Hands that wanted nothing more than to take her down upon the waiting sheets of his bed.
To touch …
To caress …
To explore …

"John!" Sam's voice suddenly made him pull away from Susan's tempting body. "Are you with us?"

"Oh yes. Sorry, miles away." He knew he had to cover his tracks, make it look like he'd been thinking about something else, something that was actually relevant to the interview in hand. "I have a question." It was something Tick mentioned earlier and at the time he'd been surprised by her enquiry as it seemed to have little or no reference to the position. He'd answered the question truthfully. But why? Why would a total stranger, and a prostitute at that, want to know how much woodland there was? "Woodland? I'm curious."

Tick suddenly leaned forward with force, her eyes widening with the look of a possessed woman. What she said next sent a shiver through John and Sam.

"Fear, Mr Taylor. Pure, erotic fear."

John felt his buttocks tighten.

"You see, Mr Taylor, I believe 1 have perfected the ultimate sexual experience. Forget your warm cosy bedrooms, your fine silk sheets. What I can offer is the chase."

Blimey. John felt his body stiffen as she explained further.

"Men, Mr Taylor." A low eerie chuckle escaped her lips as she spoke. "Some of them, Mr Taylor, need to be dominated, put in their place, drawn out like a tightened elastic band then quickly sucked back in." She moved closer to John's face, her breathing labouring with every intake. "Do you understand, Mr Taylor?" Slowly allowing the fear to heighten to the point of utter pain before being released within an explosion of unadulterated unconditional intercourse, her head shot back indicating her total dedication to her craft sending John into a state of temporary shock.

Sam sat, hardly daring to move. Even breathing had become a luxury as she stared down into the shallow dregs that covered the bottom of her mug. John was sure his simple country brain had, he feared, just been raped, sucked dry of any gentle thoughts as it now lay in tatters for all to see.

"Er, more drinks anyone?" offered Sam, breaking the awkward silence.

John waved her comment aside. "So let's get this right: you're telling us you don't need to use one of our bedrooms?"

"Correct."

"And you will do all this in the woods?"

"Correct. All I need is the full run of some woodland basic accommodation, which I'm quite happy to construct myself and permission to collect firewood as and when needed. And of course set traps."

"Traps? What, for rabbits?"

"Partially, but mainly man traps. Don't look so alarmed, Mr Taylor, they're nothing like the old man traps. Good God, I'm not that brutal! This is a business; I do want my clients to come back. No, mostly they're large nets, alarmed wires – perfectly harmless."

John pondered over the idea of having a female Rambo running amuck through his beloved ancient woodland.

"You look concerned, Mr Taylor." Tick's voice broke into John's thoughts.

"No, no. Well just a little maybe."

"Perhaps I should explain a bit more so you can understand the overall concept a little better, but it's quite simple really. Everyone has a signed and agreed contract. My clients arrive, let's say it's Mr Jones, he's kitted out with the necessary combat and protective gear, maps, compasses, basic stuff, nothing more, and then allowed fifteen minutes to run. I, on the other hand, also have the necessary combat gear, plus smoke bombs, air-soft gun, handcuffs, heavy duty rip-ties, gas mask, ten metres of five-ply roping and of course all my traps laid and ready." She paused for a moment before continuing, her back stiffening and her chin raised, trying to show her domination in all matters military. "It usually takes me well under an hour to track my target. As I said, it's all about the chase, the fear of being caught, pushing their nerves to breaking point and as for the rest, well I think you can probably work that out for yourself, but I can go into more detail if you want."

John quickly raised his hand. "No, no, that will be fine. I think we've got the picture." Visions of naked bodies romping around in the undergrowth wedged themselves in John's brain. He felt repelled by such thoughts; that sort of thing had never appealed to him – brambles, stinging nettles, biting insects. No, the possible consequences of injury had always been a risk too far for him! He swallowed hard, feeling his Adam's apple rise and fall.

Sam was willing him to back away, end the interview, politely finish their drinks and send this woman, if that's what she called herself, on her way, out of their lives forever. But John being John clearly hadn't finished. Sam inwardly groaned; she knew her husband too well and she knew that he was going to say something that they would all regret.

"So what if you can't catch them?"

There it was. Why does he do this? Why can't he just leave it alone, implored Sam. His question was met with silence, apart from the cracking of Tick's knuckles as she ran her hand over her fingers. Without warning she burst out laughing, a loud menacing deep-rooted bellow that reminded John of a cow giving birth.

"Mr Taylor, I always catch my man."

"But what if you …" The words had barely passed his lips when she interrupted him.

"I said, I never miss my target. Now, let that be an end to it." Her nostrils flared as she drew in a deep breath.

Sam shot a warning glance, threatening John to end it here and now or else.

"I see. Well, if you put it like that perhaps we should say no more on the subject. Right, I think that's all we need to know." He gave Sam a questioning look, inviting her to comment, contribute towards an already frosty conversation. "Sam?" He seemed to be willing her to say something, anything, but her expression said it all. "No? Right. Okay, then it's been great meeting you, Tick and we'll let you know either way."

After seeing her out they were back in the kitchen. The distant roar of the motorbike reassured them both that the interview was in fact well and truly over. Sam elected to say nothing while John ran his fingers through his unkempt hair.

"Interesting."

"That's one way of putting it." Sam wanted to say more but felt the time wasn't right, instead pointing to her imaginary watch, making John's heart sink in despair.

"No ... not another one." He banged his head down on the table.

"The bus comes through at three o'clock, you go get her, I'll clear up here and I'll help you get the cows in later."

The short distance to the allotted stop wouldn't take him more than ten minutes or so on foot. The hassle of getting the Land Rover out had persuaded John that walking was his best option, coupled with the fact his mother had taken the car for some meeting or other, insisting that as it was at Oakley Hall, courtesy of Lord and Lady Buxton, she couldn't possibly be seen riding a bike in such company. The sheer thought of cycling along their impressive gravel driveway on a common bicycle had filled her with utter horror. John started to walk; if nothing else it would give him time to reflect on things.

Like most country bus stops the most people you could expect to see waiting at any one time would be one or two. Today there were none. John stood alone, waiting patiently for a bus he longed to appear. Yes, it was true he had little experience in the art of standing still, and even less experience peering down a deserted country lane. There were those, he was sure, who had effectively mastered this art, but not John. His last encounter with public transport must've been around the age of eighteen, before he'd taken charge of his first motorcar. Unfortunately his memory was letting him down, mainly because it wasn't something he would've taken much notice of, but he was sure the last time saw him standing in the pouring rain on a cold November night waiting for a bus that never arrived. And here he was waiting again. At least the sun was shining, the temperature acceptable, so things had improved.

It was only then he realised he'd not been standing still at all. Far from it. In fact he had trodden a definite track around the base of the grey pole – a sign telling everyone that this was, in fact, an official bus stop, and if patient enough you may be rewarded by the appearance of some sort of transport to take you where you hoped to go. John gazed down at the mosaic artwork he'd made beneath his feet, trying to decipher the meaning of such patterns, puzzled and perfected by his own talent he took on a growing concern. His life was a mess if this was anything to go by. He looked at his watch: 3:05. He sighed – still an empty lane. Niggling doubts started to creep in, penetrating his thoughts. Why should he be subjected to this inconvenience? He stamped his foot in annoyance. No, he mustn't get angry, there was clearly a simple explanation for this lack of public convenience – a breakdown perhaps, a new driver unfamiliar with the tangle of back lanes that snaked around this part of the countryside. Heaven forbid there'd been an accident. No, John was sure there would be some simple explanation.

Ten past. Nothing. His well-used mosaic of tracks had without much effort been transformed into some mind-provoking crop circle.

Twelve minutes past. Boredom had well and truly set in, so much so that John found himself some distance away from the stop, attempting to distract himself with the riveting country pursuit of insect spotting, – spiders, butterflies, one solitary bumblebee, and two ladybirds trying to have it away. He watched as one unsuccessfully attempted to mount the other. Thoughts immediately flipped to his own sex life. He sighed. The behaviour of the female ladybird was starting to annoy him somewhat as she waited until the last moment before scurrying away leaving a rather deflated male stranded on his back with his legs flailing in all directions. Similar. He sighed again. Fifteen minutes past.

Finally, a tatty gas-guzzling bus lumbered down the lane, its whole body complaining of years of service. John watched as it opened up along the straight, all the while trailing a cloud of heavy lung-consuming fumes from its rear end. With every forward motion came hesitant gear changing until finally locking into a painfully slow crawl. Desperately trying not to look too excited given the extreme frustration only minutes earlier, John watched patiently as it trundled towards him, a weak smile creeping over his face as he stood beside the insect-infested hedgerow. But his glimmer of hope was suddenly replaced with a rush of despair as the bus continued to pass by, with clearly no intention of stopping.

John frantically waved his arms while hurling abuse at the driver who'd only moments earlier been seen sporting a casual smile. Realising his mistake, he forcefully applied the brakes, causing the bus to shudder to an abrupt halt.

Instinct now warned John to lower his erect finger as he made his way towards the vibrating metal monster. The doors jolted and jerked forcefully, trying to slot into their given place either side of the entrance, allowing John to peer up at the driver. He was a man of considerable weight, his stomach resting upon thick tree-trunk legs that struggled to clear the rotating movements of the steering wheel. He sat staring at the road ahead, seemingly oblivious to the inconvenience caused by not stopping.

"Well?" he finally spoke. "Are you getting on?"

"No." John's reply was swift and to the point.

"So what did you stop me for then?"

"I'm waiting for someone." Even to John's own ears his reply sounded none too convincing.

The driver looked somewhat irritated. "So who are you waiting for?"

It was at this point John realised he had forgotten to consult his paperwork, that valuable bit of information that made his presence at the bus stop more plausible. The driver now looked decidedly peeved off and he certainly wasn't going to like John's reply. "I'm not really sure."

He frowned, clearly not amused and lacking any humour towards the present situation as he attempted to dislodge something from his left nostril. "So let's get this right – you stop the bus but you have no intention of getting on, am I right?" John nodded. "And you're waiting for someone but you don't know who they are?"

John hesitated before speaking. "That's not technically true, I do know who she is but I don't know her name, that's all. I know it sounds a little strange, but she was supposed to be arriving on this bus, but clearly she may not in fact be on this particular one."

"Not too convincing if you ask me," replied the driver as he shuffled awkwardly in his seat to turn and peer down the length of the bus. "Look. The bus is empty."

"Yes, I can see that now, but I had no way of knowing that, did I?" hissed John, struggling to control his temper.

"No need to take that tone with me, I'm just doing my job."

John couldn't help feeling frustrated as he continued to argue his case, but now began to realise he had failed to convince this man that in fact he wasn't the local village idiot out for an afternoon stroll.

The driver rested his arm on the back of the seat while his other hand ran over his lightly stubbled chin. "Look. I feel sorry for you, I really do, but what you get up to in your private life is of no consequence to me. Clearly you've been stood up; a lot of those sorts of women can be quite unreliable. Not that I've had any experience that way – my Doreen keeps me quite satisfied thank you very much, but I can totally understand, it can get a little lonely out here in the countryside. So if you don't mind, I'll give you one last chance – are you getting on or not?"

"Of course I'm not."

"Fine, then have a nice day."

The doors sprang to life, squeezing shut in a series of painful movements, leaving John no option but to jump backwards before he became sandwiched between its closing jaws. He watched on as the bus pulled away, its rattling sound echoing through the trees, scattering a gathering of bloated wood pigeons.

John stood alone in the deserted lane, secretly pleased to not have to interview any more women. He would report back to his wife the details of what had happened, and as long as the lady in question never arrived, his day would be perfect.

Chapter 11

"Penny for your thoughts." Sam attempted to break through her husband's transient state as they both sat at the kitchen table the following morning.

John was certain of his final decision, yet found himself unexpectedly confused. Susan was undoubtedly the one for them; her whole mannerisms couldn't be better suited and if they were to venture down this idea of his they would undoubtedly owe their ultimate success to someone like her. But Tick. Ah yes, that one intrigued him. Admittedly at first she'd scared the living daylights out of him, and Sam had taken a dislike to her. He didn't think she was frightened of her, but she seemed to be offended by her whole presence. Tick certainly wasn't your typical female – bulging biceps and that short cropped hair wasn't everyone's cup of tea, yet clearly, as he was now finding, a percentage of men did actually look upon them as attractive!

She wasn't to his liking, but to give her her due she did dare to be different in her approach to what essentially was the same as what Susan was offering, just presented in a totally different format. Bizarre how they complemented each other perfectly. Tick had offered them something quite unexpected and John would go so far as to say tantalisingly interesting. The woodland, purely as an economical form, contributed very little to the overall farm accounts, firewood for the winter being the only monetary saving, but that wouldn't cease to operate just because one woman was using it for what could only be described as 'light industrial activity'. So it was tempting, very tempting, to be allowed to earn an income of whatever size with virtually no outlay.

Sam again attempted to free her husband from his deep and meaningful thoughts, only this time resorting to physical persuasion as she clipped him round the ear.

"What the ...?"

"With us now, are you? It's like talking to a brick wall. Your tea's getting cold."

John rubbed the side of his face. "Thanks for that."

"You're welcome. *Well* ...?" Sam clearly wanted an immediate answer as she sat ready to take in anything John had to offer.

"Susan. We'll go with Susan."

"Good, that's settled then."

Her husband's body language warned her to brace herself. "And Tick," he added.

"Seriously? What, both of them?" Sam looked more than a little surprised. It was obvious Susan would be chosen, she liked her, she liked her a lot, and if there was going to be any sharing of her home it would need to be someone like her. But Tick? And what sort of name was that anyway?

John took a sip of his tea. "Yep. What the hell, it's probably all illegal anyway, as everyone keeps suggesting. Think of the logistics of it. If we have two working here we don't have to do it for so long, less chance of getting found out. It could work and it's not as if they're going to be operating side by side, is it? Tick only wants the woods, I could put her in father's old cottage. No one will ever know she's up there and Susan can have the house. Can't you see it's perfect?" He desperately tried to sound positive but knew Sam didn't like Tick one little bit. "What do you think?" Perhaps he should sit back and give her space, try not to push any further. She would need time to think. Eventually she would see the sense in his decision.

It was Sam's turn to search through her thoughts, as her husband did make sense for once. Two incomes over a shorter period sounded sensible and if that 'woman' stayed in the woods and away from her home, she may never see her. "How long before we start then?" She looked her husband straight in the eye, demanding clear-cut information.

"Well, Susan's room will need to be decorated, then there's this new expensive carpet."

"John!"

"Okay, I won't mention it again, but I suppose we'll need new curtains, those cracked panes of glass need replacing and of course a new mattress." He shook his head at the mounting costs. "Anything else while I'm spending money we haven't got?"

"Clean sheets, we're going to need plenty of them. Lord knows what they'll be getting up to."

Besides the cost, John was secretly relieved Sam was

taking an interest in the venture. He needed her to be on board as without her support it would never happen; he was far too busy on the farm as it was. "Thank you." He reached over and placed his hand upon hers.

She gave him simple smile, nothing more.

"I'll ring them now." John pushed his chair back with determination and the look of a bull let loose in a field of twenty virgin heifers. "It'll be just our luck that neither of them are interested."

Sam's smile faded. "That crossed my mind too." The thought of Susan deciding not to come had already caused her to feel uneasy. Why, she wasn't sure – they'd only met once, yet already she felt surprisingly close to the young lady. "Susan's nice. I think I might enjoy having her around."

"Me too."

"Well, what are you waiting for? Go and put us out of our misery." John couldn't help grin as he headed down the hallway. For the second time in this venture he actually felt good about what he was doing. Yes, maybe in the eyes of the law it was wrong, but it was a chance he had to take. For the farm, their way of life, Luke's inheritance, even Mother's standing within the community, but most of all he owed it to his forefathers for all the blood, sweat and toil they'd put into this place over the years. No, he wouldn't dwell on the possible legal aspects, he would just damn well get on with it and hope for the best.

Sitting by the phone he dialled Susan's number. Like

Sam, he felt it would be nice to have a cheery bright thing around the place, as with Luke away the house seemed strangely empty. He rubbed along with Sam well enough but they'd become more like friendly business partners than a loving couple. He sighed. Heaven forbid if Susan did say no – he was certain he would feel the loss of a person who in effect was a total stranger.

He waited patiently as the ringtones continued one after the other, on and on, slowly deflating his morale. It was as if his twenty virgin heifers had already been got at by a neighbour's bull and the utter horror of having sex for the first time had quite simply put most of them off such a ghastly activity ever again.

Sam hovered in the doorway, standing within earshot of the anticipated conversation, that's if anyone would care to pick up the phone and answer it. He was just about to give up when a welcoming voice sprang onto the line.

"Hello?"

This simple word almost caused him to topple off his chair in sheer delight.

"Hi, is that Susan?"

"Speaking."

"It's John Taylor, Willowbank Farm. We ..."

"Yes, of course, how are you?"

"I'm fine thanks, and you?"

"Great."

Her voice sounded so fresh, so utterly inviting. John had quickly learnt over the past week or so that he needed to be more positive in the way he approached matters concerning his new venture. It was fair to say he'd been caught lacking on a number occasions, so was determined this time to come to the point, no fluffing around the edges, assert his authority.

"Susan, I, and when I say *I*, I really mean *Sam* and I, think you're by far the best prostitute for the job."

"John!" Sam's shocked voice echoed down the hallway. There was silence at the other end of the line. "Here, give me that." Sam towered over her husband with a look of utter horror. "Susan, it's Sam. Please accept my apologies for my husband's lack of manners. What he was trying to say is that we would be delighted if you would consider our proposition."

"Sam." Susan's voice came back on the line.

"Yes dear?"

"I'm not offended, really, and I'd love to come." Her voice seemed to sing down the line.

"That's excellent news! I'll hand you back to my brain-dead other half. Bye for now." Her threatening silence as she handed over the phone told John to sort himself out and not mess it up. She walked back to the kitchen grinning. Susan was coming to live in her home! The thought was almost too much to take in, a young good-looking intelligent female sharing every part of her daily life. With Luke temporarily out of reach she had become aware of how lonely she was and how much she needed company.

John composed himself. "Susan, sorry about that, I was never very good at expressing myself."

"It's fine, Mr Taylor."

"You can drop the Mr if you're coming to live with us – it's Sam and John. Only my bank manager calls me Mr Taylor and he's a twat so he doesn't count. Now, back to business. I know it's probably a little soon but we could have your room ready in, say, two weeks' time? How does that suit?" An unexpected pause indicated a possible problem with the timing. "Of course just because the room is ready doesn't mean you have to be here right away, I'm sure we can come to some sort of arrangement."

"No, it's not that. It may sound a bit presumptuous, but would it be possible to move in this weekend? You see the rent on this place runs out on Sunday and they insist on six months upfront. I could come and help with the decorating in lieu of board and lodgings until l start." She heard a solid sigh of relief in her ear.

"Is that all? Good grief, of course you can come earlier, we can always put you up in one of the other rooms until yours is ready. But what about your clients?"

"Oh, don't worry about that, I'll just reschedule them, it's really not a problem. I'm due a few days off. They'll just have to entertain themselves for a week or so. Really, it's no problem. Would Sunday be okay? Only I have a friend with a van, but he works Saturday."

"No problem, Sunday's fine. I'll get Sam to make up

one of the spare rooms."

"Oh that's really great, I can't wait." She sounded so excited. "It's such a lovely place you've got and I'm sure it's going to work out just fine, so I'll see you on Sunday."

"Sunday it is," replied John.

"She's coming then?" Sam was trying to look busy as John walked back into the kitchen.

"Sunday."

She spun round, tea towel in hand, vigorously drying a small bowl to the point where its floral pattern was in fear of being rubbed from its surface.

"What, *this* Sunday?" she said with concern.

"I thought you'd be pleased."

"We're not ready, we agreed."

"Don't worry, we'll just stick her in one of the other bedrooms for now. She understands the situation and is more than happy to muck in and help with the decorating, and at least this way we can get it right. You know how funny she got about how things should be – ambience and all that rubbish. Load of old baloney if you ask me; sex is sex."

"Yes, you would say that, wouldn't you."

"And what's that supposed to mean?"

Sam carried on drying her bowl. "Nothing important." She finally put the poor bowl to rest and pulled up a chair.

"And what about the other one?"

"You really don't like her, do you?"

"She gives me the heebie-jeebies if I'm honest."

"Why?"

"Why? You know very well why. Come on John, you're either a woman or a man, and from where I was standing she didn't seem to be one or the other. And another thing, it's not right for females to have muscles like that, it's gross, sends shivers down my back. It must be an odd sort of man that fines that attractive."

John wondered why she was getting so upset, Tick's appearance wasn't that bad. "I'm not sure these 'odd sorts of men' as you put it really think she's just attractive. It's more to do with what she is capable of doing to them that turns them on."

"*Please*. The thought of it is seriously making my stomach turn. All I'm saying is it's weird, that's all, and do we honestly want those sorts of men roaming about our farm?"

"You're over-exaggerating now."

"Am I really? I'm telling you, John, if she does come, make sure she and her perverted male friends stay in the woods. I don't want them anywhere near my house." She rose from her chair, turned and went back to the sink, leaving John to make his way to the hallway where he sat down and dialled Tick's number. It rang four times and then clicked to the answer message. *"Hi, you have reached A, B, R Carpets. Our staff are ready and waiting to show you the very best in quality handmade carpets and flooring, so for a first-class service please leave a message and your telephone number for either Rose, Candy, Charlie, or Sally and they will contact you shortly. BEEP!"*

"Hi, this is a message for Tick, or it could be Rose. My name is Mr Taylor, Willowbank Farm, could you please ring me back, thanks. Oh yes, nearly forgot, my telephone number, it's 01 …

"Mr Taylor!"

John was cut short by an unmistakable woman's voice as it barked down the phone at him. "Tick, is that you?" How could he honestly forget that orderly rough-cast tone, as if gravel had been rammed into her mouth.

"Sorry, Mr Taylor, I was just finishing with a customer."

"So is this your day job then?" John asked.

"Sorry, Mr Taylor, I don't understand."

"Selling carpets for a living. I have to say I never took you for someone who sells floor coverings."

She let out a loud, dry smoke-injected laugh. "We don't sell carpets here, Mr Taylor."

"I don't understand?" he said, with an air of confusion.

"Not to worry, Mr Taylor, it's of no importance. So, you rang?"

"Yes, woodland proposition. If you're interested, we'd like to give it a go." He thought it best to say 'we', rather than 'I'.

"Splendid, Mr Taylor. Excellent news, be delighted. Best I come down and finalise everything, want to keep things in order from the start, no misunderstandings. Would Sunday suit?"

"What, this Sunday?"

"Problem?"

"No, no of course not, Sunday will be fine. Shall we say … eleven-ish? How does that sound?"

"Eleven sharp. Never does any good to be vague. I'll be there Sunday, eleven on the dot. Bye for now."

The phone went dead, leaving John to collect his thoughts before presenting the good news to his beloved wife.

Chapter 12

Sunday arrived with a message on the answer machine informing John that Susan had been held up and wouldn't arrive until 6 pm at the earliest. Secretly he found himself breathing a sigh of relief, for the fear of both Susan and Tick descending upon the farm at the same time had been playing on his mind. It was inevitable that at some point the two would meet. They were, after all, both of the same breed as it were, but it would make life a lot simpler if it didn't happen just yet.

Tick was due at eleven. John predicted it would take two hours to show her around. One o'clock for lunch and then a quick snooze, milking done and dusted by six – just in time to see to Susan's needs. But he was starting to get the feeling anything to do with her arrival would be handled by his wife. Not that he was complaining; there was enough to keep him occupied, but still, he had to keep a hold of matters. Sam clearly had taken a liking to their prospective new lodger which was fine in itself, but he couldn't help worry that she might promise more than he was prepared to spend and she needed to understand this was a money-making venture.

Tick arrived at eleven sharp – likeable or not, you couldn't fault her time-keeping. John had been sent out to the yard long before she was due and knew very well why. It was Sam's way of deflecting their visitor away from entering her home. She had made some lame excuse that Sunday lunch would be utterly ruined to damnation if left unattended for even one second and so couldn't possibly join him on his quest to engage the services of someone she found totally unsuitable. So he'd been given strict instructions not to invite 'that woman' into her kitchen, but to bundle her straight into the waiting Land Rover and conduct their business elsewhere. Kim and Pup seemed less concerned with the company they kept, having already secured their rightful places in the back.

Tick thundered down the driveway and screeched to an abrupt halt only feet from John again. She sat for a moment before removing her helmet, revealing to the world a less than appealing new hairstyle. Naked white skin glowed in the mid-morning sun as her shorn skull sported a narrow strip of bristly brown hair from back to front. It was hard not to focus on what John considered as a step too far regarding her feminist roots.

"Mr Taylor." She thrust her arm forward determinedly, reminding John all too well of the first painful handshake and her ability to crush every single bone in his hand. He hesitated, this time resolved to give as good as he got. Taking a deep breath, he tensed his muscles and forcing every last ounce of strength down to his fingertips willed his mind to take the pain and channel it straight back to Tick. That was the plan anyway, yet as their hands met, his determination to secure any advantage simply vanished like a puff of smoke on a windy day as he felt the full power of her grip. John's instincts told him to pull away, escape while the going was good, but he couldn't. He stood, tears forming in his eyes as he tried not to show his discomfort, somehow still managing to address her through gritted teeth. "Tick."

Finally she released her hold, unaware of the trauma she'd inflicted. "I thought it might be best if we shoot up in the Land Rover," he said, his throbbing hand resting at his side.

"Fine by me, Mr Taylor, used to these old girls. A little more beefed up in the army but still the same old darlings underneath."

Her speed and agility for someone so stocky caught John unawares as she made her way to the passenger door, leaving him no time to warn her that it was jammed. To his horror the whole Land Rover rocked from side to side, sending the dogs into a state of panic and thinking perhaps it wasn't such a good idea to catch a lift after all. Her failed attempt to open the door had her standing back to study it, unaware it had been broken for a good twelve months and nothing John or a trusty crowbar could do had managed to fix it in any shape or form. As John stepped forward to explain, the Land Rover rocked once again as Tick decided her only option was sheer brute force. The two dogs peered through the partition in fear as their noses scraped back and forth against the glass, dislodging years of filth and grime. John rushed over to the other side of the vehicle, only to be met by the sight of his beloved passenger door lying flat on the gravel, Tick looking down at it somewhat puzzled by its now useless state.

"Rust, Mr Taylor. Heaps of it," she announced, pointing to two large holes where the hinges used to be attached. "And the lock's jammed solid. Give me half a day with the welder and an angle grinder and I'll have her as good as new."

John looked surprised. "You know how to use those things then?" He wondered why he was so surprised.

"Army, Mr Taylor. Take these old battery hens apart in my sleep – all nuts and bolts, a bit like a Meccano set, easy if you know how." As she spoke her hands grasped the top of the now redundant door frame and with one single pull she lifted herself up into the passenger seat. "Not just a pretty face, Mr Taylor."

It was tempting, very tempting, but for the sake of their venture relationship John's decision to stay silent was probably a good one.

"Come on, Mr Taylor, itching to see this woodland."

The Land Rover whined as it snaked down the lane, blackened lung-choking smoke billowing from her rear end clouding every scrap of fresh air in her wake.

"Hell, she's bad, Mr Taylor." Tick's voice struggled to be heard over the labouring groan of the knackered engine.

John kept his eyes on the road as she leant out the vehicle.

"Brings back some good memories, though. Would be nice to feel the wind through my hair if I had any! Ha! Mr Taylor."

John briefly glanced her way but said nothing.

"Hell, this is good," she bellowed, her feet firmly wedged in the footwell.

John manoeuvred the old battery hen down a gear, taking a left-hand turn onto a gravel track riddled with potholes. They finally came face to face with a rather rickety wooden gate, its lengths of timber barely hanging together with rusty nails weakened by years of exposure to the elements. He eased the Land Rover to a shuddering halt then leaned forward to rummage through a pile of farm receipts, used parking tickets and sun-drenched sticky sweet wrappers.

"It's here somewhere ..." he muttered, his hand bulldozing its way through the endless trail of rubbish. "Ah, here it is." His fingers grasped a single key that lay welded to the surface of a sticky hard-boiled mint.

Tick watched him as he held it up to the light, studying the state of it. "Yes, well, it's been a while since I've needed to use it," he explained, holding the key-sweet between his finger and thumb as he desperately tried to decide the best way of extracting it from its minty cell mate.

"Oh, give it here." Not giving John a chance to object, Tick snatched it from his hand and promptly popped the whole lot into her mouth. He watched on as she forcefully swirled it around her mouth, sucking and biting, constantly throwing out muffled crackling sounds. She finally stuffed two fingers between her lips and pulled out a perfectly formed padlock key, leaving the mint to naturally neutralise the acid taste coated on the roof of her mouth.

"You're not going to eat that, are you?" asked John as she unceremoniously pushed the sticky mess around in her mouth.

"Wasn't going to, but it's not half bad!" She took it down in one frighteningly large swallow, then came up for air. "You stay here, Mr Taylor, I'll go and open up." She jumped out and made for the solid padlock, inserting the damp key to allow an industrial-looking chain to fall against its holding post. "All good, Mr Taylor." A wave reassured him that all was clear.

"No need to close it," John shouted as his head poked out the passing window. "We're going to have to come back this way."

"Righto, Mr Taylor." Like some wonder woman, she threw herself into the moving vehicle. Her rapt attention went to the looming trees as they passed by. "So this is it then, Mr Taylor?" Her eyes lit up with excitement as she viewed the heavy shaded undergrowth that almost touched the side of the Land Rover.

"Yes, this is it. One hundred acres or there about. Mainly hardwood, but there's three or four acres of pine up at the top end. So apart from that it's mainly oak, ash and the old workings of past hazel coppicing."

The track slowly climbed up through a dense covering of neglected hazels, their long slender rods of old now grown into twisted heavily shaded branches that at times obscured the way forward.

"Excellent cover, Mr Taylor." She pointed to a steep incline swamped with brambles and young saplings. "This is so much better than I had hoped." Her eyes lit up as they approached a small clearing dominated by knee-high tussock grasses, every bend revealing countless possibilities for the hunter and the hunted alike. "When can I start, Mr Taylor?"

John shrugged his shoulders. "Whenever."

"Marvellous. I'll just have to set up some sort of base camp, but give me a week or so and I should have something half decent." John couldn't help but grin. "Something amusing, Mr Taylor?"

"Oh, it just so happens I may be able to help you with the accommodation. Let me show you."

The track rose sharply before John stopped and proceeded to get out. "We'll take a short walk from here." He led the way along a narrow overgrown path that suddenly dipped steeply down, their feet slipping over loose stones and rotting vegetation. They paused at the bottom, giving John the chance to point to a small grassy clearing that seemed little more than a breeding ground for the encroaching bramble. "Take a look through there." Pushing their way through, he motioned Tick to go in front, knowing full well what lay in store.

She disappeared, and then shouted with delight. "Bloody hell!"

"Like it?" John came up behind her, grinning like a Cheshire Cat. "It was my father's."

They stood in front of a half-hidden wooden shack, generous in size for something so far from the other buildings. Its timber cladding and corrugated roof were clearly in need of a little work, but nothing a week or so of hard graft wouldn't fix.

"Well ... will you look at that." Tick's eyes danced around its tired frame, leaving John gazing at the old building.

"My father used it for shooting mostly. I came up when I was a boy, but it was really his little hideaway, his bolthole from the stresses of everyday life." He paused for a moment, reliving past memories. "After he passed away, it got left to nature. I never had time to come up, far too busy trying to run the farm. It's the first time I've been up here for years, I hate to think what it's like inside."

They started to walk, Tick reaching the front door first, its surround swamped by a tangle of ivy attempting to bar entry, but of no match for a solid hard shove from a woman who worked out. She fearlessly entered, leaving John to tentatively follow, not knowing how he would feel after so many years away, of the memories that were bound to have lingered within the back of his mind waiting to be released the moment he took one step inside. Why he should be nervous he wasn't sure, there was nothing bad about the place. Perhaps it was the loss of someone he only really understood after they were gone, but whatever it was he found himself stopping in the doorway, gazing into its darkened interior and wondering. He looked around with pleasant thoughts.

"I must say it's kept pretty well considering. Not a great deal of work to do, I would have thought we'd have found it a lot worse than this. Just a few spiders to make homeless, but apart from that, pretty respectable." Admittedly he wouldn't want to live in it on a permanent basis, and he certainly wouldn't let a woman like Tick practise sexual abuse upon his body, but it wasn't him they were trying to please. He looked up at the ceiling – an odd spot of damp but nothing alarming. Moving further inside he stood in what was essentially one large single room, save for a small rear box room. Bolted to the back wall was a strange piece of metalwork that hung slightly lopsided, its bizarre craftsmanship still in operation as a number of rotting coats rested upon its twisted hooks.

Tick had already ventured into what was a less than functional kitchen, its basic cooking facilities languishing beneath a thick layer of undisturbed dust. Undeterred, she marched around like she now owned the place, inspecting points of interest and mentally taking notes for future improvement.

"So what do you think?" John asked.

She stood at one end, legs slightly apart, hands on hips, not an ounce of emotion penetrating her hardened exterior. "Bloody marvellous, Mr Taylor. Spot-on, ideal base camp. I can feel my nipples harden with excitement and that doesn't happen very often."

A comment like that coming from any other female would have no problem in rising John's inner man, but on this occasion something seemed to be missing. Perhaps it was the damp musty odour affecting his brain. Or perhaps not.

"Water, Mr Taylor?" Tick fired her question across the room like a sharpened arrow.

"Your own well out the back." John pointed through the rear window indicating its location through a dense covering of thick undergrowth.

"Excellent. Bog?"

"Sorry?"

"Bog hole. Mr Taylor. Danny long drop?"

"Oh, right, toilet." John suddenly cottoned on. Tick shook her head. Gentleman farmers!

"Ah, no, sorry. We always had a hole in the ground."

"Not a problem, had to deal with less." Her gaze wandered around the room. "No, this should do, didn't expect this. You've done well, Mr Taylor. Give me a week and you'll not recognise the place."

John couldn't help but look pleased. "Good. I thought you'd like it." A quick glance at his watch told him they'd better be getting back.

The steep pathway seemed less of a chore. Tick, with her knowledge of all things outdoors, led the way, effectively weaving her way over twisted tree roots and fallen branches leaving John to struggle with inappropriate farm Wellingtons. The two dogs, still confined within the Land Rover, had started barking constantly as they sensed movement. Unable to escape, their frustration grew stronger the nearer John and Tick got. To have allowed them freedom of the woods would've been foolhardy to say the least. Kim would almost certainly end up having to be carried up the steep path and Pup would have disappeared completely, exploring a part of the farm yet undiscovered.

John paused for breath as he approached the vehicle, pointing in the direction of a sharp bend in the track ahead. "It does a big loop around the top of the woods," he said as he looked at his watch once more. "I think we've just enough time to drive around."

They passed through vibrant green towering trees before coming to the outermost edge of Willowbank Farm boundary. With light in abundance the track ran alongside grass fields, presenting a view across open countryside. John stopped and pointed. "You won't see many people up here, but if you do they most likely come from down there. That's Dale Valley."

Tick sighed. "Not much for looking at scenery, Mr Taylor, but that's one hell of a view."

A vast patchwork of neatly kept woven fields dotted with the odd house lay beneath them, sending out every shade of green and brown you could possibly imagine, in contrast with a scattering of emerging spring colour.

John angled his finger away from the vastness of that

one particular area. "Now you see those buildings down there – that's Silverstone Barns. They belong to Nigel Duffy, and that's his free-range chicken houses dotted about the fields. But be warned, he reliably informs me that collecting eggs in the nude is a sure way of lifting production, and as long as you keep your wellies on it's perfectly decent! Dare say there are those who would disagree, the local ramblers group being one, but nothing compared to what you will be getting up to, ha!"

Tick for once didn't reply.

"Anyway, on that note we'd better be heading back, my wife's a stickler when it comes to Sunday lunch."

The Land Rover pulled into the yard with ten minutes to spare. John coasted across the gravel and pulled up beside the abandoned passenger door, still stranded under the post and rail fence. He rested his hands on top of the steering wheel and gazed at the unusual form that claimed to be a female prostitute, and like Sam, had to admit he would never have placed her in such a profession. "You keep the gate key," he said. "I've got a spare indoors and I'll get you a map of the farm with the woods marked out so you know where the boundaries lie. There's a right-of-way up in the far corner next to the pines, but apart from that it'll be all yours, and of course your clients'."

"Marvellous, Mr Taylor. And money? This is after all a business venture for profit. I'd like to get things sorted before we start."

Tick wasn't everyone's cup of tea but you had to like

her direct manner, and more importantly she was someone whom you felt you could trust. "I'll leave that up to you," John replied. "You know your business better than I do, but I'm sure whatever you decide will be greatly received. It'll just be nice to finally get some sort of income from the woods. I'm sure we won't fall out over it as long as it's fair for both of us."

Tick digested the information and John was sure he saw a glint of emotion briefly flow across her hardened shell. "Thank you, Mr Taylor, you'll not regret it."

"No, I'm sure I won't, but I'm puzzled."

"About what, Mr Taylor?"

"The name Tick?"

"Parasites, Mr Taylor. They're opportunistic, latching onto their victims and slowly drawing the blood from their bodies!"

Despite it being a warm day, the cab took on an unexpected chill that buried deep down into the very core of John's spine. He swallowed hard. "Of course, I should have realised."

Chapter 13

"Have you washed your hands?" Sam placed their meal on the kitchen table just as she spotted John pass by the door heading for the office. "It's dinnertime, John, and it's getting cold." Her voice travelled like an intercept missile searching out its intended target.

"Just got to get something before I forget it. I'll be there in a minute."

Five minutes later he appeared in the doorway waving his hands in the air. "Look, all clean." He strolled into the kitchen, sniffing like a dog following the scent. "Smells good. So what have we got today then, my dearest?"

"It's Sunday, John, as well you know, so don't try and sweet-talk me. Now sit yourself down before it gets cold."

He gazed at the steaming roast chicken with all the trimmings – enough food to satisfy a whole army. "You've done it again, haven't you?"

"I know." Sam's head drooped. "It's just, I can't seem to get used to only cooking for two." Her voice trembled slightly, trying to hide a tinge of sadness.

"Come on," comforted John. "He'll be back before you know it."

"I know, but I can't help worrying about him, and he said he would ring every day. Once, John, that's all – and that was because he needed more money."

John paused, his knife and fork hovering over his dinner as he looked at his sad wife. "To be fair I think it was you who told him to ring every day. I'm sure I distinctly remember him saying, 'Yes Mum, I'll ring,' which, technically he's done."

"Trust you to take his side."

"Come on, you know what boys are like, and us parents are always the last to know what's going on."

"You're not helping."

"Really, there's nothing to worry about, I'm sure he'll ring soon." John sat back and patted his stomach. "More for me." Sam shook her head, pulling his plate from under his nose.

"On second thoughts, perhaps I'll save some for tomorrow. It might help your situation."

"My situation? What on earth do you mean by that?"

"I mean you're starting to get a bit of a gut. Maybe a little less food wouldn't be a bad thing."

"Oh thanks." He took a moment to ponder what his wife had said. "It's not that bad, is it?"

"Well, not yet, but at your age you need to be careful, things start to bulge and once they go ..." She tutted, shaking her head.

"Why is it a woman can make a comment like that and get away with it?"

"Because we females are far superior to you males. Men are only useful for one thing and half the time they can't get that right. Anyway, changing the subject, what were you doing in the office that was so important?"

John knew it was pointless to argue, so tried to retrieve his dinner before it vanished forever. "I had to get a map of the farm for Tick, show her where the boundaries are."

"Oh, that one, I forgot you showed her around this morning."

"Forgot? You know very well that I did, so don't try and pretend just because you don't like her."

"*Her*? Are you sure about that?"

"Does it matter?" John replied. "As long as she does her job, so you just remember that." He waved a roast potato in Sam's direction.

"Are you threatening me, John Taylor?"

"Me? Never. I wouldn't dare."

They were cut short by the front doorbell, its unwanted tone echoing down the hallway like an annoying guest arriving at a dinner party.

"Damn it." John looked at the clock. "Why do people have to come during dinner, and on a Sunday?"

Sam looked at him from across the table. "You stay and have your food, I'll go."

Her suggestion was met by a look of defeat. "No, it's all right, I'll go. It's probably someone who wants to see me."

"Oh, and I don't live here then? Sounds like I'm not important enough to have visitors?"

"I didn't mean it like that. Women! Why have they always got to be so … never mind." He rose and headed for the front door, grumbling at female annoyances and the inconvenience of being disturbed during such an important part of a farmer's day. "This had better be good," he muttered. His arm grappled with a large high bolt while turning the brass door knob. He struggled to open the solid wooden structure as its poorly fitted draft excluder caught against the carpet, allowing him to only partially open it. John peered through the gap, his limited vision revealing nothing.

"You the farmer?" came a young voice from out of nowhere.

He peered around the door to see a smallish boy sitting on his bike looking up at him. "Hello, young man."

The boy repeated his question. "You the farmer?"

John thought about it. Yes, he was a farmer, no doubting that, but could he claim to be 'the' farmer when there were literally thousands of exceptionally good and capable men and women working the land? In all honesty he couldn't claim to be 'the' farmer, that would surely be rather big-headed. Maybe he was overthinking it. "Yes, I'm the farmer."

"You got cows?"

"Yes."

"Is one a big brown ugly bugger with half a horn on one side?"

An easy question to answer but something didn't seem quite right. "Yes. Why?"

"Because it's heading towards the village." The boy turned towards the farm entrance and pointed, forcing John to move onto the driveway just in time to see Ethel, the slowest cow in the herd, meandering past the entrance taking the occasional mouthful of grass with her ugly brown head and half horn on one side.

"Damn it! Do you know how many there are?" John asked.

The boy hesitated and began counting with his fingers. "Reckon four, maybe five."

"Great." John thanked the messenger boy. "Sam!" John shot back towards the door. "Sam, the cows are out!" he hollered at the top of his voice. "Sam!"

When the shout went up it was something that demanded unconditional attention. Forget your slowly cooling Sunday lunch, this was much more serious. "Sam!"

"I heard you."

He sprinted back down the hallway to where his wife was standing fully kitted out like a Formula One pit mechanic waiting to fit a new set of rubbers. Split-second accuracy saw a pair of size tens securely fastened upon John's feet. With such timeless perfection it enabled both of them to clear the back door and run out across the yard in little under four minutes flat. Kim shot out from behind the barn trying to break into some sort of arthritic rhythm while Pup, again, was passing the time licking his balls. His damp testicles became of no consequence when faced with the drama unfolding before his very eyes. With everyone assembled at the farm gate they watched as the last cow disappeared over the brow of the hill. "It'll be those cows kept back for insemination this morning."

John knew the quick pace of hormonal cows on the loose would see them arriving at the village long before they had a chance to catch up, yet, undeterred, he encouraged the four of them to run as fast as they could, soon realising their fitness wasn't what it once was. "God I'm out of condition!" He bent double with exhaustion while Sam gripped her stomach, far too knackered to even speak. Gasping, John peered into the distance. "Where the hell are they?" The lane stretched ahead, but there was no sign of them. Not a sound or a glimpse of anything resembling a four-legged bovine – they'd just vanished into thin air. He felt the tension starting to build, he had to calm down, breathe in the gentle soothing breeze that flowed through the roadside trees. He closed his eyes, listening for any distant bellowing of lost cows, the snapping of dry twigs from cumbersome hooves wandering over unfamiliar territory. But there was nothing – just an eerie silence so quiet each could hear their own heartbeats.

"Lost them then?"

"Jesus." John's eyes sprang open. "Where the hell did you come from?"

The young boy sat on his bike in the same position as back at the farmhouse. "You want me to go find them? Looks like you two are right knackered." He gave a long hard stare at the dogs. "Buggered too, by the looks of them. He pointed to Kim. "That one don't half run funny."

"Arthritis," John replied.

The boy raised the corner of his lip. "Funny name for a dog."

"No, it's … never mind." Now wasn't the time or place for a lengthy medical discussion. The boy ran the sleeve of his jumper across his nose, leaving a trail of slug-like substance for all to see. John was desperate, but how desperate? He gazed at the dirty individual with snot all over his arm; instincts on any other occasion would see such an offer of help tossed into the brambles. Any involvement with his kind would almost certainly spell trouble later on, it just wasn't wise to be beholden to the lower classes of the village, something country land owners like himself were told to never do. My God, he was beginning to sound like his mother. Maybe he was being a little hard on the boy – appearances weren't everything. He knew all too well many well-heeled country folk were right dickheads and certainly not to be trusted, so no, you should never go by first impressions. And to be fair, the boy *had* taken the time and trouble to inform him of the cows' initial escape. "All right then."

They watched the young grubby urchin speed off as fast as his rickety old bike would allow. John glanced over to Sam. "Seems quite a nice boy."

"If you say so." She stood with her arms crossed, awaiting orders. "Well, what next, Master?"

"We keep walking. Hopefully the lad will find something." Suddenly John spotted him in the distance waving one hand and then pointing to a gap in the hedge. "There, you see? All is good, he's found them." As he spoke the boy disappeared through the hedge like a magician's white rabbit. "Well, maybe not." Arriving at the gap it seemed the lad was right, the cows had definitely passed that way – there were hoof marks along the well-trodden footpath heading straight for the village. "Sodding cows, why can't they stay where I put them?"

Sam said nothing. It was best to let John have his little moan and move on. They were following a mixed trail of more hoof indents and freshly discarded dung. The path zigzagged its way across open scrub offering little or no edible fodder for hungry roaming beasts to feast upon, their lust for tender pickings pushing them nearer to civilisation. John knew the place like the back of his hand, although he hadn't crossed this way for some years. Far too busy on the farm to go wandering the countryside for the sheer hell of it. Not a luxury he could afford. He remembered as a child riding his bike this way, a shortcut to the village store where he would exchange his few pennies for a bag of assorted sweets. The store was no longer, now converted into a family home. He sighed. Those who lived there now knew nothing of the way it used to be, of the lives of those who eked a meagre living from the surrounding fields, of neatly attended vegetables forever being weeded or harvested by small gangs of gossiping women with their backs permanently bent double, swapping dirty jokes or comparing their ideal fancy man.

John glanced around with sadness. Now those same fields lay idle, abandoned by the people who cared so dearly for the land, left to grow unproductive scrub until the bulldozers, bricks and concrete arrived to plant not edible food but houses instead. He sighed, for he knew Mother Earth's hand was slowly losing her grip on when it would happen. Only those who thought they knew best would decide, possibly next year, possibly not, but all the while this rich soil waited to be stripped of her right to breathe the air we all take for granted.

John admitted his mind had somehow wandered far beyond the company he walked with, drifting between those lost years yet still vaguely taking notice of his surroundings.

"Found them, I have."

"Jesus. Will you stop doing that? You scared me half to death!" The lad had appeared yet again from nowhere as he pointed towards the village. "On the cricket pitch they be."

"What, all of them?"

He put up four fingers. "Three."

"Right, so what you're trying to say is that there are only three, not four?"

"If there be four I would've said. Not daft, you know."

John caught a quick glimpse of Sam trying to suppress a giggle.

"No, of course not."

Even Kim look confused, her head tilted to one side. Pup as usual couldn't give a damn and was more content chasing his tail than trying to fathom the boy's mathematical logic.

They arrived at the outer edge of the playing field and to John's relief the cows had moved off the cricket pitch and were grazing the longer grass of the off-season football field. His worries now fell to the seemly absent Ethel, the big brown ugly cow with half a horn on one side, due to her lack of speed, he assumed. John knew all too well a lone cow was far more unpredictable than a group. He scoured the area but sadly she was nowhere to be seen. "We'll have to leave finding Ethel. Let's get the rest back home before we lose them again."

He now needed to deploy his available helpers into some sort of efficient working team, something he wasn't too good at. It would've been nice to have an hour or so to mull over possibilities, plan out a line of attack, but such luxuries were not available. Sam, he was sure, would allow him some time to come up with a plausible plan, a tiny bit of responsibility defining his position as the head of the farm. Giving him free range to organise the operation wasn't in his wife's nature, and she would no doubt leave her suggestion till the last minute so undermining his authority yet again. She would undoubtedly have the final say but he had to give it a try. "Okay, Sam, you stay on one side of the gap, and, what's your name?" John looked down at the boy sitting on his bike.

"Josh, but my mum calls me tosser."

"Right, I think we'll stick with Josh if that's all right with you?"

"Suit yourself."

"So Josh, would you like to stay with Sam and cover the other side? That's of course if you don't mind helping?"

"Whatever, nothing else doing."

"Great! Me and Kim will go around the back of the cows and drive them towards you." He waved his hand in the direction he wished them all to go.

Josh looked puzzled. "Thought you said the dog's name was Half Titus or something?"

"I'll explain later." At this point he was sure the inevitable would happen and Sam, being a woman, would interfere and politely suggest another way. He waited, but nothing, not a sniff of interjection passed her lips. This moment had to be savoured; this unexpected victory was something he wasn't used to. He called Kim to heel and started to make his way across the grass.

"Would it not be better ..." As if she had a sharp knife, Sam plunged it deep in his back. John felt the words slowly drain away any self-respect he foolishly thought he ever had. Once, just once, is that too much to ask, he heard himself saying over and over. He turned, gritting his teeth, trying to look grateful for any positive suggestion she might possibly have. "Perhaps ..." she continued.

Oh for Christ's sake woman, just come out with it! That's what he wanted to say out loud but of course to keep the peace he quietly listened to her suggestion.

"What about if we drove them towards the lane but used that small gate in the corner – might be easier, that's all. Then we could run them along the hedge which would act as a funnel, less chance of them getting away and out into the lane, one at the front and one at the back then straight home. Just a thought. Of course there's nothing wrong with your idea, nothing at all, but I just thought ..." She left her last comment hanging in the air, knowing full well her idea was by far the best.

John didn't know whether he was more frustrated by the changing of his plan or the fact that Sam's idea was marginally better than his.

"We can go with your idea, I don't mind," she said, sensing his frustration.

"No it's fine, we can go with your plan. As always it's far more sensible than mine."

Josh grinned, revealing gaps in his teeth. "Me mum

says women are always right and us blokes ain't got an ounce of sense between us."

"Thanks for that, Josh. Let's just get them home, shall we?" No more was said as he turned and walked away, now feeling depressed about the job in hand. The cows of course played their part to perfection as if they were also conspiring to undermine his authority, but they were females after all. By the time they arrived safely back at the farm the normal chain of command had been restored. Sam seemed content with her input into the operation but for some reason sensed a tinge of resentment flowing from her husband as they all walked back in silence. Why, she couldn't understand. Josh, although totally inexperienced in the art of handling livestock, played his part perfectly and as for Ethel, she would just have to wait. After all, what harm could one cow possibly do?

"You did a good job, Josh, I'm impressed," said John, placing his hand on the boy's shoulder. "Well done, we'll make a farmer of you yet." Josh didn't say a word but grinned from ear to ear. "You wait there while I pop in and check for any messages just in case someone has spotted Ethel, otherwise we'll have to go back out and look for her."

Sure enough, the light was flashing, indicating three separate messages. John pressed the replay button ... *You have three new messages, beep! Hi, it's Dave Turner here. John me old mate, sorry to bother you but I've just had what I suspect is one of your cows in our back garden.* His words hung in the air before carrying on, warning John to brace himself. *Unfortunately she's managed to eat her way through Edith's beloved geraniums, not a problem as far as I'm concerned, can't stand the things, but Edith's a little upset. Anyway she's just trotted off towards the church – that's the cow, not Edith.* John could hear Dave chuckling at his own joke. *If you need a hand getting her back give me a nod. Good luck.*

Great.

Beep! A message for Mr Taylor. Henry Satan Jones here, Sutton Grange. Look here, Mr Taylor, this just isn't cricket, dear boy. One of your marauding beasts has just played havoc with our garden party – divots, Mr Taylor, the size of huge craters all over the croquet lawn. Absolute disgrace. Me and some chums managed to shoo her off and good riddance I say. I suggest you make an appointment to see me sometime this coming week.

The phone went dead. By this stage John was almost too afraid to listen to the remaining message. *Beep! Reverend Johnson here. Apologies for calling you on your day of rest, John, but I'm sure you're aware by now that one of your cows has escaped, but all is not lost, I can report she is happily grazing the churchyard and making a fine job of it too. I've shut the gates so there's no rush but I must warn you I believe Henry Satan Jones is none too pleased. Bye for now.*

John felt a deep pain within his chest. *Just what I need.* He slipped into his boots and wandered out to report to the others.

"Any messages?"

John raised his hand and produced two fingers. "Three," he said, which brought a half-hearted smile to Sam's face as they both glanced over at Josh. Luckily he hadn't noticed or hadn't understood John's little joke. "Apparently she's in the churchyard."

Sam looked marginally pleased. "Oh well, that's not so bad, is it? I suppose it could've been a lot worse."

"I haven't finished yet."

"Oh dear, where has she been?"

"Well, first she managed to get into Dave and Edith's back garden and massacred her beloved geraniums. Don't laugh, it gets much worse."

"I'm sorry. Poor Edith, geraniums you say?"

"It's not funny." John pointed a finger at his now giggling wife.

"Come on, John, you've got to see the funny side of it."

"Yes, but it's not so funny what she did next. Henry Satan Jones."

At his name Sam raised her eyebrows and stopped laughing. "Oh dear."

"Yes, oh dear indeed. Apparently they happened to be having a garden party and our dear old Ethel took it upon herself to have a bash at croquet, but by the sounds of it her footwear wasn't appropriate, not quite the ticket old girl. Henry is none too pleased – divots my dear, the size of huge craters. What do you say to that, my little pumpkin?"

Sam felt her face crumbling by the second as she spluttered words past her now quivering lips. "Divots, you say?" Her laughter exploded around the yard sending the dogs running for cover as she let her emotions get the better of her.

John shook his head. "You can stop that. You know what Henry's like, it'll probably be an insurance job. I can hear it now: 'You'll be hearing from my man in due course,' stuck up old fart. "You up for one last job then, Josh?"

"Yeah, I guess so."

"Good lad."

They arrived at the church as the clock struck two. John gazed up at the huge brass hands decorating the clock face. "Great, bang goes my nap." The double set of gates winced as if in pain, sending a high-pitched sound echoing around the gravestones. A dry rusty powder momentarily floated in the air before drifting off in the gentle breeze that calmly blew across the resting occupants. Ethel briefly turned her head, vaguely interested in her company, before continuing to munch her way around the undisturbed holy stones of the deceased. Luckily for John a back way to the church had unofficially been created over the years by those who used it weekly to come through from the derelict dog-walking wasteland to the village, leaving just enough room to drive a single cow back onto the lane and along to the farm.

John sent Josh through the stones, weaving his way through the resting dead to reach a small wooden gate hanging neatly between an unkempt laurel hedge. His job was to open it up and move out into the lane where Sam was already waiting a short distance up, ensuring dear old Ethel didn't run off yet again. Josh would take up the rear, leaving John and the dogs to push her safely home. Ten minutes later she was back at the farm, seemingly unfazed by her gallivanting and failed attempt at a round of croquet. With not a care in the world she wandered over to the nearest water trough and took a long hard drink before calmly making her way to the open field.

"Good! Time for dinner," John announced. He glanced at the boy sitting on his bike. "Well, thanks again, Josh. You'd better get on home or your mum will be wondering where you are. Something nice waiting for you on the table, I bet." The boy looked baffled by John's remark. "Sunday lunch, Josh. Roast chicken, potatoes, beans, carrots, yum yum." John made a gesture of rubbing his stomach, showing his delight concerning such a feast.

"Don't have dinners. Mum, she ain't no good at cooking stuff."

"Oh, right. Well that won't do, will it? Budding young farmer like yourself going without a cooked dinner? Tell you what, you come inside and the wife will find something for a man of your size to eat. After all, you've earned it, it's the least we can do. Come on."

Sam was already in the kitchen trying to bump-start a stone cold meal, looking at her once beautifully presented food in despair. It's never the same warmed up, she thought. If only they'd known about the cows a little earlier before she'd added the rich dark gravy – now they would have to scrape away the congealed skin as it welded itself to every last scrap of food on the plate. She greeted John and the boy with equal measure, not questioning the lad's presence for one moment.

"Come along in," she said. "We don't stand to attention around here." It was obvious Josh didn't have a clue what she was on about.

"Just take a seat, lad." John pointed to a chair as Josh gingerly edged his way into the kitchen. "Sit yourself down." This simple request was met with a certain amount of anxiety from a boy who was being asked to do something he very rarely did, for sitting at a table didn't come naturally.

"So what would you like?" Sam's voice bounced off of Josh's whole being as he sat staring at the choice on offer. Being a woman she instantly sensed the boy's fear as she watched his eyes constantly wandering around the room, almost as if they were trying to find an escape route. Clearly this simple task of selecting unfamiliar food had put him on edge. Sam knew to tread carefully. "Why don't you just taste a small amount of everything, then you can choose which bits you want? You can leave the rest, we won't be offended."

Josh just nodded as he watched them tuck into the warmed-up dinner. "You can start." John pointed to the knife and fork expecting their guest to take them up and start eating, but the boy only sat and stared at the instruments glaring back at him. John wondered if he'd actually heard him, but caught a discreet look from Sam warning him to back away.

"It's all right, Josh," she said warmly. "Just take your time." With this small encouragement the boy finally picked up his knife and with a puzzled look started to slice the air in front of him, swirling it back and forth like a swordsman preparing for battle. They watched as he lowered the knife, hovering it momentarily over his food before pulling it back. As much as he tried he just couldn't seem to complete the task. John glanced at Sam somewhat concerned at what he was witnessing and wishing to intervene, but once again she silently warned him to allow the boy the time and space he clearly needed.

"You all right, Josh?" The words sounded far more caring coming from a woman.

"Don't work."

"What doesn't work, Josh?"

"This stupid knife."

Sam knew she had to tread very carefully indeed; one wrong word and the boy would probably be out of the door like a jackrabbit. "Have you …?" She paused for a moment. "I mean, have you ever used a knife and fork before?" She felt she might be overstepping the mark, but it was clear he was having problems.

"Don't need them for takeaways, that's what you got fingers for, so me mum says."

"Well, yes, you're right in a way," Sam replied. "There are lots of people who use their fingers when eating fast food, but this is Sunday lunch, that's what knives and forks are for."

Josh said nothing and looked somewhat put out by Sam's comment. She could see he was starting to look a little fearful so she needed to make a decision, and fast. "But on this occasion, if you want you can use your fingers." No sooner had the last word left her mouth than she saw the knife fall with a loud clatter and two hands plunged into his food. Fingers scrabbled for whatever they could get a grip of. Potatoes proved tricky, spinning around the plate trying to avoid capture. Then to John's horror the less fortunate vegetables surrendered to Josh's immense appetite as he showed little mercy. The chicken somehow seemed to awaken from the dead, quivering with fear as it succumbed to a wave of violent attacks. Finally, to everyone's relief, Josh sat back, licked his fingers and with a look of sheer contentment forced out a large amount of trapped wind.

"Not half bad this Sunday lunch lark, apart from that – it's horrible." He pointed to a pathetic huddle of warmed-up broccoli.

Sam swallowed hard and deep as she pulled herself up from her seat. "I'm glad you enjoyed it." She collected the plates as if nothing out of the ordinary had just happened, making her way over to the sink as John casually joined her.

"That was interesting." He tried to keep his voice down as low as he could.

"I've postponed pudding until later," Sam whispered. "Rhubarb and custard."

"Good decision." They discreetly looked at the boy

who was now sucking his fingers for the second time. "Very good decision."

"I thought so too."

"Well, Josh, I'm afraid I've got to go milking now, so once again a big thank you for all your help and perhaps we'll see you again sometime?"

"Might do."

"Sam detected a slight tinge of disappointment as the boy pushed back his chair and made for the doorway. "Thanks, missus." At that moment she suddenly realised that Josh almost certainly didn't know their names.

"By the way, I'm Sam Taylor and this is John Taylor."

Josh looked at them deciding whether he needed to reply. "Righto." It was clear he wanted to say something else, but whatever it was, he was now going out the door.

"Josh," Sam called out after him. "How would you fancy going milking with John? I'm sure he'd love to have a bit of help."

"I would?" He suddenly felt the full force of his wife's expression. "Yes, yes of course I would, in fact I'd be very grateful for the help, what with chasing cows around half the day. A bit of help would be greatly received." Sam quietly thanked him with a discreet smile. "So what do you say, young Josh?"

His eyes suddenly lit up as he tried hard not to show his excitement. "Suppose I could."

*

"How did it go?" Sam asked as John wandered in from the afternoon milking.

"Well, for his first time he did really well. He's a good lad, is our Josh. Give him time and a bit more practice and he'll do well."

"It sounds like he's coming back."

"If he wants to, why not?" Sam couldn't help look rather pleased with herself. "Okay, I admit it was a good suggestion on your part. Even got the pigs sorted."

"Very satisfying outcome then." She just couldn't help but grin.

"All right, you win, I accepted it was another good idea of yours."

"Do you think he really enjoyed it?"

"You know, to be honest, I think he did, he's got the makings of a good stockman."

"What, you can see it even this early on?"

"Without a doubt, he's just got a way with animals and the animals respond to him. No, he's very good, more than I can say for his eating habits; that was shocking. What must he be, thirteen, fourteen? Something like that, and he can't use a knife and fork?" John was right in a way, but to be fair it probably wasn't Josh's fault, that sort of thing came down to good parenting, or not, in this case.

The chime of the grandfather clock flowed through the house, reminding them that Susan would arrive later. Sam had spent some time sorting out one of the spare rooms, although to be fair the whole house seemed to have had a light going over. John wondered how she ever managed it; first impressions were one thing but to go to all that trouble for a ... he suddenly stopped himself – thank goodness he was only thinking.

"I'll get tea." Sam broke his line of thought.

"No, don't bother, we had dinner late. Why don't we wait until Susan arrives, she'll probably be hungry by the time she's sorted out her room and it'll be nice to sit down and have a chat, get to know the person we're going to share our house with. What do you say?"

Sam looked surprised. "Well for once you've come up with a very good suggestion."

"Oh thanks! A little bit of encouragement always goes a long way. I'll see if I can keep it up in the future."

"You know what I mean."

"Do I?"

"Yes. Why don't you go and have a quick nap before she gets here? Clearly you're starting to get a little grumpy."

It was John's turn to look surprised. "I'm not grumpy."

"There you go, you're raising your voice."

"No I'm not."

"You are." She pointed towards the front room. "I'm not talking to you when you're like this. Off you go."

John went to protest but was cut short by a look that told him to back off. "Fine." Women!

*

"John. Wake up. Susan's here." Sam's voice drifted around him as if part of an unexplained dream. "John, wake up." The voice seemed louder, why was she calling his name and who was this Susan? "John. Come on, wake up. Susan's here." She gave him one almighty shove but still his eyes refused to open until the very last moment. "Susan's here."

He took a deep breath, rubbed his eyes and slowly pulled himself out of his trance. "Who?"

"Dear God. Susan, remember? It's six thirty." She towered over him with a disapproving look then pointed to the door. "She's outside right now."

"Just give me a minute and I'll be there."

Susan had arrived in a blue rusty transit van. Her friend sat patiently in the driver's seat smoking a cigarette and listening to a mind-numbing beat of seemingly little variation.

"Susan, it's lovely to see you again."

"And you, Mrs Taylor."

"Wrong, young lady. If you're going to live in the same house, it's first names only."

Susan's face broke into a smile. "Sam. Sorry."

"That's better. John will be out in a minute – he's just coming round from a short nap, poor soul's been on the go since five this morning, it's been one of those days. Ah, here he is."

"Susan." John appeared from the hallway, still not quite with it. "Nice to see you again."

"And you Mr ... sorry, John." She quickly glanced around and caught Sam's nod of approval.

"Don't worry," John replied kindly. "We'll get used to each other over time."

Susan pointed at the van. "That's my friend Leo." The young man saw he was the centre of their conversation and acknowledged them with a light-hearted wave, but stayed seated.

"Right." John rubbed his hands. "Let's get you unloaded then. If you can get Leo to back up to the front door, that'll be great."

They stood and watched as the van shuddered to life, the exhaust violently knocking against the under-workings of a vehicle that had clearly seen better days. Leo slowly pulled away, taking a long run-up before attempting to back towards the house, occasionally stopping before pulling up straight several times.

"Is he all right?" asked John.

Susan attempted a reassuring smile. "He's not long passed his test."

"Oh." As if that made an excuse for a poor attempt. "Perhaps I should have a go." John was given a disapproving look from the wife. "Only a suggestion. Why don't you tell him there's a wheelbarrow in the garden if he wants a little practice on something a bit smaller?"

"John, please!" Sam's voice slapped the air around her husband's face. "Sorry, Susan. Unfortunately John's lack of patience I can only put down to a total disregard towards anyone who dares not to come up to his supposedly high level of competence."

"That's fine. I'm used to men with inflated egos." She gave Sam a discreet wink, indicating that from that point on they were both going to enjoy each other's company.

Finally, and to John's obvious relief, 'Postman Pat' managed to deliver the goods, but not before he was told to stop for fear of knocking down the oak archway pillars. And still the van managed to roll another half metre after applying the handbrake, narrowly missing a concrete ornament of a gun dog grasping a pheasant in its jaws. Leo fell out the door and made his way to the rear of his trusty van. "Hi everyone. Mr Taylor, Mrs Taylor." He seemed a nice enough young man, apart from reeking of smoke. "Sorry."

"A little rusty there." John looked at the van.

There was a moment's silence until Leo finally cottoned on. "Ah, funny, got that one, rusty van, good one, Mr Taylor."

Oh Dear!

John smiled politely before Leo continued. "Did Susan tell you I'm into music? Got me own band and everything. This is our touring van, just got to give her a touch-up with a spray can and she should be as good as new."

John kicked a badly worn rear tire. "How big a spray can have you got?"

Leo had to think about this one. "Got it, Mr Taylor, large can, lots of rust, clever, like your humour."

Oh Dear!

"The Dead Legged Donkeys."

"Excuse me?"

"That's the name of my band, the Dead Legged Donkeys. Catchy, hey?"

"Very." John was sorely tempted to add more to his reply, but this time thought better of it. Finally Leo opened the back doors and stood to one side to reveal a half-empty van.

John ran his eyes around the partially carpeted interior. "Is this it?" Somehow he was expecting to be confronted by floor-to-ceiling boxes of Susan's life, but instead he looked upon a meagre collection of oddly sized containers. Three large suitcases were wedged neatly alongside the sliding door next to a curious black leather-bound chest. A small assortment of dresses and garments hung upon brightly coloured coat hangers protected by a light see-through plastic covering. "Right, we better get unloaded. The women can carry the light stuff and me and Leo can take charge of anything that's slightly heavier," John suggested.

Both women made their way along the hallway sharing out what little there was. Sam noticed one or two rather revealing garments she was adamant would never entertain room space in her own wardrobe, but Susan was young, very good-looking and could without doubt pull off such things. She sighed, thinking of her own lost youth as she peered at the girl in front of her, an exceptionally attractive young woman. Shamefully she now found herself picturing their new arrival scantily dressed in more than one of the outfits, and suddenly felt a warm glow to her cheeks; or was it just the stairs making her flush? "I've put you in the bedroom opposite for now."

Susan led the way along the landing into her new temporary accommodation and placed her clothes on the neatly prepared bed.

"This is lovely, Sam."

"Oh, it's nothing really. Now I've put some spare sheets and pillowcases in the airing cupboard and over here is a good-sized walk-in wardrobe which by the looks of the amount of clothes you've got should be ample. I'll put this lot down here, shall I? Then you can sort them out later."

"Thank you, that'll be great."

Just then John and Leo came struggling up the stairs. "Men at work, make way," called John from the landing as both men entered the room. "Where would you like this, Madame?"

"Anywhere for now, and thank you both. I'll unpack what I need – the rest can stay in boxes until we've finished decorating the other room."

John and Leo had finally come to the last piece as it sat all alone in the back of the van waiting patiently for someone to come and claim it. A chest of some age, the studded black leather almost growled at anyone who dared to venture too close. Leo rubbed his hands in preparation. "Beware of this one, she's heavy," he warned as he gripped a brass handle.

John's curiosity got the better of him. "What's inside? Do you know?"

Leo hesitated, rested his free hand on its lid, slowly leant forward and whispered to his partner in crime. "Don't know, but I could have a good guess." He gave a sly wink to John.

"What? Do you mean …"

"Yeah, I reckon."

"Blimey." John couldn't resist running his hand along the worn leather. "I bet this could tell a story or two. You can almost feel the heat."

Leo held his hand on its surface longer than necessary before pulling away. "Ah, you bugger! Had me going then."

John let out an amusing chuckle. "Come on, let's get it upstairs before it bursts into flames."

"Well, ladies, I think I deserve a beer. Come along, Leo,

coffee for you, you're driving. You can tell me all about these dead donkeys."

"It's the Dead Legged Donkeys, Mr Taylor."

"That's what I said."

Chapter 14

A cool breeze filtered through partially open curtains, occasionally causing them to billow into the room. Only birdsong could be heard as the rays of the sun reflected across the brilliance of the white ceiling. Susan watched as a spider hovered on the outer edge of its web allowing a fly to struggle for life, its every movement exciting its capturer until finally it pounced mercifully upon its prey. She shuddered.

Her senses were bombarded with the unfamiliar as she lay on her back safely wrapped in freshly scented linen. Unfortunately this lazy existence would eventually come to an end, but not just yet. She smiled, if only for her own amusement, simply because she could. This little luxury and the occasional sounds of movement reminded her she wasn't alone. Floorboards creaked as footsteps passed. The clock showed nine, a respectable time for any working girl to still be in bed, but clearly not for a country household.

She tried to lure herself to a point of no return, for she knew she had to get up. Hand gripping tight, one pull saw the sheet fall to the side, leaving her naked body barely covered by a light flowery night dress. Legs apart, she welcomed the cool breeze that gently tingled her exposed skin, and with the increasing warmth her mind drifted into a pleasant land of tranquillity and well-being.

The door flung open and George walked in with a

bucket of tools and a pot of paint. Susan broke from her trance as she lay entangled by her own nightdress, its ruffled state jammed up behind her back exposing every part of her lower body to anyone who cared to look on.

"Bugger me!" George froze. His arms shook uncontrollably as he caught the full uncensored view of everything this young lady had to offer. With the overexposure his hands fell limp, releasing their hold on the bucket and sending the contents crashing to the floor.

Susan watched as the old man swayed back and forth before his legs started to buckle beneath him. She leapt out of bed and ran to his side, just in time to catch the elderly gentleman as he crumbled to the floor. "Help! Someone? Please, anyone ..." Her distressed cry for help travelled down the landing. "Help!" Sam was already halfway up the stairs before she had a chance to call out for the third time. "Oh thank God you're here, he just collapsed, poor man."

"Calm down, it's only George." To Susan's horror Sam didn't seem overly concerned.

"You need to do something. I think he might be ..." she gasped for air. "Dead."

"Only temporarily, dear."

"Temporarily? How can you be temporarily dead?" Her voice had risen in panic.

Sam placed a hand on the young woman's arm. "It happens."

"What!" Susan couldn't believe her ears.

"It's okay," Sam replied. "All we have to do is undo his shirt like this, then, I suggest you stand back." With a raised arm and a clenched fist she laid one single blow to George's chest. To Susan's sheer relief the old man coughed and spluttered then gingerly sat up.

"That's more like it, George." Sam's voice floated through the air as she gazed at the young woman standing barely covered in the open doorway. She could see why George had taken to the floor – even with her unkempt sleep-induced wild look the girl was utterly stunning. Her eyes gently drifted over every last part of Susan's body. Yes, she knew she should look away, deny the feelings threatening to engulf her very soul, but it wasn't easy.

"Dodgy pacemaker. Nothing to worry about, you'll get used to it, but for the sake of poor old George here I suggest you get covered up before he comes round completely, or else you'll be sorting him out next time! Come along, George, just had a little shock, that's all." He struggled to his feet, leaning his weight against Sam's supporting arm while trying to avert his eyes from Susan who'd wisely wrapped herself in a pink silk dressing gown and now stood a short distance away.

"Oh thank ye, ma'am. All over shocked I were, seeing young missus here all exposed an all. I do apologise, miss, see I only come to paint the windows."

Sam tried to hide her amusement as she steadied him from toppling over. "It's all right, George, no harm done, but it's the bedroom opposite that you're supposed to be doing."

He now looked confused. "Ah, but I thought you said the one on the left?"

"I did, George, but this is the one on the right."

"Be it, bugger me, begging your pardon ladies. I'm right sorry, miss, be a misunderstanding for sure, they be tricky them left and rights, slippery as eels they be. Well I better get next door then." He leant forward to retrieve his discarded tools and felt the room move as if being shaken by a large unseen hand.

Sam had already grasped his arm. "I think we'd better go downstairs and have a strong cup of coffee, don't you George?"

"But I only just started, ma'am, not me break time for another two hours or more."

"Don't you worry about that, now come along with me. I'm sure Susan will oblige by picking up all your tools for you. Just place them out in the hallway would you dear, George won't be long. You'd like a nice cup of coffee, wouldn't you George?"

"Best be a drop of whisky if choosing, ma'am."

"I think coffee will be just fine, don't want you drunk in charge of a paintbrush, do we now?"

The old man shook his head as he was led out of the room. "Not long for this world, ma'am."

"Yes, George, I seem to remember you saying that years ago. It's a new pacemaker you need and then you'll be as right as rain, just need to go and see the doctor, that's all."

"Bloody doctors, begging your pardon ladies, poked his finger up my arse last time I went. Ain't natural for a man doing that to another man. Be not going again so you can stop your nagging, get enough of that at home."

Sam shook her head. "Come along, George."

Susan watched as they staggered off down the landing. "Are you going to be all right?" she called out. "I'm really sorry about everything."

Sam half turned. "Like I said, you'll get used to it, but it's good you found out now."

"Slippery as eels, ma'am."

"I know, George, those left and rights can be very difficult sometimes."

"Not them, ma'am, bloody doctors, begging your pardon ladies, slippery as eels."

*

The smell of fried cooking drew Susan to the kitchen like a moth to a light.

"Ah, just in time." Sam looked up from her work. "John's just come in." She pointed to an empty chair. "Take a seat, there's plenty for the two of you."

"Are you not eating?" Susan asked.

"Dearie me no, it's Monday, had mine hours ago but I might have a slice of toast. Washing on a Monday, so I like to get up early and make a start. Sorry about George, I should have warned you, but what with one thing and another it went clean out my head."

"Is he all right?"

"Yes, he's fine, but one day he won't be so lucky and the blasted thing won't restart, and sadly that will be the end of him."

"How horrible." Susan couldn't help thinking how people in the countryside looked at life, and in George's case, possibly death.

"You can't make the man go to the doctors if he doesn't want to," Sam continued.

"No, I suppose not, but I'm glad he's okay."

Sam stopped what she was doing, finding herself concerned for Susan's well-being. "And you, are you all right? It must've been a shock for you too."

"I'm fine, he's not the first man to see me half naked!"

Sam couldn't help but let out a light chuckle. "No, I suppose not, but certainly the oldest."

"Oh, you be surprised."

"Really? What, older than George?"

"Only the once, and his wife insisted on watching."

The sound of a saucepan hitting a solid object echoed around the room as Sam tried to compose herself. "Well I never." She continued to busy herself unnecessarily. "I know it's none of my business …" She paused for a moment trying to choose her words. "But can they still … you know?" There was a quick glance towards the open door just in case John might appear and catch them discussing such a personal topic. "You know?"

Susan knew exactly what Sam was trying to say but thought it amusing this older woman found it so difficult to talk about. "No, I don't know."

Sam lowered her voice to a near whisper. "You know … get it up, at that age."

"Oh yes, age doesn't really come into it with men."

"Oh good grief, just the thought of it, and his wife watching, you say?" There was a look of disgust as Sam proceeded to stab a sausage and peer at its steaming length. "Bet there's more meat in one of these chaps than in an old man's willy!"

It was the way she said it that made Susan crack up with laughter, enabling Sam herself to see the funny side. With the offensive sausage now firmly secured to her fork, Sam lifted it to eye level and gently signed. "I can see I've got a lot to learn." She was halted from saying anything further by John marching in through the open door.

"Good morning, Susan." He'd appeared from the boot room, his hands and arms recently scrubbed to within an inch of their life, but to Susan's horror his face still held signs of being far too close to a cow's rear end. He looked at both women with suspicion. "Well, are you going to let me in on the conversation?"

"No. Just girls' talk, nothing to do with you," said Sam.

The two women grinned at each other.

John looked a little put out. "Oh, so that's how it's going to be, is it, secret whispers? Very well, I'll mind my own business."

Susan looked at John in disgust as he proceeded to pull up a chair in an area where food was in the process of being served for human consumption.

"What?"

"You've got poo on your face." She stared in disbelief at the dried hardened lumps behind his ears.

"Ah, a bit of muck never hurt anyone, but just for you young lady, I'll see what I can do about removing it, shall I?"

He proceeded to rub his hand all over his face trying to dislodge any offensive material from Susan's view.

"Oh no, there's a really large bit in your hair," she grimaced, utterly repulsed.

"Poo, muck or shit, it's very important if you're going to live on a farm to understand the right terminology."

"John, please! Leave the poor girl alone."

"Only saying." He watched with amusement as Susan squirmed at the sight of him running his fingers through his hair.

"Gross, now it's on your hand!"

Sam now saw him as a probable health hazard and forcefully pointed towards the boot room.

"All right, I'm going. Great, now I've got two females on my back. Just don't you forget some of us have been working since five this morning."

"John … "

"Yes, I'm going." He purposefully looked over in Susan's direction and pointed his finger. "Your cards are marked, young lady." To her relief she saw a glint of humour on his face.

"Excuse my peasant husband, I'm afraid he's not used to other people being here when he's having his breakfast. Two eggs all right for you?"

"Lovely."

"Bacon, mushrooms, fried bread, and of course we know all about the sausages."

The young woman's eyes lit up. "Great, but you don't have to."

Sam held up a hand. "Yes I do, you're a working girl. Admittedly not farm work, but you need to keep your strength up, and I think I'm going to quite enjoy cooking for three again. Not that I've actually stopped since Luke went away, John can vouch for that." She proceeded to overload Susan's plate.

"Now that's what I call a breakfast," John announced as he strolled back into the room. "Get that down you, young lady and you'll go on all day."

Susan looked on with trepidation. The thought of actually eating her way through such a large amount of food clouded her mind as she gingerly picked up her knife and fork.

"At least this one's not using her hands." John's comment seemed a little out of the ordinary; confusing in fact. Perhaps she'd misheard – he did have a tendency to make some strange remarks from time to time. She smiled politely, hoping it was the right thing to do, and put it down to the oddities of country life, something she'd clearly have to get used to. Her first mouthful nearly blew her mind as flavours never experienced before attacked her taste buds. "Sam, this is extraordinary. I never knew food could taste so good."

"Why thank you, Susan, it's nice to have someone compliment you on the food you present on a daily basis." She deliberately glanced in John's direction.

"What do you mean? I appreciate it too."

Sam hesitated before taking another mouthful of toast. "No, John, you're just a heathen when it comes to food."

"Don't know what you mean," he replied as he shovelled a load of fried food into his mouth.

"See what I mean, Susan?"

John was first to place his used cutlery down on an empty plate and push it towards the middle of the table, indicating to all that he'd officially finished. "I needed that."

Sam stared at him. "Susan met up with George this morning." She'd finished her solitary slice of toast so rose up and made her way to the sink, not bothering to wait for a reply.

"Oh, good. Dear old George. Salt of the earth, been on the farm forever, worked for my father most of his life. Now helps with whatever Mother wants, a bit of gardening, DIY. Nothing too physical, but be warned, he does have a dodgy pacemaker."

Susan set her knife and fork down. "I know. I kind of stopped it working this morning, unintentionally of course. I think seeing me partially undressed was a little too much for him. My fault."

Sam interrupted. "I asked him to start painting the windows in the bedroom, but in hindsight I should have probably shown him what I wanted done, you know how he gets things muddled up sometimes. Well today it was his left and right and unfortunately he mistakenly walked into the wrong bedroom. Normal thing, thump to the chest and he was fine."

John couldn't help but grin. "Well, lucky old George."

Sam suddenly spun around. "That's typical of you men, isn't it, not concerned about how the woman might feel. No, just lucky old George, bet he got a good eyeful."

"Hang on, I didn't mean it like that." At this point John really should have left it at that, but of course he couldn't. "Anyway, Susan should be used to that sort of thing, being a pro—"

"Don't you dare, John Taylor." Sam's voice struck like an arrow to his unprotected heart.

"All right, calm down, I'm sorry. That last remark

didn't quite come out the way I hoped."

She looked him straight in the eye. "Now you apologise."

"Really, Sam, it's all right."

"No it's not, Susan. We asked you to come here, and yes it's to do a particular job, I know that, but certain people in this room need to learn some manners."

"Look, I'm sorry, all right? I apologise."

Frankly Susan wasn't particularly concerned about John's conduct but it seemed Sam was. She was right in a way, there were those who thought they had the right to take liberties just because of her profession, but that wasn't John. "Apology accepted."

"There you go, sorted," John replied.

Sam looked like she wanted to throttle him, but for the sake of not drawing blood in front of their newly acquired company she'd refrain. "George is scraping down the window frames, then he's going to paint them, although he might need a hand to reach the tops. I'm not keen on him climbing up the stepladder on his own."

Susan saw the chance to remove herself from the frosty atmosphere. "I don't mind giving him a hand with the hard bits." It was said with honest intentions, but she suddenly realised how it actually sounded.

John couldn't help it. "Now that didn't come out the way you wanted it to, did it?" He wasn't sure whether he'd overstepped the mark yet again, but now even

Susan was grinning.

"Come on, it was meant as a joke." He was forced to sweat it out while his wife pondered over his last comment.

"I suppose I can let you have that one."

*

Susan stepped into the room that was to be her whole life. Her dream four-poster bed stood much the same as before, yet now it was stripped of its mattress, looking somewhat sad and in much need of love. She smiled for she knew it would certainly get that, perhaps not affectionate love, but certainly lust. Either way she was sure it wouldn't complain. Her eyes scanned the room. The small rug had disappeared leaving the wooden floorboards exposed and the dreary sun-bleached curtains were gone as well, allowing easy access to every part of the window frames.

George sat on the ledge peeling off flakes of paint with some sort of flat-headed metal thing, his hands wrinkled and old yet able to move along the woodwork like a skilled craftsmen of much younger years. "Hi George."

He looked up and stopped. "Miss, you did catch me half napping. Sorry I am, be out your way in a tick."

"No, please carry on. I thought I might come and help. Sam … I mean Mrs Taylor, said you wouldn't mind a second pair of hands."

"Oh right, that be very kind of you, miss." There was a

little unease in his voice, somewhat withdrawn in the way he spoke, almost certainly brought about by their earlier incident, Susan thought. She knew it hadn't been her fault but felt she should at least try and clear the air between the two of them. "I'm sorry about this morning."

George seemed relieved the subject had been brought up. "Now, miss, was all my doing. I feel right wrong for what I done, mistake be all mine and no arguing about that." He turned back towards the window, gazing at the open view. "You be some sort of model then, miss? Of course be none of my business, just curious like."

Susan suddenly had to think; clearly no one had told George the truth, perhaps concerned it would be too much for his weak heart, so maybe unintentionally he had just given her the perfect cover story. "Yes George, something like that."

"Ah, I thought that be the case, you be a fine-looking lass and no one could say a word against that."

"Why thank you, George. I'll take that as a compliment."

"You take it as you will, miss, there be no truer than me word."

Chapter 15

"How much? I know it's for a four-poster bed but that's extortionate! What's it stuffed with, royal ostrich feathers?"

Sam wondered about her husband sometimes. "They don't use feathers in mattresses any more. They may have done the last time you thought about buying one, but not nowadays."

"But £800!"

"Oh put your tongue back in your mouth, John, you look like one of those Māori fellows, and I hate to say it but it was your idea in the first place."

"Trust you to remind me."

"Well it was."

"Yes, the initial plan, but then you wandered off in another direction and told Susan she could pick her own mattress."

"What did you expect? Of course she needs to pick her own, she's the one who's going to be lying on it and you can take that smile off your face, John Taylor. But if it makes you feel any better, she's assured me it will pay for itself in no time. It is, after all, her main bit of equipment; you'd be no good as a dairy farmer without your tractor, now would you?"

John frowned at Sam's comparison. "I'm not sure it's quite the same."

"Yes it is, there's no difference."

John knew he was onto a loser but now and again it was nice just to stretch his wife's arguments to the limit. "And what of the carpet?" he asked. "I suppose we've got the top-of-the-range shagpile being laid?"

"Now you're being silly."

"Am I? Am I really?"

"Yes you are, because that's where you're wrong – apparently shagpiles are too dangerous."

"You're kidding me?"

"No, I've been reliably informed that any carpets used must be of a medium to short length and be of a neutral colour. It's all to do with obtaining maximum grip when barefooted and not distracting the eye away from the business at hand."

John fell silent, his mind trying to make sense of the information and the complete crap that was coming out of his wife's mouth. "You really have got to be joking."

"Apparently not." She paused before carrying on. "Perhaps that's where we've been going wrong all these years." They looked at each other, daring the other to speak out over their less-than-active marital activities. "The carpet's being delivered tomorrow morning and the mattress sometime in the afternoon, they promised to ring just before they got here. So all going well it should give Susan the weekend to move all her belongings across, and be ready for Monday."

"What? Ready for work?" The speed and efficiency that was going on around him had taken John by surprise.

"If that's what you want then yes. You're the man in charge, remember? She reckons she could be up and running by the middle of next week, if not sooner."

Realisation suddenly set in – next week they could have real live men appearing at the front door with the sole purpose of employing the services of a prostitute. Dear God, what had he done? Up until now it had all seemed like some make-believe play where things could be seen to be happening all around you but everybody knew it wasn't actually real. Sam had just made it very real indeed and John wasn't entirely convinced he was prepared for it. Why couldn't it all just go away, he thought. Susan. The bank manager. His wretched overdraft. Just vanish and leave him to his own little world of self-denial.

"I think I need to go for a walk." He needed time to himself.

Sam heard the back door close as John made his way out into the courtyard and across to the garden.

"John, dear." His mother's high-pitched voice travelled across immaculately kept lawns, penetrating his line of thought.

Reluctantly he raised an arm hoping she wouldn't detect his annoyance at being interrupted in his quest for peace and serenity. She lay on a sun lounger partially shaded from the sun by a rather striking striped blue and white umbrella. Great, that's all I need, he thought. He knew his mother all too well and would almost certainly be committing himself to a lengthy conversation. But it was too late and like it or not, she was his mother, so with some reluctance he strolled across the grass, a vague look of interest upon his face. "Mother, how are you?"

"I'd be much better if my only son would show some willingness to visit his poor lonely neglected mother from time to time. But putting that aside, I'm fine dear, and who wouldn't be with weather like this?" She looked up at the clear blue sky. "Isn't it just lovely for spring?"

"It is, Mother, very nice."

"Very nice? Do I detect a certain degree of uncertainty in your voice? Well don't just stand there blocking the sun, pull up a chair and tell me all about it, we haven't had a good chitchat for ages and if I were a wise old owl I might think you were trying to avoid me."

"Nonsense, Mother, it's just I've got a lot of things happening at the moment."

"I dare say you have, dear, but farming is always busy. Or is it more to do with this new venture of yours? We've not spoken since I gave Sam those telephone numbers, clearly it must've helped, am I correct? Although I'm sad and a little put out by the lack of thanks."

"Sorry about that, Mother, and yes, they were very helpful thank you."

"That's better, even if I did have to squeeze it out of you. I have to admit I went to a lot of trouble to get those names, put my neck on the line, I can tell you. If my fellow women at the WI ever found out, my chances of running for regional chairperson would be utterly ruined."

John leant back in his chair and looked at the large dark lenses of his mother's sunglasses. "How did you get those names anyway?"

"My little secret, dear, and the less people that know the better. So please tell, I'm dying to know what's developed. I've even resorted to questioning George but he's about as much use as a pair of Wellingtons with holes in, so come on John, speak to me."

"Well, if you must know, George has done an excellent job in the bedroom."

His mother waved a frustrated hand as if being pestered by an annoying fly. "Not George, dear, the man is a buffoon. "No, the girl. I've seen her wandering about and I must say she is a rather pretty little thing. Who is this young lady? I need a name, dear."

"Susan."

"Susan who, dear?"

"I'm not really sure."

She raised her sunglasses and gave John a look of bewilderment. "You mean to say you've taken on this girl but don't know her surname? Really, John, sometimes I wonder about you. Your father was the same, trying to get him to get the whole story was like shovelling muck up a hill with a pitchfork."

"Sorry, Mother, you'll have to ask Sam, she's sorting everything when it comes to our new lodger so I've left them to it. But yes, Susan is a very nice young lady."

The glasses slipped back over her eyes. "George likes her, that much I have managed to get out of him."

"Yes, he's seen quite a bit of her this week." It wouldn't do to elaborate any further on that.

"I caught a glimpse of her hanging out some rather revealing washing yesterday. It's hard to believe she's a … you know what."

"A prostitute, Mother."

"Really, John, I prefer you didn't use that word."

"You too? Sam's not that keen on it either, must be a woman thing."

"It's so vulgar, dear, surely we can come up with something a little more presentable to the ear – perhaps a working girl would be more appropriate. I believe it has a softer edge to it."

"If you wish, Mother."

"And what of poor Samantha, is she really happy about all this?"

"Yes, I think so. She really likes Susan – she's even been busy making new curtains for her room, and to be honest I think she's looking forward to having a bit of female company."

His mother's head shot round. "And I'm not a female, is that it?" she said with a rumble of discontent.

"Yes, of course you're a female, but Susan is ..." He paused, knowing whatever he said next would almost certainly get him into trouble.

"Younger, John? I think that's the word you're looking for. I'm not a fool, dear, I know exactly what you're implying and I'm not bitter or twisted about it. Let's face it, the years have passed by far too quickly and perhaps I'm not the best company."

"I'm sorry, Mother."

She waved a dismissive hand. "Forgotten already. But John, what of all those weird men passing through the house, surely Samantha can't be pleased about that? I know I wouldn't want it."

He slowly edged his way to the front of his chair, hoping his mother would realise he needed to get on. "We'll just have to wait and see, won't we. I'm not denying it's going to be strange at first, but I'm sure we'll all get used to it."

"You don't sound too convincing. Are you really committed to this venture of yours?" His responsive silence told her all she needed to know. "I understand, dear, you have to do something, I realise that."

John went to get up. "We need money, Mother, and right away. I'm not saying this will solve our problems, but it has to be a step in the right direction."

She rested her hand upon his. "You're so much like your father, dear. I know he would've been proud of you. As I am."

"Thank you, Mother, that means a lot to me."

Their hands parted and she looked him straight in the eye. "Now can I please have my gardener back? Just look at the state of my borders."

"Tomorrow, Mother."

"Well that's a relief."

John pulled himself up and gently kissed a waiting cheek. "I have to go." There was little point bothering her with any further details, such as taking on a second woman. A woman who could only be described as the nuthead of the forest with alarming tendencies towards physical human torture. Perhaps not someone his mother would instantly warm to.

Later, John walked through the house and past the half open door of his office, spotting the farm map on his desk. It was over a week since he'd shown Tick around and although he hadn't expected to hear or see anything of her, he felt a tinge of curiosity seeping into his cluttered brain. He needed to deliver the map to her, but perhaps it was too early. Convincing himself she had probably done very little in the time given, John wondered if it was pointless spending precious time going up to the hut. Yet the more he thought about it the more that tiny niggling voice perched on his shoulder kept telling him he should at least make the effort.

With the folded map and a large stone holding it firmly on the passenger seat, John and the two dogs travelled up the lane, made a sharp left-hand turn and stopped abruptly in front of the entrance to the wood. With renewed vigour he leapt out towards the gate, its padlock and chain firmly secured indicating that perhaps no one had passed through recently. Yet as he leant forward to insert the key he noticed a number of narrow tyre marks clearly not from his Land Rover, but more of a motorbike nature. Tick must've passed through by the looks of it, and on more than one occasion, but whether she was here now was anyone's guess.

The oversized lock sprang open just as a chilled breeze whipped up through the surrounding trees, their leaves breaking the silence with an eerie rustling that drove a shiver up the length of John's spine. The dogs lay silent, not daring a single bark, something John instantly found strange. They crouched like statues transfixed by some strange force, staying safe within their confines. John glanced up expecting someone to be standing beside him, but saw nothing, only the leaves gently swaying in an increasing wind.

He stood for a moment, studying the darkened track and could've sworn the undergrowth moved. "You're cracking up, John, pull yourself together, man." It was said in a less than convincing manner and with no one to listen he made his way back, occasionally glancing over his shoulder just in case. Urging the Land Rover into her lowest gear, John and two rather nervous passengers clawed their way through the trees, steadily climbing, until he finally spotted Tick's motorbike, parked sideways across the track making John park a short distance back. With some apprehension he sat for a while studying his surroundings, why he didn't know. He was only delivering a map, for goodness' sake. He looked back at the dogs for reassurance but found little more than two quivering wrecks.

"A lot of good you two are." They stayed silent, hoping their master would turn and follow the track home, but were sadly mistaken as he opened the door and walked away. With map in hand he followed the well-trodden path down the steep slope over familiar territory, picking his way along until eventually the small wooden structure came into view. To the naked eye nothing much had changed, and if it hadn't been for Tick's transport John would've found it hard to believe she had troubled herself towards any improvements, yet she must have done something. He made his way to the front door, bracing himself for the unknown. Ownership of everything around him made no difference to his own manners – this was now Tick's and as such warranted respect. He wondered what, if anything, awaited him. He knocked three times on the weather-beaten woodwork and stood back to wait.

Nothing. Not a sound, a movement or a voice. Should he wait a little longer? He wanted nothing more than to turn and walk away, but he had promised. He gave another two loud raps on the door, the noise rattling through trees, scattering a few birds from their resting branches. Still nothing.

After making every effort to get noticed he placed a

hand on the crude brass doorknob he remembered so well from his youth, one that had a tendency to rotate one full turn before engaging the locking mechanism. It didn't disappoint, then with a gentle nudge of his shoulder he peered into the eerie silence. "Hello?" he called. "Is anyone home?" His well-mannered upbringing wouldn't allow him to enter further, certainly not until he'd called out several more times, but there was still no response. A final failed attempt had him stepping inside while trying to convince himself his decision was the right one.

His eyes adjusted to the dim light that hung heavy in the room, throwing out lines of unfamiliar objects that dared to dance before his face. As they became clearer he felt a surge of shock rumble through his veins, his face muscles tightening as they reacted to what confronted him. Normal movement was impossible as his gaze fell upon a sight that scared the living daylights out of him. Virtually every hint of his father was now gone; he was sure Tick would have a perfectly good explanation for every single item that now decorated the room. John couldn't for the life of him understand why anyone would pay good money to be subjected to such things. The door creaked on its hinges and he turned with a gasp, convinced someone was standing there, but no, just an empty hole in the wall. This wasn't natural, he thought, as a sudden cool breeze cut across his face – not an uncommon experience, cold winds occasionally whipped up on a hot spring day – but this felt different somehow. He put the map down and ran a hand over his chin. Pull yourself together, John, you're a grown man for Christ's sake. This was stupid, he had to keep telling himself that. It was just a room, what was in it wasn't going to jump out and bite him on the leg. Or was it!?

Moving deeper into the room, he studied every piece of crafted metalwork, every hanging chain, every dangling shackle. Dear God, *why*? Why would a man, or a woman for that matter, want to be subjected to such torture, a word he found all too easy to explain what he was looking at. To be bound hand and foot, to be held against spikes that jutted out in all directions and then to be simultaneously tortured for the sheer hell of it. *Why*? A single wooden chair stared back at him. Innocent at first glance, it seemed to offer a safe resting place for those who chose to sit upon its wooden frame, but on closer inspection it offered little more than two small clips that attached themselves to long wires running to a twelve-volt battery! *Why*?

John's mind felt numb. Happy childhood memories battered and bruised, dislodged by everything around him. With relief the small kitchen came into sight, its worn enamel sink showing signs of years of neglect. He looked at the familiar objects – a kettle, a toaster, everyday things that surely even Tick couldn't use for anything else other than preparing food and drink. As for the rest of the room, it stood shielded by a heavily lined pair of curtains stretching from wall to wall. Probably a sleeping area, perhaps even the final resting place for those poor tortured souls who may be allowed at least a little comfort for their money. John paused as he felt the stiffness of the curtains. He was tempted to push them aside, have a quick glance, but that would be wrong, and for all her bizarre imperfections Tick still deserved her privacy.

The light in the room changed. It was almost as if something had momentarily blocked it. The hairs on the back of John's neck sensed a presence as he began to turn …

"Hello, Mr Taylor."

The words pounded in his ears, blocking out any other sounds. He felt the air being sucked from his lungs. "Christ, Tick! You scared the living daylights out of me!"

"Sorry, Mr Taylor. Hungry?" She held up two freshly killed rabbits, eyes bulging as if their last moments on earth had not been pleasant. John himself had shot and trapped hundreds of their kind in his life, but never had they looked so fearful, so utterly macabre as these two. He almost felt sorry for them, but at least now they were dead, relieved from their seemingly torturous death. Tick laid her victims to one side. "Used to sneaking up on people, Mr Taylor, habits are hard to break. Please take a seat. I'm sure you'll have a cup of coffee – no tea I'm afraid, can't stand the stuff."

John looked around, trying desperately to find something that wouldn't electrify his buttocks and send them into uncontrollable spasms. Tick watched with amusement. "There's a couple of ordinary chairs out back, you stay there and I'll go get them."

"Ah, right, good."

She returned with two rather rickety chairs John thought were equally capable of inflicting just as much pain and discomfort as the others. Clearly of his father's making, they were lashed together with baler twine and dodgy looking half screwed-in plates.

"So where are you getting your electric from?" John asked as he tried to balance on three legs, the fourth one clearly too short to come into contact with the floor.

"Rigged up a couple of solar panels, straight into three deep cell batteries. Day like today all the power I need."

"I'm impressed."

"Thank you, Mr Taylor, don't do jobs by half – waste of time. Army for you, Mr Taylor. If you're going to do a job, do it well. Sugar?"

"Just one thanks."

She reached out, grabbed the bowl and placed one spoonful into John's drink, then shovelled a good six or seven into her own. John looked on in horror as she produced what looked like a life-sized replica of a man's willy, pressing a button and making it spring into life.

"Is that what I think it is?" John couldn't help but ask.

She held it up as it twisted and turned like a hand-held lap dancer, a vibrator. "Yes, bloody good things for getting the white head on your coffee." She plunged it head-first into his mug. "Don't look so horrified, Mr Taylor, I've got two! Never used this one for what it was intended for, but a great tool, don't you think?"

"Yes, great."

"You still don't look to convinced, Mr Taylor."

"No, it's fine."

"That's the spirit."

John reluctantly placed his lips against the enamel rim and found the experience far more pleasing than he had hoped, but then noticed Tick studying the vibrator in some detail.

"Something wrong?" he asked as a mouthful of coffee disappeared down his throat.

"Identification, that's the trick to these big boys. Without it you can never really be sure."

"But you said ..."

"Sorry, Mr Taylor, mistakes happen, but I'm sure I would have given it a good clean. Funny, never done that before."

The contents of John's mouth travelled at speed out of his mouth and over his lap.

"You all right, Mr Taylor?"

He hastily used his hand to wipe away the remnants of a possibly used willy-enhanced coffee. "Fine, just a little hot, that's all."

"Good man."

John was rapidly losing the will to go on and had visions of a dancing willy rotating in his mug – all it needed was for a thick crop of curly hair to sprout out around the rim and he was sure he would throw up.

"Looking a little pale there, Mr Taylor, are you sure

you're okay?"

His head dropped as he started to feel seriously unwell, and to cap it off there seemed to be an unwanted rumble developing deep down in his stomach. "Oh God, I think I'm going to be—" With little time to finish his sentence, he shot from his chair and ran, reaching the open door just as he projected the entire contents of his breakfast out across the grass.

"Didn't think you looked to well." Tick had followed him outside.

Bent double, John desperately tried to wipe away an embarrassing trail of slime that hung from the side of his mouth. "Thanks for that." His words showed little interest to what she was saying as he tried to regain his composure, only to be met by a mug of coffee forced under his unwilling noise.

"This will settle your stomach, Mr Taylor."

Without hesitation his head thrust forward for the second time, bringing with it the last dregs of his beloved bacon and eggs. "Perhaps not now, Tick, if it's all the same to you. Just give me a minute and possibly a glass of water?"

"No problem, Mr Taylor, if you're sure you're okay?"

"Fine, just water please." With a much clearer head John stepped back into the hut.

"Water, Mr Taylor."

John was presented with what looked like a perfectly

normal glass, its contents looking as it should. Water. Why was he so surprised? He took a couple of mouthfuls. "You'll have to excuse me, probably something I ate this morning." It sounded plausible, at least to his ears. "Anyway, I brought you the map," he said, pointing to a sliver of paper poking out beneath two dead rabbits. "It looks as though you're finding your way around already but at least now you'll know the boundaries, and don't forget the right of way. I'd stay away from there, you don't want to tangle with anyone from the local Ramblers Association – one or two can be a bit unfriendly."

"Not a problem, Mr Taylor, no one will know I'm here."

John didn't doubt that for one second. "I see you've settled in all right."

"Just the necessaries, Mr Taylor, can't operate with too much clutter around. Everything has a job, functional and effective, that's how it should be. I run a tight camp here, Mr Taylor, got taught that in the army, only carry what's necessary."

John glanced around the room. He didn't necessarily agree with Tick's choice of home comforts, but that was her business.

"You disapprove, Mr Taylor?"

He paused for a moment. "Well, not disapprove, just a little naive concerning such things I suppose, but I'm sure there are those who would think differently."

"There are, Mr Taylor, and willing to pay good money for the privilege, but understand this, I'm not in this for the fun of it as some might think. No, Mr Taylor, I'm here to make money, as much as I can, and if I can do that by supplying these men with their deranged world of abnormal sexual fantasies, then so be it."

John placed the empty glass aside and studied the woman in front of him. "I apologise."

"For what, Mr Taylor?"

"I fear it may have seemed like I was misjudging you, but you must understand I've never had to deal with anything like this before."

"Anything, or any*one*, Mr Taylor?"

"Both, I suppose. Look, Tick, I'm a farmer first and foremost, that's all I really care about. Nothing else matters and unfortunately that's under threat – my life, my livelihood and to a lesser extent the whole farm, and I won't let anything happen to those things I love most. So the truth of the matter is, I need money too, so perhaps in a way we're both very similar. And you, Tick, you talk about making as much money as possible. For what?"

"Wales, Mr Taylor. Buy myself a small place surrounded by woodland, that's me. Somewhere where no one can judge me. I don't ask for much."

"Lets hope it works out for both of us then." John went to get up. "You know where I am if you need me."

"Don't worry, Mr Taylor, something tells me we are both going to get along just fine."

"I hope so, Tick, I really do."

Chapter 16

The doorbell gave two long blasts from a slightly tired-looking box of cobwebs. Sam was busy preparing lunch, a bowl in each hand she headed for the freezer in search of last season's fruit. "Susan? You couldn't see who that is, could you? It's probably the men with the new carpet. If it is, just show them where to go and I'll be up when I'm finished here."

Susan had just come down after spending an hour or so sorting out various boxes ready for her big move later that day. All that remained to be done now lay in the hands of tradespeople. Her main concern was that it happened to be a Friday and if she knew anything about anything, counting on men to do anything this late in the week was a big ask, but she stayed upbeat and hoped Sam was right. The thought of at least two drop-dead gorgeous hunky tradesmen with large hammers hanging between their legs made her almost skip towards the door. She felt a tingling of excitement over the prospect of having them ready and able to spend the rest of the day on their hands and knees servicing her every need.

Sadly her carefree fantasy was just about to take one humiliating hit as she found herself tugging helplessly at a stubborn bloody-minded lump of ancient wood. After what seemed an eternity she finally managed to open up a gap just big enough to poke her head through revealing her knights in shining armour who, on first inspection, had been turned into a stubby little toad and a lanky stick insect!

"Hello, love, come to lay a carpet," the short stubby toad croaked as he glanced down at his clipboard. "A Mr Taylor, Willowbank Farm."

"Yes, that's right." Susan stretched her slender neck slightly further through the door. "I'm afraid you'll have to give the door a bit of a push, unfortunately I don't seem to be strong enough myself."

"Anything for a good-looking lass like yourself."

Susan felt anything but good-looking as she pulled back and waited to one side. "Come on, Justin, give us a hand." Susan heard the two men grunt as the heavy oak door slowly gave way. "There's your problem, sweetheart, someone's fitted the draft excluder too far down, and this carpet!" He shook his head in disgust. "This carpet's not been laid too well. See that, it's all loose, it's getting pushed up as the door opens."

Susan had already learnt one very valuable lesson in life: if you've got it, flaunt it, especially when it comes to tradesmen. "Do you really think that's the problem?" Her voice had changed, taking on a more innocent damsel-in-distress kind of tone. "You're very clever, aren't you," she added, eyelids flickering.

"Oh, nothing to it really." He stretched his back and raised his chin, trying to show superior knowledge of all things to do with the mysterious world of floor coverings. "I'd stake my reputation on it, sweetheart, and believe me that goes a long way in the carpet world."

It was time for Susan to perform at her best. "I'm very impressed, I always admire a man who knows his trade." She watched his cheeks glow with pride as he fumbled with a tie that wasn't there.

"Comes with years of practice, love. Of course, when you get to my level of competence you learn to spot these problems, all to do with the eyes. Take young Justin here, he's got a lot to learn but he's in good hands, aren't you boy?" The young silent lad nodded.

"Do you think it's a job I could do?" Susan swiftly asked, her words a softer sultry tone. Of course she had no intention of mending anything. "I'm sure I haven't got the right tools," she continued, "but I could probably find one of those ..." she made deliberate useless gestures with her hand. "You know what I mean, one of those long-handled things with a funny heavy grippy thing at the end."

There was a look of sheer shock from both tradesmen. "What, you mean a hammer?"

"Yes, that's it. I'm sure they've got one on the farm."

Stubby little toad puffed his cheeks in total disbelief. "Dearie me, you wouldn't want to be going at it with such a tool, be like cracking a nut with a steamroller. No, you need slightly different tools, more specialised."

Susan knew she almost had him. He paused for a moment, gazing at the problem in hand. "Tell you what we'll do, if I get young Justin here set up in the bedroom I'll come back down and fix this for you, how's that?"

Got him. "Oh, are you sure you can spare the time?"

"Won't be a problem, sweetheart – someone with my skills, I'll have this done in no time. Anything for a nice young lady such as yourself."

"Oh, that's really good of you." Even to her own ears she was starting to sound perfectly annoying.

"My pleasure, love. Now where is this carpet got to go?"

"Follow me." She deliberately strutted in front of them, her buttocks swaying from side to side, occasionally stopping to fiddle with her shoelaces and giving them both a good old eyeful. By the time she had subjected them to a visual erotic stair climb they were like putty in her hands. "Here we are," Susan announced.

Stubby toad strolled around the room croaking every so often then stopping mid-stride. "Well, looks pretty straightforward, but this bed might be a problem – technically the room should be clear of any furniture and suchlike before we arrive, and this old girl looks a bit heavy. Health and safety you see, we're not here to move clients' belongings. We're carpet layers, not removal men and even they would grumble over this one."

Susan felt her muscles tightening by the second. She surely wasn't going to be outdone by some health and safety claptrap, her carpet would be laid today or else. "Perhaps if I give you a hand, I'm sure the three of us should be able to move it." Her toad in shining armour looked unconvinced as he scratched his head. Susan knew she had to do something fast or this carpet would never be laid. "I'll just open the window a bit, shall I, while you're having a think. They say fresh air is good for the brain, it's so very hot in here, don't you think?" She proceeded to undo the top two buttons of her blouse revealing slightly more cleavage than necessary when contemplating moving a large bed.

Both watched on as she wandered over to the window and reached full length, her figure silhouetted within its frame, the bright light dancing upon the curves of her young body. She hovered there a long moment before turning back to two open-mouthed tradesmen. "There, that should do it," she said, deliberately running her hand across her breasts. "Now, this bed?"

"Not a problem, love, nothing we can't handle, eh Justin." The silent lad didn't look so convinced. "Righto boy, grab hold of the other end, we can't have the young lady moving something like this. After three – one, two … cor blimey, she's heavy!"

Susan deliberately moved closer, making sure the men got a good glimpse of her open top. "You will be able to move it, won't you?"

"Ah yes, not a problem, sweetheart. Me and Justin have it sorted."

She watched as the two struggled under the weight of a very well-made four-poster bed, moving it inch by inch across the bare floorboards, causing the toad's back to creak more than the bed itself. The pain on his face made Susan feel slightly guilty, but she brushed it away with a flicker of her eyelids.

"There you go, love." She watched him try to straighten up, his hand firmly grasping the corner of the bed. "Right, we'll go and get the carpet."

"Thank you, you're wonderful," she cooed.

"Not a problem, sweetheart. Come on, Justin, we'll get you going on this and then I'll mend that door." They disappeared down the stairs, the young silent apprentice and the toad whistling 'Rule Britannia'.

Susan made her way to the kitchen, drawn in by the smell of freshly baked bread.

"Ah, Susan." Sam looked up, her face lightly powdered with a fine dusting of flour. "Sorry I haven't been up yet, this is taking a bit longer than I thought. John will be up in arms if his dinner isn't ready. I assume those two men are here to lay the carpet?"

"Yes, they're just making a start now and the one in charge, sweet little man, is going to fix the front door."

Sam gave her a look of concern. "John won't be pleased about paying extra for a job I've been nagging him to do for years."

"He's not charging for it."

"Isn't he? Whatever prompted him to offer to do that?"

She ran her fingers through the flour scattered across the table, suggestively making odd little swirly patterns as she feigned a look of innocence.

"Susan!"

"I can't help it if the sweet little man has taken a liking to me, now can I?"

"What have you been up to?"

"Nothing. Just a little bit of flirting, that's all. It's amazing what you can get done if you show a little, let's say, *encouragement* in certain directions."

"Susan! You never! You little minx!"

"I've always loved the smell of baking."

"That's right, change the subject. Too good-looking, that's your problem."

A smile appeared on the young girl's face. She simply blew a kiss in reply, and their eyes locked, each of them wondering what the other was thinking. Sam was the first to break the silence. "I thought we'd have a salad today, but I think the bread is cool enough to eat if you want a slice? Blackberry and apple pie for afters."

"You're going to get me fat with all this good food."

Sam glanced at an almost perfect figure. "I hardly think so; you could do with a bit of flesh on you if anything."

"What are you saying, that I'm skinny?"

"No, of course not, you're young, that's all. I've just forgotten what that looks like, stuck in this house most of the time, you almost forget what the real world's like. So I'll correct myself – you've got a lovely figure, is that better?"

"A little, but seriously, Sam, if I carry on eating this much halfway through the day, I'm going to have to keep my afternoon appointments for the less energetic clients. You try getting your legs up over your head when you've just eaten a large meal. You either end up getting cramp or farting, and both are totally unprofessional."

Sam stopped shelling the eggs. "I wouldn't know," she said wistfully, her hands hovering over the sink.

Susan moved closer. "Look, I'm sorry, I didn't mean to ramble on about what I get up to. I suppose it starts to become second nature after a while. Anyway, I'm really sorry."

"No, it's fine. Believe it or not I'm genuinely interested in what you do, having never met anyone in your profession before."

Susan didn't know whether to stop the conversation and just step away or dig a little deeper. She'd noticed, even in the short time they'd known each other, that this woman was hiding something and perhaps now was a good time to delve under the sheets as it were. "You can tell me to shut up if you like," Susan continued, "I won't be offended, but I'm guessing your sex life isn't ..." She hesitated briefly but was cut short by Sam's immediate confession.

"None adventurous. I think that's what you were going to say."

"Something like that. Look, it's really none of my business."

"No, it's not, but I don't mind. In fact it's quite a relief to have someone to talk to and yes, it's certainly not adventurous. It's more … what's the word I'm looking for? Not boring. Just … functional. That's probably the best way to describe it. There's a need occasionally from a man, you know that as much as I do, but it's as if it's a woman's duty to spread her legs when those needs arise. Don't get me wrong, I don't dislike it, but there's just something not quite right and I'm not sure it's John's fault." An uneasy pause lingered in the air. "In fact I know it's not."

"What are you saying?"

Sam looked away. "I don't know what I'm saying. Sex for me is just something to endure. John, well he's a bit like how the bull on the farm does it, then wanders off and has a sleep under the nearest tree."

Susan sat silently, allowing the older woman the freedom to offload her thoughts and concerns. If she was happy to continue then she was willing to listen.

"We tried to spice it up once." A light chuckle escaped Sam's lips.

"Just the once?" Susan asked.

"Yes, well, I did warn you. Sad, isn't it?"

"What happened?"

"We attempted it in the shower. I remember we'd been watching some film, can't recall which one, the name doesn't matter. God, I can't believe I'm telling you this."

"Sam, remember what I do for a living?"

"Quite. Where was I?"

"In the shower."

"Oh yes, rubbing soap all over themselves they were, I mean it's not the sort of film we usually watch, you understand."

"Sam, I'm not judging."

"No, of course not. If we'd known, we wouldn't have started watching it." Her mind drifted back to lost memories. She sighed. "Quite exciting, certainly got me going, and it even kept John from falling asleep and we're talking ten in the evening."

"Really, that late?"

She shook her head at Susan's slightly sarcastic remark. "You're clearly not married to a dairy farmer, are you? Anyway, in the film, one thing led to another and they ended up having sex while in the shower, so we both looked at each other and agreed, why not?"

They had to agree to have sex, Susan thought, have a discussion – weigh up the pros and cons of such an outrageous act of human lovemaking? Dear God, if this is what happens when you've been married for any length of time she'd rather stay single.

Sam was on a roll. "The soap part was actually quite arousing, apart from John getting it in his eyes, but the sex, that really needed more practice and how that woman in the film managed to stay upright while the man did his bit I'll never know because I'm damn sure

I couldn't do it! Looking back I think we overdid it on the soap. More running water perhaps? Slippery as eels, George would say. John lost his footing, fell back and cracked his head on the soap holder, ended up with a nasty gash above his eye, but even before he went over there was no way he was going to perform. It was a total disaster."

Susan felt it was time to say something. She really didn't want this conversation to stop and felt Sam wanted to say more, but whether she would was another matter entirely. "You said it was your fault?"

"I think it was definitely the soap."

"You know what I mean."

Sam silently continued with the last of the eggs, content to stare out the window. Susan was sure she would speak out but her thoughts were broken by the sound of continuous banging from upstairs. Then Justin passed by the kitchen door trying to balance a large green flask and two sizeable lunch boxes in his arms. Shortly after the women heard muffled voices and then silence as the men settled down for their mandatory one-hour break. Then to cap it all John wandered in and sat at the table looking as though he expected the food to miraculously appear before his very eyes while he moaned about everything under the sun.

Susan noticed with some humour that Sam had perfected the art of appearing to listen while casually nodding now and again to keep the peace.

"Did you see they arrived with the carpet?" She

deliberately interrupted John's flow of verbal criticism as he had reached the point whereby he was starting to repeat himself.

"Yes, I saw the van outside. How are they getting on?"

"Fine, I think. I've not had a chance to get up there yet. Susan showed them in and told them what to do, didn't you, dear?"

"Yes. They seem quite nice."

"She even managed to get them to fix that rub on the bottom of the front door. For free!"

"Yes, well, it's amazing what men will do if you flirt a little," said Susan.

"My, my, starting to earn your keep already. Good girl. Of course I've been meaning to get that job done for a while now."

Sam spun around. "No you haven't! I've been on to you for ages, and let me remind you it was your own doing. If you'd done the job properly in the first place, you wouldn't be always putting things off. You could've got George to look at it but oh no, we're to save money, do it ourselves, and how many years have we had to put up with that damn door sticking?"

"Okay, calm down."

"Don't tell me to calm down, John Taylor." Her raised voice bounced off all four walls. "God! Sometimes you make me want to scream!"

No one said a word, leaving John to contemplate his next move. Even with his apparently pea-sized brain he could sense a ripple of hostility creeping over his wife, and like so many times in the past sometimes it was just best to agree and move on.

"Of course, you're probably right."

"I *am* right."

He raised his hands in defence. "Okay, you're right, I'm sorry. I was wrong all the time."

"Now you're patronising me."

"No I'm not, I'm agreeing with you."

"That's not agreeing, that's just being sarcastic."

He should have stopped at this point but he just couldn't let this one go. "First I was patronising, now I'm being sarcastic?"

"It means the same thing, John."

"Does it?"

"Yes, it does."

"Okay, if you say so."

"There you go again." They were cut short as the older carpet layer wandered past the kitchen door, also sensing hostility in Sam's voice – he was yet to meet her, but thought perhaps now he'd rather not. He'd had intentions of popping his head around the door and informing Susan of his impending plan to start on the front door, but like the man now sat at the table receiving untold abuse, he felt on this occasion the best thing was to just walk on by.

"Who was that?" John had caught a quick glimpse of a man going about his business while whistling 'Rule Britannia'.

"That's the carpet layer," Susan replied.

This small but invaluable distraction had come exactly at the right time. John had never claimed to know anything about female behaviour, but there was one thing he was extremely good at and that was grasping an opportunity to get the hell out of it. "Probably best if I go and check up on how they're coming along. I'll see you later."

"But what about your dinner?" barked Sam.

"I'll have it later."

Sam slumped herself into a chair. "Why do I put up with him?"

"Because you love him?"

Sam's honest reply was tempting, but then she thought better of it.

"I'm not sure you realise just how lucky you are, Sam." Susan pointed to herself. "Look at me."

The older woman snapped back. "Yes, look at you, shall we? You're young, well-educated and you've got a figure most men would die for. Anything else I've missed out?"

"Quite a lot, actually. That's my trouble – men just want me for my body."

"It *is* your profession. Apologies, that didn't come out

well."

"It's okay, but it's always been the same – even the boys at school only wanted one thing."

"I think you'll find that's nothing unusual, anything half decent at that age will get their hormones racing. I'm afraid, dear girl, beauty can be a curse sometimes. Not that I speak from experience and that's fine by me, couldn't see what all the fuss was about. Give me a good book any day. Look, Susan, I appreciate your concern, but John and I are fine most of the time. That's when I don't what to throttle him, but if anyone's going to find love and happiness you'll be first in the queue."

"Nice words, Sam, but let me remind you that I'm twenty-five years old and single, yet I have more sex than the average baboon."

"Lucky you."

"Yes, but I don't have *real* sex. I think that says it all, doesn't it?"

Susan felt a warm hand gently rest upon hers. "It'll come."

"Will it? You have it all. Yes, John might moan from time to time ..." Sam's head tilted to one side, "... okay, a lot of the time, but I'm sure you've never stop loving him. Sorry, this is your home, we hardly know one another and it's none of my business." She rose and made for the door.

"Susan."

She turned and faced the older woman, a woman she'd warmed to over the short time they'd known each other. "Thank you."

Susan smiled. "You're welcome, and we can work on the sex thing."

*

John stood in the bedroom doorway pondering his new purchase. Justin was carrying on while his mate fulfilled his promise and could be heard raising the draft excluder having already relaid the loose flooring. "Ah, Susan, I'm sorry about that, I'm not sure what's come over Sam lately, she's not normally so short with her comments."

The young woman stood peering into her new bedroom. "It's all right, whatever it is will pass, I'm sure, you know what we women are like."

John shrugged. "That's half my problem, I don't know what women are like, never have done. The only females I can sort out have four legs and don't mind if I fumble their teats twice a day." He rested his arm on the door frame. "Anyway, take a look at this." Half the underlay was now covered with a pale pink grey-flecked carpet, something John struggled to get excited about, but for Susan's sake he would show some interest.

"Oh, it's just how I imagined it would be, not too bright and yet not too dull. Get the bed in place and a few bits of furniture and it will look great."

John forced a smile; to be honest he detested anything

pink. This wasn't much better and it cost him a small fortune! Justin kept his head down, slowly working his way around the edges having no opinion of his own, although Susan could see he wasn't daft. Perhaps that's what you did when entering people's private homes, she thought, you hear and see things that possibly you shouldn't, but professionalism forces you from airing any opinions. What you discussed at a later date, however, was another matter entirely!

Susan retreated to her temporary bedroom, leaving John to ponder over a colour she thought he liked, but it was Sam's voice that eventually shattered his thoughts as she shouted up the stairs.

"John! The mattress has arrived – can you come down and sort it out please?" It sounded more like a demand than a request.

Susan raced out onto the landing like a small child on Christmas morning, taking the stairs two at a time in her excitement.

"Whoa, slow down, it's only a mattress."

She met John lumbering slowly down the stairs. "Don't be such a stick-in-the-mud – it's my mattress, so there." Her hand deliberately ran through his hair as she passed by.

"Oh, is that right? Then perhaps you wouldn't mind paying for it."

"Can't hear you," she shouted back as she ran along the hallway and opened the door that now swung with ease.

"Women!" John grumbled, but no one was listening.

The carpet layer, propped up against the post and rail fence, was talking in some depth to the delivery man. "Here she is." Susan's stubby knight in shining armour greeted her with a wide grin as she came running up. "Ah, you're enough to brighten anyone's day, sweetheart." She greeted his compliment with her infectious excitement that made both men wish they were thirty years younger. "Bet you don't get a welcome like that every time you deliver a bit of furniture?"

The delivery man shrugged his shoulders. "More's the pity, the world would be a brighter place if we had more like her."

"Not a truer word said, and if there were more like her I could trade me missus in for a bright new model. Wouldn't get much for her, but think of the fun I'd have running the younger one in." Both men started laughing.

"I heard that!" The men grew silent, knowing how unprofessional they'd been, and that some might take it the wrong way. Susan tried to look serious for a split second, making them squirm but just couldn't hold herself back any longer. "You're naughty, both of you, but I forgive just this once." She leant forward and placed a gentle kiss on the cheek of her ever so helpful knight. "I think you'll have trouble keeping up with me, best you stick with the older model. And thank you for mending the door."

Speechless, he felt a nudge in his side. "Don't get that

every time you lay a carpet, I bet." They were all still laughing when John appeared, somehow incapable of matching the bright spring day with his mood. "Ah, a Mr Taylor, I assume? One mattress for you, sir."

John glanced into the almost empty van. His mattress stood beside a small bedside cabinet. "Not much on today then?"

"Nah, just yours and one other, but as long as I'm back before five I'm not worried. It's that cabinet that's going to be the problem, got to go all the way over to Singleton, forty-five-mile round trip. Madness travelling all that way just for a small thing like that."

John had to agree. "Can't be any profit in that, surely?"

"You're right there, sir, but try telling them back at the office." He shook his head, showing his concern. "But they won't have it. Stupid thing is I'm out that way again tomorrow. Could've taken it then; complete madness if you ask me, and that's the trouble, they never ask, and us drivers are the ones in the know. I was telling my mate Tony only the other day, Tony, I said, we're the ones on the ground but do they consult us? No they don't. Still in nappies most of them, couldn't figure out one end of a paper clip to the other and I'll tell you another thing, them computers are the worst invention out, makes people lazy, trying to tell us old boys what to do. Load of old tosh if you ask me."

John was getting just a little annoyed; he had work to do. "Shall we get this mattress indoors and you can be on your way?"

The van driver took a deep breath and seemed

determined to carry on the conversation. "You know how long I've been working for this company?"

John felt his will to live being stretched to its limits. "No. Anyway, we'd better get on ..."

"Go on, have a guess."

Damn the man, he just wasn't listening. John's hands tightened. All he wanted to do was get this overpriced mattress in the house, up the stairs and in the room. Not much to ask, was it? "I don't know."

"Go on, have a guess," he insisted.

This was what John really hated – a total stranger – asking him to guess something which was clearly impossible to get right, having never met the man before and not knowing his life history. So any suggestion, unless a complete and utter fluke, would be wrong, so the whole exercise was defined as a total waste of time. "I don't know, forty years?"

The driver looked somewhat surprised. "Don't be silly, I haven't been with them that long. No, ten years."

"Really." John didn't think this warranted that much of a mention. He gazed at the man's rounded stomach as it flopped over his trousers stretching the base of his shirt to almost tearing point. It definitely wasn't ten years of hard graft, he knew that much. "Well I'm afraid I can't stand around talking all day." John knew it sounded a little blunt but he could see no way of ending this man's constant chatter.

"Righto, sir. So where do you want it put?"

John had to think, and quickly, or else this overfriendly driver might start talking again. "It can go on the top of the stairs for now until they've finished laying the carpet."

The man glanced down at his delivery notes. "No, I'm afraid I can't do that. Sorry, there's nothing down here saying anything about taking it up any stairs."

"You're joking."

"Sorry, union policy, unless it's written down here on this ticket then I'm not officially allowed to carry it anywhere but to the front doorstep." He glanced once more as his notes. "And nowhere here does it say otherwise, so stairs are a definite no-no."

John now saw this man as the enemy of the state. "Correct me if I'm wrong, but you do sell bedroom furniture?"

"That's correct, sir."

"Surely most bedrooms are upstairs?"

"Look, Mr Taylor, I completely understand where you're coming from, but like I say, if it's not written down then I'm afraid I can't take it up any stairs. Nothing to do with me – union policy."

"Dear God, what's the world coming to?"

"What's that, sir?"

"Nothing. Can we at least put it in the hallway?"

"If it doesn't involve stairs, then no problem."

After what seemed like a lifetime the mattress appeared out of the shadows and into the sunlight where it took a short trip on the van's hydraulic lifting platform, and there it stayed. The man stood and waited, seemingly unwilling to proceed any further, his arm resting upon the item in question with little or no incentive to go on. John could only assume he was stopping it from toppling over before completing his task.

"Okay everyone, if you could all just give me a hand, we'll have this done in no time."

"Hang on." John now looked slightly confused. "If we weren't here to help, how would you get it into the house? Clearly you can't carry it by yourself."

"Like I say, Mr Taylor, if there is nothing written down then I must assume there will be help,
otherwise I'm afraid it'll have to be taken back to the warehouse."

John heard his heart pounding in his chest. "Let's just get the thing in the house, shall we?"

Chapter 17

Sam entered the room, her arms loaded down with a pile of neatly folded bed linen. "You'll be needing some of these, I'm sure."

Susan's bedroom was now finished. The four-poster bed victoriously dominated the room, showing off its new pristine mattress. The pale pink of the carpet blended perfectly with pastel shades thrown out by freshly painted walls, while the brilliant white sash windows captured the elegance of the gardens and trees beyond.

Susan sat on the edge of the bed gently bouncing, her feet barely touching the floor. "I've always dreamed of something like this."

"Well, now your dream is coming true. So, young lady, it's Sunday afternoon and I've done everything I need to do, so why don't I give you a hand and make this into a real bedroom? That's if you want me to, of course."

"I'd love your help, and thank you."

"Go on with you, we women need to stick together. Let's get going, shall we?"

Sam was met by an assortment of boxes, some open and partially empty, while others hadn't been touched, still taped and ready to be moved. One wide-open suitcase lay on the floor, the other two stood to the side along with the black chest that seemingly tempted those of a curious nature to wonder over its contents. "So what's first?" asked Sam, rubbing her hands.

"Let's take the boxes. The small ones we can carry, the big ones we'll have to push across the landing."

"Righto."

One suitcase was so heavy both women needed all their strength just to push it. The dresses Sam took as a cautious challenge, knowing full well there were items hidden behind the wardrobe doors that she'd rather not handle. Glimpses of one or two the day Susan moved in were enough to tell her these were extremely personal to someone in her profession. The doors swung open and she was faced with an array of colours and fabrics hanging upon delicately designed padded coat hangers. Her first pick almost certainly wasn't a dress. She held it at arm's length and studied it with curiosity. "Well this one is different."

Susan peered over her shoulder to identify the item. "Ah, yes, that's a police uniform. Not a real one of course, but to the untrained eye pretty near to the original."

Sam raised an eyebrow. "Men like this sort of thing?"

"Some do, it's a uniform thing. I've also got the navy, the army and a really popular one's a nurses outfit – for some reason a lot of men find that a turn-on." She moved forward and rummaged through the hangers, stopping at one in particular. "But this one is almost definitely the most popular of all. What do you think?" She held it up against her slim frame, its shortness taking advantage of two slender legs.

Sam look dismayed. "No. Really? A school uniform? They make you dress up in that and then what happens?" She suddenly realised what she'd said. "No, don't tell me. I'm far too old to know about such things." Yet seconds later she changed her mind. "Oh, what the heck. Go on then, shock me."

In the intimacy of the quiet room Susan showed off her talent, slowly slipping into character, her mannerisms changing as if performing to a packed audience. Sam watched as the years melted away before her very eyes. Susan was now a girl of tender means. "Whatever you want, Sam, my dear." The older woman's cheeks blushed with embarrassment. "Perhaps a little playtime," Susan continued. "You'd like to play with me, wouldn't you, Sam? Mummy says I have to be home before dark so that gives us lots of time …"

Sam was transfixed, unable to pull her attention away as she gazed into the sultry eyes of the young woman who'd entered her life. How long had she stood there? She didn't know, possibly only seconds, yet it felt like an eternity.

Susan suddenly broke free. "Like I say, there's a lot of men that find this one very appealing."

Sam took a moment to snap out of her trance, her unsteady heartbeat slowly recovering. Something wasn't right, she thought. Her feelings shouldn't be like this and yet she had no regrets. "Beats me why anyone would get turned on by a grown woman dressing up as a schoolgirl." Lying didn't come naturally, but surely it would be seen as wrong in every possible way if her real emotions were aired.

Susan deliberately ran her fingers down the outfit's open top, the buttons of the white blouse slowly relinquishing their hold as her hand pretended to rub against an emerging pair of young breasts. "You never know, John might be into something like this."

"Good God, I hope not! Can you honestly see me dressed up in that with my figure? I'm sure I'd end up looking like an ugly sister in Cinderella, so thanks, but no. Although if you had a pantomime cow outfit we might get some reaction." She glanced at the open door half expecting someone to walk in. "I think we'd better get all this lot moved and out of sight before my husband claps eyes on it."

Susan lowered the offending item. "So you're not denying John's interest could be, let's say, heightened just a little with something like this?"

"I'm sure it would, but only if you were wearing it. Me, on the other hand, wouldn't be able to stand the humiliation of being laughed at and can I remind you that I'm trying to spice up my love life, not dampen it to a smouldering heap."

Susan hadn't quite given up. "Oh, well I can see I've hit a brick wall, but if I know men John will have a surprising soft spot – we just need to find out what it is. I'm sure there's something a country woman like yourself could excel in, but we'll keep the cow idea as a backup, shall we?" Grabbing an armful of clothes she started across the hallway. "Oh, by the way, I had a text this afternoon – one of my regulars wants to come tomorrow if that's all right?"

Sam knew this would eventually happen, but had put it to the back of her mind, deliberately trying to avoid the inevitable intrusion of a third party, someone whose only purpose of entering her home was to use this young lady for their own pleasure. She felt uneasy; until now the whole venture had simply swirled around in her head like some imaginary child's game seeming to hold little or no end consequence, but now she realised with a sinking heart that things were going to change. Susan was here to do a job, playtime was over and she didn't much like it. Her new companion, her soulmate, had already started to fill a longing. Luke had always occupied that empty space; his laughter, his tantrums, oh how she longed for one of those, but now Susan had unintentionally taken his place. She felt an unexpected tightening of her stomach by the sheer mention of her name. A stranger, yes, but someone who she now … no … thoughts of that nature were unthinkable and she even found herself ashamed for allowing them to enter her head. She kept telling herself it was just because Susan was new and refreshing, a bright spark in an otherwise darkened existence that occasionally came with country life. Youth could do that, such was the energy that radiated from a young body, an energy that could literally swallow up its surroundings and everyone within it, but secretly she wished things would just stay the same.

"Of course it's all right. What sort of time?"

"Around eleven in the morning," Susan called back.

"That's fine. I'll tell John when he gets in." She tried to sound enthusiastic towards the prospect of Willowbank's first ever paying customer, but deep down she felt nothing more than an unwilling loss. "Good, well, that's really exciting, isn't it," she said, raising her voice as she scurried in behind carrying an armful of dresses. She entered the room and paused for a second. "He's all right, this person? I mean ... actually I'm not sure what I mean."

Susan didn't hesitate. "Yes, of course. You've no need to worry about him, he's quite quiet on the whole, very well-spoken and has impeccable manners. Used to live with his mother before she died about a year ago. I think he's just a little lonely, that's all."

"That's good." Sam hoped she'd managed to cover up her disappointment towards this intrusion, this unknown person. If she hadn't, Susan was making a very good job of not noticing. The fun of creating a comfortable environment for Susan to enjoy and relax in had vanished. All she wanted to do was walk out the door, try and shake off this strange feeling of resentment engulfing her. Why had she suddenly felt so withdrawn? It was as if this young woman had cheated on her, been found kissing her boyfriend behind the bicycle sheds. "I must go. There'll be hell to pay if John's tea isn't ready." As she went to leave the room she added, "I'll get John to give you a hand with the chest later."

Sam's hasty departure left Susan feeling slightly

confused, and yet she sensed the change in her mood was a matter that needed a cautious approach. She decided that now wasn't the right time.

Half an hour later Sam called down the hallway warning Susan not to be late for tea. "I'll just finish here and I'll be down."

*

The following day felt strange to everyone. John had, as usual, risen from his bed at five, milked the cows, fed the calves, cleaned the yard and checked over the expectant mothers for any signs of imminent births. He now sat in the kitchen sipping a well-earned cup of tea while Sam kept herself busy baking an assortment of cakes to refill the ever dwindling supply kept in a highly decorated tin of delights. Susan had already eaten lightly, pointing out that a full English, although delicious, may not in fact be the best meal to have before her first workout in over a week. John glanced at the clock just as it turned ten forty-five. "Not long now," he noted, his impatience evident by the constant tapping of his fingers on the table.

"Yes, I can tell the time," Sam said.

He shrugged his shoulders, continuing to tap. "I wonder what he's like?"

Sam turned and looked at him with annoyance. "Same as any other man, I suppose."

"Sounds like you're implying any man who pays for sex is somehow different from your
average male."

"I didn't mean it that way."

"Maybe not, but that's how it sounded."

She was about to reply when the doorbell rang. John stared at his wife, but she held her ground, realising he was expecting her to go. "Oh no, I'm not going."

Her statement was met by a shake of John's head. "Well I'm not going, it's not right for a man to greet another man when he's come for sex. It could be embarrassing for both of us."

"It was your idea, now go." Sam pointed to the open door. "And do try and smile."

"But ..."

"No buts, John. Go, the man's waiting."

Reluctantly he made his way down the hallway, a heavy feeling of sickness rumbling deep down in the pit of his stomach. "Try and smile," he muttered. "It's okay for her to say that. Why? Why on earth am I doing this? I'm a farmer, for Christ's sake." The door swung open and a rather slim, well-manicured man with brown wavy hair stood looking a little lost.

"Hello," he said, "I'm not sure if I've come to the right place." His eyes seemed to dance around the interior of the open farmhouse. I'm here for Susan."

John looked him up and down, trying hard not to show his embarrassment. "Susan, yes, sorry, you must be her eleven o'clock appointment."

"That's right." The man looked uncomfortable, having

expected to be greeted by the young woman in question. "I'm afraid I'm a few minutes early, I do hope it's not inconvenient?"

John shook his head. "No, please come in, just go along the corridor and through to the kitchen, you can wait there. I'm sure Susan won't be long."

John glanced towards the stairs. Where was she? This wasn't part of the deal, having to entertain clients while lady muck powdered her nose or whatever these women did prior to an engagement. As he followed the man down the hallway he found himself just a little disappointed with the whole appearance of their first ever paying customer. He seemed perfectly normal. His mind wandered, perhaps it was the tight-fisted farmer in him, but he just couldn't see any enjoyment of having sex and knowing full well you were going to part with hard-earned cash at the end of it. It was madness as far as he was concerned, and God forbid if you fell asleep halfway through and still had to pay. "Please take a seat," he smiled, not knowing what to do next. "Let me introduce you to my wife. I'm sorry, but I'm afraid I don't know your name."

"Paul." No more was said as the man's eyes wandered around the room.

John gestured towards his wife. "Mr Paul, this is Sam. Mrs Taylor if you prefer, and I'm John, we own this farm."

"Mrs Taylor, Mr Taylor." Mr Paul politely nodded, yet it was clear he was starting to feel uncomfortable as he lowered his head and focused on the tiled flooring.

"Susan won't be long, I'm sure." Sam's comforting voice somehow managed to take the edge off the situation as she watched him nervously playing with his fingers and thumbs, trying to avoid eye contact.

John once again started to tap on the table, feeling increasing unease over the whole affair. "Would you like a cup of tea?" he asked. For a moment there was no response to the sudden offer. "Coffee perhaps?"

"Thank you, but no."

"Right. We've got a very nice organic orange and lemonade juice." John was met by a somewhat puzzled look on the poor man's face, but once again he refused the offer.

Sam suddenly spun around from her baking and began to leave the room. "Will you excuse us for a moment, Mr Paul? John, please." Her mannerism did nothing to convince John that she was after a pleasant mid-morning chat as he pulled himself out of his seat and scurried behind, not sure what he'd done wrong but wisely leaving a safe gap just in case of any unexpected retaliation against a crime he'd clearly committed but knew nothing about. They both stood in the hallway, Sam's arms firmly held across her ample breasts awaiting an answer, while John cringed like a naughty schoolboy, hands behind his back waiting for his punishment. "What are you doing?" she hissed with as much authority as possible while trying to keep her voice from travelling through the whole house.

"What do you mean?"

"I mean, John," she looked towards the open kitchen door, lowering her voice to a mere whisper, "I mean the man is here to have sex, not take part in some village coffee morning. Christ, John, next you'll be offering him some of my home-made caramel slices or perhaps a little nibble of a butterfly cake!"

"I was only trying to be polite, put a personal touch to the job."

"Well don't." With that she walked back into the kitchen followed by a rather battered looking husband. "I'm sorry about that, Mr Paul, I really don't know where Susan is but I'm sure she won't be long."

She was greeted by a half-hearted smile followed by a brief silence, allowing Mr Paul to compose himself in preparation to ask a question.

"Mrs Taylor, I hope you don't mind me asking, and it's probably going to sound a rather strange request, but I couldn't help overhearing you saying you made caramel slices." He cleared his throat and straightened his posture. "You see, my mother, bless her soul, I believe made the best caramel slices ever, but since her death I have been unable to find anything that remotely comes close to what she achieved in the confines of her own kitchen. I understand this is asking a lot as we find ourselves total strangers, but I was wondering if I could possibly indulge in a small mouthful of one of yours, for I suspect by the wonderful smells that linger here that your culinary delights may equal that of my mother's."

Sam took her praise with the utmost pride,

straightening her back and holding her head slightly higher than usual. "Mr Paul, I would be delighted for you to try one." Within seconds the tin had appeared and now balanced upon her right hand with the lid removed.

Mr Paul was confronted with the pick of some ten or so evenly sliced caramel beauties. Sam and John watched as he leant forward sniffing the air, the aroma filtering up through his nostrils for a brief moment of unadulterated pleasure. Eyes flickering with excitement, and with the utmost care, he slowly reached into the tin and selected his prize. Delicately holding it between his fingers, the heavenly caramel length drifted over the rim of the tin as he lifted it towards his open mouth. He stopped momentarily, rotating it beneath his nose as if it were an expensive Panama cigar, enchanted by its perfect form glistening in the sunlight. Then he slowly sunk his teeth into the smooth upper layer of semi-hard caramel, its coated chocolate crushing beneath gentle pressure. Mr Paul let out a long satisfied breath of contentment as the dryness of the crumbly but firm base blended perfectly to create an experience he had been longing for.

Sam stood, still clutching her tin in the hope of a response that she knew she so justly deserved but rarely received. John, on the other hand, seemed totally bemused, still sipping his tea as he watched a total stranger behaving rather oddly in his kitchen. Mr Paul sat with his eyes shut, head tilted, seemingly unable to speak yet savouring every last mouthful before reluctantly swallowing with sheer satisfaction.

"Heavenly," he announced, his moistened lips allowing his tongue to catch the last few crumbs. "Sheer heaven, Mrs Taylor."

No sooner had he composed himself than Susan appeared at the door. "Paul, you can come up now."

He briefly hesitated before rising from his seat. "Mrs Taylor? I wonder if I may possibly …" A nervous finger pointed towards the open tin.

"But of course," she replied. This simple gesture allowed a rather satisfied man to hesitate briefly before he plucked his prize. He finally stood, his posture showing his overwhelming delight. "Thank you, Mrs Taylor.

For the first time since he'd arrived, Sam was sure she caught a glimpse of a smile, clearly only intended for her eyes. Sam watched on as their first ever customer made his way out, and as much as she didn't like Susan being used by these men, Mr Paul had at least softened her concerns.

John, meanwhile, was waiting patiently for the right moment to say something. He knew he had to make sure Susan had led her client upstairs and into her bedroom, but on hearing the door close he slowly turned and faced Sam, who seemed very satisfied with herself.

"What are you doing, John?" he mimicked, his rather sarcastic tone reverberating across the room. "The man is here to have sex, not participate in a village coffee morning." Sam was forced to break from her thoughts as John continued. "Next thing you'll be offering him some of my home-made caramel slices. God forbid something like that should ever happen. I wouldn't mind so much, but he had two! I'm never allowed more than one a day."

Sam glared at her husband. "Oh for goodness' sake, stop your moaning and take one."

John couldn't believe his luck as he seized the opportunity and quickly grabbed a slice from the tin, showing none of the gentle finesse of Mr Paul. His next move confirmed Sam's long-held belief that in fact he had little in the way of manners when it came to food as he plunged his hand back in, securing yet another piece.

She looked on in disappointment as his fingers attempted to remove two at the same time. This she would not tolerate, and without hesitation she reached out and landed a short slap across the back of his hand. "Just one, you know the rules."

"But he—"

"No buts, it will be dinnertime soon and haven't you got some paperwork to do before then?" She pointed in the direction of his office. "Go. John, go. I mean it."

John was about to argue but thought better of it when Sam glared at him. He slowly ate his slice in silent protest then reluctantly made his way out of the kitchen. He stopped in the hallway, hovering as if up to no good.

Sam couldn't help noticing him at the bottom of the stairs. "What are you up to now?"

"Shush! I'm trying to listen."

"John, have you no respect?" She tried unsuccessfully to sound shocked at his behaviour as he strained to catch the slightest noise from the bedroom above, but in reality Sam wanted to eavesdrop too. This was, after all, her Susan that was being used. The morals of what they were doing briefly held her back, but only for a moment as she found herself joining her husband. "Can you hear anything?"

"I might if you'd just keep quiet for a minute." Hunched like naughty children, a long drawn-out silence followed. "Nothing," John whispered. "Not a dicky bird."

"What did you expect?" said Sam, amused at her husband's obvious disappointment.

"Shush, I'm trying to listen, damn it."

God, what's wrong with the man, thought Sam.

"I know if I was paying for sex I'd want at least a squeal or a small cry of excitement, something."

"Would you?" Sam looked surprised at John's take on the situation and his obvious need for noise during lovemaking.

"Would I what?" he replied.

"Want some noise when lovemaking?"

He looked slightly confused. "What are you talking about?"

"You just said ..."

"Shush, I can hear something," he whispered, raising his hand in an attempt to silence Sam.

Men, she thought. They're impossible.

Suddenly John's head sprang to one side forcing his ear towards the bedroom. "Did you hear that?"

"No, I didn't hear anything. I think you're just imagining things, and if Mr Paul's anything like you he's probably fallen asleep by now."

"Funny."

"Anyway, what were you expecting?"

"I don't know, an odd bump would be nice. I know that bed can give a good old squeak when she gets going. Remember us using it when my parents were away that time?"

Sam couldn't help but daydream of lost years. "You had a little more go in those days, but now? No squeak, and definitely no thumps. Sound familiar?"

"Quiet! Someone's coming."

John grabbed Sam's arm and hurriedly dragged her back into the kitchen. "Quick, make yourself busy." He glanced at the open door and had only managed to open the first page of a crumpled newspaper when Mr Paul walked in, followed closely by Susan as he gave a less than convincing rustle of pages. "Ah, it's you two."

Sam groaned under her breath. The sight of her husband trying to look surprised almost made her want to speak out and apologise. "Everything all right?" he continued.

Susan could smell a rat but didn't push the subject. "Yes, fine." Her reply gave little away, much to the annoyance of John.

"Mrs Taylor," said Mr Paul, seizing his chance, "may I say once again a big thank you, your baking is of the finest quality. My mother, bless her soul, I believe would approve, but for now I must be away, work never stops." He moved forward and gently lifted Sam's hand giving it a light kiss of appreciation. "I hope to have the pleasure of seeing you again quite soon, dear lady. Mr Taylor. Susan, my love, I will be in touch. The pleasure as always is mine." Susan went to move. "No, please, I am quite capable of seeing myself out. Good day to you all."

The front door shut with a gentle thud, leaving John itching to know more, needing to know more. No, he *had* to know more, if only for the sake of the growing warmth that was developing in his groin. Just thinking about Susan having mad passionate sex with a stranger, and in one of his bedrooms no less, was enough to send any red-blooded male into a frenzy. He knew Sam wouldn't approve. Susan's business was her own affair, but he had now convinced himself it was perfectly acceptable behaviour to know what was going on. After all, Susan did technically work here. Not every last detail, that wouldn't be right, just the basics.

As for Susan, she knew men all too well and John, bless his soul, was no exception. "Go on then, ask me," she said. John pathetically tried to turn to the second page of his newspaper, something he was clearly not reading.

"Sorry Susan?" The page shook a couple of times. "Ask you what?"

"You know very well what, you're dying to know what happened upstairs, aren't you?"

"Susan, what do you take me for?"

Her finger gently pushed the page down, enabling their eyes to meet. "A man."

Sam appeared to agree with Susan's observation. Silence followed as John weighed up his options. "Okay, you win. Give it to me, tell me all." He placed the newspaper on the table and waited with excitement for an uncensored flow of naughty titbits.

Susan smiled inwardly. "Well, what would you like to know?" This question pleased John immensely, but he didn't know whether he could contain his boyish excitement if she shared every last detail. "Well … and I'm not judging the man, you understand, but he wasn't here very long, was he? I would've thought things … took a bit longer than that?"

"What, sexual intercourse you mean?"

John could hardly catch his breath; the mere mention of such human behaviour had him shifting in his seat. "That may have crossed my mind. Of course," he continued, "I realise there are those who take longer than others, it's just the way it is."

Susan grinned. "If you must know, he only had time

for a quickie, had a meeting to go to."

"A quickie?" John now looked a little confused.

Susan leant over and grabbed the kitchen broom and proceeded to gently run her fingers up and down its wooden handle, slowly at first, then to the accompaniment of the occasional moan. John's eyes were transfixed on her rapid hand movements, faster and faster she went, her breathing deep and throaty, as both John and Sam's watching heads bobbed up and down, until the broom rose up then forcibly banged its head upon the floor, as Susan let out an almighty scream, her head flying back from the seemingly pulsing wood as it fell to the floor with an almighty crash.

John and Sam sat in sudden shock, their unease only heightened by the absolute silence that now fell upon the room.

Susan composed herself as she flicked back a lonely stray length of hair from her face. "That's a quickie."

John ran his hand through his hair. Christ, lucky old Mr Paul. "So you ...?" He didn't really want to say the M word out loud – it wasn't something men talked much about in public.

"Yes, John, I jerked him off."

"Susan!" Sam looked her in the eye. "That's a horrible word to use, it sounds so crude."

"But that's what it is."

"Not in this house it's not."

John felt obliged to air his concerns. "What sort of man is he if he can't do it himself? Save a lot of money."

Susan shrugged. "He could, I suppose, but not the way I do it."

She placed a number of notes on the table as John looked on with curiosity. "What's this?"

"It's your share of the M word, if that's what you wish to call it."

He glanced down at the money. "You charge that much for a ...?"

"John!" Sam quickly pulled him in line. "I think we've got the idea."

He almost stumbled over his words. "That much for no more than twenty minutes or so!"   Dear God, at this rate I'll be able to tell that bank manager where he can stick his overdraft."

Susan couldn't help but smile as she made for the door. "Oh, and I'm going to need a vacuum cleaner," she called back.

"Damn it, Susan, what sort of sexual activity are you performing with an electrical appliance?"

"It's not for my clients, silly, I've got crumbs on my bed. Mr Paul would insist on eating a newly acquired caramel slice while we did it. Wants to know if I can make it a regular part of his visit." She looked over at Sam. "Apparently you're responsible for this culinary sexual delight."

"I'm sorry, Susan, but I couldn't deny the poor man a little pleasure."

"Really? And there I was thinking that's what I was here for."

John said quietly. "Now that's what I call adding value to a product."

Chapter 18

"John, you haven't been shooting recently have you?"

"No, of course not, you know I haven't. Why?"

"Because there are four rabbits out here." Sam stood in the garden pointing towards freshly killed bunnies crudely dangling by their feet on rusty nails, gutted and ready for skinning.

John made his way over. "Yep you're right, they're definitely rabbits." Mildly curious, he shrugged. "Could've come from Jack I suppose, he's often out shooting, but why just leave them and not say anything? Nice size though, shot well too, one single wound to each head. Takes some doing, especially with an air rifle." Yet as he spoke an icy chill ran down his fingertips.

"What's wrong?" Sam asked.

"Nothing." But he knew who'd killed – no, murdered them – there was no mistaking those torturous eyes. He couldn't forget that vacant stare when Tick suddenly sprung upon him at the hut armed with her kill. He went to lift them down and noticed something stuck inside one of the hollowed out stomachs.

"What's that?" Sam asked, curious as to what lay within the animal's ribcage.

"I'm not sure." He gently opened the creature's knife wound to reveal a small plastic bag no bigger than a tennis ball, the contents marred by an unsightly smearing of fresh blood over its surface. Although Sam was a country woman, she'd never got used to the sight of blood. Despite the tradition of a farmer's wife being expected to deal with such things, she'd always insisted John handle them. She looked on in disgust.

"Best run it under the tap," she said. "But don't be messing up my kitchen."

John made his way back inside to the sink and held the offending item under the water, carefully rinsing it until he was satisfied every last trace of blood had gone. Sam had followed and looked on curiously as she moved closer. "Is that what I think it is?"

John silently removed a bundle of notes tightly bound by an elastic band. This was Tick's style all right, he thought. Who else would leave four recently assassinated victims with a wodge of money crammed into one of the carcasses? Clearly a professional job. The money sprang open before their eyes. Tens, twenties. "Blimey." John's eyes lit up. "Looks like a hell of a lot." He laid them out neatly on the table, flattening each one, then his eyes fell upon a written note.

He picked it up and read aloud. "Dear Mr Taylor, please find enclosed your share of the first few weeks' takings as agreed." John couldn't remember agreeing but that was of no concern, he carried on. "Apologies for not being as much as hoped, new business and all that but I think still acceptable. Should be in full swing very soon. P.S. Hope you enjoy the meat. Tick." He slowly counted his money – correction, *their* money – he needed to remember that. Shaking his head he looked at his wife. "And she's apologising! Add this to what Susan is bringing in and I could soon become a gentleman farmer."

"Oh yes," Sam replied, "and you'd miss your cows in no time."

John grinned. "Only joking, but you've got to admit this is good money and almost all profit. I told you this would work." Sam could see he was starting to get excited, his eyes glazing over, a sure sign things were heading in the wrong direction, and soon he'd be starting to repeat himself. "This is too good to be true." He held the money in front of his face, transfixed as he drifted from fantasy to the real world and back again. "Straight profit," he muttered. "Sam, look, and we've hardly had to do any work."

Oh dear, she thought, he seriously needs to be brought back to earth, for this wasn't a John she liked to see.

"Look at all this, Sam."

"John!" she chastised. "Calm down." Finally her request seemed to register as he looked up from the wodge of cash.

"Calm down?" he repeated. "Aren't you just a little excited? Damn it, woman, this is brilliant. I've just done a quick calculation ..."

"John!"

"No, hear me out. I've worked out that at this rate we're looking at thousands by the end of the year, straight profit."

"Yes, so you said, but you're forgetting one thing."

"What's that?"

"This is unearned income, probably illegal unearned income to be precise."

"But—"

"No, John, no buts. Have you any idea how we're going to lose that amount without any questions? This can't go near the farm accounts and you know there's only so much cash we can spend without suspicion. Yes, I'm certain the bank manager will be delighted to see that much rolling into our account but he's going to want to know where it's from. The odd thousand wouldn't be much problem, but with that amount, someone's going to ask questions. She glanced down at the money. "I don't mind admitting it's more than I was expecting, and don't get me wrong, I realise your reasons for doing this, but I just worry about the amount."

John silently digested his wife's concerns. "Perhaps we could put a load of it down to private hay sales, no one knows how much I make and it always varies from year to year. The bank manager wouldn't have a clue and everyone pays in cash anyway, so we could do that."

His efficient wife had already grabbed a calculator and spent the next five minutes working out various simple mathematical scenarios. She shook her head. "I'm not convinced. To lose that amount in hay sales we would need to be seen cutting at least an extra one hundred acres of grass. One *hundred*. John, we don't have that amount of land going spare, the whole farm is only two hundred and fifty acres and that includes the farm buildings, tracks, the house, the gardens and the woodland and anyone with any sense could easily work out you can't make hay from trees. And what happens when the organic inspector comes round? You know how thorough they are, it just won't work. I'm sorry."

John's bottom lip drooped slightly. He really thought his bogus hay sale scam was a good one, but as always logic had come into the equation and yet again Sam unfortunately was right. He had nothing but frustration rattling around in his head. "We still need to eat away at the overdraft, that was the whole idea of this venture," he continued.

"Yes, of course, I know that. Just leave it with me, I'll think of something."

Just then Susan appeared at the door and glanced at the two of them. "Bad timing?"

Sam looked up. "No, of course not, just discussing farm business, that's all. Never a cheery subject at the best of times. So what can we do for you?"

"I was wondering if John could come up to my bedroom with his toolbox?"

His eyes lit up with excitement. "Well there's an offer you don't get every day."

Sam couldn't help but chuckle. "Good luck there, young lady, his toolbox hasn't been used for a good many days and what's in it is probably rusted solid from lack of use."

"Very funny," John replied as he gazed at Susan. "What's the problem?"

"It's one of my hand restraints, it seems to have got jammed."

John shook his head in bewilderment. "I wish I hadn't asked now. Restraints?"

"Yes," she replied. "Just the one, a little squirt with the oil can should do it."

Sam gave out another light-hearted chuckle.

"Now what's so funny?"

"A little squirt, just about sums you up!"

If looks could kill! "And whose fault is that?" The humour in the room evaporated, leaving an awkward silence. "Okay, give me a minute and I'll be up," sighed John, rising. "The things I do to make money." He disappeared, leaving Susan feeling somewhat out of place.

"I'll go and wait for him upstairs."

Sam said nothing at first, but called out as Susan went to leave. "Susan? It's okay."

Susan turned and their eyes met. She gave Sam a sympathetic smile then carried on.

Having collected his tools, John went upstairs and gave a short sharp rap on the door.

"Come in." Susan's muffled voice carried out onto the landing giving permission to enter.

The thought of all that extra ill-gotten money followed him into the room, lifting his spirits. "Right, let's have a look at what you've got." His flippant almost suggestive statement was met by the sight of Susan sitting beside a half-naked middle-aged dark Mediterranean man, dressed in nothing more than ladies underwear. His right arm rested beside him while his left dangled helplessly above his head, firmly secured by a bright shiny handcuff.

"What the …?"

"John, this is Gino, he's from Italy."

John stood and stared, then desperately tried not to look as poor old Gino sat like a trussed chicken wearing a highly tensioned G-string and matching boob holders. It was evident he clearly worked out with his bulging biceps, and what was with all that chest hair? Jet black and curly, the likes of which John had never seen before. It certainly wasn't to his taste, smothering the entire upper body like some tropical undergrowth and oh dear God, was that what he thought it was? Like some dozing python, Gino's manhood lay crammed beneath a narrow strip of red material waiting to pounce upon unsuspecting victims. "Sorry Susan, I didn't realise you had company."

She smiled with that look that never failed to turn John's heart. "You don't have to worry about Gino, he's not a shy man."

"No, I can see that."

"How do you do, Signor John?" Gino offered his free hand, leaving John little option but to shake it. He tried not to recoil at the damp clammy feeling of his sweaty palm.

He forced his lips into a sort of welcoming gesture. "So it's your other arm that's giving you problems, then?" John's half-hearted humour battled to break through the Italian's understanding of the English language.

"Ah yes, you are right, it is stook." He rattled the offending handcuffs, indicating to everyone that John was correct in his assumption.

"Yes, you're right," John replied, "it's definitely stook, probably just needs freeing up." Retrieving a battered oil can from his toolbox, John unwillingly caught sight of a potentially embarrassing development evolving between Gino's fishnet covered legs. Gino himself seemed unconcerned as his ever enlarging manhood gently tightened itself against expanding fabric. Averting his eyes, John blindly fumbled with his can, behaving erratically as he injected a small amount of oil into a tiny keyhole while standing far too close to another   man's erection. He had an overwhelming desire to complete the job immediately for it was plain to see that the G-string could only hold for so long. A second squirt overfilled the keyhole but John didn't much care, for the sooner he got away the better! He forcefully applied increasing pressure to a stubborn key that wouldn't budge as sweat trickled down his overheated cheeks.

For Christ's sake, work! The words pounded his head as he tried to persuade the key to move but to no avail, and he was sure Gino was getting even more aroused by the sheer presence of another man's efforts. Then, like a synchronised swimming team, both lock and Gino's highly tensioned underwear sprang open. John jumped back as a sun-baked member popped up like a spring-loaded jack-in-the-box, leaving him no option but to grab his toolbox and head for the door. "Should be fine now," he called back. "Don't bother seeing me out!" Stumbling along the landing his legs almost buckled beneath his weight.

"I thank you, Signor John," Gino's voice trailed after him.

John vaguely heard Gino's voice as he legged it to the stairs. "No problem, have a nice day."

Sam caught a glimpse of her husband as he silently shot through the kitchen, hands clutching his toolbox. "All done then?" she called out after him, as she watched him scurry along the back passage.

"I'm a farmer, I shouldn't have to do this sort of stuff! I'm going milking." The door slammed behind him, leaving Sam quietly grinning to herself. Ah well, she thought, it's just something he's going to have to get used to.

Chapter 19

A month slipped by and to John's relief things seemed to be going worryingly well. The dodgy handcuffs were replaced with a more user-friendly, high-quality leather item complete with buckled straps to eliminate possible malfunctions. Susan had embraced living and working in the countryside and to her surprise, actually enjoyed it. She seemed blissfully happy with life. Tick, John assumed, was equally content in her world of erotic seductive torture as nothing had been heard or seen of her since, just the regular supply of fresh rabbits bearing gifts. Sam still found it hard to come to terms with her, but those weekly drops suggested all was well and another thing he didn't have to worry about. Sam, as usual, was busy in the kitchen, preparing a never-ending supply of food and now a constant trickle of caramel slices for the more discerning of Susan's clients. As for John, he was just happy to eat, sleep, work or just sit in his counting house counting his money.

It was Friday evening and he and Sam had retired to the front room. John sat watching the news and Sam lay stretched out across the sofa, totally immersed in a randy novel with highwaymen getting their wicked way with the young village maidens.

Susan entered and sat on the last remaining chair. "I was wondering if I could have a word."

"Of course you can." Sam broke away from her page and rested her novel face down on the floor. "John,

Susan wants to talk to us."

"Yes, just a minute, the weather's nearly finished." He shook his head in bewilderment. "I don't believe it!" he protested, throwing his arms up in dismay. "Just look at that dirty great low sitting smack in the middle of the Atlantic! Isn't that just typical, here we are desperate for rain and it's all being dumped out at sea. By the time it gets to us there'll be nothing left." He slumped back with a disgruntled snort but carried on ranting, much to Sam's annoyance. "Well if we don't get any rain soon, the grass is just going to burn up."

"John! Susan." Her harsh tone dragged him back into the real world.

"Yes, all right, I'm listening."

She glanced over at the young lady. "Take no notice of him, he's always like this when the weather comes on. It's a farmer thing, they've got to be grumbling about something or else they start worrying things are going too well. Never satisfied."

John took offence to this observation of his normal everyday behaviour as his weary eyes tried to stay alert. "Yes, go on, criticise if you must, it's all right for you lot sitting indoors, you haven't got to find enough feed to keep the cows going. I'm telling you, if we don't get any rain soon things are going to start to hurt."

Sam couldn't help but grin; she knew it was wrong and she should be more supportive, but it was so funny the way he went on. "I think we're onto a losing battle with this one, Susan."

"Perhaps I should come back another time?" said Susan, clearly feeling a little awkward.

"Nonsense, you can always talk to me. So what was it you wanted to say?"

Susan slightly rearranged herself. "Well," she continued, "it's like this … I have a friend."

"Oh God, not Leo again."

"Be quiet, John. If you've got nothing good to say then shut up."

"Thanks a lot, just remember a man's home is his castle."

"Yes, and if you can't be quiet his castle will be in the shape of a dog kennel."

John folded his arms in protest at his ill-treatment. "Fine."

"Carry on, Susan, we'll pretend he's not here."

Feeling slightly uneasy she wished she was somewhere else, but decided to continue. "Like I say, I have a friend and she's looking for a room. She was operating out of a two-bedroom flat but the landlord has started to get a little funny."

John's ears immediately pricked up. "She's operating – does that mean she's a …?"

"John."

"Only asking."

Susan quickly interrupted. "Yes, John, she's in my line

of business. It's a long story, but let's just say the landlord's suggesting personal favours, if you know what I mean, and if she doesn't oblige he's threatened to get the law involved."

John ran his hand over the stubble on his chin. "I didn't think it was illegal to operate from your own home."

"Technically it's not, as long as you're sole traders, but landlords can get a little funny sometimes and the law isn't there to take the side of any woman in our line of work."

It was clear John's brain was ticking over. "So let's get this right – you're asking us if we can put this girl up in one of our rooms? And I assume she'll want to carry on working."

Susan nodded. "I know it's a lot to ask, but she's a really good friend and I feel I should do something to help, but she doesn't know I'm asking. As there are some spare rooms it seems a shame to let them go empty when they could be earning money." Her intense eyes unsettled John.

"Don't look at me like that, young lady. It might work on your man friends, but not with me, and certainly not at this time of the night. He rubbed his tired eyes. "I don't know. Yes, the money would be nice, especially with this drought. If it carries on I'm going to have to buy in extra feed and that isn't going to be cheap, but would we be starting to push our luck? Everything's working just fine as it is – another set of clients coming and going might get people talking and they're a suspicious a lot in the village.

Susan went on the defensive. You wouldn't have to worry, my friend's what we call a high-class operator and only entertains one client a day. She's more of an escort, gets taken out on business trips, private functions, that sort of thing, so most times she ends up back at a hotel or the client's residence." Susan took a long deep breath. She knew she couldn't stop now; John was clearly longing for bed and would agree to anything if only to shut her up. She heard him quietly groan under his breath as he watched her lips move. "So you see, there would only be the odd man wanting to come back here."

He was far too tired to bother with the finer details of any proposal, but something had caught his interest. "So she charges a lot of money, then?"

"Oh yes."

"What, a lot more than you?"

Susan knew she had him in the palm of her hand. The mention of money had clearly done the trick. "Yes, quite a bit more. You won't be disappointed in that area, but then she is incredibly good-looking, and when you look that great men will pay almost anything."

The thought of more money still couldn't hold back John's falling eyelids as his vision started to wander around the room searching for a way out, but with some effort he finally managed to focus on his wife's presence long enough to ask her opinion. "Well, what do you reckon?"

She simply shrugged. "Cows need feeding. It could be a good way of losing some of the money. Money we'd have to find somewhere and if I'm cooking for three, another one wouldn't make much difference."

"Okay," John reluctantly agreed. "But I need to see her first."

"Great," Susan replied, "because I told her she could come tomorrow."

Too tired to protest, John looked on in defeat. "Whatever. Now can I go to bed, because some of us—"

"—have been up since five o'clock this morning," said Sam and Susan in unison.

"Cheeky buggers, and maybe another one of you lot coming. I must want my head tested." Contemplating that, he went to get up out of the chair just as Susan dropped a kiss on his forehead.

"Thanks."

There was a giggle from the sofa. "That was brave, he hasn't washed yet!"

Susan hastily wiped her hand across her lips, looking as if she'd just found half a maggot in an apple.

"Serves you right, young lady, but don't thank me just yet because nothing is decided. If I think she's not suitable then I'm afraid we can't help, understand?"

"I understand," Susan replied, "but I'm sure you won't regret it."

*

The following morning John was given strict instructions to stay in the house after breakfast. Although he claimed there were a hundred and one things to do out on the farm, he was to stay put and wait for Susan's friend. He'd been coerced into sorting through a large pile of neglected farm-related papers that he had conveniently forgotten for a good two weeks. "Sam?" he shouted through to the kitchen, "did Susan tell you what this girl's name was?"

"No. I just assumed she told you."

"Great, just what I need. How odd is that going to look if I haven't even bothered to find out her name? Is Susan upstairs?"

"No, I think she's gone out for a walk."

"Never mind."

Sam heard John muttering under his breath, meaning he'd probably finished talking to her, but no sooner had she returned to preparing the food for the midday meal than she was interrupted by the doorbell. "That'll be for you, John," she called.

"Yes, all right, I can hear it."

A strange relief settled over John as he pulled himself from his chair, quietly pleased for a distraction taking him away from his desk. Although he didn't enjoy interviewing, today he would make an exception. Admittedly he was a little apprehensive as to who might be on the doorstep, but that was of little concern. His worries were more towards the difficult position of agreeing to meet a stranger he had no name for, and worse, a person who happened to be Susan's very good friend. He'd only just realised she might take offence if he found this mystery woman was totally unacceptable. Would he be seen as the big bad ogre? Why was life so complicated? All he wanted was a simple existence, just him and his cows, but he had made it quite clear that his was the final decision. He smiled as something occurred to him – if he said 'yes' he could be her knight in shining armour. He liked Susan – he liked her a lot, probably more than he should, so perhaps a small act of kindness would warrant another kiss. Or maybe two! John swung the front door open and was greeted with a familiar face.

"Hi, Mr Taylor."

His mind took a moment to register as he gazed upon a heavenly being. "Antonia!"

"Tony, please."

"Yes, sorry. Tony, what a surprise."

She could see he looked a little on edge and slightly agitated as he kept glancing behind her, almost as if he was expecting someone else to arrive any moment. A rather unorthodox manner of greeting someone, she thought, but chose to ignore it. "I said I'd pop round and see you both one day, so here I am." She casually glanced around her surroundings. "I must say it hasn't changed at all."

John still looked preoccupied. "No, well, this really is a surprise," he replied, not sounding at all convincing.

"Are you all right, Mr Taylor? You look a bit concerned about something. I've not come at bad time, have I?"

He peered past her again; this could potentially be rather embarrassing, he thought. What if Susan's high-class hooker arrived now? His mind worked overtime, not panicking just yet but he could certainly feel his temperature rising. "No, not at all, come in. Sam will be surprised to see you." If he could get Tony offloaded onto his wife he could channel Susan's friend into the office and hope the two wouldn't meet. His hands went clammy, instantly reminding him of Gino. What was happening to his farm? This thing seemed to be swallowing him up, to the point he couldn't even have someone popping round to visit for fear of being found out! Everything seemed so simple at the beginning, but he had to stay focused. "I'm afraid I'll be a little tied up for a while, I'm expecting someone."

"But Mr Taylor—"

John had his hand up. "No, it's okay, it's not a problem, you're welcome any time. We'll talk when I've finished. I shan't be long and it'll be good to catch up. Right, Sam's in the kitchen, follow me. Sam, look who's just arrived – Tony Chapman. Remember I told you I bumped into her in the bank?" He tried to wink, his words slow and precise as if trying to talk to a deaf person. "She's come completely out of the blue just to see us, a social call, nothing to do with anything going on around here." He waved his arms. "Totally out of the blue."

Sam looked at her husband with concern. "Are you all right?"

"Never better. Well, Tony, it's great to see you again."

"But Mr Taylor, I—"

"No buts, you have a nice chat with Sam. I'll be back. The doorbell will ring and I'll be gone, but I'll be back."

"Tony." Susan walked into the room with a wide grin on her face. "You made it then."

"Of course. I knew how to get to this place blindfolded."

The girls embraced each other, rendering John almost speechless. "You know each other?"

Susan wasn't sure how to reply. "We do. This is my best friend Tony, the girl you're going to interview today. I thought you realised that?"

The penny dropped like a lead weight causing a rather impolite finger to point in Tony's direction. "So *you're* Susan's high-class …?"

"John!" Sam immediately cut him down like an annoying weed. "Language! Sit down, you're making the place look untidy."

"That's one way of putting it, Mr Taylor." Tony wasn't sure if it was too early to call him by his first name so thought it best to carry on being formal. "Susan always likes to make out I'm somehow higher up on the entertainment ladder than she is. Yes, I may charge slightly more, but in reality we both do the same thing, just in a different way, that's all."

John returned to the real world but still couldn't believe this gorgeous female was in his kitchen waiting for him to allow her to stay. As far as he was concerned it was a mouth-watering 'yes', but he had to be careful. Looking too excited, too keen this early on would never do; he needed to play it cool. "Sorry, Tony, I really thought you were here for a social visit. I didn't for one minute think it might be for any other reason." His mind shot back to when they had first met. "But didn't you say you were in public relations?"

"I did," she replied, "and in a way I am."

John looked a little confused. "I'm not sure I know what people in public relations do."

Tony shrugged her shoulders. "Does anyone? It is a rather vague description for any job, but it seems to work for me."

"I suppose it does suit your profession in a funny sort of way." He was intrigued to know more about this stunning individual. Susan was right – she was utterly gorgeous and if he had to, he would choose her any day with those looks and figure. Oh dear me, that figure, it was no wonder men paid handsomely for her. His mind was longing to drift off to its happy place, but he had to stay business-like. "So, Tony, do your parents know what you do?"

"No, they don't. I've no plans to do this any longer than I need to, so hopefully they'll never find out. As far as they're concerned I'm in public relations, and as we know, no one has a clue what they do." She paused.

"So I'm guessing everyone thinks you're still making all your money from farming?"

"Yes, apart from my mother. But George, you remember George the gardener? I don't think he knows, but he's a sly one, I wouldn't be surprised if he knows more than he lets on."

Tony looked surprised. "George is still alive? He was old when I was a little girl so he must be ancient by now! No disrespect, of course."

"That would about sum him up. My mother's always moaning about the poor man but secretly she'd be lost without his company, and like him, none of us are getting any younger, so you make the most of your youth."

Tony gave a cheeky grin. "I am, Mr Taylor, and making money from it."

"Yes, well, apart from that."

She looked at him intensely. "I know what you mean, Mr Taylor, but the business allows me to do both – make money and play a little. What else is there?" She could see him pondering over his next words.

"Marriage, kids, a nice house … you know, those small unimportant things in life."

He was met with a look of defiance but noticed a hesitant pause before she replied. "I'm quite sure there will be plenty of time for that sort of thing later."

Sam suddenly spotted an underlying weakness in this young lady's armour. "As long as you're aware of what you could be missing, young lady, then I suppose that's fine."

"I'm still young, Mrs Taylor, and it would only complicate matters."

John was sure Sam's words were a genuine concern for Tony's future, but for some reason he could sense a gentle rift developing between the older wiser shoulders and the inexperienced views of someone unburdened with quite so many years. Perhaps it was time to break the conversation up, he thought. Sam was clearly marking out the boundaries and in doing so could very well be showing this newcomer where she stood. Yet Tony wasn't a total stranger. Still, she didn't seem to have been greeted with the enthusiasm John would've expected. "Tony, would you like to go and look around the available bedrooms?"

Sam glanced at him from across the room. "That sounds very much like you've made up your mind."

"No, but we need to know which one Tony would prefer if I decide to offer her the opportunity. Well, Tony, shall we?" He'd already made for the hallway, making a deliberate point not to look back at his wife or even consult her any further on the subject. As far as he was concerned he wanted this young lady more than anything. Maybe his decision had been ruled by his heart but that was fine, for he needed to see more of this stunning individual and yes, he was not ashamed to admit that he had fallen under her spell.

Chapter 20

"What's this?" John peered at several papers on the kitchen table as Sam nudged them closer to him.

"It's a timetable. With Tony here things are getting busy, so I thought it would be a good idea to get everything written down. Easy enough to print off each evening, then we'll have a clue of what's going on, because frankly, I have no way of knowing who's arriving at the door, and I can't work like that. This is my home, John, and I need to have things organised."

"Fine," he replied. "I don't have a problem with that as long as you're happy."

Sam wanted to say more but instead pushed the sheets towards John. "So at the top there's Tony's name, underneath are appointment times, names of clients, and a time for each session here. I've left a space for any comments so when she's away for the day all she has to do is write it in. Fairly easy with only one client a day, but it's nice to know if she's coming in late or not at all. Freaks me out when I hear unusual sounds at night – could be anyone wandering about and as we know it takes more than a few creaky floors to wake you."

"Just remember some of us have to get up at five each morning, if you hadn't noticed."

At his comment Sam screwed her face up in despair. "If you say that one more time I'll …" She just managed to stop herself from saying what she really wanted to say.

"You'll what?"

"Never mind, just be thankful I haven't throttled you yet. Right, where were we? Oh yes, so Susan has the same format and if you look here," she pointed to another sheet, "you can see at a glance all her appointments, names, times and the odd comment."

"Busy girl. Says here Tony's got two appointments today."

"Yes, that's unusual for her, but at least we know what's going on. She's got one at the moment and another this afternoon. Simple, really. You can see she has a Mr Sparrow, then a Mr Goldfinch.

John studied Tony's time sheet, inspecting it in some detail. "Mr Sparrow and a Mr Goldfinch? What's she doing, a cheap day out for the local ornithological club?"

"Trust you to make a joke of it. If you must know she names all the clients after birds. It's so they don't have to use their real names."

John rubbed his throbbing head. "This is really getting silly. So our Mr Sparrow just happened to fly in on his Range Rover, did he? I saw it parked outside."

"Keep your voice down. It's nothing to do with us, we just supply the facilities."

"But it's my house."

"No, John, it's *our* house."

"Okay, *our* house, satisfied? No need to take that tone."

"Oh, do stop your moaning."

"Well! Next I'll be made to tiptoe around the place just in case I disturb any frolicking."

"At least there *is* some frolicking going on around here."

"And what's that supposed to mean?"

"You know exactly what it means."

"I'm tired, that's all."

"You're always tired, and don't you dare say it, John, I'm warning you."

He was on a path to nowhere so felt it best to just move on and keep life simple. "So let's get this right: we've got a Sparrow roosting in one bedroom, and Susan," he looked down at her sheet, "oh surprise, surprise, she's got the Caramel Kid."

"I said keep your voice down."

"It's our house!"

"Not any more it isn't, so get used to it. You wanted the girls here so you need to respect their workplace and not make fun of the clients, so no more taking the mickey, understand?"

"Suit yourself. So what's this one then, a Mrs Radcliffe 3 pm. Susan's not batting for the other side now is she?"

"If you must know, Mrs Radcliffe has a twenty-year-old son," she said, lowering her voice, "who has never had a girlfriend." She glanced towards the open door, hoping no one would enter. "So he's obviously never had the chance to experience the ways and temptations of the opposite sex. Apparently his mother was getting a little worried as he spends most of his time playing computer games. She thinks a little motivation in the female direction may encourage him to go out more, build up his confidence. She wants Susan to ... you know."

Sam made some sort of funny hand gesture which John didn't really understand. "I know what?" he replied.

"You know. Come on, John, keep up." But there was still nothing. "Dear God! Do I have to spell it out? Sex, John! I think it's quite nice," Sam continued.

He looked bewildered. "Nice? What, to lose your virginity to a ..."

"John! I told you before, I don't like that word."

"I was going to say working girl."

"No you weren't." She watched his lips pout with defeat.

"Okay, I wasn't, but it's still the same thing whichever way you look at it. Can you not see the poor boy's going to be stripped of his innocence, forced over a matter of an hour or so to suddenly become a man?"

"Bullshit! And you know it. I've never heard such a load of nonsense! Are you seriously telling me a twenty-year-old virgin male isn't going to enjoy his first encounter with a woman like Susan – a *woman*, John – we're not talking about some giggly immature teenager here."

"All I'm saying is, perhaps he should be saving himself for someone special for that first moment with a willing girl, someone who really loves him."

His wife gave a resounding shake of her head. "That's very romantic, John, but in reality things like that very rarely ever happen."

"Well it did for me."

Sam looked somewhat surprised. "John Taylor, I'm flattered." She leant forward and gave him a little kiss on his cheek. "It's not very often you pay me a compliment like that."

"That's okay, but I didn't say it was with you."

Without warning he felt a hand connected with his right ear. "In your dreams, John Taylor. When we first started going out you didn't even know what your right hand was for except for shoving up a cow's rear end."

"There may have been someone else," John sheepishly replied. He watched as his wife desperately tried to hold back her amusement.

"No, John. I can categorically say I was your first. I'll never forget the sheer horror on your face when you came that first time. Such earth-shattering realism only happens once in a man's life. So no, totally clueless and completely bewildered by the whole event." She waved a mocking finger at him.

"I remember you wouldn't talk to me for a week afterwards."

"I did nothing of the sort. Just happened to be in the middle of hay-making, that's all. We were busy carting bales. You know what Father was like, every field had to be cleared before there was any possibility of getting away. You were lucky to get what you did!"

"Oh and I was supposed to fall for that, was I? I wouldn't have minded a little romp in the hay, you could've found a way if you'd really wanted to. Instead I had to wait nearly three weeks before we did it again and that was only because your parents went to a funeral and stayed overnight, but you still insisted on going to that draughty cobweb-infested attic. One lumpy single bed is all I got for my patience because you had to constantly peer out the window just in case your parents came home early." Sam felt herself pulled along as every detail of John's pathetic attempts came flooding back. "And don't even remind me of that time we did it in your tractor!"

John grinned with a certain amount of pride. "Now that was fun."

"No, John, it wasn't. You were fine, sat in your seat, but you try getting your legs between the gear stick and a mass of hydraulic levers, not to mention that dirty great steering wheel stuck up your arse. Every time you thrust it sent me spinning off to one side. What are you grinning about now?"

"Just thinking back. She was a wicked tractor, that Ford. I'm sorry we ever sold her now."

"John! Is that all you can remember?"

"No, of course not. The stereo was good too."

"Oh for ..."

"Language! You know I don't like that sort of thing in my kitchen," he said sarcastically.

"Don't push me, John. Now what are you grinning about?"

"Do you remember the time we did it in the cornfield?"

"Yes, John." Sam almost spat the words out. "I also recall you stopping halfway and pulling your trousers up just because a jumbo jet flew over.

"Ha! Hang on, in my defence those planes have lots of windows, you know. We could have been spotted."

"John, it was miles up in the sky, you could hardly see it. I think they'd need pretty good eyes to spot your tiny little pink buttocks."

John's memories were flooding back. "Didn't you get some sort of rash on your body?"

"No, John. It was a burn mark. Oat straw I could have handled, that's a lot softer, but wheat! And I got covered in tiny black mites. I had red blotches for days. Not so romantic, was it."

John rested back in his chair looking decidedly pleased with himself. "You still married me, so I couldn't have been that bad."

"Better the devil you know." Sam knew it was a

confession rather than a statement.

"What's that supposed to mean?"

"Well, it's a small village, the choices were a bit thin on the ground in those days, and to be totally honest I only married you for the big house—"

Her words were suddenly interrupted by a loud thud from upstairs. They both looked to the ceiling. "What was that?" Sam looked decidedly concerned.

"Beats me. Probably that bloody sparrow trying to make a nest, randy little bugger." Laughter rang around the kitchen as they waited for an aftershock.

"John, stop taking the mickey."

"You're a fine one to talk. Oh, come on, you've got to admit this whole venture is as mad as they come. Who else would ever dream of turning their farm into a guest house for prostitutes, I ask you." He took his wife's hand and gave it a gentle squeeze. "And who else would have a woman who would agree to it?"

"Thanks!" It was said with such feeling that Sam almost shed a stray tear.

They sat for a moment listening to the rhythmic ticking of the grandfather clock pushing the arms of time constantly around its decorative face. "Quick! Make yourself busy," whispered John, suddenly breaking the silence. "Someone's coming."

Their hands instantly parted just as Mr Paul popped his head around the door. "Ah, Mrs Taylor, many thanks for the delicious treats, quite superb as usual.

NEIL ELSON

See you next week if I may?"

Sam looked up. "Without fail, Mr Paul."

"Excellent. I will see myself out, good day to you dear lady. Mr Taylor."

They heard the front door shut leaving John gazing at his wife. "See what I mean? This whole thing is as mad as it gets. Ah, Susan, having a nice time?" John picked up the sauce bottle and seductively rubbed its neck, instantly receiving a swift clip around the ear.

"I warned you, now behave. Sorry, Susan, you'll have to excuse my childish immature husband. I really don't know what gets into him sometimes. Cup of coffee? You must be thirsty?" Rebelling against his punishment, John was now into a mind-buckling blur as his fingers showed little sign of slowing down. "Stop it, John! You're worse than a kid and you can wipe that dirty grin off your face, what's got into you? You're all ..." she paused mid-sentence, "what's the word I'm looking for ... that unusual word that's very rarely used in this house? Oh yes, I know – happy! That's it. What are you up to, John Taylor?"

"Nothing. Perhaps it's just because the sun is shining, there's money coming in, the grass is finally growing and I'm surrounded by three gorgeous women. What more could a farmer want?" They all heard the back door open, then close with a loud bang as John's dream world was just about to be turned on its head.

"John! Sam! Anyone around?" Heavy footsteps marched down the back passage. "Hello there."

John spun around just as Jack Whitlock came into the kitchen. "Thought I might catch you having a cuppa. How are you, Sam my dear?" Much to her displeasure Jack planted a large damp kiss upon her unwilling left cheek.

"Good thanks, Jack."

"John, me old mate!" John received a slap to the back as their visitor pulled up a chair and sat down. "And who's this pretty young lady?" His eyes ran over Susan's entire body, meticulously inspecting every curve, every dimple.

John's heart pounded for he knew this would eventually happen, the time when someone would question the girls' presence, but like a fool he hadn't come up with any feasible alibi. How do you explain the presence of not one but two extremely attractive twenty-five-year-olds? In sheer desperation his mind wandered to the unbelievable lie of two long-lost nieces, but even he could see future problems that might cause, and how would he explain the constant visits by men? People weren't daft, half the time village folk knew more about your private life than you did.

Susan could see he was starting to panic and stepped forward. "Susan Swan," she said to Jack, offering a handshake.

"The pleasure's all mine, Susan Swan," he replied, shaking her hand enthusiastically.

"They were right then." Jack's voice travelled across

the room like an unwanted smell.

"Who was right?" John worryingly asked.

"Them down the pub, talk, rumours of pretty young women up at Willowbank Farm. Course I never believed them. I said, 'What would old John Taylor be doing with young females?' But you know how rumours get started." Jack licked dry lips while glaring eyes focused on Susan's exposed cleavage. "Seems I was wrong. So, little Susan Swan, what brings you to this out-of-the-way village of ours? Doesn't look like those hands do much hard graft, if you don't mind me saying, so that rules out farm work. Not much else around here."

Susan didn't like this man. He smelt of beer and looked like he hadn't washed for a good week. "Modelling, Jack. Myself and Antonia are professional models. We rent rooms from Mr and Mrs Taylor, these large houses are ideal for photography shoots – light and airy, perfect to show off high-class clothing. And the landscape is to die for – a photographer's dream. The clothes are sent out, then they come and do the shoots; it's a lot cheaper than working from an expensive studio." She took a short breath. "Naturally each company is different and insist on sending their own people, so there's a lot of coming and going, but it's working just fine. The Taylors get a guaranteed income for the rooms, use of the house and grounds and we get somewhere nice to live and work. What could be better?"

Jack's smug expression melted before their eyes as Sam gave Susan a subtle nod of approval, leaving him the unpleasantness of pulling himself up from his deflated cocky stance and focusing his attention upon the confident young lady herself. "Oh. I see. Well, that sort of makes sense I suppose, and all these men are photographers, you say?"

"Yes, Jack. And delivery men."

"Right."

Susan knew what kind of man Jack Whitlock was and he was clearly hoping for more than the explanation she'd given him, but now it was time for her to dangle that organic carrot just far enough away so he couldn't quite take a bit and test the real flavour of what was going on. "Of course we don't just model everyday clothes."

Susan's comment seemed to please Jack as his eyes lit up with curiosity. Perhaps there was something juicy he could report to his pals at the pub, he thought. "You don't?" His mouth drooled with excitement as Susan openly flirted while slowly reeling him in by his own unwillingness to walk away with at least some sort of scantily dressed gossip.

"No, Jack. Occasionally we're asked to wear far less."

His tongue ran across moistened lips. "You are?"

"Oh yes, far less." They all heard him swallow hard and deep.

"What, like women's ..." He could hardly bring himself to say it out loud but somehow with the determination of a randy old billy goat he forced the words out. "Women's underwear?"

Susan purposefully moved closer and in a soft erotic voice whispered, "Lingerie." Jack almost fell off his chair. "Nothing too revealing," Susan continued, "that would never do, but you understand what I'm saying, don't you, Jack?"

"Quite understand."

"Good. We wouldn't want people thinking we're those sorts of girls, now would we?"

"Definitely not. I never thought otherwise, totally respectable. I can see that and don't you worry, Miss Swan. It is Miss, I assume?"

"As pure as a virgin snowfall, Jack."

John almost choked.

"I'll put them gossips to right, no fear of that."

She gave him a reluctant light kiss on the cheek. "That's a good boy, Jack. We wouldn't want any nasty rumours getting about, now would we?"

"Certainly not, Miss Swan, you can rely on me."

"Thank you, Jack. Now if you'll excuse me I have some more clothes to prepare." She sent a velvet covered kiss floating through the air, causing their visitor to rearrange his seating position. "Bye for now, Jack, it's been nice meeting you."

"Likewise, Miss Swan." They all watched as she sauntered out of the room, purposefully running a hand through her hair in a somewhat provocative manner.

Jack turned back to his hosts. "Lovely young lady, very pleasant indeed. Anyway, I must be off, wanted down at the church. Vicar needs some furniture moved, said I'd go along with the farm trailer, be seen doing me bit for the village. I must say, John, this modelling lark seems ideal for you both. Not prying, you understand, but I got the feeling things were starting to get a little tight. Always handy to have extra cash. Only wish I'd thought of it, me stuck in my big house all alone. Never mind, your gain. Right, I'll be off, good to see you again."

"Jack?" John looked at his old school friend.

"Yes me old mate?"

"You came round for a reason?"

"No, just passing, thought I'd just pop in and say hi, all neighbourly like, nothing more."

"Oh, right." John wasn't convinced as to Jack's motives but Susan had put him in his place good and proper, and what a performance. He inwardly grinned as he watched the man leave the room. "See you about, Jack."

"Aye, you will."

The back door finally closed, allowing John the pleasure of a massive sigh of relief. "Whoa, that was close, but what about Susan? She's a clever little thing. Modelling, who'd have thought of that one, and did you see the way she gave poor old Jack just enough to chew on? Brilliant! They're going to love it down the pub."

Sam started to clear the dirty cups from the table. "You do realise it'll be all round the village by tomorrow? Let's just hope it's enough to keep them happy for a while, but if I know men, John Taylor's going to be the envy of every red-blooded male for miles around."

"God, I hadn't thought of it like that. You're right, I can hear them now – lucky old John, surrounded by gorgeous young women. I like it. I like it a lot."

"Men!" Sam placed the cups into the sink. "You're so easily pleased."

Chapter 21

Tony was settling in just fine, and after the little scare with Jack's suspicions, John asked the girls to keep work steady – only regulars and definitely no new business, certainly not until he was absolutely convinced Susan's modelling alibi had been circulated and accepted by the villagers. Jack was well liked by most, especially in the local watering hole 'The Dog with no Tail', so John was hopeful once he got talking over a few pints that those who were itching to tell tales would be satisfied with the explanation. Yes, there would be the odd one who just had to elaborate whatever the circumstances, but even infectious rumours had their life and John was sure they would soon be picking on some other poor soul and Willowbank's unorthodox country behaviour would be forgotten, or at least put to one side.

John himself was more relaxed, partially due to the pound coins trickling into his overdraft – small amounts seemed to be the answer. Their weekly deposits had been gratefully received by the bank manager with little concern to origin. John found the man constantly apologising concerning bank policy; nothing personal, he continued to point out. Yet for all this, John still looked upon him as a complete twat; nothing personal, you understand.

So financially things were ticking along nicely. The girls, much to everyone's delight, were loving the farm and often seen venturing further away from the garden. Tony had taken on the role of head girl and with great pleasure wandered familiar fields showing Susan hidden trails of past youth, sadly some overgrown and impossible to venture down, but new ones had been discovered and happily carved out of the glorious countryside they now called home.

John often saw them exploring like wild teenagers, desperately hanging onto their precious years, chasing butterflies or simply lying on grassy banks watching clouds drifting by. Their innocent acts of freedom made him feel warm inside, only too pleased to see them enjoy the place as much as he did, but for all their childlike innocence he couldn't help but feel a tinge of sadness knowing what these bubbly young women did for a living. Yet he was happy to offer them somewhere safe to do so. Sam openly admitted she relished their company and although they'd been at the farm for a fairly short time, she'd willingly accepted them as part of the family. John sensed Susan was her favourite over Tony – perhaps it was just a personal thing, he wasn't entirely sure, but he got the distinct filling she didn't quite trust Tony.

Tick, on the other hand, would never be trusted, but that was fine by John. She still left regular gifts hanging by their feet and always with their brains blown away, a single shot to the head with torturous eyes bulging out of cracked skulls. Something John never quite got used to – why, he couldn't understand. They were vermin and as such demanded little respect, but these poor creatures had him often wondering about his own existence upon this planet. His concerns soon melted away with the sight of tens, twenties and even the odd fifty. He never saw Tick and wisely chose not to go up to the woodland hut, a place that worried him. She would, he was certain, leave a note if any problems arose.

The Caramel Kid had started to open up, possibly seeing Sam as a replacement for his dear departed mother, only too pleased to experiment with golden treacle flapjack, and when the fancy arose, the odd butterfly cake. Much to Susan's displeasure he would insist on trying Sam's culinary delights while in the throes of being entertained. Susan, bless her soul, had brought her own vacuum cleaner. So life on the farm seemed to be running along just fine.

*

"Christ! You scared the living daylights out of me!" John was suddenly confronted by Lizzie Blackman staring straight at him as he attempted to mend a broken strand of barbed wire.

Her arm raised, she pointed an accusing finger at him. "I know what you're up to, John Taylor." He carefully studied the grey-haired woman standing in front of him.

"Is that right, Lizzie?"

"It is. You might be able to fool those mutton-headed numbskulls down in the village, but you can't fool me. I know what's going on in those bedrooms, seen it with my own eyes. Ha! Them girls are no more models than I am. Loose women, that's what they are, ladies of the night. Sinners!" She looked like a woman processed by the devil himself, vacant eyes glistening in the sunlight, her top lip trembling with fear. "Naked flesh, John Taylor! Young female bodies entangled in the act of fornication, seen it with my own two eyes." She pointed a shaking finger at her own face as her body swayed back and forth against the winds of sin.

"Don't know what you're talking about, Lizzie. Reckon your imagination's got the better of you." John tried to sound calm and unconcerned, but Lizzie's comments sent a worrying ache deep down into his gut. He lifted his hammer, forcefully hitting the last of the staples into a waiting post and then looked up. Lizzie had vanished, disappeared as quickly as she'd arrived.

*

The three women sat in the kitchen talking about nothing in particular when Sam noticed John wasn't his normal greedy outspoken self, half-heartedly picking at his food.

"Are you all right, John?"

"Sorry?"

"I said, are you all right?"

"No, not really. I think we might have a problem." The two younger girls stopped their conversation and turned.

"It's Lizzie Blackman," he announced.

"Really, is that all?" Sam laid her knife and fork to one side. "What's she been up to now?"

"Who's Lizzie Blackman?" Susan asked.

"She's a scary old witch."

"That's enough of that, Tony."

"Well she is, we used to call her lesbian Lil."

"They still do," John interrupted, receiving a scolding look from Sam.

"That's enough, I said. You know very well she's just a lonely old woman."

"Batty as hell if you ask me."

"John. Enough! She's just broken-hearted by the loss of a loved one."

"Poppycock. She's doolally. How can anyone be right in the head when they garden stark naked and stand for hours, sometimes in the pouring rain, just waiting, hovering under that massive oak tree along at Back Lane? Scares the living daylights out of passers-by."

"You know very well why she stands there, she's waiting for Jane to come home."

"Who's Jane?" Susan now looked confused.

Jane Bromley, she was a lovely woman. Lizzie's partner. She died of cancer, probably about ten or so years ago now, broke poor Lizzie's heart. True she's never been the same since, but she's not mad."

"If Jane's dead, why does she wait for her?" asked Susan.

Sam looked at the innocent face of a girl who had clearly never truly been in love. Perhaps one day you'll understand why bereaved people do certain things," Sam replied.

"But gardening in the nude? I can kind of understand the waiting bit I think, but what has losing someone got to do with stripping off and weeding your beds?"

"Well said, young lady."

"John! Please don't encourage her. If you must know, Lizzie and Jane belonged to a naturist group, that's partially why they bought Rose Cottage, because of its position. You would never know it was there unless you were local, and she waits under the tree because Jane used to cycle to the village to do the shopping. I think it's quite sad, but rather sweet."

"Batty as hell, like I say." John waited to be shouted down but Sam had clearly had enough. "Anyway, it still doesn't solve our problem," he continued.

"Which is?"

"I unfortunately met up with her today down at bottom field. I reckon she's been spying on us, claims to have seen naked activity in certain bedrooms."

Sam couldn't help but chuckle. "That rules out ours then."

The two glared at each other, Sam being the first to look away, allowing John to pick himself up and carry on. "Young ladies, she says, carrying on in the most inappropriate manner. She's put two and two together and come up with ten."

Sam just shook her head. "No one will believe her, you know. Most of the village thinks she's mad so I wouldn't get too concerned about it."

John shook his head. "There's always those who'll take her side whether they think she's mad or not. They're just born gossips. I'm telling you, I really don't feel happy about this, especially after Jack sniffing about and almost accusing us of harbouring loose women!"

"But we are." Sam glanced over at the two girls. "Sorry, no offence."

"None taken." They both spoke at the same time.

"I know," John continued, "but that's beside the point."

"Is it?"

"You know it is, stop complicating matters."

"No, John, all I was saying was we are."

"Why do you women have to be so politically correct?"

"Because—"

"No!" He raised his hand. "Leave it. Enough!"

"Okay, you don't have to get all uppity about it. So if you're not happy, what do you intend to do? Shoot her before she tells the world?" Sam carried on eating.

"Naked flesh!"

"Excuse me?"

"That's what she said: 'Naked flesh, John Taylor, young female bodies entangled within the act of fornication, I've seen it with my own eyes!' Then she disappeared."

Sam stopped eating. "Okay, let's say your worries are justified. What then?"

"I don't know. Shooting could get a bit messy; I'm not the best shot. I could chuck her in the slurry pit." John grinned at the two girls. "Your faces! It's only a joke."

"There's really nothing you can do," Sam replied. "If she wants to spread rumours then she will." She could see her husband's mind churning away. "If you're still thinking about the slurry pit, forget it – she'll block the tanker when you finally get around to cleaning it out. Lumps of straw are bad enough, but decaying old women have no hope."

"Really, Sam, you're just as bad as he is."

"Country humour, Susan. You need a bit of it in farming or you'll go mad. Just like Lizzie."

"John!" chided Sam. "You're very quiet, Tony."

"I was just thinking we could sweeten the old girl up a little, give her something else to occupy her mind."

"Go on."

Tony looked over at Susan. "Sadie."

The moment she heard that name her face lit up like a Christmas tree. "Yes, of course, Sadie! What a brilliant idea, she'd be perfect."

"Who's Sadie?" John asked.

"Satan Sadie."

"What are you talking about?"

The room filled with youthful laughter as the two girls congratulated themselves on such a clever idea.

"We're sorry, it's just that she would be perfect."

"Yes, you've already said that, now do you mind telling us what the hell's going on?"

"It could work, Susan."

"Ahem." John loudly cleared his throat, showing his impatience.

"Okay," she paused for breath, "Sadie Brooks, she's an old friend of ours – well, still is, I suppose."

Tony butted in. "More of an acquaintance, really."

"Yes, you're probably right, more of an acquaintance, but for all that she's a really nice woman. Admittedly a little rough around edges, but a heart of gold. Only ..."

"Only what?"

"If looks and mannerisms are anything to go by, she'd be the last to board the train and as such normally ends up taking everyone's rejects or weirdos. Yet, and this is the best bit, she's a self-confessed lesbian. So can't you see? It's perfect. She could become Jane – a good wash and a little makeup, problem solved."

"Are you seriously suggesting we make her out to be Lizzie's long-lost lover, the one that happens to be dead?"

"Well, yes."

"Well, no. Sam, help me out here." He was met by a doubtful look. "Oh, so that's how it is. You're on their side, you of all people. Doesn't it worry you that we'll be tricking her?"

"Funnily enough, no. Clearly this Sadie can't be Jane, so I don't think we'll be tricking anyone, and Lizzie is a lonely woman, perhaps a little companionship wouldn't be a bad thing. You never know, they might hit it off. I say we give it a go."

John slumped back in his chair. "So let's get this right – you're saying we take on this woman to effectively give Lizzie one to shut her up?"

"John! There's no need to be crude about it."

"I say it as I see it and we need to know where we stand on this." He looked at the girls. "Well?"

"Technically, yes," Susan replied.

"No, none of this technical stuff, a simple yes or no will do." They both nodded. Fine, that's all I needed to know. All right, I can't say I like the idea, and it's risky, but I think we need to do *something*. The last thing we want is Lizzie ruining everything, doesn't matter how slim that case might be."

*

Later that evening Tony sat in the front room and pressed Sadie's number into her phone. She wasn't even sure if the woman was still around, but what else could she do? Sadie's unconventional lifestyle saw her moving or being moved frequently; she could even be in prison. Unlikely, for she was well known to the police and locking her up would be seen as a total waste of tax payer money – better to turn a blind eye and hope she finally decides to move on to someone else's patch.

The other three sat busying themselves, only too happy to allow the evening's charming effects to lighten their day's toil. Tony paced the room as she waited for Sadie to pick up. John pretended to watch the news, sound down to a minimum so he could conveniently eavesdrop on any possible conversation, only to be disappointed by Tony's disappearance down the hallway. He strained his ears, and a few moments later detected a muffled voice, but to his annoyance nothing of any clarity. For all he knew she could be talking to anyone.

Sam was reading another book and Susan was listening to music, her headphones securely wrapped around her head. Tony finally walked back in, a look of satisfaction on her face, but as yet no real indication of any victory. John tried to feign disinterest, attempting to give the impression that he was more intent in painfully viewing the commentary of some cricket match that had been played earlier – a sport he loathed but for the sake of appearances he would endure until Tony announced her findings.

She sat back down knowing full well John was itching to be informed, but found it highly amusing to let him stew for a while longer. "Okay, you win," he finally burst out. "Did you manage to talk to her?"

"Wondered how long you'd last."

"Don't get smart with me, young lady. Well?"

"Yes, very interested as it happens. She's just been busted yet again, this time for trying to give an undercover police officer a blow job outside

McDonald's – claimed she mistook it for a happy meal!"

"She sounds different." John was unable to hide a look of concern.

"Oh yes, she's certainly that."

"What will they do to her?" John asked. "Only we need her here, like *now*."

"Probably just slap her hand and move her on." Tony paused. "You look worried."

"That's his normal look." Sam placed her half-read book face down on the carpet. "Let me guess. John, you're worried she might bring the police round here?"

"Something like that. Last thing we want is the local constabulary sniffing about."

"That won't happen," Tony replied. "My guess is when she tells them she's leaving town they'll be too busy celebrating down the pub and the last thing on their minds will be finding out her next destination."

John still didn't feel overly convinced by Tony's prediction, but what else could he do? "You explained our situation, told her what we discussed earlier?"

"Yes, John, stop worrying."

"Just checking. I'm still not convinced it's the best way to go."

"It'll be fine, and the good news, all being well she should be able to get here on Saturday. Wants to stay overnight then see about starting on Sunday. The money side can be sorted out later, but if I know Sadie, a good clean bed and a hot meal will be enough for starters."

Sam looked at the clock. "Good, that's sorted then. I'm off to bed."

Tony gave Susan a prod in the ribs. "Ha, bedtime."

"What?" She pulled a headphone away from her ear.

"I said it's bedtime."

She gave Tony a disgruntled look. "Bossy so-and-so."

"I try to be. Sadie's hoping to be here on Saturday."

"Brilliant! She's a bit of a rough one, but I like her."

"Me too."

The girls' comments did nothing to alleviate John's concerns, but he too felt it was time for bed.

"Oh, and John," said Tony as she paused in the doorway, "Sadie said she'll be coming down on the bus. If it helps, me and Susan can walk down and meet up with her, if that's all right?"

"Not so bossy with him, are you?" Susan said.

"He's the boss, you're just a worker," she said with a wink before disappearing down the hallway.

"Whatever suits." John's eyes were almost shut. "I'm off to bed."

*

It was Saturday morning and John was finishing off milking when he saw the girls head off up the drive. His attempt at a wave unintentionally drifted off in the breeze leaving him hosing down the concrete and wondering if asking Sadie to the farm was such a good idea. Slight doubts still niggled, questioning the reliance of someone who sounded to him as rather dodgy. Perhaps he was overreacting to a problem that may never arise, but that vision of Lizzie kept coming back to haunt him. It would only take a tiny spark to reignite those earlier suspicions of wrongdoing at Willowbank Farm ... He stopped short of thinking of the consequences. No, he had to be positive, it'll be fine. So why was his body sagging with uncertainty?

John had just sat down at the kitchen table when the front door opened and a chorus of female voices came down the hallway, reminding him of a barn full of turkeys. He braced himself as a nervous tingle of apprehension shot through his veins, yet he must have accidentally voiced his thoughts.

"Excuse me?" Sam turned and looked at him.

"What?"

"You said turkeys."

"Did I?"

"Yes."

He tried to hide behind a blank expression; it was better just to play dumb than to admit his basic level of male humour.

Men! Sam shook her head in bewilderment at her husband's somewhat strange behaviour. They were interrupted by their two young attractive bubbly females strolling into the room, shortly followed by a less than appealing creature of maturing years.

"John, Sam, this is Sadie Brooks." Tony raised a hand and introduced their guest.

One look and John was convinced this could be one huge mistake. Rough around the edges was an understatement; he'd never thought himself a snob, but his thoughts were telling him he would gladly pay good money to ask this one to leave the bedroom. "Nice to meet you, Sadie." He reluctantly offered a handshake.

"Morning, Mr Taylor, Mrs Taylor."

John was taken aback by the frank tone of voice and wanted nothing more than to pull away, but it was too late as he felt her grip tighten around his fingers. Christ! Could Tick have a sister? Yes, she does, she mentioned it on her first meeting, but the name was Marigold, wasn't it? Certainly not Sadie. His hand fell away, leaving a sour taste in his mouth as he wondered what the hell he had done.

"Peaceful place you have here. Grew up on a farm meself, not as nice as this one though. Dartmoor, bloody freezing, and that was the summer. The winters, well, they were enough to ice your nipples over." Rough laugher echoed around the room as everyone else smiled out of sheer politeness.

John was sure he could detect the odd whiff of body odour which, mixed with the smell of fried food, saw his stomach do an almighty flip.

Sam saw he was starting to look uncomfortable and decided it was time to step in. "Why don't you girls show Sadie to her room? That'll give me time to cook up the breakfasts."

Sadie's eyes lit up. "Smashing, Mrs Taylor. A good old English fry-up, can't beat it, ha, Mr Taylor?"

"No indeed, best meal of the day."

"You're right there."

Susan made for the hallway. "Won't be long." She eagerly escorted their guest out as it was only too plain to see it had been a bit of a shock for John to finally meet the elusive Sadie Brooks. He clearly needed time to come to terms with her slightly overpowering presence.

"I hope you like your room, Sadie," smiled Sam. "First bedroom on the right, girls. It has a nice outlook over the fields."

"Grand, Mrs Taylor. Be down for me grub in a jiff."

John waited until the girls were at the top of the stairs before he dared say a word. "God, I hope this is going to work."

"It'll be fine. Admittedly she's a bit forthright, I'll say that much."

"That's an understatement. If Lizzie doesn't take to

her, which at the moment I seriously have my doubts, then we're in big trouble."

Sam broke two eggs into a waiting frying pan. "I'm sure you're worrying for no good reason. Give her time to settle in and I'm sure she'll be a different person."

John looked at her doubtfully. "You know what Jane was like when she was alive? Any resemblance to our endearing Sadie?"

Sam paused for a moment, trying to choose her words carefully. "Well... she was a woman... and a lesbian ...." Then fell silent.

"Great!" John replied. "Just what I need."

Chapter 22

"Psst." Tony stopped dead. "In here." She spotted John's nose poking out of a small gap in his office doorway. "Tony, quick, come in." The door opened just enough to allow her to enter, leaving John to nervously pop his head out and look both ways before gently closing it shut.

"You all right, John?"

"Fine. Look, it's about Sadie." His voice trailed off to a mere whisper.

"You don't like her, do you?"

"No, it's not that, it's just, she's ... how can I say it ... don't get me wrong, she seems a nice woman, but I think you were right when you said she's a little rough around the edges. I'm just a little concerned she's going to be too different from Jane, and Lizzie won't like her. If we're to succeed I think we should at least try and get her to look similar."

"So what are you saying?"

"I'm saying perhaps you could have a go at her, you know?"

"No, I don't know."

"Spruce her up a bit, give her a makeover. Nothing too drastic, simple things to start with, like a shower, and progress from there. Look, I'm sorry to be frank, but she reeks of BO."

"You noticed too?"

"Couldn't help but notice. And perhaps try to do something with her hair. I know there's not much to work with, but I'm sure you can do something. Anything half decent would be nice. Have a quick word with Sam beforehand, she'll tell you what the old Jane used to look like. I'm sorry to be so blunt but I just can't see it working as she looks at the moment. Is that all right?" He hoped he hadn't overstepped the mark. Sadie was, after all, a friend to the girls.

"It's fine. Leave it to us girls, we'll knock the old bird into shape."

He couldn't help but catch the young woman's gaze. "Anyone tell you you're a beauty?"

She placed her hand gently down upon his and leant forward. "Most days." Then, to John's delight, she landed a light kiss upon his willing cheek. "Now be a good boy and stop worrying, everything's going to be just fine." She stood and made her way towards the door. John sprang to his feet. "What are you doing?" he demanded.

"It was just a friendly kiss, John."

"No, not that, although it was nice. People don't need to know we've spoken to each other." John opened the door a crack to make sure the coast was clear. "We'll leave separately," he whispered. "I'll leave first, and when the coast is clear, I'll knock on the door three times, understood?"

"This is ridiculous, John!" she whispered back. "Okay,

fine," she relented, seeing the serious look on his face.

John slipped out of the room first and left her standing like a lost child on their first day at school. With some relief she finally heard three muffled knocks and slowly opened the door to find herself alone in the hallway. "John Taylor," she whispered, "you're as mad as they come, but I'm beginning to like you." Her thoughts drifted along the impressive hallway that held her dream home together. One day.

*

"Mother, how are you today?" John pulled a patio chair closer to the sun lounger. Her giant sunglasses reminded him of dustbin lids, hiding her eyes from the brightening sunlight while the warmth from a gentle breeze whipped up around the garden.

"John, dear, I was beginning to wonder if you'd left home. Can I remind you I don't live on the other side of the world?"

"Sorry, Mother, but it's been rather full-on lately."

"Excuses, excuses. And yes, I'm fine, at least someone pops in to see me occasionally."

"Sorry again, Mother."

"Not you, Samantha. If it wasn't for her and the WI ladies I would surely be a lonely old widow, compelled to watch ghastly daytime television. Have you any idea what rubbish they serve up nowadays? I've a mind to complain but I really haven't got the time nor the energy, so I must leave such things until I am wheelchair-bound, God forbid."

"Yes, Mother, if you say so."

"Don't patronise me, John. You know I can't stand such things, and being ignored by my own son." Her hand swept across her face in a most threatening manner.

"No one's trying to ignore you, Mother. As I said, there's a lot on at the moment."

"So you keep saying. And what of your young lady?"

"She's not my young lady, Mother, she just works from here, remember?"

"Yes. Business brisk, is it? And when were you going to tell me about Antonia?"

"How did you know about her?"

"Samantha told me, you cloth head, we women talk you know. Fancy Antonia, who'd have thought it? Such a sweet child, a little dominating at times I remember but boys are only miniature versions of men, easily led. Clearly she had it in her even at that age, poor Luke."

"Mother, that's a terrible thing to say, they were just kids."

"Yes, well, everyone's allowed their opinion. She's a grown woman and quite attractive by all accounts, but I worry about George. It's not good for a man his age to see scantily dressed women roaming about. Caught him lingering around their underwear the other day!"

"What?"

"Don't look so shocked, dear – hanging on the washing line at the time, but concerning nonetheless."

"Mother. I hardly think the girls are going to walk around half naked; all that sort of thing happens in the bedrooms."

"Lucky them. But John, lines of erotic undergarments are not what an elderly gardener with a dodgy pacemaker should be mowing around and I'm sure he was sniffing them on one or two passes. Quite unacceptable, and I have to say some are hardly worth wearing – even a sparrow would have trouble making a nest in them." She drifted momentarily into another world before drawing in air. "Your father always insisted on choosing what I wore, said they needed to make a good oily rag when finished with! Once a farmer always a farmer I suppose, but these modern things are not enough to blow your nose let alone wipe your hands."

"They're G-strings, Mother."

She turned back and rested her head on the pillow. "Is that so? A poor effort for an onion bag if you ask me, so don't come to me when you're desperate for rags."

"No, Mother."

Her body seemed to slump. "I'm lonely, John. So many people about but hardly anyone to talk to, and while you're all having fun in the big house poor little me sits here all by myself."

"You have George."

Her head dropped to one side in protest. "That hardly counts for anything, dear. I couldn't possibly have him indoors, he has bowel problems, you know. I was convinced there was something wrong with the mower the other day, it sounded dreadful. Constantly backfiring, but on further inspection and to my horror I realised the malfunction was from George's trousers. So no, dear, I don't have or wish to have the man for anything but horticulture."

John had to feel sorry for his mother, yet a lot of her troubles were of her own making. "What if I get the girls to come round one afternoon, it would be good for you to get to know them a little better, how does that sound?"

She looked suspicious. "I'm not a charity case, dear, but if you must, I accept your suggestion. But only if the girls really want to – I would hate to think they were being pushed."

"I'm sure that won't be the case, Mother."

"Of course I will have to consult my diary." She sat and thought for a while. "How does tomorrow afternoon sound?"

"I thought you had to look in your diary?"

"No need, I've just realised it's Sunday tomorrow, church in the morning, but any time after lunch will suffice, they can't possibly be working on the Sabbath.

John was about to agree when he remembered Sadie.

"Ah, slight problem, the girls have a friend staying for the weekend." He felt slightly guilty raising his mother's hopes; it couldn't be nice living on your own and having people make up excuses as to why they couldn't spare a small amount of time to come and see you, and yes he was as much to blame as the next person. Even now his visit wasn't entirely a sociable one but he dared not admit that. In truth he'd actually come round to see if he could borrow her old bike. If Sadie was to stand any chance of getting in with Lizzie they needed to use every means at their disposal. "Mother, I was wondering ..." he paused briefly, "I was wondering ..." He was beginning to think this was a bad idea, his mind racing headlong towards the inevitable consequences of his next actions.

"Yes, dear?"

"I was wondering if you would like to come around for supper tonight?"

"Oh John, that would be lovely, you are a dear, and there I was thinking you had an ulterior motive for coming to see me."

A false smile pushed its way onto his lying face. "Would I ever?"

"Well I must apologise for being so suspicious."

"Really, you don't have to, Mother." With every word he spoke John could feel the long rope of deception slowly tighten around his neck.

"No, I insist."

"Fine, Mother, if it makes you feel better, but it's really

not necessary." The speed his invitation was accepted had temporarily taken John by surprise. There was no 'Oh that's so kind but', there was no 'I'm perfectly happy eating on my own and I wouldn't dream of disturbing your evening'. No, there was none of that, not even a 'Tell Samantha thank you but no thank you'. Nothing. Sam was going to kill him. Why, why had he done it?

"What time would you like me to come around, dear?"

For some reason her time of arrival seemed insignificant compared to the terrible things that awaited him, and then there was still Sadie to sort out. Why hadn't he just come clean and asked about the damn bike? He was such a fool sometimes. "I'll go and check with Sam."

She pulled her glasses off and squinted at her son. "She does know about this, I hope?"

"Yes, of course she does, it was all arranged this morning." A weak gesture of acceptance rose into the air, desperately trying to shoo away any possible worries that would almost certainly arise. "She may have said a time, but you know what I'm like."

"Umm, you're to be excused, dear. After all, you are a man."

*

"What! You did *what*? And *tonight*?"

"All right, keep your voice down. I'm sorry, okay, but she kept going on about being lonely and no one taking the time to go around and see her."

"Bullshit, John! She always pleads poverty, have you not learnt yet? She's out and about more than you and me put together. You're such a fool, John Taylor, and *tonight*? Any other evening I could have coped, but with trying to sort out Sadie and nothing in the fridge it's not good timing, and you know how fussy she is. Sometimes I wonder why I married you."

"Steady on, it's not that bad."

Her hands flew up in frustration. "You did ask about the bike?" John tried to avoid eye contact. "Tell me you did."

"Well ..."

"Oh John, one thing, that's all you had to do, just go around and politely ask."

"That's two things." Why did he have to say that? Suddenly he could feel that rope cutting off his air supply, hoisting his body off the ground leaving him dangling for life. A damp smelly dishcloth smacked the side of his unprotected head.

"Out!"

"Seven o' clock all right?" Seeking out the safety of the hallway, he legged it.

"Get out!"

Mother arrived via the back door smack on seven, knocked twice and waited. Just walking in unannounced was something that would never enter her mind on occasions such as this. One had to be escorted into the house. Normal visits were seen as a totally different affair, knowing she had the right to enter her old home and a quick shout down the passage would solve any embarrassing moments, but not tonight.

"Mother, you're looking lovely this evening." John had learnt this was always a sensible way to start. Women liked to be complimented on their efforts.

"Cut the crap, dear, you know you don't mean it."

Well, that went well, he thought, but then looking at his mother more closely perhaps she was right, there was certainly very little loveliness from where he was standing. This time she had well and truly gone over the top and wouldn't look out of place leaning up against a lamp post in a shady part of town. "This way, Mother."

"I know my way around, John, remember I did used to live here."

He didn't bother replying, what was the point? She was back to her normal self, but occasionally you just dared to hope, foolishly perhaps, that she had mellowed. But that was her way and he could see why his father ruled with a rod of iron, for to do otherwise would have surely spelled disaster. Thankfully Sam had risen to the task and with little pre-warning had produced a meal fit for any country gentry. Earlier that day the girls had handled Sadie's makeover leaving Sam to get on with preparing the food. She'd allowed them free access to her wardrobe, apologising for its sparse appearance, claiming the odd trip to market via the abattoir never warranted anything special. The girls looked at the dresses determinedly and seized the opportunity to create something out of very little. So Sam had left them to it and as yet no one outside of Susan's bedroom had so far seen the consequences.

A trip to the village had partially replenished the dwindling supplies of foodstuffs, all courtesy of surplus cash that found its way into various hiding places around the house. Yet Sam was always careful not to be seen flashing too much money about as she knew people were still on the lookout for the next bit of gossip, and to be seen to be too wealthy wasn't something a farmer's wife should ever be allowed to experience.

Sam hadn't seen or heard anything of the girls since suggesting they try a rather out-dated flowery dress that looked like it should take pride of place in a museum of past country life but looked like it would fit Sadie's fifty-plus frame without too much pushing and shoving. John had used milking as an excuse to stay well out of it, figuring he had caused enough upset for one day, and hadn't been seen for hours.

The meal was to be held in the grandeur of the old dining room, a place no one used on a normal daily basis. Susan didn't much care for it due to the cold uninspiring walls and odd stuffed animal head, their glazed eyes constantly watching. A vulgar statement, she thought, of country status that did nothing to warm her heart. John would inevitably take great pride in showing off paintings of past occupants who frankly looked just as scary as the poor animals themselves, but the decision was made so she'd just have to put up with it.

"Sylvia." Sam quickly wiped her hands on her pinny, John trailing in behind. "How are you?"

"Fine, my dear Samantha." John always felt it strange his mother called by her Christian name, it just didn't sound right.

"Go on through, dinner's almost ready." Sam caught a lung full of highly scented mothballs and looked slightly concerned at her mother-in-law's dress sense, discreetly catching John's attention. He just shrugged as if to warn of a possible lengthy evening and then disappeared.

The table was laid for six. John watched his mother relishing the prospect of dining the night away within such a large gathering as she ran her finger around the silverware lifting the occasional knife and fork, inspecting its state of cleanliness before returning it to the table in the correct position, as far as she was concerned. "Very nice, dear."

"Thank you, Mother."

"Six places." It was said as a statement rather than an observation.

"The girls have a friend staying, I think I mentioned it earlier."

"Oh yes, quite. A young lady, I assume?"

John thought about his next words very carefully. "A little older."

"And is this person trading?"

"Trading, Mother?"

"I think you know what I mean."

"If you're implying is she on the game, then yes."

"Quite vulgar, John, but one needs to know these things, less embarrassing that way."

"Quite right, Mother."

"I must say there does seem to be a lot of it about, I never knew but it just goes to show you can never tell a normal person from one of them."

"Glass of wine, Mother?" John grabbed a bottle and laid it across the lower part of his arm, forcing someone who knew nothing about wine to gaze down at a New Zealand label.

"Looks fine, dear, but I'd much prefer red, white gives me wind. You'd know that if you asked me around more often."

"Right, red it is. He rummaged through the selection of past Christmas gifts and grabbed the first red. "Here we are then, one of the best." A lie, he didn't know much about wine but this one was no more than cheap French vinegar, but if she insisted then that was fine by him. Leaving his mother sipping, he casually made his way back to the kitchen.

Sam pulled away from an array of steaming pots and pans. "How's it going?"

"Um. Fine."

"Oh, that good?"

John plucked a piece of chicken from a waiting carcass. "I've got a horrible feeling about tonight and she hasn't even met Sadie yet."

"Well, too late now, so make yourself useful and take these vegetables in. I'll finish off and then we can start." Sam placed the last of the food down just as the girls came in. She could see the wine was being topped up at an alarming rate and Sylvia's sips had turned into large gulps, the alcohol flowing like water from a tap. John's mother was halfway through the first bottle and they hadn't even started yet. What was her irresponsible husband up to?

She knew there were only two bottles of red but if Sylvia consumed both, God knows what the evening would end up like. Her only option would be to try and outdrink her and hope the dislike for white would somehow stop her dead in her tracks. It was a risky strategy on her part as she herself loathed reds of any kind and she really couldn't hold her drink that well either, but for the sake of not ending up with a disastrous night she had to give it a go. "John, if you please," she said, waving a large empty glass in front of her husband's nose.

"I didn't think you liked red?"

"Silly, of course I do. Now pour and make it a big one."

"Fine, red it is. Say when." Much to his surprise he watched the level rise until it hit the rim.

"Thank you, John." The glass had only just connected with her lips when Sadie walked in.

"Evening, everyone." Her commanding presence almost knocked John off his feet.

"Sadie, is that you?"

"'Tis, what do you think?"

"It's amazing," John replied. "What a transformation. Let's take a good look at you, give us a twirl." He suddenly remembered his manners. "I'm sorry, Mother, very rude of me. This is Sadie Brooks, the girls' friend I was talking about."

Sylvia's upturned nose ran across the woman's entire body and then with some reservations she held out her hand. "Nice to meet you, Sadie."

"Of course you know Susan," John continued.

"Hardly, dear. I believe my gardener has seen more of you, much more, so I've been informed." An uneasy feeling floated across the table.

"And this is Tony."

His mother studied the pretty young woman in front of her. "Antonia, you don't mind if I call you by your proper name? Tony seems so common, hardly fit for a female." Another mouthful of wine found its way past her lips. "I must say you've changed from the last time I saw you, so sweet and innocent back then." She paused. "Never mind."

Sam was struggling halfway through her glass when she asked John to top it up. When he hesitated, she just sat and stared at him, warning him to do as he was told.

Now with glass almost spilling she invited everyone to take their places. "Well, this is lovely, everyone getting to know one another. Shall we eat?" Her rapidly glazing eyes searched for the serving spoon but only found her husband's concerned look. "John, perhaps you could do the honours?" The room started to sway. Food, that's what's needed, drinking on an empty stomach was never advisable, not for her anyway. She watched John top up his mother's glass. Damn, at this rate she'd have to have a third refill. The thought made her stomach churn with displeasure knowing how she detested red wine, especially cheap stuff. Oh how she longed to reach for the quality white, but there was no option – she had to keep going.

To John's relief the evening was ticking along just fine with the conversation mainly focused around politics, and for all of Sadie's rough edges she did seem to have a keen mind when it came to world affairs. But now he could see his mother feeling the effects of her sour grapes and slowly but surely her airs and graces were gradually showing as she raised her glass and took another sizeable swig of her vinegar-enhanced liquid.

"Tell me, Heidi," she slurred.

"Mother, it's Sadie."

"Yes, dear, that's what I said." Her body rocked back and forth to the rhythm of an irregular heartbeat while her eyes searched the room for her intended target. "So, Heidi, John tells me you are one of them." Her arm came down with an abrupt thump upon the table top.

Everyone else held their breath while Sadie contemplated. "No, Sylvia, I'm a prostitute."

A red wine induced finger rose in the air and attempted to tap the side of a waiting nose. "Don't worry, my dear, I won't tell a soul."

Now John was getting warning signs from the other end of the table. "Okay, Mother, I think perhaps it's time I took you home."

"Nonsense, dear boy, we haven't had dessert yet." Her wandering eyes scanned the table. "Or have we? More wine, John." She clumsily pushed her empty glass towards a waiting bottle. "I've been without far too long."

"Really, Mother, I insist."

"Is that you insisting on filling my glass or you insisting," she rocked backwards, "on insisting."

"Mother, we need to go."

"Quite the demanding fellow, aren't we? Oh for goodness' sake, sit down. You're making me feel quite dizzy. My glass is still empty, dear." Her nose pressed against the glass as she tried to peer through its circular form. "Naughty boy, haven't been doing your job, have you?"

She flipped it upside down and shook it several times, proving as she had suspected that indeed it was empty.

"John." Sam tried to catch her husband's attention. "Can you give me a hand with these dishes please?"

"Ah, good, dessert." His mother's voice stumbled as she spoke. "Why don't you get Heidi to do it, the woman looks like she's used to manual labour."

Sadie went to get up but was immediately stopped by John's hand. "No, Sadie, you're our guest, the girls and I are quite capable. Sam, you stay put, you've had enough tonight … I mean you've done enough." He briefly gazed at the gathering of people at his table. "Let's all try and enjoy the rest of the evening, shall we?"

He heard the clink of a toppling wine glass. "Nonsense, John, the woman's clearly below us so let her do her job."

"Mother, that's enough." He turned to Sadie. "I apologise for my mother's rude behaviour, Sadie."

"Have it your own way, dear, but if it was up to me the servants wouldn't be allowed at the table in the first place."

John clenched his fists in anger but Sadie just smiled, forcing him to back away before he said something he may regret later. The two girls had already started to clear the table and Sam had defied orders and somehow managed to get the cheeseboard safely to the table without dropping it, a risky procedure given her wine-induced state, but she needed to get away from her shameful mother-in-law, breathe in the calm of the kitchen and apologise to the girls. They'd both shrugged it off but it left Sam feeling let down by her adopted family. Tony smiled as she brought in a large pavlova while Susan carried a bowl of fresh fruit, both fearing the evening was a long way from finishing as they made their way back to their chairs. They were met by a raised glass which still hadn't been filled.

"Cheers everyone." Sylvia's raucous dry laugh echoed around the room as she sat staring at the arrangement of fruit. "Look," she pointed with her unstable finger, "look, it's a man's dingly dangle!" The fruit in question had unfortunately been placed between two shiny bright red nectarines and lay in wait for the attentions of a rather tipsy elderly woman. Sylvia leant forward and with a wobbly hand stroked its long bent yellow shaft with her fingertip. "Oh how I miss your father, John, he was such a big man." A faint chuckle passed over her partially numb lips as she touched its hardened skin. "Do you know what we used to call it?"

"Mother!"

"No, it wasn't that, try again."

"No, Mother. I think it's time to go, you've had quite enough for one night."

"John?"

"Not now, Sam."

"But John. I think your mother's going to be—"

Her warning was cut short by the horrific sound of an inebriated pensioner depositing her entire evening's meal across the table, her head rocking upon her shoulders before being thrown forward for the second time. Then finally she sat upright and held out her hand. "Hanky please, John." The remains of her meal hung from her lips as she noticed everyone had discreetly moved away. "Ladies, I think it's time I went. John, your assistance please."

She felt a reassuring hand grasp her arm, and then everything went blank.

Chapter 23

"How are you today, Mother?" John found a sprawled body resting on the sun lounger, beside it a large glass of tomato juice and next to that an open box of pain relief tablets. A slight movement indicated that it wasn't in fact a decaying corpse but a live human being.

"I don't what to talk about it."

John stood to one side knowing if he hung around long enough his mother's curiosity towards her company would eventually break her. He waited in silence, admiring George's work and listening to nature as it went about its daily life.

"My God, John, I made such a fool of myself. You must be so ashamed of me."

"Nonsense, Mother. It really wasn't that bad."

"Crap, John. I was a complete disgrace and you know it. Christ's sake, boy, I threw up all over the pavlova."

"Oh, you remember then?"

"Of course I remember. And that poor woman, how could I insult her like that? What must she think of me? What must they all think of me? I should be shot at dawn."

John briefly gazed up at the sky. "Bit late for that, Mother, the sun's already up."

"Very funny, John."

"The girls will understand."

"I've told you before, I can't stand being patronised." She painfully rearranged herself. "They'll hold it against me you know, and who could blame them. I'm just a stuck-up old bitch and my head hurts, so if you've nothing good to say I suggest you go away, I'm in no mood for any of your hollow sympathy." Her head lifted a fraction then dropped back. "Just go."

"Very well, Mother, but I hope you feel better soon." He started to turn, trying to make out that his only reason for visiting wasn't just for selfish gain. "Oh, there was just one other thing."

"What is it now?"

"Can I borrow your bike? Only Sadie wants to do a bit of cycling while she's here and as it's such a nice day it would be a shame to waste it."

Her hand fumbled for the juice. "Take the wretched thing and leave me in peace."

"Thank you, Mother, I'll come and see you later shall I?"

"If you must. Now go."

*

"You can ride, can't you?" John looked on as Sadie tried to cock her leg over a saddle the size of a giant tortoise.

"It's this damn dress," she replied.

Tony was standing at the rear firmly holding the wheel between her legs while Susan gripped the handlebars. In sheer frustration Sadie lifted her frock up around her waist and flashed rather too much red underwear.

"That'll scare the pigeons away." John's grin stretched across his face.

"Oh, hilarious, think you can do any better?"

"No, just saying. Try and touch the ground with your toes." She looked utterly bewildered as she tried to balance on the seat, eyes watering, fearing her buttocks would never close up again. "I can't even reach the pedals, let alone the ground. It's no good, I can't ride the damn thing as it is." She wobbled about, hands attempting to grip anything that wasn't moving.

"Just give it a go. You never know, you might get used to it after a while."

"No, John, I can't reach the bloody pedals. Look!" A stretched out foot instantly showed him what they were up against. "See?"

"Okay, off you get, I'll have to lower the saddle. That should do the trick."

With some discomfort Sadie slid to the ground. "Me arse feels like someone's rammed a fence post up it and it's still got barbed wire connected." She looked at the others. "Yes, go on, laugh. I tell you the best place for that bloody thing is on the scrap heap."

John grabbed the offending article and headed towards the workshop. "Won't be a tick." He could still hear the girls' laughter as he reached the barn.

Like innocent young teenagers they sat cross-legged making daisy chains while listening to distant swear words concerning a bloody-minded stubborn saddle. Tony had noticed a sudden change in their friend's mood and perhaps it was the trick of the light but she was sure a tear or two had formed at the corners of the woman's eyes.

"It's lovely here," Sadie announced. "Just like when I was young. Of course it was nothing as grand as this, but us kids thought it was the best place in the world." They saw her body sag under the hidden pressures of life. "Now look at me."

The two girls sat silently, allowing the woman to offload her troubles. "What have I to go back to?" She wiped a moistened eye trying not to show any emotion. "I'll tell you, shall I? Some smelly one-bedroom flat, that's what, where sodding kids find it funny to piss outside your front door and drunks think they can do what they like to you for twenty pounds," she sobbed, her lip curling in disgust. "I wonder sometimes how the hell I got to where I am now."

Tony placed a hand on her shoulder. "It'll be fine, something will work out for the best, I've got a good feeling."

"Feelings are all very well, love, but rarely get you anywhere. It's all right for you girls, you've still got youth and look at me, I have to take what's left and it isn't usually very pretty. Men can be bastards sometimes."

Susan rolled onto her back and gazed up at the sky. "But you're gay, why put up with men?"

"Beggars can't be choosers, that's what my old dad used to say and hell he was right. So that's about the sum of it, my life in a cracked nutshell, but when Tony rang and explained what John had in mind I thought to myself, why not? This may be my way out, play me cards right and I could even get permanently hooked up with this Lizzie character. Let's face it, anything is better than what I've got now."

Their conversation broke as John trundled back. "All fixed, only one grazed knuckle. So what do you reckon, ladies?" He stood beside his efforts waiting to be congratulated.

"It looks too low now." Sadie wasn't one to mince words as she studied the new height, but could see John's ego was slightly dented. "Sorry, it does look a little low, but not to worry, never the one to turn away from a challenge, that's me. So just for you I'll give it a go."

They watched on as a rather inexperienced woman attempted to ride a bike that looked like it should be used by a performing clown at the circus.

"It's definitely too low, John." Her distant voice floated across the gardens as she narrowly missed Kim who was stretched out under a tree and was now wondering what on earth was going on. Unfortunately a sleeping Jack Russell caught a direct hit, sending the bike careening across the lawns where it ended up in a woody shrub.

"Keep trying," John shouted.

Not what Sadie wanted to hear. "Keep bloody trying! It's okay for you lot stood laughing at me." A sudden unwelcome thought of urine-infested alleyways spurred her to jump back on. "Don't worry, I'll get there." With her legs almost knocking her teeth, she pedalled for her life.

"That's the way to go!"

She knew it wasn't impressive by any stretch of the imagination, but John needed to be impressed. With speeds that made her eyes water she gradually gained confidence.

"You look the part now, Sadie," John shouted.

Susan discreetly turned her head and gave Tony a cheeky grin. "I think a certain Mr Taylor is starting to like our Sadie."

"What was that?" John, just out of earshot only managed to catch part of what was said.

Susan looked up against the bright sunlight, unable to see the face of the man she had just spoken about, his whole presence framed within a blue background. "I was just saying how nimble our Sadie looks."

"Yes, she's doing great," he replied, pulling a spanner from his back pocket and waving it in Sadie's direction. "What is it they say? Never judge a book by its cover!" The sound of screeching brakes brought their conversation to an end as John lost all thought of what he'd just said. "Off you get and I'll bring her up a bit." He deliberately peered at Sadie's bottom. "It's a lot to ask, but I think she'll take it."

"Cheeky bugger! You're all the same, want me to show a bit more knicker elastic, do you?"

"Couldn't be responsible for my actions if you did."

"I'll stick to scaring pigeons then, shall I?"

The girls were well aware of what Sadie was up to. Her desire to change her life showed in all she did and they knew that if you dealt with men as much as they did it was easy to play the game. Correctly executed, you could happily lead a man to water and made him drink.

Sadie shot off at speed, sending the dogs scurrying towards the safety of the barn. "It's much easier to ride now, John." With confidence rising, a convincing wave managed to leave the handlebars as she cycled the whole length of the drive and back, eventually coming to an abrupt halt next to John's feet.

"I think you're ready." John looked at the woman he'd placed his faith in, a woman with her skirt wrapped around her hips showing off a light touch of ruby red underwear. Was he worried? No. Did he question his own sanity? Yes. He smiled.

*

It was late afternoon and John had sent out undercover scouts to verify Lizzie's whereabouts; it would be pointless sending Sadie out on the road if their target wasn't there. The two girls had managed to climb Clay Hill, the highest point in the valley, a hill so ideally placed it gave uncompromising views of back lane snaking its way through open countryside. Armed with an oversized lump of 1940s binoculars they nestled themselves on flower-rich grassland and waited. Lizzie's roadside retreat had been described in detail, and true to John's word a large towering oak stood on a bend in the road with afternoon sun casting a shadow far beyond its thick heavy canopy. It was hard to be sure from a distance, but with the help of the binoculars they were confident Lizzie wasn't as yet present.

A good hour or so later the only point of interest was in the shape of two young lovers clearly out for a passionate afternoon snog. Susan, out of sheer boredom, followed their progress as they discreetly parked a little way along the lane and now sat hidden from passers-by but in full view of their hilltop position. She focused intently on the rampant intimacy that happened to be evolving before her very eyes. Tony had refrained from such peeping tom antics and instead chose to keep her attention solely on the job in hand, but much to her annoyance was now compelled to listen to a running commentary.

"Oh no, I wouldn't do it like that! What is she doing?"

"Really, Susan."

"What?"

Tony briefly took her eyes off the lane below. "Don't you get enough of that sort of thing?"

"Nothing else to do. I admit it could be classed as a poor man's country porn, but it's something to do.

Anyway, it looks like they're finishing, hardly worth the petrol getting out here from what I could see." She placed the binoculars to one side. "You ever done it in a car?"

"Once, my first ever boyfriend. He had a Robin Reliant."

"What's that?"

"You really don't want to know. What about you?"

"No, just doesn't look comfortable."

"It isn't, believe me."

The lovebirds could be seen driving back the way they came. "I'm bored." Susan perked up. "We've been here over an hour now, perhaps she isn't coming today."

"John said she always comes, we'll give it a little longer," suggested Tony. Susan sighed in protest as she lay back, allowing the feather-light grasses to wave around her body.

"Too much countryside is bad for your health, you know."

Tony gazed at her friend with surprise. "I thought you liked it here."

"I do, most of the time." She rolled over and rested her head upon a supporting hand. "But you, on the other hand, are a real country girl."

Tony looked away and up at the sky that seemingly engulfed their simple hilltop existence. "This is home, I love it here, have done since 1 was a child. I've always fantasised living in the Taylors' farmhouse and working in the country. It just has something, I don't know what."

"And John!" Susan's remark didn't take Tony by surprise as she sat agonising over what to say next. "Oh dear, your silence says it all."

"There she is."

"Who?"

"Lizzie of course, or have you forgotten what we're here for?"

"But Tony."

"Not now."

The moment was lost as the two of them spotted a lone figure barely visible in the shadows standing perfectly still, partially shaded by the darkened overhang of the great oak. Susan felt a shiver run across her entire body. "Spooky. Do you think that's her?"

Tony grabbed the binoculars. "It must be, who else could it be?"

"It's giving me the creeps, I don't like this."

"She's just a woman standing under a tree, you're letting that imagination run away with you. Sort yourself out."

"I don't know."

"Cut it out, you're like a scared little kid."

"Fine by me. Come on, I'm going, suddenly this job doesn't seem very appealing."

To Susan's relief they started back down only to be confronted by a dark solitary figure standing near the bottom of the hill. It was impossible to tell who it was – even with binoculars the bright light of the day gave little away. Susan suddenly realised after a second look that the figure had vanished. "Oh god, she's come to murder us!" she wailed in a state of panic.

"What is wrong with you? It's Sunday afternoon, the countryside's riddled with footpaths,
it's probably just someone out for a walk."

"You said probably, so you're not convinced. Oh Tony, I don't like this, I'm too young to die."

"Will you please pull yourself together? No one's going to hurt you."

Susan suddenly let out an ear-piercing scream. "There!" She pointed to an unknown person moving slowly across the intermittent gaps in the hedgerow. "We're going to die, be murdered and buried in a shallow grave, it'll be years before anyone finds us."

"Stop it!"

"Don't leave me."

"I'm not going to leave you, as much as I would like to. Now come on."

Susan's eyes constantly darted all over the place. "Where is she? Where's she gone?"

"How do I know? Be quiet! I've had enough." Tony stormed ahead, somehow trying to distance herself from such negative thoughts.

Susan hurried behind, constantly looking over her shoulder, stumbling as she went. She saw Tony trying to pull further away but was having none of it. "We must stick together or she'll pick us off one by one."

That's it, Tony thought, her arms up in the air in annoyance. "You've seriously lost it, Susan." She felt a nudge from behind.

"Let me go in front. I watched this film where they walked through the jungle and every so often a hand would grasp the poor soul at the back and no one even knew, it was so silent."

Tony stopped and faced her so-called friend. "You do realise if she's set a trap you'll be the first to cop it?"

Silence fell. "I'll take my chances, let me by." Head down, Susan marched on and almost instantly collided with a hunched effigy. A curdling scream echoed around the valley as she came face to face with George. With a heart threatening to explode at any minute she tried to pull herself up to his height. "What the hell. George? You nearly made me wet myself."

"Begging your pardon, miss, but this be what we do every Sunday. Me and the missus, see, we always go for a walk."

"Sorry George." Tony attempted to look apologetic concerning Susan's behaviour. "I'm afraid my dear friend here isn't herself today."

"My fault, miss, 'twasn't intentional, I can assure you."

"Course not, George. Take no notice of Susan, she's just been watching too many late-night films, that's all."

George took a sideways glance at the young lady in question. "Been to the cinema have you, miss?"

"Sorry?"

"Films, miss?"

Tony saw Susan hadn't a clue what he was on about. "Something like that, George, yes."

They all stood for a moment not really knowing what to do next until Tony peered down the path from which George must have come. "So where's your wife, George?"

"Ah, she be along in a minute, always complaining I walk too fast. Can't be having all that moaning, ruins a good afternoon stroll. I'll be home before she shows up."

Tony looked at the old man who showed little signs of exhaustion. "So you don't actually walk together then?"

"No, miss, not done for a good ten years or more, she be a bit like an old walrus with a twisted ankle."

His description of his poor dear wife somehow lightened the situation to a point where both the girls found it hard not to giggle. "Well it's nice to see you again, George, and give our regards to your wife, that's if we don't bump into her in a minute," said Tony.

"Will do. Be seeing you tomorrow, I'm sure."

"Yes, George, tomorrow. Bye for now."

He raised his hand to a waiting cap. "Ladies."

The girls walked into the yard and almost bumped into Sadie strolling out of the farm buildings, kitted out in an oversized check shirt, faded jeans and ankle-length wellies.

"What have you been up to?" Susan looked the woman up and down with curiosity.

"Been helping John milk the cows. I tell you, it brings back some memories. Mum and Dad used to have a couple of house cows. John's just coming."

He appeared smiling as if he'd won the lottery.

"You look pleased with yourself." Tony couldn't help notice a slight twinkle in his eyes.

"Do I? I suppose it's just nice to have a bit of company in the milking parlour, that's all."

"I see Sadie's becoming quite useful then."

John was a little slow on one or two things but he wasn't a fool – he knew what Tony meant so decided to change the subject. "Well, is she there?"

"Yes, we think so, having never seen Lizzie before, but there's definitely a lone figure standing exactly where you said."

John rubbed his hands. "That'll be her all right. Sadie,

quickly go and get changed, me and the girls will discreetly go and pick some of Mother's flowers. Sam reckons Lizzie and Jane always had flowers around the house, a little sweetener you might say."

Twenty minutes later Sadie stepped out of the house wearing Sam's chosen dress, her hair bundled together at the back by a bright yellow ribbon and the wellies ditched for more fashionable practical footwear. Riding a bike in high heels would have certainly been a step too far. John looked on as she came down the garden path. He still thought she was rather plain but to her credit she had come a long way from that unkempt, smelly individual who had turned up a mere day before and it pleased him that in the short time they'd known each other a comfortable relationship had developed. You still needed to be wary of her nature and it was obvious to those who spent any time around her that life hadn't dealt her the best hand. As the girls pointed out, she had a heart of gold, it just needed the chance to shine, and as much as people thought he was somewhat naive on certain points, he was no fool. She was playing him for her own gain and he knew that. And why not? Wasn't he too running with this idea of his for his own future? He glanced at her smiling face. He could see she enjoyed being here much like the others, but he hadn't really thought about having another woman around the place. Two working girls he could just about handle, but three? And he couldn't forget Tick, the elusive blood-sucking parasite of the woods. "You look great, Sadie."

"Thanks, John." A quick twirl of the dress showed her

absolute delight at being appreciated. "Not bad for an old tart," she replied, revealing a glimpse of her underwear.

"Very nice," he said, averting his eyes.

Sam watched from the back door, listening with growing envy to the laughter assaulting her ears. A wave of sadness brushed across her face forcing her to look away. She paused then headed back into the kitchen. Like so many other days on the farm she found herself back at the sink, her hands gently playing with the soapy bubbles. It felt good to have so much life about the place, yet she didn't feel right. Her hands disappeared beneath the water. Yes, it was right for a big house like this to be spoiled by so much energy and she'd wished they'd had more children, but that decision had been cruelly taken away for reasons no one will ever know other than the human body was a complex lump of existence.

"Now, Sadie, you know what you've got to do?"

"Yes, John."

"Are you sure? We can go over it again if you want?"

A look of defiance told him to back off. "I'll be fine, stop worrying. I'm damn sure I've come up against a lot worse."

"Good. Right, so here are the flowers and be sure to mention you're good friends of ours and you're staying at the farm for a while, it'll explain your presence a bit better. Whether it helps at all is a different matter entirely, she's bound to ask questions, but just try and get her confidence, pull her in and stop her from talking to anyone."

"Yes, John, we've already gone over this ten times before. Calm down, I know what I'm doing. Believe me, by the time I've finished with her she'll be licking my fanny."

The thought made John's Adams apple rise and fall. "You have such a way with words, Sadie, I'll give you that. Now, you know which way to go?"

"John."

"Only asking."

"Right, give us twenty minutes or so, then take off. We'll be watching from the top of the hill."

"Hang on a minute." Susan's voice sounded rather too sharp for John's liking. "We haven't got to climb that hill again, have we?" She stamped her foot in protest.

"That's enough." Tony really couldn't put up with any more of Susan's childlike behaviour. "Why don't you do us all a favour and stay here, have a rest, paint your nails or something."

"Sounds fine by me. Perhaps I'll have a long hot soak in the bath, my feet are killing me."

"Excellent idea, as long as you're happy, we're happy."

Susan turned without saying another word and headed into the house.

The two spies had only just managed to reach the top when Sadie was spotted cycling down the lane. "Good, there she is," puffed John, pointing to the valley below.

"You're out of condition, old man, especially for someone who works outside all the time. You surprise me."

"I'm a farmer, not a mountain goat! Besides, we're not here to talk about my health. Pass me the binoculars." His first attempt at locating anything of interest failed miserably as he somehow set his sights on a distant faraway clump of trees in the middle of a large field.

"Bird-watching, are you?" Tony looked amused as the angle of the lens indicated John's total lack of direction. "I think it would help if you tilted them down a fraction – not trying to tell you how to use your own binoculars, you understand, but I think the action's down there!"

"You don't say." Finally John locked on to his intended target who was now travelling at some speed and was desperately trying to cling on to a wavering bunch of carnations.

"What's she up to?" He paused for a moment, taking in the scene before him. "Oh dear, it's not looking good, she's wobbling out of control and far too fast for the bend. She needs to slow down." Sadie was cycling to and fro across the lane, her skirt billowing against the prevailing wind while she desperately tried to grip on for dear life. "Slow down, you fool. God, I can't watch, she's just going too fast."

Tony calmly shook her head. "No she's not, can't you see she's doing exactly what you asked her to do?"

"I don't understand."

"No, because you're a man, that's why, you only see the obvious. She's acting, John, making out the bike's out of control. She's not daft, you know."

"I never implied otherwise, but if that's acting then she's making a damn good job of it because there's a dirty great milk tanker coming the opposite way. Now we'll see who's playing to the audience." They heard a loud blast from the oncoming lorry. "I'm not sure I want to watch."

Tony grabbed the binoculars in time to see Sadie career off into the long grass verge, her wheels channelling along an unseen rut, limbs flailing in all directions. The seemingly unconcerned lorry trundled on, leaving Sadie sprawled on the grass looking decidedly deflated. "Oh no, she's gone down."

"Not so much acting now, hey!"

"Shut up, John, this is serious." In a blind panic Tony went to get up, her intention to go and help.

"No, don't." John gripped her arm to stop her.

"John! We need to do something." Her desperation was met with a determined shake of the head.

"No, we can't, it'll ruin everything. Give me the binoculars." Tony was torn between doing what she thought was best or obeying orders.

For a moment John thought she was going to throw them at him. "Please." He held out his hand as she stared into his very soul. "Thank you."

Carefully raising them to his eyes he scanned the area for life. "She's all right, she's sitting up." He handed the binoculars back to Tony, hoping this small gesture would restore the peace. "Just give it a few more minutes, that's all I'm asking."

Tony stayed silent, her only concern for a woman who had yet again been used by a man for his own means. Perhaps that was too harsh, she needed to remember it was her suggestion that Sadie became involved. She'd had her own reasons for helping her out, knowing full well that she herself could end up being that woman. She peered down at the fence line below and immediately spotted Lizzie helping her friend to her feet.

John couldn't hold his curiosity any longer. "Well? What's happening?"

"Look for yourself." In his haste he almost snatched the binoculars from Tony's eyes.

"All right, calm down."

A brief silence fell as John finally locked on to what was going on. "Oh, this is perfect. Lizzie's got her arm around Sadie's waist. We couldn't have planned it any better."

"John! She could have been badly hurt and all you're worried about is your damn plan."

"Yes, but she wasn't hurt, was she?"

"We don't know that, do we? It's hard to tell from all the way up here."

He trained his vision back to the ongoing proceedings. "She's walking about – good enough for you? Anyway, one or two cuts and bruises could be a good thing – Lizzie's more likely to take pity." Tony could almost see him patting himself on the back. "This is working out brilliantly."

"Really, John, is that all we are to you? Just part of your major plan? Never mind we could possibly have feelings, oh no." She grabbed a handful of grass and tossed it into his face.

"Tony, I didn't mean it like that. You know very well this has to work, not just for me but for everyone's sakes. If we get found out we're all in trouble and you'll be back on the street. I'm sorry, I didn't mean that the way it came out, it's just everything's working so well at the moment and ..."

"And what, John?" She looked him straight in the eye. "Well?"

"And I like having you and Susan around." He paused for a moment, afraid of what he was about to confess. "And especially you."

Tony reached out and took his hand. "Go on," she said. It was clear John wanted to say more.

"I don't quite know how to put this, but you've brought something special back to the farm and I want it to continue." There was a sincerity in his voice that told her John meant every word. She knew men and it would have been difficult for the male of the species to put such emotion into words if they hadn't come from the heart.

She shuffled closer and pulled him towards her. John's body trembled beneath the weight of his self-imposed guilt. This shouldn't be happening, he thought, but nothing really mattered any more. The farm. Sam. No, not even her. He was powerless to stop what he hoped Tony would do next.

With the utmost care their lips met, and a soft warm feeling flowed through his body. She was so young, he longed for it to go on forever but then she pulled away, picked up the binoculars and focused them down towards the lane. John raised a finger to his lips and sat in silence. He was confused but relieved at what had just happened. The morals, right or wrong of the matter didn't come into it, yet he had to keep telling himself it was just a kiss.

"She seems to be walking around all right." Tony's words shattered John's thoughts.

"That's good." He wasn't sure what else to say.

"And the bike doesn't look too bad."

"Tony?"

She lowered the binoculars for a brief moment and glanced at him. "It's all right, John, I wanted it to happen."

John was even more confused. Perhaps that's how these women worked, he thought, playing with a man's emotions with no particular meaning to it, and he'd just become one of her victims. He slowly pulled himself out of his complex mind and looked upon the girl he had now fallen in love with.

"What's happening now?" he asked.

"You won't believe it."

"I might if you let me have my binoculars back."

"Later. This is far too interesting. Our Sadie's just put her arm around Lizzie's waist. No, hang on, she's backed off."

John was almost tempted to stand up and scream at every female in the valley, 'What's wrong with you women!' "Why doesn't she just get on with it instead of playing around?" He wasn't sure who he was aiming his comments at, but he just needed to get them off his chest.

Tony shook her head. "You don't have an ounce of romance in you, do you, John? These things take time. Wait. She might be going to do something ... and ... no."

"Oh, for pity's sake!" Tony felt a deliberate huff very close to her ear.

"Now they've put the bike in the bushes and they're starting to walk away."

"Damn and blast, Tony, enough is enough. Hand me my ruddy binoculars back."

She ever so slowly peeled them away from her eyes and handed them to their rightful owner just as the two women disappeared into the trees.

"Great! Now they're gone."

Chapter 24

It was a Monday morning and the last of the cows were wandering down the track, their lumbering forms ploughing through unsettled dust, heads lowered, tails swishing, biting flies that dared to latch onto their body heat. John watched for a moment, satisfied he'd done his best for them until they returned in the afternoon. With thoughts of a hearty breakfast he turned and walked straight into Josh who happened to be standing right behind him. "Whoa!" John's startled voice broke through the silence. "Josh, you all right? Didn't see you standing there."

"All right, Mr Taylor."

John peered at the lad who seemed unconcerned about the collision. "It's Monday, Josh, why aren't you at school? Not playing truant, I hope?"

"Na, one of them teacher training days, reckon some of them need it too. Mum told me to get lost. So here I am." He stood immobile, hoping or perhaps expecting some sort of encouraging reply, eyes searching the yard, willing John to offer him sanctuary for the day.

"Well, I must say it's nice to see you again – thought perhaps we'd put you off farming after chasing those cows halfway around the countryside."

"Na, had to look after me mum, broke her ankle the silly cow, been run ragged I have. Here and there and back again and all the time she sits on her fat arse eating takeaways and watching crappy daytime TV.

Damn near drove me mad, but she's up now so don't want me about the house, told me to lose meself for the day." He shrugged and scuffed the ground with his right foot, somehow warning John that he would probably have the pleasure of his company for the rest of the day whether he liked it or not.

"Okay, we'd better find you something to do. I'm about finished here, only the calves to feed so you can start with helping me carry the milk over to the barn." He was met by an eagerness to do just about anything asked, a simple look of willingness nudging John's thoughts back in time when he too longed for his father to give him a job on the farm. "Watch that calf at the end, it's a stubborn little rat, spent a good while yesterday trying to get it to drink. Gave up in the end, so it should be hungry this morning."

Josh seemed to take this as a personal challenge and went straight to the stubborn creature, an animal blessed with a look of cast-iron determination to foil any attempt at coercing it into drinking any form of liquid, yet a quick rub of the head saw it slowly show willing. John looked on as both boy and calf seemed to melt into one, the lad's body language telling of a national stockman in the making. Unsupervised, he'd managed to master the art of coaxing the happy-go-lucky baby to its warm milk using only his fingertips, and as if the animal was responding to an unspoken command to obey, it started to drink.

"I'll leave you to it for a minute, need to get some more milk." John had barely turned away when he was stopped by the sound that he himself had unfortunately experienced in his younger days. He turned back just in time to see the contents of the bucket shoot up in the air by an impressive calf head butt that any inner-city gang leader would be proud of. Milk dripped down the faces of boy and calf. John held back a light chuckle; it wouldn't do to gloat, he thought. "Never mind, Josh, it happens to the best of us. I'll go and get a bit more milk and then I think you'd better come indoors and get cleaned up."

"Sam, look what's appeared on the doorstep."

She wiped her hands on her pinny as their newly acquired apprentice walked into her kitchen. "Josh. Oh, been feeding the calves, I see. And why are you not at school, young man?"

The boy stood silent, his senses bombarded by the savoury aromas drifting across the room, the dried milk splatters still clinging to his face.

"He's got a teacher training day apparently."

"Has he? So you've come to help John for the day have you, Josh?"

The boy unwillingly looked away from the steamy delights and turned to Sam. "Yup."

"Umm, not like that, you're not. Off you go and get washed up, otherwise you'll stink to high heaven." Sam pointed to the boot room facilities.

"But I done me hands, Mrs Taylor."

"Not good enough, my boy. You just take a look at your face in the mirror."

She waited until he had gone and immediately turned

to face her ever forgetful husband. "You do realise you've got a fête meeting at eleven?"

"Damn, I forgot about that."

"And you know you can't just let Josh wander about the farm unsupervised, it's too dangerous. Perhaps he could help George until you get back?"

"Good idea. Wondered why I married you."

"Ah, Josh, slight problem. I've got a meeting this morning so how about a spot of gardening?" John saw disappointment on the lad's face but knew Sam was right, gardening was a much safer option and George, although old and a little slow was a good teacher when it came to all things horticultural. "Tell you what, Josh, a good plate of food first and then gardening, how does that sound?"

Begrudgingly the deal was accepted. "Unless of course you've already eaten?"

"No, I ain't."

"Now sit yourself down and we'll see what's spare." Sam knew she always had a bit left over.

"That would be real nice."

Sam returned, purposefully hovering the plate under a wondering nose. "And?"

"Ta, Mrs Taylor."

"Very good, Josh. Now we've taught you some manners you can have your food." The odd leftovers had somehow transformed into a meaningful amount for any budding young farmer, causing his eyes to pop out of his head.

"Bloody ..! I means it looks nice."

"Quite, Josh." She stood back and waited in hope. After the boy's last attempt at eating she wasn't expecting too much, but to her surprise he seemed to be doing all the right things. "I see you've been practising your knife and fork skills, Josh."

Barely coming up for air, he explained. "Told me mum she had to start using them, course the old cow couldn't argue being laid up and all. Fish and chips is all right. Burgers not too bad, but sausages! They be right slippery buggers and Chinese, well, you've got sod all hope."

"Josh! You were doing so well."

"Sorry, Mrs Taylor."

"I should think so too, but nevertheless I'm impressed with your table manners, apart from the language. Well done." Sam looked around as Tony wandered in, bleary-eyed and in a state of partial undress as she stood in the doorway, her tightly fitted shorts stretching around the contours of her lower half while a loose cotton shirt did little to conceal a braless upper body. "Ah, there you are."

"Morning, everyone."

Josh briefly stopped eating and sat staring.

"And who's this young man?"

"This is Josh, he's from the village," Sam announced.

"He's come to give John a hand for the day; we're trying to make a farmer of him."

"Morning, Josh."

For a moment the room lay silent as he eyed the girl in front of him. "Real pretty, you are," he said, then carried on eating.

"Right, well thank you, Josh." She gave Sam a curious look before making her way across the room, Susan following behind.

"Morning, everyone."

Josh cast his eye upon yet another good-looking female.

"This is Josh, Susan."

"Morning, Josh."

"You're real pretty too," he replied, before tucking back into his food.

"Okay." She pulled up a chair and sat down, hoping Tony would make her a hot drink. "Coffee would be nice."

"Would it?"

"Just one sugar."

"Ah, Sadie, there you are." Everyone watched as she marched in wearing a red blouse and large baggy bright yellow shorts that did nothing to hide a number of bulging varicose veins, their weaving tracks sneaking down her right leg like an Ordnance Survey map.

"Hello, young man." Her fingers shot out and ran through his hair, giving the boy little chance to protest. John could see he was going to open his mouth and say something that may not be acceptable within his wife's kitchen.

"Josh, all finished? Good man." John quickly rose from his chair. "I think it's time we went." Before the boy had a chance to say something unpleasant, John interrupted. "Back garden, Josh. I'll be out in a minute then we'll see if I can find George, he can't be too far away."

The boy pulled himself out of his chair looking none too pleased and started to make for the back passage. "Ah, Josh," Sam called out as he passed by. "Forgotten something?" He glanced back at his chair expecting to see a mislaid object or perhaps an item of clothing, but there seemed little clue as to Mrs Taylor's concern.

"Don't reckon so, Mrs Taylor."

Arms crossed over her ample breasts, Sam stood her ground, willing him to think. "You sure?" A shrug of the shoulders warned her not to expect too much.

"Don't know, Mrs Taylor."

"A thank you would be nice, don't you think?"

"Oh right, sorry, Mrs Taylor. Thanks, tasty bit of grub."

"Umm, I suppose that'll have to do."

Minutes later they heard the back door slam shut. Susan took a sip of her coffee. "You've got a right one there."

"Oh he's not that bad really, just needs a bit of training, that's all."

"Right."

John turned and looked at Sadie, wanting to know of any progress with Lizzie. "Clearly no broken bones then."

"Well I'm glad you're so concerned, and no, just my pride and one buckled wheel."

"So how did you get on with our Lizzie? I'm dying to know."

"John?" Sam's voice interrupted any further questioning, her finger pointing out towards the garden. "You might like to see this." She'd spotted Josh waist-high in a sea of early summer blooms, his hands gently brushing across their delicate heads.

"What is it?"

"Look."

John made his way across the room and peered out of the window, followed by the girls who clambered for a position. "Well, will you look at that? Now you see, girls, there is hope even with the roughest ones."

"But he's trampling on your mother's flowers. I wouldn't say the word hope springs to mind." Susan couldn't quite understand what John was getting at. They stood in silence for a moment, taking in the scene. "Nope, still don't get it."

Sam was just about to say something when she felt a

comforting hand gently touch her waist, channelling a warm glow through her entire body. She was conscious that Susan was standing directly behind her, but surely … She suddenly realised it was John's hand resting and cursed herself for even thinking or wanting it to be anything else. She turned her attention back to Josh, who was running his fingers through each flower in turn, seemingly exploring every possible texture before lowering his head and indulging in their heavenly scents. "Do you think he's all right?" Her whisper met an understanding nod.

"He'll be fine," John replied. "But I'd better go and explain a few things. Leave it to me."

"I still don't get it?"

Sam turned around and came face to face with the young woman she had become extremely fond of. "You will one day."

"Well I think it's lovely." Tony went to move away. "I get him completely."

Sadie had sided with Susan and with her matter-of-fact approach to life saw only a naughty misfit in someone else's lovely well-tended borders. "Tell him to sling his hook, John, he needs to be taught a lesson. If I had done that sort of thing when I was his age, Dad would have taken the belt to me."

Sam looked at her in horror. "Sadie, that's a terrible thing to suggest."

"I didn't mean the belt for him, but it wouldn't do him any harm as far as I can see. But times have changed," she continued. "Too soft nowadays, if you ask me." She was happy with her own observation and if the others had a problem seeing the bigger picture, so be it.

John slid his boots on and made his way outside. Josh was still standing in the flowers, his eyes glistening with emotion. The man paused; perhaps it was best to allow the boy his moment of discovery to take its course. John could see Josh was in a world of his own and as such surely no one had the right to break that bond between boy and nature.

"Mr Taylor, sorry." A look of worry gripped the boy's face.

"For what, Josh?"

"Flowers, Mr Taylor. I ain't damaged any." As he spoke he gingerly made his way out onto the lawn, taking the utmost care not to tread on a single stem. "I ain't done no harm, I was real careful, honest." A grubby sleeve quickly wiped away moistened eyes. "Don't know wot came over me, Mr Taylor."

"I do."

"You do?"

"Yes, Josh."

"And what be that then, Mr Taylor?"

"All this, Josh." John waved his arms around in the air. "All this."

"Wot you on about?"

"Nature, Josh. The flowers, the trees, the birds, and

let's not forget the insects, oh no. Can't you see, Josh, we live in such a wonderful world but without all this we as humans would be nothing. Nothing, Josh."

"If you say so, Mr Taylor."

"I do, Josh." With a steady hand John gently persuaded a wandering ladybird to rest upon his finger and with care placed it in front of the boy's face. They both watched as it spread out its wings and flew off. "Nature, Josh."

"You all right, Mr Taylor?"

"Never better, Josh, and let me tell you something else. You, my boy, have it. It's a rare thing indeed but you've definitely got it."

"Got wot, Mr Taylor?"

"*It*. You either have it or you don't, and you can't teach it, oh no, but you have it."

"You really all right, Mr Taylor?"

"One day, Josh, when you're older, it'll suddenly hit you and then you'll remember this day."

"If you say so."

"I do, Josh, and I'm so pleased for you because it's the best gift anyone can have." John stood for a while simply gazing into space. "Well, this isn't getting the work done. Now, I wonder where George has got to. Follow me." Their march took them back past the kitchen window, John storming ahead leaving Josh to ponder over what had just happened. His thoughts were suddenly interrupted by a voice calling out from the house.

"All right, Josh?" Sam was at the sink, her hands once again submerged within the hot soapy bubbles of yet more washing up.

"He's gone mad, Mrs Taylor."

"Who's gone mad?"

"Mr Taylor. Gone completely loopy, reckons I've got 'it' but I never asked for 'it' and I'm damn sure I don't want 'it'. Freaking me out, he is."

"Oh don't worry, Josh, rambling on about the birds and the bees, was he?"

"Something like that. Can't stop, he's buggered off somewhere."

"Josh, language!"

"Sorry Mrs Taylor."

"Don't worry, Josh, you'll get used to it," Sam called.

"It, Mrs Taylor? I wish someone would tell me what 'it' is. Mum don't like me bringing stuff home, bad for her chest." He slowly disappeared across the garden. "Bloody mad, the lot of you!"

"Language!"

A fading voice travelled back along the garden path. "Sorry Mrs Taylor."

*

"Ah, there you are, George." John finally tracked him down, working in his greenhouse. "Another beautiful day."

"'Tis, sir, you're right there."

"George. I was wondering if you'd mind looking after young Josh here for an hour or two, try and teach him some basics of gardening, let him get his hands dirty. Only till lunchtime."

The old man gazed at his approaching new apprentice with an eye of suspicion. "Not up to me either way, sir." He eyed the boy from a distance. "Here, ain't you Mollie's boy?"

"She's me mum."

"I, well, never mind, can't all be perfect."

"Is that all right, George?"

"I suppose so, sir."

It was clear the old man wasn't too pleased with the arrangement but John didn't have time to ask why. "That's fine then, just send him into the kitchen when you go for lunch. Sam will look after him from there."

George looked more than surprised. "He be eating with you then, sir? In the house?"

The man's concerns weren't entirely unexpected given the fact that John's mother never let him anywhere near the house. Such liberties were unheard of and even during the coldest of winter days she would quite happily let him freeze in the potting shed while her open fire roared away with the logs his cold aching bones had brought in that very day.

"Okay, excellent." John turned to leave the greenhouse sensing George wanted to say more, but it wasn't his place as an employee to disagree with orders, no matter how pleasantly John had tried to present them. Josh was left staring at the floor waiting for instructions from a man who clearly didn't want him and probably had little confidence in his ability to perform any sort of task correctly. "Oh, I almost forgot." John stopped and turned back. "Tony has a problem with one of her legs, apparently it's coming loose. I would do it myself, but I've got this meeting."

"One of her legs, you say, sir?" George gave the boy a discreet wink. "Always happy to help the young ladies out."

"Great. Apparently it needs to be done before this afternoon, she's got a photographer coming around later and they want to use the bed to bring out the best in the shot."

"Is that so, sir? Perhaps that's where me and the missus be going wrong as we only use ours for sleeping." John, mind elsewhere, totally missed George's humour. "Leave it to us, sir, dab hand at legs I be. We'll just finish this here planting and then me and Josh here will be on it."

"Good, I'll see you later then."

The two stood for a while, unwilling to break the silence until George pushed his hat back and scratched his head. "Better get on then, got me cabbage plants to put in before midday. 'Tis the moon you see, planting day today, no good this afternoon –

she be gone over with. Just like me missus, need to catch her right, one day out and you're buggered." Josh had started to wonder if they were all totally mad. "Oh well, reckon we'll get you started on marigolds, good safe job for someone like yourself, untrained and all. Can't go wrong with marigolds. You mess this up and there be no hope for you, ha."

Josh stood and waited for his instructions, his eyes wandering from one unfamiliar object to another. George was concentrating on filling small trays with some sort of dark brown substance.

"First lesson, lad," said George, lifting a single tray in front of the boy's nose. "What do you see? Use your eyes, it be the only way in this game. No books can teach you how to be observant."

He nervously reached his hand out and tilted it towards his face. "Dirt?"

George mumbled something under his breath. "*Compost*, it not be dirt. Feel it be like dirt to you?"

Josh hesitated for a moment and then poked a solitary finger into the soft material. It felt like nothing he'd ever handled before, allowing his senses to connect with something deep down inside him.

George could see something evolving in front of his eyes, reminding him of past years and of the thrill of himself connecting with nature. "Well, have you worked it out?"

The boy just nodded for they didn't need to say anything.

"Good lad, now we need to water them ready for the plants. Not too much mind, doesn't do to try and drown them." The old man handed over a watering can, showing the lad in as little movements as possible what he wished him to do. A smile formed across the elderly gentleman's face. "That's the way."

His voice, Josh thought, had changed, now a much more reassuring tone.

"Always look and learn, best way, and remember that goes for farming as well. Need to use your eyes before you do anything, might save your life one day. Always learning, even an old timer like me, that's what makes it so interesting. You can keep them office jobs, this be the real world."

"Okay, Mr George."

The old man continued to smile. "Mr George. I like that, lad. Bit of respect for your elders goes a long way in my book."

Josh moved over to the half empty bag of compost. "Com … com … pound?"

George could see the boy was having problems. "Compost. You see," he pointed to the side of the bag, "COM. POST. You'll get used to it. This be potting compost, just right for small plants like these." He held up a lonely seedling. "You remember its name?"

Josh hesitated for a moment, trying to think back to what he had been told earlier. "Mar … Maribold?"

"I, well, nearly right, they be marigolds."

"Marigolds, Mr George."

"See, learning already. Now let's see how good you are at pricking out." A comforting hand rested upon his shoulder. "Reckon we're going to get along just fine, nipper. Just fine."

Chapter 25

Susan placed her empty plate on the draining board just as Sam finished drying the men's breakfast things. "Oh just leave it there, I'll wash it up when the other two have finished."

"Are you sure? It doesn't seem right you doing all the cooking and washing. We can help, you know."

"I know, but really I enjoy it. Since Luke went away this place had started to get me down, but you've all brightened it up so much, it's like you're my family now."

Susan placed her arm around the older woman's waist. "Thanks."

Sam tried hopelessly to brush off the warm sensation threatening to run through her entire body. This was the second time today someone had put their arm around her. The first, she shamefully admitted, found her longing to be held by the arm that now felt so natural, but sadly she'd been disappointed. Yes, it was nice in a homely sort of way, but nowhere near the feeling she had at this exact moment. She stood perfectly still, wanting nothing more than to reach out and hold Susan's hand, fall into her arms and feel wanted. This is shameful! What was she thinking!

"Sadie, how did it go with Lizzie? You were about to tell John before I interrupted you." She needed to concentrate on something else, take her mind off the feeling that burned within her stomach. Susan moved her arm away, relieving her of some of that feeling, but she knew she would never be able to rid herself of it completely.

"Like I was telling the girls, it's early days yet. Perfect timing though, that truck coming around the corner like that. Scared the living daylights out of me, but it did the trick."

Tony was quiet. She'd been furious with John at the time, but here was Sadie saying the exact same thing. Perhaps she'd overreacted and needed to remind herself that Sadie and John were very alike in the way they looked at things. Much more down to earth, no shades in between, just black and white. Her vision was always slightly blurry, certainly not as bad as Susan but still not as clear-cut as the others.

Susan sat down, not particularly interested having heard most of the details already. She had time on her hands for once, her afternoon appointment having been called off leaving her free for the rest of the day. "Still gives me the creeps." Susan didn't have to say anything, but something inside her pushed the words out of her mouth.

"Don't start that again."

"Well, she does."

Sadie looked slightly amused at the girl's comment. "She's all right, she's really kind of sweet."

"You can get sour sweets, you know."

"Susan, you're impossible sometimes." Tony shook her head in frustration.

"Sorry, Sadie."

"Oh that's all right, but I have to say judging a person before you've got to know them isn't good practice in my book." She hoped it hadn't sounded too abrupt – the girl was, after all, still young and probably had a lot to learn about life. "I know I've only spent a short time with her but I reckon I'm a pretty good judge of character. Hell only knows I've seen enough bad ones in my time. Me husband being the worst, but no, she's not a bad one. Don't like the thought of tricking her, though, doesn't seem right, but if I tread carefully you never know, her duvet could be keeping us both warm this winter. She's got a lovely place, reminds me of our old farmhouse on the Moors. I could see myself pottering around that garden."

"Blimey, sounds like you've already moved in. Rather you than me."

Tony gave Susan another cautious glare. "Don't start."

"Just making a comment."

"Ignore her, Sadie, she's just jealous."

Sam kept out of it. This was what she enjoyed, a house full of people, a lively conversation. Silence did nothing for her.

Sadie rose from her chair. "So I'm off again this afternoon. If it's all right I'll have an early lunch, not sure when I'll be back, might even stay the night."

"Oh please, no more information."

"Susan!"

"That's all right, Tony, skin as tough as a rhino's backside and probably as good-looking, that's me."

"You put yourself down," replied Tony.

"Thanks, love, but we all know I'm not a patch on you two girls. Had me time and I wasn't that good then so a nice little cottage in the countryside with not a man in sight will do me fine. Sometimes it's the most unlikely of people who end up satisfied in life." She just couldn't help but look at Susan, unintentionally drawing the young woman down a peg or two as their eyes locked.

Susan's defeat was swift and sharp; she knew when to back off. "Then I wish you all the best, Sadie. Take no notice of my bitchiness." She knew the older woman had hit a tender spot – her life certainly wasn't a bed of roses. The other two could sense an uneasy truce had developed between beauty and brawn, but perhaps that was to be expected.

Tony pushed back her chair and went to leave. "Well, I've got to get on, my afternoon appointment can be quite demanding so I'd better be ready for him."

"I hope he doesn't treat you badly?" said Sam, with a look of concern.

"No, nothing like that, I wouldn't have him back if he did. No, he just likes things neat and tidy, that's all."

"Yes, well don't we all?" Sam replied.

"I know, but he takes it to the extreme, you can see why he's divorced. If he so much as finds a speck of dust he'll be out of that room before you can blink. I don't really like having him here, it's a farm after all."

"What are you saying? That my house is a pigsty?"

"No, of course not. I didn't mean it like that, but you really don't understand what he's like. This is a man who insists on hanging his clothes up when he undresses, knickers and all."

"Good grief, I have trouble peeling John's off he keeps them on so long!"

"Aren't men funny."

Sam still couldn't get used to the girls' way of life and what they came out with sometimes. She knew it wasn't her place to pry but this one sounded quite unusual. "So if he's that way minded, what's he like when he ... when ... when he's having sex?"

"Well that's the thing, he doesn't."

"What do you mean he doesn't?"

"Exactly what I'm saying, he likes to watch, there is no sex involved."

"I've got one like that," Susan interrupted. "Finds it a turn-on watching me undress while he plays with himself."

"Mine doesn't even do that, he's a stickler for hygiene so anything of that nature is quite out of the question. Far too messy."

Sam now looked totally confused. "So what does he do, then?"

"He gets his fix from watching me take my clothes off, then iron them. I have to do his as well, he hates creased clothes, just can't stand it."

"Lord have mercy. I've heard it all now." Sam almost dropped a soapy plate. "So he doesn't touch you in any way?"

"No, just watches me ironing the clothes."

"But surely he must do something, what's the point otherwise?"

"Beats me, but if he's prepared to pay, why should I argue?"

No one seemed to know what to say next.

"Well, I'd better go, got me an ironing board to oil up!"

The whole room erupted into uncontrollable laughter. Sadie was the first to calm down. "It's a joke, right? You're pulling our legs?"

Tony lifted her head and made for the door. "That's for me to know and you to wonder over. Either way I get paid well for it, so who cares. See you later," she sang, waving a dismissive hand as she left the room.

Sadie looked to the other two. "Well, this won't do, got things of my own to sort out. See you for an early lunch."

She disappeared through the open door leaving Sam tentatively looking at Susan. "And what are you going to do today, young lady?"

Susan sat staring into space. "Sorry?"

"I said, what are you going to do today? Miles away, weren't you?"

Susan sighed. "I was just thinking about life."

"Oh, that. You really must stop thinking too deeply, it's a far too complicated topic to ever try and work out. I'm just in my fifties and I can still hardly manage to figure it out on a daily basis, so you've got no hope." Sam paused. "It's a nice day, why don't you go for a walk? There are plenty of footpaths around about here, I'm sure I've got a map somewhere. It'll give you time to think – there's nothing like the solitude of the open countryside to reflect on life.

"Yes. I think I might. It was great fun when me and Tony went exploring." Her eyes brightened at the thought of being outside in the fresh air, so long as it was in a totally opposite direction to where that Lizzie character lived.

*

"My, my, look at you. Can I remind you that you're only going for a walk, not some fancy evening dance?"

"Do you like it?" Susan spun around, forcing the pastel shades to blur into one bellowing mass of material.

"Do I like it? How can I not, it's lovely, so 1940s if you don't mind me saying."

"Not at all. It's the new look, I bought it from one of those vintage online stores. I know it's not very practical for the great outdoors but I just had to wear it. I'll never get the chance otherwise. Do you like it, really?"

Sam could only gaze on. "You look absolutely gorgeous, I mean beautiful." She fumbled with her dishcloth. "I mean .." Their eyes met for a brief moment. "It's perfect, that's what I mean."

"Thank you."

"Don't thank me – you're the one they'll be whistling at." Sam paused, and as seconds slipped by their minds seemed to speak to each other as they both felt something special slowly float between them like a passing cloud. "Anyway, here's the map, so hopefully you won't get lost, and I've packed you a couple of things just in case that pretty little stomach of yours happens to get hungry. So off you go and find a nice spot to watch the world go by, and don't get too deep and meaningful, it's not good for your health."

Susan moved forward and gently brushed a light kiss on Sam's cheek. "What would I do without you?"

"Never mind that. Now off with you, and remember to stay on the footpaths, some of the landowners are not as friendly as we are. So shoo, out of my kitchen, I've got work to do."

Susan strolled out of the yard, the light fabric of her dress gently brushing against her skin as a cool breeze fought the warming sun. A steady walk took her down the lane to a signed pathway. Lifting her dress, she climbed over the wooden stile and found herself standing within a small copse. The path snaked its way up a gentle incline, disappearing briefly before reappearing into what looked like an open field. She moved on at a leisurely pace. There was something about the countryside that demanded you took control of your life, the heart to beat only to sustain life, nothing more, allowing you to appreciate your surroundings.

She reached the far end and was rewarded with a patchwork of coloured fields – golds, browns and greens of all shades. She remembered the first time she'd viewed such beauty – it seemed so long ago when John picked her up from the station and she'd stared out of the Land Rover window, amazed at the ever-changing colours. According to the map, Tony had shown her most of the land resting on one side of the farm, but this area was yet to be explored. Left or right? She knew from past experience even this simple choice had the ability to lead your life into the most unexpected directions, and sometimes not necessarily to your advantage.

The long grass that hugged up against the woodland edge seemed to invite her to explore the wealth of life it supported. Brown butterflies clung to simple flower heads, their existence as fine as the stem they rested upon. She took a closer look – what at first glance seemed drab and uninteresting suddenly held her attention, a showering of finely patterned eyes adorning each wing. Barely noticeable, these marks competed to show through the shadows of the overhanging trees. Susan watched as they gripped onto their temporary home. The breeze buffeted against surrounding grasses yet somehow the delicate creatures weren't inclined to move on, but she knew that eventually they would tire of their solitary bloom and find other willing companions. Making a decision that she would let nature choose her next direction, she stood and waited. Such luxuries of wasting time amongst nature seemed of little consequence as she watched on for signs of movement. Then, to her delight, the breeze fell to a mere breath, allowing the warmth of the sun to rest upon the outstretched wings of her chosen subject. It hesitated briefly, taking full advantage of the calm air and took flight, fluttering a moment before heading off to the left. Susan's decision had been made. She followed on, allowing her butterfly to flitter about, itself undecided which way to head before finally landing on another unsuspecting flower.

"Thank you for that." Her whisper fell upon unconcerned wings as it carried on with its daily task of survival, unaware of the responsibility placed upon its tiny frame. Susan descended steadily, sloping fields stretched out either side with the odd small cluster of houses nestled in the valley far below. The open landscape put up little defence against the stiffness of a determined wind that took it upon itself to whip her dress up above her knees.

She'd been walking for a good half hour, but time was of no importance. Her lungs full of warm fresh air, any concerns towards her whereabouts seemed pointless. She was enjoying the solitude and had given up on taming her inflated dress, allowing it to rise and fall at will. "What the heck," she heard herself say. If a stray farmer caught a glimpse of her knickers then so be it. It would surely make interesting banter down at the pub. If anyone chose to believe them, it was of no concern to her.

Another decision was needed as she stood by the gate at the end of the footpath. It led onto a narrow lane, hardly used judging by the amount of grass growing through the cracks in its poorly laid tarmac. She looked about for another friendly butterfly – consulting the map would surely go against Mother Nature's wisdom and could only suck her afternoon adventure back into that organised world of prescribed routes, something she wasn't in the mood to do. That first butterfly had served her well, but now she needed a sign. Perhaps a sudden wind change, a distant sound of a wild animal, something to point her in the right direction, yet all seemed peaceful. Left or right, she wondered. Her eyes peered up then down the lane. Left. Yes, if only because it was downhill and her feet were beginning to ache. The latest fashion in shoes they might be, but country footwear they were not!

A short walk later she came across an overgrown track. If travelling past in a car, this neglected break in the hedgerow would have certainly been missed, but clearly someone or something had been using it, for a partially trodden trail could be seen leading to a clump of trees. They looked slightly out of place, standing amongst normal woodland varieties. This itself may not have encouraged her to take a look if it wasn't for the sight of one single little brown-winged friend, but perhaps this one had little interest in showing her the way. She couldn't help but smile, for it was all nonsense, there must be a thousand and one of their kind flitting about on a warm and pleasant day such as today, but it was fun to be allowed to play with your imagination. So she would once again trust the unknown guidance of this perfectly formed little creature as it made its way up the path.

To her delight she was soon rewarded with the twists and turns of an overgrown fruit tree, its neglected branches seeking light at every given point. But she was more interested in the presence of a partially broken gate that told her this was more than a forgotten parcel of land. She remembered what Sam had told her – that not all landowners were as friendly as the Taylors, but what harm could it do? She hadn't met or seen a living soul since leaving, so why would she meet anyone now? A quick look down at her dress convinced her that it wasn't particularly well designed for scrabbling in the undergrowth, and now she wished she'd worn something else, but it was too late for that. With temptation seeping into her mind the thought of turning around and walking on by, quite frankly, seemed unthinkable. A light push of the gate saw little movement. She hesitated, unsure whether to proceed further; this was, after all, someone else's property. But a voice was telling her to ignore such trivial details, and so she pushed harder.

Her efforts were rewarded as the gate swung open. She'd walked a short distance when to her surprise the path opened out into what had clearly been a garden at some point. Still visible were the flower borders, with the more dominant species towering above thick green undergrowth, and yet for all its unruly appearance the whole place still had a heart, as if Mother Nature now controlled what was rightfully hers. Susan suddenly gasped at the sight of hundreds of little brown butterflies everywhere. Coincidence?. Nonsense, she told herself. And yet was it? She pushed on through the stems of seeding weeds, their heads bowing to the ongoing heat of the day, her weary feet walking on uneven cobblestones alive with a mass of living things. And then, as if framed within a tatty broken wooden surround, a tired white thatched cottage appeared at the end of the path, seemingly greeting her with open arms as it sat wrapped within a tangle of wild red roses.

Susan stopped, eyeing up the wooden archway seemingly hanging on for dear life, its timbers precariously held together by invasive woody branches. She stood back, not wanting to be seen. But surely no one was living here? Yet something was telling her to trust her instincts to have a peek. What harm would that do? she thought. Convinced she'd made the right decision, she slowly moved forward only to hear the front door send out a long creaking sound, forcing her to step back and find safety behind a large unruly bush. Her heart pounding, she crouched as low as her dress would allow. With her head slightly raised she watched as someone appeared from the dark interior, only fully showing themselves once in the open sunlight. A man, definitely a man, bent with old age as he left the door ajar and proceeded to puff up the pillows of a well-worn rocking chair. Susan looked on as he slowly rested a frail body into a comfortable position. She could hardly breathe; after being spooked by Lizzie's shadowy figure this was enough to send her screaming all the way back to the farm without stopping. But she was beginning to feel a little calmer – her heart had slowed to an acceptable level as her curiosity grew by the second.

Why should she be afraid? He was only an old man and by the looks of his body he was hardly in a position to chase after anyone. Strangely she could feel the warmth in his eyes as he sat, sometimes rocking, staring at nothing in particular, his body motionless except for the occasional movement of his leg as it pushed. Another decision to make; he could be there for hours! If she moved to go back he would almost certainly spot her, not that that made any difference – she could be out the gate before he even had time to get out of his chair. But if she made herself known would he be angry that she was technically trespassing?

She gazed at the butterflies, longing them to give her an answer. Run or stay? It sounded so simple, but the moving sun had cast a shadow and most of them abandoned her in her hour of need. With trembling hands she quickly tidied her hair – she would make herself known. Yes, that seemed the most sensible. The dress had fared well, not a mark or tear to spoil its fresh look and with no wind to cause an embarrassing uplift, she hoped the old man wouldn't be struck down by a passing heart attack.

Holding her breath she stepped into the open and stood for a moment, hoping he would see her. If his reaction wasn't what she wanted, there was the option of running away. She stood a little longer, but nothing. Perhaps his eyesight was letting him down. She moved nearer, and for some strange reason she didn't feel scared, in fact quite the opposite. She was within talking distance when the old man staggered to his feet. Susan could see right into his staring eyes as a hand grasped the arm of his chair, precariously trying to steady himself from swaying, but it seemed the shock had taken every last ounce of strength from his frail body.

Susan felt helpless as she watched the old man struggling to stay upright, but something told her to walk forward as if he knew she would stop him from falling. Now almost running, her arms instinctively reached out and with sheer luck caught his weight, bringing him slowly
back down into the safety of the chair.

"I'll get you a glass of water." She went to move away, but felt a surprisingly firm grip on her arm.

"No, please. Just give me a minute and I'll be fine." His voice wasn't what Susan had expected. Most older country people around about spoke with an accent born and bred, but this man sounded different – softer in nature, more refined. Yes, he had that distinct elderly way of talking, the words crackled somewhat, but still there was something about him. Not knowing what to say, she stood watching the eyes of a man who didn't seem to be a stranger. Allowing time to slow to a mere breath, he finally spoke. "Forgive me – that was rude to stare, I must have startled you. Please accept my deepest apologies."

"No, really, I should be the one apologising. I had no right to wander into your garden unannounced, frightening you like that."

"You're very sweet, my dear, but I feel no one could possibly be frightened by you." His eyes momentarily locked onto the young woman who now stood in front of him. "I hope you don't mind me saying, but you remind me so much of someone I used to know."

Susan felt a heavy silence between them as his mind clearly drifted off to another world. "Many years ago now," he continued. "She was also beautiful." His head dropped slightly. "Forgive me, I have spoken out of turn, but I only speak the truth. Seeing you walk up the path in that dress, it's as if the years had vanished." He fell silent again, leaving Susan struggling to think of something to say. Clearly her sudden appearance had upset him, whether he wished to acknowledge it or not.

"Perhaps I should go. I'm sorry to intrude."

"No, please stay."

Susan wanted to, longed to, and something was telling her she needed to stay. "If you insist."

"Thank you, my dear. It would be a shame to lose your company so soon, and I must say in my defence it's not every day I get to have a lovely young lady come visiting." He held out his hand. "Vincent, my dear. Vincent Wheeler."

"Susan Swan."

"Delightful name. Please take a seat, Miss Swan. It is Miss?"

"Yes, it is, Vincent."

A quick glance revealed nothing more than a rickety old wicker chair. She wasn't sure she could trust its capability to hold any weight let alone hers, but there seemed little choice. She sat down gingerly, avoiding leaning back as she heard a cracking sound.

Vincent smiled. "It has been a while since anyone came knocking on my door, so I find myself apologising once again, but I'm sure I can find more suitable seating for the next time you come visiting."

His presumptuous statement would have almost certainly made many young ladies feel slightly uneasy, but not Susan. All she felt was relief that he had asked her to return. "That sounds like an invitation, Vincent?"

He nodded. "Please accept it as one."

"But you don't know me, I could be anyone."

The old man could only chuckle. "I will take that chance, my dear. But have you not thought I could be the undesirable one?"

Susan was the one smiling now. "It had crossed my mind, but I'll take my chances too."

Their laughter echoed around the garden before Vincent finally regained his composure. "I believe, my dear, we are going to get along swimmingly."

A cool breeze swept through the garden causing Susan to look up at the gathering clouds. "I'd better go, it's starting to cloud over and I've only got this light dress." She wanted nothing more than to stay, to find out more about this well-spoken gentleman, but she knew her questions could wait for another day.

"You will come back?" he asked in earnest.

"I have an invitation, don't I?"

The look of sheer relief on the old man's face told her she had better keep her promise. "Quite so, my dear, and I will look forward to it. I must warn you I have a busy schedule, but any day until the day I die will suit."

Susan leaned forward and placed her hand upon his. "Well that leaves plenty of time then."

"If only that were true, my dear." Their hands parted, allowing her to finally relieve herself from the discomfort of ancient woven willow as she arose. "May I ask, where is home?"

"Willowbank Farm. John and Sam Taylor, do you know them?"

He looked bemused. "But of course, the Taylors and I go back a long way. Are you related?" Vincent politely enquired.

"No. I'm just staying for a while."

"Excellent. Well, goodbye for now, Susan Swan, and do give my love to John and Samantha. I must say I haven't seen them in such a long time."

"I will and goodbye, Vincent Wheeler, it's been a pleasure."

Walking down the path saw her almost skipping with

joy. She knew he was watching her – she could almost feel those warm eyes tingling into the back of her neck.

*

"Ah, Susan, just in time. Another half an hour and tea will be ready." Sam looked up from her work. "My, you look worn out. Long walk?"

"It did end up that way – well, long for the likes of us townies," she smiled, leaning over to pinch a warm shortbread biscuit.

"You, young lady, need a good spanking."

"Sam! If I'd known you were that way minded I would have stolen two!"

The older woman suddenly felt her cheeks glow. Dear God! "I'm sorry, that didn't quite come out the way I wanted it to, how embarrassing!"

Susan gently tapped Sam's bottom. "And there I was hoping." She took a rather erotic mouthful of biscuit and went and sat down. "I met up with an old friend of yours today."

"Really? Who was that?"

"Oh, some lovely gentleman called Vincent Wheeler."

"Vincent! How on earth did you meet up with him?"

"I just happened to stumble upon his cottage, purely by accident, but I'm afraid I may have taken him by surprise. Poor man nearly collapsed with shock when he saw me walking up the path."

Sam sat down at the table, her face showing concern. "Poor old Vincent."

"Is there something the matter?" Susan asked.

"No, not exactly, but it's no wonder he didn't have a heart attack, what with you wearing that dress and your hair done up in a bun like that."

"What's with this dress? Vincent made a comment too, said I reminded him of someone."

"Dear Vincent," Sam continued, "he must have thought she'd come back from the dead."

"Who? Who's come back from the dead?"

"Alice."

"Who's Alice?"

"Vincent's fiancée. They got engaged during the war." Sam felt Susan's hand meet hers.

"Tell me everything."

"Not much to tell really. He hardly talks about it, but as far as I can work out Vincent was opposed to the war. He hates killing of any sort, even animals. In his opinion everything has a right to live, but of course in the end he had to go. There were those who started to look at him, gossip, you know the kind of thing. His family were important business people back then so there was little choice, he couldn't disgrace them like that just because of his own beliefs. Like I say, I don't know all the ins and outs but I do know he saw a lot of action. Lucky to come out of it alive, but he never talks about that side of it. Would any of us, with all that death and destruction? You'd want to block out that sort of thing or it could drive you mad over time. I think he felt it should have been him that got killed, not Alice."

Susan felt a sharp pain in her chest. "Alice died? That's so sad. How?"

The older woman paused, warning Susan she was about to reveal the worst of the story. "Killed by a bomb. Not only her – Vincent's parents as well, all three in the same night. Vincent couldn't handle it when he came back, he just wandered from place to place until he came here. The old cottage was for sale and Vincent bought it. He was still reasonably young at that stage but he just shut himself away. So sad. John's grandfather gave him some work, he did the odd job but nothing much. John's known him all his life but he's not made it easy for anyone else to get to know him. I suppose I see him more than anybody now and that's not often, so you're honoured, young lady. True gentlemen is our Vincent, and good-looking in his younger days, could have had the pick of the village they say, but there was too much hurt for that sort of thing. He and John think much alike when it comes to nature, the wildlife and organics, but he isn't a true farmer, just cares passionately about the countryside. Anyway, look at the time, John will be in soon and tea won't be ready. I saw Tony earlier; our Mr Wren looked very smart in his freshly ironed clothes."

"You're mocking."

"Me? Never! Nothing surprises me any more – it

amuses me though, yes. Oh, and Sadie's not back so it's just the four of us. Best get out of that dress – don't want to be dropping food on it, do we."

Chapter 26

All four were at the table having tea. The kettle had slowly built up steam and was whistling to itself, prompting Sam to rise. She looked up as Sadie came down the back passage and couldn't help noticing the way the woman held herself, showing not a care in the world.

"Sadie."

A chorus of welcoming voices greeted her as she found a chair and sat down, deliberately choosing to stay silent for she knew a barrage of questions was sure to come her way.

It was John's curiosity that finally got the better of him. "Well, how did it go?" With building frustration he needed information, and to his annoyance everyone in the room apparently seemed to know much more than he did.

Sadie couldn't hold back as she sat like a cat that had rummaged through the rubbish and had found a discarded kipper. "I've had a wonderful afternoon," she announced. "Satisfied?"

John looked on in disgust. "Is that it? 'Oh, I've had a wonderful afternoon', isn't the world just lovely. No, sorry Sadie, I'm not satisfied."

"John, tone yourself down."

"Well, it seems I'm the only one around here who doesn't know what's going on."

Sadie pulled herself up. "It's all right, Sam. If you must know, I think I've fallen in love."

"Oh good grief, I wish I hadn't asked now."

Sam was still making the drinks. "Sadie, that's great news."

The two girls were just about to put forward their congratulations when John butted in. "Hold on a minute, she hasn't said who or what she's supposed to have fallen in love with! For all we know it could be the postman."

"Really, John, do you have to spoil it? This is a big moment in a woman's life, finding someone she truly loves. You're ruining it and it's not funny."

"Sorry I spoke."

His wife mumbled something under her breath. "Carry on, Sadie, take no notice of him." The two girls wisely decided to keep out of it and were finding normal married life highly amusing.

"We spent the whole afternoon sitting out in the garden just talking."

"Sounds fun."

"John!"

"Hardly said a word."

"Go on, Sadie." Sam placed four mugs on the table.

"Where's mine?" asked John with concern.

"You can get your own, you know were the pot is. And

don't say a word, I'm not interested."

"Fine. I'll leave you women to gossip amongst yourselves. I've got work to do."

"But you haven't finished your tea."

"Save it. I'll have it later, got to get ready for this farm inspection. Next Wednesday, ladies, so no booking up anyone for the morning. Afternoon should be fine, we normally finish around lunchtime. Any problems ask my dear wife – she seems to know more than I do."

No one dared reply as they watched a rather disgruntled man leave the room.

"That was a bit harsh." Tony took another sip of her coffee. "He only made a little joke of it."

"I know, but he makes me want to scream sometimes. Anyway, let's forget him. So, Sadie, now it's just us women, do tell all."

Everyone gathered close to the table, clutching their hot drinks.

"It's like ..." The room quietened as they waited for Sadie to continue. She sighed with pleasure. "It's like I'm a teenager again. I can't really describe it but I'm in my late fifties for Christ's sake, things like this don't happen to older people, it's just not right." She looked down at the table, her mind turning back to just a few hours ago when she and Lizzie had taken their first kiss. A finger touched the place were another female had dared to go; yes, she'd been with other women; that was her job. Some were enjoyable, others not so much, but never had anyone made her feel the way

Lizzie had. John had asked how it had gone and she had answered truthfully to a point. Yes, they had spent the afternoon together but not in the way he'd assumed, for she knew that first kiss had opened the floodgates to a mix of emotions neither of them ever thought possible. She'd been well aware Lizzie had only lain with one other, but her inexperience didn't seem to matter for that second kiss had found hands wandering into forbidden territory, and then …

"Sadie!" Tony gave her a nudge in the ribs. "Hello? Are you with us?"

"We made love."

"Sorry?"

"We made love. All afternoon. I can't believe it."

Sam placed a comforting hand upon the woman's shoulder, her own emotions pulling in all directions. She didn't have to say a word, they were all women together; true love was a precious thing that in truth few experienced. With the silence driving home the realism of all their individual lives, Sam sat back allowing her confused heart to find a place to hide as her eyes traced the contours of Susan's face. "I'm so pleased for you, Sadie." Her voice was genuine for she knew Sadie had found what she'd been longing for all her life.

"So what happens next?" said Tony, always the level-headed one.

"I'm not sure. Best if we take each day as it comes, but we're going to meet again tomorrow."

Susan was now curious. "Will you stay the night?"

"Seems like the next stage. We'll see."

"And I hate to ask this," Susan continued, "but does she know your history? It could change things."

It was something all three of them dreaded the most. Finding happiness was one thing, hanging on to it was another.

"No, she doesn't. I'll have to tell her of course, if she ever found out from someone else I'd hate to think what would happen."

Chapter 27

Sam came out of the bathroom loosely wrapped in her dressing gown, hair still wet from a late morning shower. As she forced a towel through her matted locks she thought how glad she was to have some time to herself. John had gone off to a farm sale with Jack Whitlock, his pocket stuffed with cash courtesy of the girls and had pointed out when leaving that in fact it would be a good way of getting rid of some of it, no questions asked. Tony meanwhile was out for the day with a Mr Robin with intentions of being entertained at the races before going back to a country hotel for lunch then using the facilities of their private suite to enjoy their possible winnings, something Mr Robin was greatly looking forward to. So that just left Susan in the house.

With her head down and the towel obstructing her view she walked straight into the young woman coming in the opposite direction. As their bodies met Sam felt her robe slacken, exposing clean lightly powdered skin. Although only for a brief moment, it was enough for the girl to view everything her middle-aged body had to offer.

"Susan! I didn't see you there." Her hands scrambled for the cord as she desperately tried to cover up her embarrassment.

Susan couldn't help but smile. "You shouldn't be ashamed of your body, you know, you're a very attractive woman."

"What, for a woman in her fifties you mean?"

"No, I didn't mean it like that."

She finally managed to tie the cord, this time far more securely. "Maybe not, but it's true what they say – time has a tendency to creep up on you and it normally drags the body along with it."

Susan lowered her head. "That's what I'm afraid of."

"You young people, you worry far too much, you'll be fine. It's the rest of us that should be worrying. Well, I'd better get on, things to do as normal. Just the two of us for lunch today. Sadie never came back last night, but if she does turn up there's plenty to go around. Oh, and I've got some ironed sheets for your bed, I'll bring them up when I've got dressed. No one for you today, I see."

"No, Gino had to go out of the country at short notice."

"So a day to yourself then? All right for some."

"I could help, you know." Susan caught a look of defiance. "Fine, do it all yourself then."

"I'm sorry, it's not that I'm not grateful for the offer, but I just need to keep busy, takes my mind off things."

"Things?" Susan asked.

"You know, life in general. Anyway, I'd better get on so I'll see you shortly. If you're not in when I come up I'll leave the sheets outside the door." Sam could have asked the girl to collect them herself as she was clearly at a loose end, but secretly she wanted to have a quiet word, and with everyone away it seemed the perfect time.

She went and got dressed and then headed upstairs with an armful of neatly folded bed linen. She made her way along the landing before allowing herself to stop and take in the calm of the house then slowly she made her way to Susan's door, gently tapped with her free hand and patiently waited. Perhaps the girl had gone out, she thought. She'd pop the sheets on the floor as promised and catch up later, they could talk over lunch. Not the most private place but with no one around it would have to do. She had just bent down when the door opened.

"Susan! I thought you'd gone out. Sheets all ironed and ready for action. I mean ready to put on the bed, that's what I meant." Linen held out at arm's length, she felt the warmth of embarrassing cheeks making her drop her gaze.

Susan grinned. "You and John will never quite get used to what we do, will you?"

"I'm sorry, is it that obvious?" The girl gave a funny sideways look. "Clearly it is."

"Would you like to come in?"

"Oh, I don't know … Well, why not? If it's not inconvenient."

"Sam, come in, I told you I have all day. You obviously want to talk about something."

The bed felt soft to the touch. It played with Sam's mind, making her feel slightly uneasy towards what went on between the sheets, willing her to get up and leave. Perhaps this wasn't such a good idea after all.

Susan could see by Sam's body language that this wasn't just a general discussion over what they'd have for lunch. Her job often entailed breaking the ice, allowing the client to feel more relaxed. Sam was no different and given a little encouragement she too would open up – it was almost as if they needed to become giggling teenagers again, able to trust each other's company, indulge in each other's problems, and the only way to do that was to have a little fun. With this in mind she made her way to the wardrobe and rummaged through the array of hangers, deliberately looking for one thing in particular. "While you're here," she said, "I'd like your opinion." Her voice sounded smooth and calming to an otherwise anxious woman. "Ah, here we are – my new outfit. What do you think?"

Sam's eyes nearly popped out of her head. Susan had lied – it wasn't new at all, but if this didn't warm the hesitant chill in the room, nothing would. "It's leather. Have a feel, go on, it won't bite. Well, not until I put it on, that is!"

"Susan! Have you no shame? I don't know …" Sam hesitated, but then felt a hand grab hers, forcing her to touch the material, igniting her imagination. Fingers now running over its shiny black coating, a willing excitement tingled through her body.

"I had it made specially."

Sam embraced the whole experience. "It's so soft, I

never thought leather could be like that."

"Smell it."

The older woman almost leapt off the bed at the suggestion. "I can't do that! Who knows where it's been. Nothing personal, but no, it's not you I'm worried about, it's the other person."

"I do clean it. Not that I've had a chance to use it that much, being new and everything." She had to remember to cover her tracks.

"I'm sure you do, but no, I couldn't. Just the thought."

"Please yourself. Hardly stays on for very long anyway. You know what men are like, you get dressed up and all they what to do is rip it off you. Funny how the male brain works, isn't it?" She heard a light chuckle.

"I wasn't aware men had brains where sex was concerned."

The ice was slowly melting – time, Susan thought, to raise the heat a little higher as she laid the garment out on the bed and started to undress.

"Susan! What are you doing?"

"Putting it on of course, show you what it really looks like."

"I don't think that's a very good idea."

"Hush now." A single finger found its way to Sam's lips, making her stomach ache.

"Susan?"

"Relax, you know we're all the same underneath."

"Now we all know that's definitely not true. I think you'll find there's a lot of difference – have you ever wondered why they invented clothes?"

"Oh don't be such a prude. We're alone, there's no one else in the house, you said so yourself, so what are you afraid of?"

Sam's heart pounded so hard she could hardly hear the girl's voice; her lips were moving but the words sounded muffled.

"Have it your way. So tell me, what did you want to talk about? Clearly something is worrying you." She was met by a hesitant silence. "Sam, come on, speak to me."

"It's about me and sex … this is so awkward … I've … I've wondered, about not having any more children, that maybe something is wrong with me … I'm sorry, Susan, you're young, I shouldn't be offloading my troubles onto you. Let's forget I ever said anything." She went to get up.

"Sam, sit down. I'm here to listen." She put her arm around Sam's waist. "You can't blame yourself. Feel free to tell me to mind my own business, but when you *do* do it, are you being satisfied?"

"What do you mean, satisfied?"

"Really, Sam, do I have to spell it out? Orgasm."

"Oh, right." She deliberately turned her head, not wishing to confront the truth.

"Tell me, you have been getting them?"

"I may have."

"What's that supposed to mean, 'I may have'? Believe me, I think you would know if you'd had one."

"There could have been once."

The girl couldn't believe what she was hearing, dear God. "It's worse than I thought. How long have you been married?"

"Not saying."

"Sam."

"All right, thirty years, if you must know. That's not counting the years we were courting."

Her arm instantly left Sam's waist. "Thirty-odd years and you haven't had an orgasm?"

The older woman felt she needed to fight back and promptly folded her arms across her chest in defiance. "I didn't say I hadn't had one."

"Stop there. One possible or maybe isn't the basis for a strong argument."

"We'd had a Chinese just before."

"What has that got to do with anything?"

"I'm just saying, that's all, it could have been wind."

"Damn it, woman, you're not taking this seriously."

"Susan, it's really nothing to get hung up about, so what if I haven't had one?"

Susan's arms flew up in the air. "I can't believe what I'm hearing. Can't you see it's every woman's God-given right to experience a full-blown orgasm!" She was shouting by the time she'd finished.

"Keep it down, they'll hear you in the village at this rate. I wish I hadn't told you now."

"Sam, dear Sam, don't you understand? You'll never be fully fulfilled if you don't start with the basics."

"Oh, so it's a basic thing now, is it?"

"Yes, it is. All sex is basic, it's just another thing a consenting man and woman do with each other and an orgasm comes under that category." Susan rose from the bed and started to pace, her fingers constantly tapping her knuckles for inspiration. "Wait here and don't move." She shot out of the room and ran down the stairs, leaving Sam to wonder what on earth the girl was up to. She appeared moments later, out of breath and holding a knife in her hand. "Right, you're not leaving this room until you know how to sort yourself out." Locking the door she stood in the middle of the room, brandishing the knife.

"Susan, what are you doing? You're beginning to worry me."

"No more talk, Sam. We need to do this here and now."

"Susan, I'm not sure I like what you're saying. I think I need to go, I've got work to do."

A pointing blade told her otherwise. "You, my girl, are going nowhere. Surely not until you've learnt. Chinese indeed! Right, close your eyes."

"Susan, this is getting out of hand."

The knife moved closer. "I said close your eyes. Just trust me."

If only through sheer fear, Sam did as she was told and sat praying the girl hadn't gone completely mad. She could now feel the presence of someone very close to her.

"Open your eyes." Slowly, unwillingly, she opened her eyes only to be confronted by a bright yellow fruit. "It's the best I can do."

Sam tilted her head to one side, questioning the sudden appearance of a rather sizeable melon. "I don't understand?"

"You will." She rotated it in her hand, proudly showing off its suitability to the job in hand. "This is your new vagina."

"But it's a melon!"

"You have no imagination!"

"I think I'd need a lot of that with this one."

She watched the girl place it on the floor and cut a small slice out of one side. "There, now what do you think?"

"It's a melon with a hole in it."

Susan shook her head in frustration. "Still no imagination. Never mind, just stick it between your legs."

"I will not. Be like giving birth again without the gas."

"You're really not taking this seriously, are you?"

"How can I when I don't know what's going on?"

"Do I really have to explain?"

"Yes, I'm afraid you do."

"You are going to give this melon an orgasm. Simple, really."

"I don't think so."

"Yes you are. Right, now give me your finger."

Sam clenched her fists.

"Don't! Give it! That's better. Right, I'm going to show you how to satisfy yourself without the aid of a man. So, we just place your finger in the hole like so. As you can see it's very similar in shape and texture. Then we move up to the top and ..."

"No!" Sam instinctively pulled away. "No, Susan, I can't do it this. Whoever heard of molesting an innocent fruit for your own pleasure?"

"You clearly don't get out into the real world much, do you?" Susan replied.

"Not if it involves this sort of thing, no. Oh my God, I've suddenly had a thought." Sam just couldn't help herself.

"What is it now?"

"How did you know which was the front or back of

this poor melon? For all we know I could have stuck my finger up its arse!"

"Damn it, woman, you're impossible. Okay, clearly this isn't going to work."

"Good, can I go now? I know you mean well, but I've really got to get on. Susan, you're not listening."

"Be quiet, I'm thinking. Regrettably we're going to have to ditch the melon."

"Why do you have a melon in your bedroom anyway?"

"Don't ask. We're going to have to do it for real."

"What!"

"Yes, that's what we'll do. But it isn't going to work with our clothes on."

"Susan!"

"Don't look so shocked, I've already seen most of your body today and I can't imagine it's changed much."

"Well I did sneak two caramel slices and a butterfly cake just before I came up – those wouldn't have done the waistline much good." She heard a foot thump against the carpet.

"No more jokes, understand? My God, you're getting worse than your husband!" A clenched fist warned of a determination to get the job done no matter what. "Take my hand."

"Why?"

"Sam, do as you're told." Suddenly all the humour

vanished. "That's better."

"Susan, we shouldn't be doing this."

"Be quiet, you'll thank me for it afterwards. Now let's take some of these clothes off."

Sam knew she should get up and leave but something pulled her back, something deep down telling her this was what she'd been longing for all her life. Letting go and laying her trust in another woman seemed so natural, like nothing she'd ever experienced before. She waited for that voice to warn her of the consequences but all was silent. It was like she'd been given permission to allow this gorgeous young lady to take her to a place she'd never been before. As paralysed limbs held her to the bed she felt the buttons of her blouse slowly being released. She could only wait, hope and share every last moment of what could be the start of her life as experienced fingertips ran over trembling skin. Then she felt the loosely flowing material slip off her shoulders leaving her gasping for air.

"Susan!"

"Hush now." Playful fingers traced along waiting straps teasing aching breasts, willing them to show their true selves and to allow this beautiful female to caress their naked form. She felt the weight of Susan's body upon the bed as the girl's hands firmly grasped the clasp, sending everything into free fall. This couldn't be happening, she would wake up, as with so many other nights, and be compelled to listen to the snoring of her worn-out husband. But this seemed different, so much more real. With warm air drifting across erect nipples she was compelled to believe in the unthinkable, for never had she experienced the damp sweat of so much emotion as she sat in a trance, barely able to think about anything, and then from out of the mist of her dreams came a familiar voice.

"Open your eyes."

"I can't."

"You can. Now open them. Trust me."

There was that word again, trust. A final deep breath persuaded her to do as she was told, yet her eyes seemed reluctant at first. Flickering lids allowed only partial vision, but slowly she watched as the outline of Susan's form gradually came into focus.

"Find yourself, Sam. Let everything go, it's just you and me now, nothing else matters."

Mesmerised by the sight of her dreams she sat and stared at the curves of a partially naked body. This was what she'd longed for, cried out for ever since she was a child. Now understanding all that pain, that anguish of past years and why she'd always felt like she had, it all seemed to slot into place now. My God, what was she confessing?

Susan smiled as she released the tension of her jeans, allowing both hands to pull across slender hips. Sam could do nothing more than watch as this tender sweet girl glanced down at her own aroused nudity, unashamed.

"Stand up."

The command didn't seem to worry her any longer as she rose from the bed, willing the body to move forward and take her into her arms.

"Take your skirt off."

Sam did as she was told, forcing it to stretch over rounded hips and finally drop to the ground.

"Good girl."

She stood viewing the delicate lace work of Susan's finally crafted panties and was suddenly reminded that her own were oversized, plain and lacking, forcing her to realise how old she really was. Perhaps Susan was being polite or didn't care, whichever way she wasn't showing it; all she could see was warmth and kindness and a willingness to go further.

"Take them off."

More demands, but Sam knew that was how Susan worked. She had the beauty and the youth to command any man to do exactly what she wanted, and that's what she was doing to her, but she didn't much care and without hesitation pulled them off with the willingness of a teenager on her first ever sexual encounter. Was this wrong, she wondered. Did a long and trusted marriage make any difference? No, with what she had now she had to answer a definite no. Such thoughts of wrongdoing were pushed to one side and allowed to float away downstream, possibly never to be seen again. No, this felt so right. Yet the sight of another woman's private parts made her want to cover her own rampant growth spreading like an unkempt hawthorn hedge, sprigs poking out in all directions, but it was too late for that.

"Sit down."

Another command, each more exciting than the last. She watched as Susan got down on the floor. My God! What was she doing between her legs, could this be it? A cold sweat settled upon ageing skin as her breathing, hardly bearable, gripped the back of her throat and then the unmistakable touch of the girl's hands sent her to a place where she could feel the gentle pull of her socks from her feet. Oh, she thought, was that relief or frustration that now raced through her body? She wasn't sure.

Susan rose and then gently lay on the bed, her exposed body sinking into the covers as she invited Sam to join her. A brief moment's hesitation found little regret. No, she had come too far to stop now as every nerve in her body screamed at her to lie beside the woman that she wanted with all her heart. Trembling with uncontrollable want, her eyes danced across a naked form, then a gasp escaped her mouth as a hand dared to venture to a place no other woman had been before. Their eyes locked, showing a warmth that demanded full and utter commitment allowing their lips to touch. Nothing else mattered. It was a long hard kiss, a kiss that had the ability to suck every last breath out of her lungs. They pulled away only to return time after time. This was what Sam had been longing for, but then with shock she suddenly realised that all she wanted to do was touch another female like nothing else in the world.

Susan pulled back, her voice as soft as the sheets they now lay on. "Are you all right?"

"More than all right, thank you."

Susan smiled and then pulled herself up, indicating she wanted her lover to lie flat. This was it – this was what it was all about, the undressing, the gentle touches and finally the kisses. There would be no more holding back. Sam knew she would finally know what it really felt like to be a complete woman. Eyes closed, she willingly fell into Susan's care; no fear, just a relaxed mind that told her things were going to be fine. Both hands gripped the sheets as she felt the dip of the bed between her legs, encouraging her to feel the hand that now stroked the insides of her thighs, ever playful fingers moving closer to that mass of hair that she now so regretted. Unable to breathe she drifted off into an unknown world.

*

Susan rolled over and gently blew a kiss across Sam's face. Her eyes slowly opened. She didn't want it to end; she felt exhausted but satisfied, letting a shameful giggle pass over her lips as a light soothing voice begrudgingly dragged her back into the real world.

"Wake up, sleepy head."

Sam lay for a moment, just gazing up at the ceiling. "Christ!" she shouted. "What time is it?"

"One o'clock."

Her whole body sagged with relief. "Damn it, I nearly

had a heart attack. What if John had come home and found me here?"

"Stop worrying."

"Oh Susan, what am I going to do?"

"Calm down, you don't have to do anything. No one will know except us two." A comforting arm wrapped around her naked body. "By the way, how do you feel?"

"What, after cheating on my husband, you mean? Fine, perfectly fine, never better."

"Sam, stop it. Now give me a kiss and let yourself settle down, you've just had your first orgasm. Well two, actually, you need to rest."

"Oh Susan, all these years. Why are you looking at me like that?" The girl pulled a stray hair from Sam's face.

"How long have you known?" Their eyes locked, demanding a straight answer.

"What? That I prefer women?" She sighed. "I don't know, forever I think. I thought it would pass and it was something that naturally happened to you when you were young. You couldn't talk to anyone about it, certainly not in those days. You can only fight it for so long, but if that's how you feel what can you do? I suppose over the years I learned to push it to one side and get on with life. Well, the life that people expect you to lead, so I got married hoping it would change things. Had no choice really, it's the way of the countryside – find a farmer, get wed, have children, life sorted."

"I'm sorry, Sam."

"Nothing to be sorry about, that's how it is." She was stopped from saying another word as a warm set of lips pressed against hers.

"You're not thinking of leaving John, are you?" Susan heard a ripple of laughter that reassured her, but still she needed to know.

"Good grief no. I love it here, this is my home, it's where I had my baby. No. I'll be a lot more content from now on, thanks to you."

"Glad to be of service, and if you ever feel the need again, just call."

"You're a little minx, young lady."

She gently touched Sam's face. "But seriously, I'm here."

"Thanks, but now I know how to do it, the world's a far different place, and John will be happy. He needs his sleep, poor soul, and he's gone long before I get up, so while the cat's away the mice do play. And believe me, I've got a lot of catching up to do."

Susan placed another kiss on her willing lips. "Now who's the little minx?"

"And who did I learn that from, I wonder? So, on second thoughts, if it's all right by you, I might hold you to your offer. After all, I know where you live."

Susan pulled the sheets over their heads. "Lunch can wait," she whispered.

Chapter 28

"Morning everyone." John strolled into the kitchen, his nose following the overpowering smell of fried food. "I'm starving!" He looked at the gathering of women at his table. "You sure there's any left? This is like being back at school, last one in gets the leftovers."

"Morning, John." He was met by a chaotic jumble of female voices as Sam rose from her seat. "Here, you can have this chair, I've finished. There's an extra sausage and another egg today so no pleading poverty, and if you're still hungry there's more fried bread."

"Well, I might have to be a straggler more often – thank you, my dear wife."

"You're welcome, my dear husband."

The women giggled with amusement. John looked at them, slightly concerned. "What are you up to?" he asked.

"Nothing. Can't a wife treat her husband once in a while?"

"Suppose so, but I still think there's something going on."

Sam pointed out the window. "The sun's shining, the birds are singing and the cows, I assume, are happy, so what more could you want?"

He waved an empty fork in her direction. "I know why you're so chirpy, it's because of what you and Susan got up to yesterday, isn't it?"

An empty saucepan hit the floor with a clatter and all heads turned to see Sam cursing her clumsiness. "Don't know what you mean." She could hardly hear herself speak over a heart that refused to stop pounding in her ears.

"Oh yes you do, just because the rest of us were out you two thought you'd have a little fun, and don't deny it."

Hands now trembling with fear, she held her breath, watching John turn his attention to Susan. "And you, young lady, are a bad influence on my wife. All play and no work, that's what I found when I got back. The chickens hadn't been cleaned out, the cake tin was almost empty and there was nothing ready for lunch. It was a good job I'd had something at the sale. Out wandering the countryside, I bet. A farm can't run on its own, you know."

Sam was almost beside herself as she finally allowed a small amount of relief to enter her shaking body. This was going to be harder than she thought. Turning back to the sink she gazed into the empty washing-up bowl and was completely engulfed with visions of Susan's naked body. God, this was definitely going to be harder than she thought!

"I think Sam deserves a day off now and again," said Susan in a cool, calm voice. "She works far too hard and yes, it was my fault. I admit I led her astray with my wicked ways, and I apologise."

"Umm, maybe you're right," John added. "Perhaps she does deserve an odd treat now again, as long as you two don't make a habit of it. But I'm not convinced having time off actually does you any good. By the time I got in after milking so late my wife was nowhere to be found, completely exhausted she was, fast asleep in bed before me."

Sam grabbed the side of the bowl while Susan played the innocent little girl. "We just had a wonderful time, that's all. It was nice to relax and get to know each other a little better, and I've learned so much about your wife, John."

Sam was struggling to contain herself. Susan was playing with fire and if she didn't watch it they were all going to be burnt to a crisp.

"So you're telling me you spent most of the day just talking?" John continued.

"Pretty much."

Sam discreetly turned her head, sending a warning shot in Susan's direction pleading her to stop playing games. To her relief John lost interest and was more concerned with filling his stomach than delving into his wife's as yet undiscovered love affair. Still wanting answers, he focused his attentions on Sadie. "I suppose you and Lizzie just sat around all day as well."

"That's about the sum of it, yes."

"But you're managing to keep her quiet?"

"Of course."

"Good, that's all I need to know. But just sitting around all day, it's not good for the body; you need to be doing something physical." If only John knew, the women thought. "Hard graft, that's what's needed," he carried on. "Those hands were made for solid work – you need to feel exhausted at the end of the day, that's how you achieve satisfaction in life."

"We were satisfied, weren't we, Sam?"

"Sorry, Susan, miles away."

"I was just pointing out to John that we were very satisfied with our efforts yesterday."

"Yes, Susan, we were. Now if you'll excuse me I really must hang out the washing."

"Sam?"

John's voice shattered her thoughts. "You okay? You look a little flushed. Not coming down with anything I hope?"

"No, I'm fine, be back in a minute."

"Before I forget," John announced, "a reminder to you all that the farm inspector is here next Wednesday, so no appointments until after lunch." He pushed his plate to the middle of the table and stood up. "Oh, and I nearly forgot, village fête here weekend after next, I've booked you all up to help."

"What!"

"I thought you'd all be pleased. Look on the bright side – you get in for nothing and you might even get to do a bit of hard graft for a change! See you later." He shot along the passage at high speed, trying to dodge the abuse now being hurled at him.

"But, John?"

"Too late, Susan, he's gone."

Sadie rose. "I bet you anything I'm the one with me head locked in the stocks with everyone chucking wet sponges for 50p! I'm off to me room, not seeing Lizzie till later, we're going for a bike ride and she's lending me Jane's old bicycle seeing as mine is knackered."

The other two girls looked at each other and discreetly nodded. "Getting serious then?" Susan asked.

Sadie paused at the door. "I hope so." Her tone didn't sound like a woman head over heels in love.

"Something the matter?" Tony asked as she stood to leave. "If you need to talk, I'm around."

"Yes, Sadie," Susan agreed.

"Thanks, girls. To be honest I'm worried sick, I'm going to have to tell Lizzie about what I do for a living sooner or later and I'm afraid when the truth comes out she'll want nothing to do with me."

Sam wandered back in and caught the tail end of Sadie's plight. "Problem?" she asked.

"Sadie needs to tell Lizzie the truth about her past."

"Oh, right. Tricky one, but of course you might be worrying for no good reason – she might love you so much that she doesn't care about what's gone on in the past. Let's face it, everyone has a few skeletons in their cupboard and you have to hold on to the fact that women are different from men and are more understanding about things." She couldn't help but look at Susan as she spoke.

"I hope you're right."

"Wait, Sadie, I'll come up with you. We can have a nice long chat, mull things over, how's that?"

"Thanks, love, that would be great."

Sam waited as she listened to footsteps making their way up the stairs before lowering her voice. "I had kittens earlier, I thought John had found out. Nearly wet myself, and you didn't help playing your little games."

"We're fine, no one's going to find out. So how was it, by the way?"

Sam wondered at first what she was on about but saw that look on her face. "Don't know what you mean."

"Come on, you're not telling me you didn't have a go by yourself this morning?"

"Susan, keep your voice down."

"Your cheeks are glowing, Sam. Dead giveaway."

"Will you stop it!" They briefly looked at each other. "All right, I may have done."

"You may have done a likely story, of course you did, it's written all over your face. I'm surprised the others didn't notice it. John, well he's a man, he wouldn't notice a brick wall until he walked into it. That's why you were so clumsy earlier on, I'm not a fool."

"Earlier was partly your fault, pushing the boundaries

like that."

"You're changing the subject. So I'll ask again, how was it?"

"Great, if you must know, but I think I might need a bit more practice, took me ages and I got cramp in my finger!"

"Not as good as me then? You're blushing again, Sam."

"You're impossible, young lady, now stop it. And no, not as good as you, you're ..."

"I'm what?"

"You're amazing, and that body, I'd have an orgasm just thinking of you." Sam's heart flickered at the thought.

"Glad to be of service."

"Stop it."

Susan put on a cheeky grin. "We could have sex again."

"You're not helping, but it's a good idea." She looked Susan in the eye. "What about you?"

"Oh, most mornings. It's the best way to start the day, but I quite often do it just before an appointment."

"Why?"

"It's business, I get paid to do a job, can't be having all the hassle of feeling randy, far easier to fake what they want. You need to be in control, bogs you down otherwise. But now I might save myself for you."

Sam quickly glanced at the open door. "Don't talk like

that," she said in a low voice.

"Why, don't you want me?"

"Of course I do but it's complicated. You know that what happened yesterday was something even I was surprised with."

"Surprised! That's not a very emotional word."

"What, do you want me to say the truth?"

"Which is?"

A silence developed between them as they both grappled with their own thoughts. "I think ..."

"Say it, Sam."

The young woman watched as tears trickled down the older woman's face. "I think I've fallen in love with you." A deep ache ripped through Sam's body as she spoke and with a trembling hand she wiped her face and waited. What a fool she was, someone of her age falling for a twenty-five-year-old, and a woman at that.

Susan stayed silent and just sat for a moment, staring at the woman in front of her. "I'm going to my room. Please, Sam, don't follow."

"But, Susan."

"No. I need time to think."

*

Tony held Sadie's hand. They had talked over so many scenarios that both their heads were starting to spin.

"I think you should leave it a while," Tony finally suggested. "You've only known her for a short time; the shock might be too much for her."

"But what if she finds out in the mean time?" Sadie replied. "She's already raised concerns about what she claims to have seen through the windows. She's not daft."

"What did you say to that?"

"What *could* I say? I told the truth in a roundabout way, said you and Susan occasionally have man friends around but you were models, both young and attractive so it was only natural to be involved with the opposite sex. Me, on the other hand, couldn't be seen as modelling potential, I think we all know that's stretching the imagination a little bit too far."

"But surely she still thinks you're an old friend of the Taylors staying for a while, there's nothing wrong with that. I think you're over-worrying it, I say get to know her a little better, make it so she can't possibly live without you. Like Sam said, women are different from men, she'll understand."

"I don't know, Tony. I feel I should tell her now and hope for the best." She felt her hand being gently squeezed.

"You're the only one who can make that decision."

"Sod the world, Tony. And damn this business we're in, it'll ruin all of us given the chance, you'll see. My advice to you, love, is to get out and take Susan with you before it destroys you both."

"You don't know that."

Sadie gazed into Tony's inexperienced eyes. "Play with the devil and he'll want paying back, that's what me old mum used to say." They sat in silence, each in their own worlds.

"Sadie?" Tony's voice brought the other woman back to the real world. "I know it's probably not the best time, but could I ask a favour?"

"I'm not sure I like the sound of this."

"It's just a tiny little bit of a favour, nothing much."

Sadie already looked resigned to the fact that whatever it was she'd probably end up doing it. "Go on."

"I've got an American client coming over from the States next week and unfortunately the only day he can make it is Tuesday morning, and I'm already booked up all day so I was wondering if you might ..."

"Hang on there, Missy, if you haven't noticed you're young, extremely good-looking and have got all the necessary energy. I, on the other hand, haven't. Can you not see these streaks of grey hair and bags under my eyes? You really think he's going to want to play with me?"

Tony knew whatever she said next could very well stifle her chances of Sadie agreeing to help. "Actually, it doesn't matter about your looks."

"Oh thanks, love, for someone who's looking for a favour you're not going about it in the best way."

"Thought you might say that. I'm sorry, Sadie, I didn't mean it like that. What I meant was you'd be wearing a costume, so it wouldn't matter."

"Oh great, is that supposed to make me feel better? What sort of costume?"

"A chicken. Well, a hen to be precise."

"You're joking, aren't you?"

Tony managed a half grin. "'Fraid not. It's a very nice costume, wing feathers and everything."

"You can say that, you're not going to have to wear it, and when I'm dressed up as an old broiler what's he going to come as?"

Tony could see she was losing the battle and her reply certainly wasn't going to help. "A rooster." There was no other way of putting it.

"What! A bloody cockerel?"

"It won't be that bad."

"Sure it won't, love, because I ain't doing it."

"Please, Sadie, just this once, he's my best paying client."

"I don't know, Tony. I've got a good thing going with Lizzie, I need to start leaving all this stuff behind."

"He pays really well."

"How much?"

Tony leant forward and whispered a figure in Sadie's

ear.

"How much? And he'll know it's me?" Tony nodded. "Christ, I wouldn't make that in a month! Okay, deal."

"I knew you wouldn't let me down."

"I must have 'mug' written all over my face. Now be off with you before I change my mind, which wouldn't take much."

*

Sam, as usual, had her hands in the washing bowl but no enthusiasm for the job. There were certainly no sexual visions of Susan emerging from the bubbles, just an overwhelming fear of what to do for the best. She knew leaving John wasn't an option – that was sheer madness. She'd read of other farming couples having to sell the farm to pay each other out. She couldn't do that to John, she'd rather walk away with nothing; this was his home, his inheritance. No, she couldn't do that, especially as none of this was his fault, she could only blame herself. Perhaps not blame, no, that wasn't the right word, no one can help how they feel, how they'd been born. All those years of confusion, self-doubt and denial which had finally led her to accept her own sexuality. Poor Susan, she had unfortunately been sucked into that journey of discovery and it didn't help she was young and attractive. Her hands violently splashed the soapy water, sending it racing across the worktop. Damn it. Damn this world. Her hands clenched in despair, tears running down her face as she cursed herself for being how she was.

"Sam."

She spun around, hoping the voice belonged to the one she had come to adore. "Susan!" Instantly she wiped her face, leaving a trail of bubbles that somehow caused them both to laugh. "You must be hungry." She grabbed a towel and brushed it across her face. The tears had stopped but the pain lingered, causing Susan to look concerned.

"You've been crying."

"You too, by the looks of it. Let me get you something to eat."

"No. Sam, sit down." There it was again, that commanding tone. "Sit down, please."

They both sat in silence, waiting for the other to say something. "If you want me to leave, I will," Susan whispered.

"Leave? You're not walking out on me now, young lady, not after what we did yesterday."

"You may want to keep your voice down."

"I don't give a damn about who hears me!" Sam knew she had to be strong for once, it was her turn to make the rules otherwise she could very well lose this girl. Clearly no good would come of it, but did she care? Hell no, and she'd come to the conclusion life without her wasn't an option. "We need to work this out, get things straight, that's all. So let's sort this problem so we can move on." She suddenly realised she was perhaps being a little harsh, but a smile from the girl told her otherwise.

"It makes a change for me to be put in my place," Susan confessed.

"I'm sorry, I didn't mean to be so blunt, but I can't lose you, mad as it might be. I need you around me. I said I wouldn't leave John and nothing's changed there, and yesterday, well, I can't describe how I felt lying beside you. And I want more." She grabbed Susan's hand. "We can work this out. It's not ideal but we can be together for as long as you want. John's happy with the way things are so why mess it up? Let's look forward, and we can do this, it can work, I know it can. Do you love me?"

Susan lifted her head. "Yes, you cloth head, of course I do." The girl held up her hand to stop Sam from saying any more. "I want to have a baby."

"Oh, well that could be a problem. I'm sure John would be only too pleased to oblige, but I'd rather keep you to myself if you don't mind."

"I'm serious, Sam. One day."

"Of course you do, it's every woman's right to be given the chance to bring a new life into the world. Sadly not everyone achieves their dreams, but you're still young. Who knows what will happen in the future? So long as whoever you have it with loves it as much as I'm sure you will, then that's just fine."

"Would you?"

"Me?" Sam felt floods of past emotions clouding her vision. "Never you fear on that score, young lady. I've still got a lot of love to give, but hopefully one day you'll find that handsome husband of yours and I'll gladly be Auntie Samantha."

Susan's thoughts found no peace, only concern, but she knew one day she would have her baby.

Chapter 29

The sound of the phone rattled down the hallway, making John groan. He sat at the kitchen table, having finished his breakfast after being early for a change. Milking had passed almost without thinking, maybe because he had a lot on his mind as tomorrow was inspection day. It wasn't that big a deal, just something that would play on his mind until the inspector was satisfied everything was up to scratch. There had never been a problem in the past and probably wouldn't be now. Tick all the boxes, show the animals and land are at the level expected and all would be well.

The girls hadn't come down yet, probably wasting time chatting on their phones or still sleeping. How anyone could lie in this late baffled John constantly, but would he dare say? Maybe not, but for now he was more concerned with the continually ringing phone. "Bloody thing," he said in frustration. Sam wasn't around, having clumsily dropped the sugar bowl and contents into the washing up water, and had gone over to his mother's to ask for a backup supply until she could get down to the village store. He wondered if she was coming down with something for she didn't seem herself lately. Pulling away from the peace and quiet of the room he made his way through the house with the sound still ringing in his head. "All right, I'm coming! Hello?"

"Ah, is that Mr Taylor?"

"Speaking."

"Joy Butterworth here, your organic inspector. How are you today?"

"Oh hello, fine thanks."

"I'm sorry to bother you, Mr Taylor, but I've just had my appointment for today cancel on me, domestic problems, and I'm not far from you as it happens."

"Right." John could almost predict what was coming next.

"I was wondering if it was at all possible to come today rather than tomorrow? Swap the two of you around as it were. I know it's a bit sudden but I'm up from the West County and I've only got two days for this area."

The girl sounded quite young but rather sweet, so like a fool and without thinking he'd offer to be her saviour and agree to her plight. "Yes, that should be okay, one day is no different from the next. What sort of time?"

"I could get to you in about two minutes, I'm sat outside your gate."

"Right, how convenient, see you soon then."

The phone had hardly gone dead when his ears pricked up at the sound of a car making its way along the driveway. Then he heard Sam's voice calling from the kitchen wondering where he'd gone. The young lady would have to wait, he thought.

"Oh, there you are," Sam said. "You can have tea now, I've got more sugar."

"You'd better hang on for a minute, the inspector's just arrived."

"But it's Tuesday! The appointment's not until tomorrow!"

"She just rang and asked if we could do it today, her other appointment cancelled."

"Really, John, you don't think, do you? I suppose she's young and has a nice voice."

"Might have, I didn't take much notice."

"Liar. Really, this isn't good timing, you know Sadie's got a client coming this morning. How are we going to explain that if the two meet up?"

"Well it's too late now."

"When is she due?" She was answered by the doorbell.

"Now!" replied John, stating the obvious.

"Damn it, John, I could strangle you sometimes. What about Sadie's appointment?"

"You'll have to sort it out. I'm sure it'll be fine, they'll be in the bedroom anyway so hopefully the two won't meet."

"But John."

"Got to go." He opened the front door and found himself confronted by a pretty young girl holding a clipboard.

"Mr Taylor?" John was greeted with a pleasant wide

smile as she offered her hand.

"Miss Butterworth, nice to meet you. I'm assuming it's Miss?"

"Most definitely, far too busy for that sort of thing. I have a horse – equines and men I find don't mix."

He looked her up and down, struggling to imagine this girl without nappies let alone being the owner of a horse, but for all that she held a certain degree of authority, with her hair pinned back and a pair of dark rimmed glasses that instantly gave the impression she'd done many years of hard study. Yet let that long brown hair flow upon those shoulders, remove the glasses and John was sure she'd keep many a good man warm at night.

"Please come in. Carry on through, it's the open door on the left, my wife's in the kitchen." He found it a pleasure to follow on behind, allowing his eyes to wander over the curves of her extremely firm buttocks.

Sam looked up as they both entered the room. "Sam, this is Miss Butterworth."

"Nice to meet you, Miss Butterworth."

"Mrs Taylor. It's very good of you and your husband to have me at such short notice."

"Yes, it is, isn't it?"

The conversation broke as the two girls strolled in for breakfast. "Morning. Oh, sorry." Susan eyed the girl up as they stopped mid-stride. "We didn't realise you had company."

"No, don't worry, girls, come on in, this is the organic inspector, Miss Butterworth."

Tony looked concerned. "But the inspection's not until tomorrow."

"No, it's been changed."

"But Sadie?"

"She'll be fine, John and Miss Butterworth are just going to have a cup of tea and then they'll be off."

"Yes, but ..."

It's fine, Tony, they won't be back in until lunchtime, will you, John?"

He caught a stern look from across the room. "Er no, sometime like that."

Miss Butterworth stood wondering. Not coming from a farming family, she was still trying to come to terms with some of the odd behaviour of many country folk. After a quick cup of tea at the kitchen table John ushered her out, closing the back door behind them.

"Have they gone?"

Sam peered down the passage. "Yes, I think so."

"What are we going to do?" Tony's voice had an air of panic to it. "Sadie's entertaining my client this morning."

"I know, a Mr Rooster. I can only imagine what he's like with a name like that."

"I wouldn't joke about it because I don't think you quite understand the problem we're in."

"I can't see any problem so long as they stay in the bedroom, and I'll make sure our Miss Butterworth is kept out of the way during lunch. We should be fine."

"You really don't understand, do you? Our Mr Rooster doesn't want to stay in the bedroom."

"What do you mean?"

"I mean he might want to wander around a little while. He's … you know?"

"This wasn't on the appointments list."

"I'm sorry, I meant to tell you, but what with one thing and another I forgot."

"You forgot! This isn't a minor detail, Tony."

"I know, and again I'm sorry."

"Does Sadie know about this?"

"Yes, I did mention it."

"And you, Susan, did you know?"

"I may have been informed."

"Great, so all of you just happen to have forgotten to tell the owners of this farm that we would have a man running around the farm doing who knows what to a female! Did it not occur to you all that there are other people who occupy this place?"

"Sorry again, but if it's any consolation he'll be dressed

up, and so will Sadie."

"Great, another little detail you forgot. So do I want to know what they'll be dressed up as, or should I just go out in the garden and scream with frustration? Well? I'm waiting."

"The clue is in his name," Tony replied.

Sam's mind was ticking over, until she suddenly clicked. "No!"

"Afraid so."

"And Sadie?"

"A chicken. Hen, actually."

"Oh, just great!"

"The outfits are up in my room."

"I really don't want to know."

Tony suddenly looked down at her phone and started to move towards the door. "Sorry, but I've got to go, Mr Sparrow is waiting outside."

"But you can't leave us to sort your mess out."

"I've got to, sorry again. See you later and good luck!"

"Tony!"

"Bye."

"But you haven't had anything to eat."

"I'll grab something when I'm out." She left the room at speed, not daring to look back. "Sorry," she shouted again as the front door slammed shut.

"What are we going to do?"

Sam wandered over to the kitchen window. "Quiet, Susan, I'm thinking." Sam felt a hand rest on her bum. "You're not helping, young lady, but carry on."

"Naughty." Susan's last word was interrupted by a voice behind them.

"Cosy."

"Her hand dropped as they both turned to see Sadie standing in the doorway. No one said anything as she waited to see what excuse the two of them would come up with.

"Sadie, there you are." Sam was now glowing with embarrassment.

"Well?"

"Well what, Sadie?"

"Don't play games with me."

"Games? We were just looking out of the window and saying how nice it is today."

"That's a load of old tosh and you know it." She pulled up a chair and sat down, waiting for a proper answer. She watched as Susan slowly placed her hand upon Sam's and gently kissed her on the cheek.

"That's all I need to know, my love, but a word of warning, don't do it in public. You were lucky it was only me this time, but if it's any consolation I wish you both all the best because as I see it you're going to need it." She pushed back the chair, stretching her legs out beneath the table. "So apart from you two lovebirds, what's happening?"

"We have a problem," Sam announced.

"What, another one?"

"I'm afraid so. The inspection has been moved, and it's happening right now."

"Shit."

"Exactly, and a rather big load of it. John's taken her out the way for now, but where they are I haven't a clue. I suspect by the time they've looked at the cows and walked around the fields your Mr Rooster will be knocking on the front door, so I think you need to hole up in the bedroom for as long as possible, try and persuade him it's a better option."

"I don't think that's going to work, he's paying good money for a chase. How my old knees are going to hold up, I'll never know. Lizzie had me ride a ten-mile round trip yesterday and I'm knackered already."

"Umm, okay, we go with Plan B. Susan, stay in your bedroom and keep the door slightly ajar. When you see them come out give me a signal from your window – I'll be out in the garden somewhere, that should give me time, if they're around, to divert them long enough for Sadie to draw Randy Rooster out the front door. I'll leave it open so you can head for the trees by the drive, you've got plenty of places to hide. You look worried, Sadie."

"You weren't much of a group leader at school then."

"It's the best I can come up with on the spur of the moment, it isn't that bad is it?"

"Let's say I can see one or two flaws in it, but hey, what could possibly go wrong?"

Twelve o'clock sharp Mr Rooster appeared at the front door, his oversized Jeep towering over the inspector's Ford Focus. Sam answered the door and now stood staring at someone who clearly needed a big vehicle to compensate for his lack of stature. He was certainly not what she was expecting – instantly reminding her of a pufferfish crossed with a beetroot. Rich he may be, but handsome he most certainly wasn't.

"Good day to you, ma'am."

Sam smiled. "Mr Rooster, I presume?" A tilt of the head reassured her she was right. "How nice to meet you."

"God darn it. I just love that English accent." He looked at her with hungry eyes. "I must say, ma'am, it looks like I'm going to be a lucky man today." The words trickled out of the side of his mouth as he spoke. "Tony warned me you were a mighty bit older but damn sure she forgot to mention how pretty you were, and it doesn't do a chicken farmer any harm to get his teeth into a mature bird now and again."

Sam realised with some disgust that he was looking at her, fully plucked, trussed and ready for stuffing. "I'm sorry, Mr Rooster, I think you're mistaken, it's Sadie who is your appointment for today. My husband and I own this farm, Samantha's the name."

"Begging your pardon, ma'am, no offence meant."

"None taken, Mr Rooster."

"Well that's just dandy." His eyes quickly scanned the exterior of the house and surrounding landscape. "Quaint place you got here, Samantha."

"We like it, suits me and my husband perfectly well."

"God darn it. There you go again, I'd pay good money just to have you talk to me with that accent."

Why was she talking like a country snob? Perhaps subconsciously she was trying to put this arrogant little American in his place – quaint place indeed. "Sadie's waiting for you, if you'll follow me." She led him up the stairs and deposited him, with some relief, in front of Sadie's bedroom door. Two knocks were greeted with a faint 'come in'.

Mr Rooster turned before entering. "If your husband ever tires of you, ma'am, be sure to give me a call." She watched with growing concern as he rummaged in his jacket pocket and produced a shiny bright business card in his sweaty little hand. "Ma'am." He was clearly hoping his offer would at some point in the future be accepted.

"I very much doubt that will happen, Mr Rooster." she replied, quickly glancing down at his card. "Or should I say Chad Memphis? Quaint name. Good day, Mr Memphis."

"Ma'am."

*

Susan was in position, a slight crack in the door allowing her to view without being seen. Now all she had to do was wait. She could hear the odd sound along the landing, but nothing more. She was just wondering if Sadie had actually managed to persuade Mr Rooster that the privacy of the bedroom had far greater merits than roaming about a dusty farm when the door sprang open, allowing an oversized battery hen to stagger out, large feet tripping over the carpet, forcing its head to flop forward. Susan just managed to hold back a giggle as the lumbering bird staggered down the stairs, its obscured vision missing the occasional step, sparking muffled swear words.

"One, two, three, four ... twenty! Coming, sweetheart!" Suddenly a portly pantomime character leapt through the open door, tail feathers erect and ready for action. The randy old bird strutted to the top of the stairs then turned without warning, staring up the landing as if sensing someone's presence. Susan took a sharp intake of air, holding it for as long as possible as the bird's head slowly moved from side to side then turned and made its way down the stairs. She exhaled with relief, channelling the air out of her lungs so fast it sent her head spinning out of control. She turned and made for the window, then without bothering to look started to wave and was met by Sylvia waving back, her hand moving in a regal manner whilst surrounded by a gaggle of WI members.

"Sod it! Where is she?" A scout around the whole garden only managed to spot George weeding one of the flower beds, but no Sam. Panic setting in, she sprinted across the room and out onto the landing. She could hear noises from below like muffled screams persuading her to take the stairs two at a time, but upon reaching the bottom she was confronted by what could only be described as a crude country pursuit. Mr Rooster dismounted and eyed Susan with the look of sheer want.

"Well, well, a young chick, I'll be damned."

"Run, Sadie. I'll sort this moth-eaten heap of feathers out."

Sadie's only way to freedom was via the kitchen; not the intended route but she would take any way out from the claws of this sex-starved over-sized pheasant. Susan had seen enough as she brought her right leg up into contact with the only tender bit of meat that this tough old bird had to offer. A howling crow rang out as she watched the horny Rooster drop to the ground, leaving her to follow Sadie to relative safety.

"You're supposed to have gone out the front door," she said, as she caught up with the staggering slightly plucked chicken.

"Bloody thing was shut. You try opening it with this outfit on – before I knew it he was on me." Sadie could hardly breathe as the muffled words escaped through her beak. "Oh great, I can hear him coming. He can't catch me again so soon, he's paying good money to chase me." They suddenly spotted John, the young inspector and Sam standing next to the barn.

"What's Sam doing with them?" Susan asked.

"Beats me, but I need to get out of here."

"You can't go that way, you'll be spotted."

"Great. You wait until I get hold of Tony – I'll ring her bloody neck, that's if mine doesn't get stretched first." They looked around to see Randy Rooster coming at them through the kitchen. "Got to go, I'll just have to shoot through the garden."

"But—" Susan was cut short by a large beak appearing at the back door. "Run!"

Sadie picked up her sagging feathers and lumbered across the lawn, her top-heavy head bobbing to the ungainly rhythm of her strides. Susan ran in the opposite direction, hoping to attract Sam's attention while horny Rooster peeled off and was seen gaining on his original target, waddling between the flower beds trying to take a shortcut. Luckily for all concerned George was on a break and Sylvia had retreated to her kitchen to reload the teapot, but unfortunately she'd left Joan and Martha Snodbury, the twin daughters of Lord and Lady Snodbury of Dartfield Manor, discussing the intricate process of setting marmalade. They looked on as Sadie limped by, closely followed by a five-foot talking bird.

"Afternoon, ladies." A courteous wing shot up.

The two ladies raised a hand in response. "Good afternoon."

"God darn it, don't you just love that accent!"

Their heads moved, following the unusual creature

before it finally disappeared from view, leaving them to casually resume their discussion on all things jam related.

Susan found herself crouching behind a bush, peering over the top in an attempt to attract Sam's attention without being spotted.

"Is that one of your girls?" Miss Butterworth rearranged her glasses so she could get a better look at the continued odd behaviour of the Taylor household.

"Ah, yes," replied Sam, trying not to panic. "Will you excuse me for a minute? That's Susan, a sweet thing, but two bales short of a full load, if you know what I mean. I'll just go and see what she wants."

Sam looked at John pointedly as she left the two to their business. "Susan, what are you doing?"

"I was just about to ask you the same thing. Where were you when I signalled?"

"They came back sooner than I thought so I've been trying to stall them for as long as possible. How's it going anyway?"

"Not great. Sadie got caught in the hallway, apparently the front door was shut."

"Ah, I forgot about that. Where are they now?"

"That's the problem, I don't know. I lost sight when they took off across the lawn, they could be anywhere by now."

"Just what we need, but the good news is we're almost finished, we've just got to have a look over the pigs and then I'll take them indoors for a spot of lunch. You go and see if you can find the love birds and try and head them away from the orchard. I'll see you later."

"Pigs next." Sam rejoined the two. "If you'd like to follow me, Miss Butterworth." She gave John another warning shot but by now he really hadn't a clue what was going on. The orchard lay still, just the odd rustle and grunt of rooting pigs, their mother stretched out enjoying the shade of an overhanging canopy.

"Oh, this is so idyllic, Mr and Mrs Taylor. I was told you had a model organic farm and I have to say I haven't been disappointed. You should be congratulated for your efforts – I only wish others would follow your example."

John took his praise with open arms and was now prepared to discuss various organic topics at length, only too pleased to have a willing ear listen to his life's work, while Sam was looking at something moving amongst the trees. On closer inspection, and to her horror, she saw a knackered old hen weaving its way through the tangled branches of neglected apple trees. To her relief Miss Butterworth had her back to the proceedings and was happily discussing attracting new members to the organic movement. Sam discreetly kept one eye on the moving object, knowing full well it was poor Sadie. Struggling to stay upright, her body showing near defeat, she took shelter within the relative safety of the old chicken hut, but no sooner had she closed the door than Mr Rooster was spotted and unfortunately followed suit. A large bang of the wooden door echoed around the orchard, making Miss Butterworth turn with growing curiosity.

"What was that?" The young woman's eyes scanned the surrounding landscape but could find nothing out of the ordinary.

"Probably someone shooting, that's all," Sam replied. She'd just quietly congratulated herself on a spur-of-the-moment white lie when they were all subjected to an ear-piercing "Cock-a-doodle-doo!"

"Is that a cockerel, Mr Taylor?"

"No." John immediately shook his head. "We don't have a cockerel, can't stand the things, can get nasty if you don't watch it."

"But I'm sure I heard one." Her eyes scanned the trees with suspicion, waiting for a sound, any sound, to verify her concern, but there was only an eerie silence. She'd almost given up when the hen house shuddered, rocked from side to side and produced another spine-chilling crow. "There, Mr Taylor, definitely a cockerel. And that hut seems to be moving. You understand I must inspect all animals that are being kept on the premises."

"But we don't have a cockerel."

"Mr Taylor. I hope you're not trying to hide anything from me – we at the Organic movement take a dim view of such practices." As she spoke, a blood-curdling howl sent the hut into spasms of violent jerking. "Mr Taylor, what on earth is going on?"

"Beats me."

The young lady paled by the second as she was subjected to the sound of raucous sexual noises. Sam had to do something, and quick. "Miss Butterworth, I can explain."

"You can?"

"Yes. John, don't you remember? It's almost certainly that big old cockerel from next door again. It's becoming quite a nuisance, Miss Butterworth. I'm afraid he has a bit of a wandering habit when the urge grips it, and I'm afraid will kidnap one of our hens from time to time, and I'm sorry to say strips her of any dignity."

"How horrible." The poor girl now looked positively shocked.

"Yes, quite horrible, Miss Butterworth. Powerless to do anything about it bar shooting the creature."

The inspector removed her glasses and with a clean hanky wiped the sweat from her eyelids. "Extraordinary. I don't think I've ever heard of such a thing. And big, you say?"

"Huge," Sam replied. "He can have his way for days, the poor hen's quite buggered by the time he's finished. Literally," she added.

The young girl's glasses almost fell out of her hand. "You mean … from behind?"

Sam nodded, trying to keep a straight face. "I'm afraid so, plucked to an inch of her life, won't lay for months afterwards." Their ears were assaulted by yet another loud thump followed by a thrust that sent the hut rolling onto its side.

"This is shocking, Mr Taylor."

"You can say that again."

"Mr Taylor, Mrs Taylor, I must strongly advise you both to correct this situation as soon as possible. The mixing of organic and non-organic livestock is not something we will tolerate and I suggest you have a stern word with your neighbour, this cannot continue. However, I will let this matter pass on this occasion, but you must sort it out. The well-being of your chickens are of paramount importance. Please correct it, Mr Taylor."

John just nodded, still not knowing what the hell was going on.

"Very good, Mr Taylor." She turned to Sam. "Quite bizarre, Mrs Taylor."

"I agree, Miss Butterworth."

Sam knew she was pushing her luck but she had a hunch this rather traumatised young lady wouldn't accept. "Miss Butterworth, would you like to check on the hens' well-being?"

Sam saw her remove her glasses for the second time, her hands visibly shaking. "That won't be necessary, Mrs Taylor." Her last word was met by yet more grunting sounds. She stepped back and prepared to bolt to the safety of the house. "Paperwork, Mrs Taylor."

"Excellent idea, Miss Butterworth."

*

That evening a veil of calm had settled upon the farm. Miss Butterworth had eaten very little of her lunch and left in a hurry with strict instructions to get things sorted before the next inspection, which she had booked for twelve months' time, underlining the fact she herself would not be attending that particular appointment using the excuse that it was policy not to send the same person for two inspections in a row. Sam didn't believe this for one minute, watching with amusement as her Ford Focus left the farm in a cloud of dust.

John had finally been filled in on the bizarre happenings of the day, but found it all too much and was now asleep in the front room. Mr Rooster had been more than satisfied with his quaint little farm experience and had paid handsomely, stating upon leaving that if Samantha were ever wanting to sell he'd be more than interested. She'd politely shown him the door, ripping up his card as the Jeep made its way up the drive.

Tony arrived back to a chorus of abuse and was told never to invite that horrible little American again. The Snodbury sisters had raised concerns on Sylvia's return, telling of an encounter with a rather large bird sporting an American accent. Sylvia had promptly pushed the home-made whisky-based marmalade to one side, suggesting perhaps they had overindulged and strawberry jam may be more to their liking.

Sam stood at the sink washing the last of the tea plates, her hands submerged in warm bubbles allowing the odd chuckle to escape her lips, for this was what her home was built for, to be filled with mischief and mayhem, something raucous children would have provided in bucket loads. She felt that ever present pull to the heart as tears clouded her vision, then carried on as if nothing really mattered.

Chapter 30

"Ah, Susan, just the person I wanted to see." Sam placed a freshly baked cake into a rather tatty looking tin and could clearly see the girl questioning its condition. "It was my mother's, I haven't the heart to throw it out and let's face it, a new one wouldn't do any better a job, it's just the outside that looks a little dated."

"I wasn't going to say anything."

"Nice try, young lady, but it's written all over your face. Anyway, I've made this fruitcake for Vincent after you saying you almost gave him a heart attack the other day. I felt a bit guilty for not going to see him in ages so I thought this might go some way towards a peace offering." She paused for a moment. "And I was hoping you'd like to come with me?"

Susan hesitated. "I don't know, I'd love to come, of course I would. He did invite me back, but I don't want to cramp your style."

Sam gave a light chuckle. "You youngsters do come out with some strange things. For a start, you won't be in the way and secondly, I lost my 'style' as you put it years ago – that's if I had any in the first place. I'm only going to deliver a cake, not chat the old man up. Please, say you'll come, it'll be good to be alone together again."

Her eyes lit up. "Well, if you put it like that, how can I refuse?"

"Great. Now, it's Sunday, so there's not much to do – Sadie's over at Lizzie's and Tony's helping John move some heifers. Apparently this afternoon she's going to help with milking."

Susan detected a slight resentment in Sam's voice as she secured the lid of the tin.

"They're spending quite a lot of time together, aren't they?"

The older woman ran her finger around the tin, trying to force unwanted thoughts from her head. "I suppose it's only natural. Tony loves this farm, that's pretty plain to see, and for all her good looks she's definitely a country girl at heart."

"That sounds like you shouldn't be in the country if you're good-looking?"

"I didn't mean it like that, but you do wonder. Anyway, it doesn't matter."

Susan moved closer. "It's not just that, is it?"

"Perhaps not. I'm no fool, she's an incredibly good-looking girl, what man could resist that?"

"You don't mind?"

"I can hardly plead poverty, now can I? But no, it's still hard, I just hope she doesn't make a fool of him, that's all."

"She's a good person, Sam, and I'm sure she wouldn't do anything if she didn't mean it."

"Yes, that's what I'm afraid of."

Susan looked at the older woman. "Incredibly good-looking, is she? Should I be jealous?"

"Not my type, sweetheart. Now are you coming with me? Because I'm going in half an hour."

"Give me a kiss and I'm all yours."

Sam shook a warning finger. "You know what Sadie said – not in public, and anyway, you're mine already so go and get yourself sorted. Half an hour, now shoo."

*

The climb over the stile brought back memories of that first encounter with Vincent, and Susan felt a tingle of excitement knowing they would soon meet again. Why, she couldn't explain – he was, in the eyes of anyone who cared to look, a total stranger, but there was something drawing her to him. They made their way through the trees heading for the light of the open fields. She watched as Sam gazed up into the oak's heavy dark green canopy.

"I love trees; don't they fill you with joy? So peaceful, so undemanding. I don't get out nearly as much as I should." There was the ever-changing scent upon the breeze as she allowed her body to race with excitement as Susan's hand moved to her waist. It was as if the mere touch could take her into another world. The other hand wandered up to waiting breasts, gentle strokes at first for she was unsure as to the response.

"Susan?" As Sam spoke a finger went to her mouth, pleading her to stay silent. Their heads turned and found each other's waiting lips. It was this soft unconditional meeting of two willing females that had the ability to suck the air out of her lungs. The forgotten tin dropping to the ground. The kiss went hard and deep, manipulating their minds into submission as Susan felt her own breasts being caressed by the one she knew as hers, the one person she envisioned every morning as her hands explored beneath the sheets. Sam wanted this so much, yet somehow her hand pulled away, signalling they needed to stop. "We shouldn't be doing this, not here."

"Why?"

"I'm sorry, it's not you. I'm afraid of messing things up. We need to be careful, and this isn't being careful, we're on a footpath – anyone could spot us. Village life can be cruel if you don't obey the rules."

The young woman stepped back off the path. "Does this make any difference?"

"No, it doesn't, and don't pout your lips at me, public footpaths or not."

Susan fluttered her eyelids. "Just one more kiss then and I'll let you go."

Sam knew she was beaten. "Okay, but only one." Their lips met, but this time the passion had gone; it felt more like a farewell embrace, a 'goodbye until we meet again' sort of kiss. They pulled away and noticed the discarded tin laying on its side.

"Oh dear." Sam examined it for any damage. "Just another dent to the side, nothing too serious." But as she carefully opened the lid she saw that the poor cake had taken a direct hit, its pristine surface now blemished by loose broken pieces. "Oh well, look on the bright side, I thought about making an iced chocolate one – that wouldn't have fared so well!"

This light humour was enough to break the tension as they carried on towards the wide open fields. As Susan ran ahead up the long drawn-out slope, Sam was reminded of the age difference and began to wonder what the hell she was doing. That niggling doubt that had successfully been pushed to one side suddenly reappeared like a bolt of lightning from a near-perfect blue sky. Why was someone so young and full of life prepared to tie themselves down to a middle-aged crone? Surely she would tire of her company in the end? She waved to the girl in the distance and felt a gut-wrenching pain in her stomach, not through illness but simply worry for the future.

Vincent heard the gate, his elderly eyes peering down the path waiting for whoever dared to venture into his little world. Sam led the way, her composure recovered. The old man pulled himself out of his rocking chair and welcomed his old friend. "Samantha. What a pleasant surprise." His eyes quickly found the younger woman. "And Susan Swan, this is a delight. I am blessed indeed with two beautiful women – I don't believe my poor heart will cope."

Sam moved forward and placed a gentle kiss upon his cheek. "Always the gentleman and charmer. How are you, Vincent?"

"I am fine, my dear."

Susan followed with a kiss to the other cheek. "Vincent." It was a mere whisper in the old man's ears.

"My dear." He touched his face where her lips had been. "I believe I won't wash for a week." It was difficult to pull his eyes from the girl's face. "I must apologise for my lack of manners, I'm afraid you'll have to find yourselves a chair, there's a few around." His hand waved about as he gripped his own chair for support. "You will excuse me, my legs are not as good as they were, I think perhaps it may have something to do with old age."

Susan stepped back; it didn't seem the same with the three of them. He sat down while Sam rescued two moth-eaten specimens allowing them to chatter about the weather, village gossip and John's work on the farm, all topics that were designed to draw out their visit to the maximum, but none of which Susan found particularly interesting.

"Oh, I almost forgot, I brought you this." Sam held out the dented tin.

"Samantha, you are a dear."

She pried the lid open enabling Vincent to view the damaged fruitcake. "I'm afraid it got dropped along the way."

"It looks and smells heavenly, thank you, Samantha."

She quickly glanced at her watch. "Look at the time – I should be off. If lunch isn't ready John will throw his wellies out the window."

"So soon?" he said, unable to hide his disappointment as he placed the tin to one side.

"Why don't you stay and talk some more, Susan?" Sam suggested. "I have to get lunch but it won't be ready for a while and I'm sure Vincent wouldn't complain." Her suggestion had clearly gone down well as she was confronted by two rather pleased looking faces. "If Vincent doesn't mind, of course?"

"Not at all, my dear, I'd be only too pleased to have Susan's company."

"There you are then, sorted." The women's eyes briefly connected, showing their love for one another, something that didn't go unnoticed.

"I'll see you soon, Vincent."

"Goodbye, Samantha, and thank you for the cake, but the tin?"

A dismissive wave of the hand reassured him he shouldn't worry. "I'm sure one of us will be back soon, isn't that right, Susan?"

"Yes, very soon."

"Right, I must go." She turned and wandered down the path, hesitating before disappearing out of sight. Two's company, she thought and carried on.

Vincent slumped back in his chair. "She's a lovely woman, as kind as they come."

"Yes, she is."

Her tone of voice told Vincent everything he needed to know as he watched a wanting soul pull herself into a moment's silence. He sighed. No good would come of what he'd just seen but it wasn't any business of his, people had to sort their own lives out. He looked back at his own with nothing but heartache and lost moments, but at least for him the pain would soon be gone and all those years of waiting would be over.

All Susan wanted was to run after Sam, spend precious time alone with her, but the voice in her head held her back, telling her to stay and comfort this man, a person she hardly knew. Vincent, out of respect, held back, not wishing to unlock the girl from her thoughts. Just looking at her was pleasure enough; all the years of waiting and now she was here. All he wanted was to just hold her, if only for a moment, if only for one last time to touch those lips without fear of them vanishing into his shadowy dreams.

"I'm sorry." Susan's voice shattered his thoughts.

He looked surprised. "Whatever for, my dear?"

"Sam told me about Alice, and me wearing that dress, it must have been an awful shock. I hope I didn't upset you too much?"

He said nothing for a while as she noticed his eyes glistening. "On the contrary, my dear, you made an old man very happy."

Without thinking she went to him, kneeling down to rest her head against his frail leg. She heard the sound of a grown man crying as he gently ran his fingers through her hair, her own eyes watering. They sat listening to the giant echo of the surrounding countryside, both content to be allowed to follow their own paths. Susan then pulled away, returning to her chair, allowing Vincent to wipe his face.

"Thank you," he said, raising his head.

She smiled, finding herself swimming within the love of two lost people. "She must have been very beautiful?" Susan dared to push the boundaries, but felt sure Vincent was ready to open up his soul.

"Yes, she was. They say time heals the pain, but I can assure you it does not. How can it when I see her every time I go to sleep, waiting for me to come back from a war no one wanted, a war that I loathed with all my heart, but one we had to fight." He clenched his fists with regret and anger. "She waited, but in the end it was me who had to suffer the agony of passing time, but you, dear Susan, gave me that brief passage back in time, something I will treasure until my last breath."

She looked him straight in the eye. "I'm not Alice, Vincent."

"No, dear, I'm no fool. Old, yes, but for a moment I dared to believe, and after all these years I felt justified in doing so. I hope you don't mind. And no, you are not Alice, but we will be together soon. I'm sure this life can't go on forever, but I hope until that time comes you'll accept me as a friend and admirer, nothing more."

Susan wiped the moisture from her eyes. "It will be a pleasure to get to know you, Vincent."

He gazed out into the distance. "I think Alice would have liked you." They continued to sit in silence, nothing allowed to complicate the deafening sounds of Mother Nature until the old man spoke again. "I think a slice of cake is in order, don't you? I feel all this emotional turmoil is making me rather hungry." He went to rise but was held back by Susan's hand.

"I'll go."

"No, dear, you wouldn't know where anything is. You just sit there and enjoy the peace and quiet." With some effort his old bones made their way into the house, taking him back to his hidden world of the past leaving Susan wondering about the part of him he wished to keep private. She was certain he was lonely, but he had chosen to be so.

"Here we are then." With slices that wouldn't feed a mouse, Vincent made his way back to his chair and carefully repositioned the cushions before resting his body back into place.

Susan's first mouthful saw her hand brush a stray crumb away from her lips before she spoke. "It's lovely here."

"Yes, it is. I remember the first time I saw it. I was lost in a world of grief, still mourning the loss of three people I truly loved. Sam told you about my parents, I suspect?"

Susan nodded.

"Of course." His plate balanced upon his knee. "I'd drifted from one place to another hoping maybe that

I would find them but knowing deep down they were dead, yet you never seem to give up." A faint grin appeared on his wrinkled face. "It was a day like today when I just happened to notice a 'for sale' sign hanging from the gate. The trees were mere saplings back then, it was far more open and you could see the cottage from the lane, but even then it had a charm, a homely presence to it. You can't really describe that feeling. Of course there was no such thing as locked doors in those days, so I found myself walking around its empty rooms. It was in a shocking state but it felt right. Have you ever had that feeling, Susan, when you knew something was meant to be?" He knew her answer before he had finished.

"Yes."

It was tempting to probe deeper; that look in the two women's eyes as they had parted had said it all, but how deep those emotions went he wasn't sure. "So I bought it – that was nearly seventy years ago and here I am still waiting."

Susan looked up, her face showing concern. "Do you want to die?"

"I'm ready to die, if that's what you're asking, but do I want to?" He looked around at his overgrown patch of England. "On a day like this and with your company? No. Who would want to leave that? But this is such a brief moment of my life, tomorrow may be different."

"I can't imagine wanting to die." Susan sounded confused.

Vincent chuckled. "That's because you're young and

in love." He suddenly stopped himself from saying another word, wishing he hadn't said the last.

Susan looked at him. He knew! Dare she confess to this man? She longed to tell someone about her love for a woman she couldn't have, yet that voice was telling her he could be trusted and was worthy of her confession. "You know." There, it was said. All she could do now was wait and take the consequences.

"About you and Samantha? I had hoped it wasn't so, but I recognised that look and I can still see it in Alice's eyes, even after all these years."

"You think it's wrong, don't you?"

"I think it could be complicated. As to whether I think it is wrong, I'm too old to be concerned about such things. Your life is just that – yours. Mine is almost at an end."

The young woman tried to look serious. "That doesn't answer my question."

"What, if two women should fall in love?" He rested back in his chair, lightly holding both hands together. "It's not something I have ever had to contemplate. I had love and lost it, that's all I know, but it's something no one should go through be they a man or woman, so perhaps unintentionally I have just answered your question."

Susan knew it wouldn't be wise to push any further. Whether Vincent truly approved she would probably never know, but for now it was clear he had started to tire. They'd arrived unannounced which in itself was a strain, and she was sure older people needed a good week to prepare for a social visit. "You're looking tired. I should go."

Vincent's gaze twinkled behind paper-thin eyelids. "You're an observant young woman; I confess I am a little worn down by all this entertaining." His bony hand stretched out. "I wonder if I could ask you to help me up?" He knew he could rise by himself; living on your own and at his age warranted that daily struggle, but he needed to touch her one more time, remind him of the girl he had lost, and for that brief moment, as their hands gripped one another, he saw Alice staring back at him. "Thank you, my dear."

"May I come again?" Susan asked.

Vincent looked surprised. "I would be most disappointed if you didn't. We have much to talk about, Susan Swan."

She leant forward and gave his cheek the lightest of kisses. "Take care, Vincent. Next Sunday?"

"I'm sure I can fit you in."

Her pace took her halfway along the path before she decided to turn, but Vincent had gone, the door still partially open, but no sign of the man she now felt so deeply for.

She arrived back to cheerful voices flooding out from the kitchen. Sam turned as she entered. "Good, just in time. These two might have eaten the lot if you were any longer." John and Tony looked like two naughty excitable children innocently playing with the other.

"You two look pleased with yourselves." Susan went to wash her hands, discreetly giving Sam a sideways glance.

"We've had a wonderful time, haven't we, John?"

"We have that."

Tony was grinning from ear to ear. "We've been moving some heifers to the top fields – well, trying to."

"Lost one or two," John butted in.

"And whose fault was that?" Tony replied.

"Okay, blame me."

The bubbly young woman nudged John in the ribs with her elbow. "Good fun, though." They giggled like teenagers, then without warning John placed his arm around Tony's waist and proceeded to announce, "This young lady's going to do her first milking this afternoon. I tell you it's nice to have someone to come out and help me on the farm. Don't get enough of it, but she is a treasure, aren't you, girl?" His hand squeezed her fine waist.

"You're a good teacher, John."

Giggles danced around the room, hitting Sam on the back of her neck as she gritted her teeth. Susan smiled politely but felt the embarrassment hard to swallow; such affection in public wasn't the done thing. She looked towards Sam, longing to hold her for it was plain to see the woman was hiding the hurt, but what could she do? These two giggling hyenas would've missed an elephant walking through the room they were so into each other, and it wasn't as if Tony was a dumb brainless creature. Tony was well educated, possibly far cleverer than she was, which got her thinking that perhaps she was playing John like a fiddle.

Tony finally came up for air, swallowing a mouthful of food before speaking. "I hope I don't get my hands dirty, wouldn't be good for my line of work."

"Don't you worry about that," John replied. "I can give you a good scrub down afterwards."

"Cheeky so and so."

Susan cringed with every word. This wasn't like Tony – she was definitely up to something. Yes, it was common knowledge she loved the farm, but John? That was another matter entirely.

"Well, work stops for no person; we can't all stay indoors doing nothing. Come on, Tony, we've got cows to milk."

They heard the back door slam, causing Sam to throw her dishcloth to one side.

"Are you okay?" Susan placed her knife and fork to one side and watched the older woman's anger grow by the minute.

"Fine! Never better." She spun around and looked Susan straight in the eye.

"What?" asked Susan with concern.

"Can you work on a full stomach?"

Susan tilted her head to one side in confusion.

"Well?"

"I'm not that hungry, so I've not eaten that much. Why?"

"Good, because I want you upstairs in your bedroom right now!"

Susan looked at the remains of her meal. "I knew there was a reason why I wasn't hungry."

"Right, up there, now." Sam pointed to the open door. "I'll show those two sniggering jackasses. Keep me indoors while he plays with his new toy, will he? Well, I'm going to make the most of it!"

Susan could only smile. "I like it when you're so dominating."

"You haven't seen anything yet, my girl." Sam took her by the hand and pulled her up the stairs.

Susan looked on as the bedroom door slammed shut. She didn't know what was about to happen but had a funny feeling it could be very enjoyable. "You're not worried if they come back then?" she asked.

"Young lady, do I look like I give a damn? Now strip off." Sam had already started to undress, flinging her top on the floor in a frenzy of fumbling fingers.

Susan was having trouble keeping up as the urgency showed on Sam's face, but eventually her shirt went the same way, exposing her half-covered breasts.

"Off with the bra. Now." Sam had already stripped to

the waist, then with a quick flick she saw Susan do as she was told. They stood looking at each other, daring one another to make the next move. "I said strip."

Susan couldn't believe what was happening – exciting yet slightly worrying, it had all been a bit of a game up to now. Serious, yes, but a game nonetheless.

With glowing eyes Sam demanded Susan did as she was told. "I said take them off," she ordered, pointing to Susan's jeans. Her frustration rising by the second, she ran to Susan and began to undo the zipper herself. "When I tell you to do something you do it, are you listening?"

"Yes, Sam."

"Good girl."

Susan was powerless to stop her body from being willingly raped, but then Sam suddenly stepped back, her urgency melting. Susan stood virtually naked, her only shred of decency a finally woven black pair of panties.

"Take them off, but slowly."

Reaching to either side Susan gently, with the utmost care, slid the fine material over her hips and let them drop.

"Now come here."

As Susan walked slowly towards her, Sam took in Susan's naked body. "Kneel down and take the rest of my clothes off." With a pounding heart Sam felt two delicate hands remove them. "Get up. Now go and lie on the bed." She wanted nothing more than to grab Susan and touch that perfect smooth youthful skin, but she would savour her, she would show that arrogant husband of hers she wouldn't be humiliated in her own kitchen. "Part your legs." Susan gladly did as she was told, bracing herself for the ultimate lovemaking experience as she felt the bed move beneath her.

*

Sam woke first and glanced at the bedside clock. John wouldn't be in until six – it was now four-thirty. A look at the beautiful girl lying beside her confirmed she was doing the right thing; she couldn't fight those feelings any longer. How she had come to be with someone so perfect was a mystery. She leant over and carefully kissed Susan's lips, forcing her eyes to slowly open. "Hi." Sam didn't say another word, just rubbed her aching lower half against Susan's leg.

The next time she looked, the clock screamed five-thirty and she knew the only option was to get up. John would be in soon expecting his tea, yet her legs felt like jelly as she pulled herself out of bed. It wouldn't do to have too much time to herself, God forbid the thought. She pictured the two chuckling clowns. Who is laughing now, John Taylor? she muttered to herself. Her problem, as she could see it, was actually getting dressed and down the stairs without falling flat on her face. She needed to keep telling herself that this orgasm lark could be overdone. Her first attempt failed miserably. Ten dizzy minutes later she staggered into the kitchen.

Desperately still trying to coordinate her fingers, she attempted to lay the table. As she turned she heard the two so-called workers making their way along the back passage, Tony's voice sending her nerves on edge.

"I'm going to smell for days at this rate."

"I did promise to rub you down earlier, the offer still stands."

"John Taylor, don't you let Sam hear you say that."

"I wasn't going to invite her."

"Cheeky thing."

Sam couldn't help but congratulate herself on a good afternoon's workout; if only these two knew. Her legs were still a little unstable but it felt so good to have the upper hand. She politely smiled as the two wandered in. "Hello you two, had a pleasant afternoon?"

"Great thank you."

Sam watched as Tony placed her scrawny little backside onto one of the chairs.

"Tony nearly got covered in shit, I had to pull her out of the way."

"That was good of you, dear." Sam clenched her teeth as John picked up a dry piece of bread that could very well kill a duck from a hundred metres away.

"This is a bit hard, haven't we got any fresh stuff?"

Not for you, you snivelling pile of mouse droppings. "Ah no, I'm afraid not fresh. Tomorrow, when I pick it up from the store, sorry. Hope you both choke on it," she muttered under her breath.

"What was that?" John asked.

"I said I could make toast of it."

He tapped it on the surface of the table. "Suppose it will have to do. You really should make sure we have reserves with all these extra mouths to feed."

Sam could almost feel steam blowing out of her ears. "No, you're right, John, it was silly of me not to order more."

"Good girl, you'll get used to it."

He was chewing his way through the first mouthful of something that had been lying in the pig bucket only minutes earlier when he noticed someone was missing. "No Susan?"

"She's upstairs having a lie down, I think she's a little tired."

"Right, but she doesn't do anything all day. Not like this one – we've both been hard at it
since this morning."

"Really? Don't forget we went over to see Vincent. It's quite a walk across to his place."

"Oh, and that counts as a whole day's work, does it?"

Even Tony was starting to feel uncomfortable. "I think I'll take this up to my room. I've got some things to do before tomorrow, I'll bring the plate down after. See you later, John."

"Yes, okay, and thanks for your help, we must do it again."

"Love to."

John waited until he heard the footsteps reach the top of the stairs and then turned to face his wife. "What's your problem?"

"Don't know what you mean."

"You know exactly what I mean. You've been like a cow with a sore udder since lunch, and don't think I haven't noticed."

All Sam wanted was to rip into him, grab his wandering dick and do a Chinese burn on it. That would slow him down for a day or two, but she couldn't. It was too risky getting angry with him – she'd only end up saying something she'd regret. Sadie already knew about Susan; she couldn't have anyone else finding out, certainly not her husband. "I'm sorry. I'm a bit under the weather. Probably coming down with something, there were some people coughing and spluttering in the store the other day. I had a long lie down this afternoon yet I still feel exhausted, my legs have no strength and there are parts of me that ache something rotten."

John suddenly realised he'd probably overstepped the mark and was feeling a little guilty. "I didn't realise. You should have said. There we were having fun and you're here suffering. Do you think Susan's coming down with the same thing?"

"I wouldn't be surprised; she does seem to have almost

identical symptoms as me. I'll take her up some soup later."

"Yes, good idea."

"Then maybe I'll have a good hot bath and perhaps go to bed early."

John nodded. "Sounds like the best thing. I've got too much work to do, don't want to be coming down with anything."

His shallow concern didn't go unnoticed. "I would be very surprised if you did."

"Nevertheless, these things can be contagious, so you make sure to have that bath and get off to bed, all ready for tomorrow."

"What's happening tomorrow?"

"Well, there's all the cooking and washing to do, a house doesn't run by itself."

Sam wondered why she'd ever agreed to marry this man. She thought he'd been genuinely concerned up until that point. "Thanks for caring so much."

"That's all right, what are husbands for?"

Sam said nothing.

*

With hot soup in hand she stood at Susan's door and knocked twice.

"Come in."

She slowly pushed the door open and made her way

in. "I've brought you some soup, you're supposed to be going down with the same bug as I've got."

"I don't understand?"

Sam winked. "Cover story for why we both spent the afternoon in bed. Separately, of course."

"I see. Clever."

She placed the tray to one side. "To be on the safe side I think I should take your temperature, you can never be too careful with these things." She ran a hand under the sheets and placed it between Susan's legs. "Umm ... a little hot, but nothing to worry about." They both started to laugh. "Shush, we're supposed to be ill."

"Love fever more like it."

"Oh dear, Miss Swan, that could be quite fatal. No cure, I'm afraid."

"I sincerely hope not."

*

Sam watched John dozing off to sleep while the telly chatted away to itself. "John?"

"What?"

"I'm off to bed."

He casually looked up from his armchair. "Oh, good. And how's Susan?"

"Much better. It's amazing what an afternoon nap does to the body." Reluctantly she left Tony alone with her husband, but for the sake of her supposed illness she had to be seen to be doing the right thing. "Goodnight, Tony."

"'Night, Sam."

The girl was laid out on the sofa reading a book, long slender legs sprawled across the cushions and those shorts doing little to cover much of her lower region, allowing anyone with a good eye to see over to the next county. John, she was sure, would be turned on, but that didn't much worry her any more – there had been time to think while soaking in the hot scented bathtub about the situation they all found themselves in, and she had come to the conclusion she was no better than him. Worse, in fact, so she decided to let him have his fun.

Sam climbed the stairs, stopping briefly at Susan's door. It was tempting, very tempting. Their afternoon had been amazing, and being bossy was quite a turn on, something she would have to do more often. But for now she must play the sickly patient and be content with the memory of the past three or four hours.

She couldn't sleep. It was far too early to go to bed, but these bugs could be tricky little things. She lay with her eyes wide open listening to the sounds floating up from downstairs. At first she thought it was the TV, but the clock told her it was well past the weather, surely he wasn't still watching it. Straining her ears, she could just make out Tony's voice, then John's laughter. They were at it again! She mustn't get upset; there was Susan now, that's all that mattered. She rolled over, trying to block out her concerns before finally drifting off into a light sleep.

She was woken by John coming into the bedroom. She heard him undress and then felt the bed sink to one side as he climbed in. Then nothing. She knew he would simply fall asleep, leaving her to yet again pass the time away until sleep took over. She wasn't sure how long it was when she felt movement. John was clearly restless, mumbling to himself, tossing and turning, touching her in the back. Then to her horror a hand wandered all over her body, acting like a demented octopus, his tentacles trying to sneak into every nook and cranny. Mumbles subsiding, he started a rhythmic motion as Sam lay perfectly still, hoping he would end his dream and sleep. Normally his snoring was the only problem, and that could always be stopped by a quick dig in the ribs, but this?

Suddenly he rolled over. Sam held her breath as realisation set in – he'd hardened like a pogo stick and was intent on using it. She felt the rod of iron trying to find its way up the crack of her arse. Gripping the pillow she lay still, but if it went any further she'd have to give it a sharp slap around its head. Now his hands had found her breasts; what had gotten into him? And to cap it all his thing was getting far too close to her back passage. She only had one option left and regrettably the time had come to roll on her back, part her legs and think of Susan. It was a cruel thing to do to an absent lover, but she hoped she would understand. She'd only just managed to roll back when she felt John's full weight bearing down on her as he called out Tony's name and shot at will. So that was it; her husband was making love to her while thinking about another woman, and a young stunningly good-looking woman at that. God, no wonder he'd come so quick. She'd been used and all she had to show for it was a damp rapidly cooling mess between her legs.

Sudden crazy thoughts shot into her head – what if she got pregnant? No, surely not at her age and with her history, but Sod's law, it could happen. What if the child came out looking like Tony? With such passion anything could happen. My God, the thought of carrying another woman's baby! Could she ever find it in her heart to love it, or would it be resented for the rest of its life? She felt the slime get colder by the second. "Damn you, John Taylor."

Chapter 31

The village fête had arrived. John stood alone, taking in the morning silence as he gazed over the empty marquees, the trestle tables waiting for the onslaught of the ever burdened helpers, village folk that arrived as if by magic and run everything as years past. He felt a sense of pride over his family's continued efforts to keep this quintessential English tradition alive and kicking, and quietly thanked his grandfather who first allowed this occasion to be held on the home lawns. Despite his mother's confession concerning dodgy dealings and a seaside mistress, he felt more in tune with this man than ever before. A mistress? How exciting! The thought made him smile.

He still loved Sam, he was certain of that, but they had lost something along the way, that excitement of being together as one. Not one to point the finger, but sex had never been eventful; it was as if she held part of herself back. He couldn't quite explain it, but rampant it definitely wasn't. Perhaps that's why Grandfather had taken another woman, given him that something marriage quite often failed to supply? The shock of his confession took him by surprise as he realised what excitement a mistress could bring. He quickly glanced around in fear of someone overhearing his thoughts. Stupid, of course they couldn't.

He went to move away but caught sight of Tony's distant figure walking towards him. Could he possibly? he thought. He dreamed about her every night. It wasn't just because she was attractive – although that would be enough – it was also the fact she loved the countryside, this farm and the animals. All of that had taken him totally by surprise. "Tony."

"Morning, John." She looked around the deserted scene. "It is today, isn't it? Only there doesn't seem to be much going on."

John couldn't help but laugh. "It's a pretty casual affair, nothing gets going until about two hours before, then all hell will break loose."

"John?"

"Yes, Tony."

"Me and Susan are a little concerned – we don't really know what we're supposed to be doing, and time's getting on."

"Just look pretty – that should get the punters in."

"If you think I'm going to show off my wares to the oldies of the village, you can think again."

"Wouldn't dream of it, you're for my eyes only."

She tapped him lightly on his nose with a mischievous finger. "I'll see what I can arrange, but seriously, John, what are we doing?"

"Best go and see Sam, she'll sort you out."

"I might just do that, and you be a good boy while I'm away or else. Oh, and Sadie's called off, apparently Lizzie's not happy about coming to this sort of thing. I think it's more to do with the villagers' attitude towards her that she doesn't like."

"Just tell the wife."

Tony wandered off across the lawn knowing full well John's eyes were drooling over her every movement. Men! she thought. They were all the same.

As John predicted, people arrived carefully carrying jams, cakes, clothes, books, trays of flowers, everything and anything that seemed to rattle or clank to the enthusiasm of the willing helpers. The girls watched with amusement as the seriousness of the organisers took hold, gladly giving advice on such matters as prices, labelling, and scolding the odd elderly gentleman who unknowingly placed something in the wrong section then claimed it was nothing to do with him – he'd only helped carry it in.

The notorious Miss Goodman flew from stall to stall checking on this and that, seemly trying to make sense of it all while constantly tapping the side of her head in an attempt to keep her reserve hearing aid from malfunctioning. Sylvia had mastered the art of looking busy when in fact she was doing very little with her commands over the WI members, reducing the girls to tears of laughter.

"Ah, there you are girls." Sam appeared from nowhere brandishing a clipboard and looking like she was the one you asked if you wanted to know anything. "Bric-a-brac stall." She pointed to a mountain of clothes, games, stuffed animals, shoes and just about anything else people didn't have a home for. "That's your job for today, sort that lot out and try and sell it." She glanced at the growing pile of other people's throw-outs. "Try your best. I'll leave the pricing up to you, whatever you can get for it. If it doesn't sell it will most likely end up in the local dump." She suddenly spotted someone in the distance. "I'm wanted, see you later."

They looked at each other and then down at the pile of jumble. "Well, looks like we're old rag and bone women today." Susan rolled up her sleeves. "Better get stuck in." She gingerly picked up a rather large heavily reinforced bright red bra. "You have got to be joking."

Tony glanced over her shoulder. "Suppose we could sell it as a hanging basket."

"Look at it all, are people actually going to buy this lot?"

A pair of near-new shoes found their way into Tony's hand. "I don't know, there are one or two better things here." She placed them on the table and stood back. "There, it's a start."

Susan didn't look overly convinced but suddenly spotted something she recognised. "Oh look, my gran used to have a set of these on her wall."

"What, ducks?"

"Yes. Well I suppose looking at it now it was an odd thing to have in your front room, but each to their own. Oh look, this might be interesting." She picked up a small carved wooden box. "And it rattles."

"Go on then, open it up and see if you've made your fortune."

"It's quite heavy," Susan replied, "and the lid's a bit tight but I think I can—" She suddenly let out an ear-piercing scream, causing a number of people look around. Her hand shot up to her mouth. "God, I think I'm going to be sick."

Tony raced to her side only to be confronted by a smiling set of false teeth wedged in cotton wool. "Is that all?"

"They're gross! We're never going to able sell those."

"Bet you a fiver we do."

"You're on, but just don't put them anywhere near me."

Half an hour later things were taking shape. They stood in front of the stall admiring their handiwork, complete with bright yellow marigold kitchen gloves stretching up to their elbows.

"I think we've done a pretty good job. Not so sure about the pregnancy testing kit though."

"We could give it to George to test the pH in the soil."

"Hark, listen to you." Susan looked at her friend's confident expression. "You're starting to sound all country-like. And how do you know about such things anyway?"

"John was showing me how to test the soil only a few days ago as it happens."

Susan lowered her voice to make sure no one could hear. "What's going on there then?"

"Where?" Tony thought Susan had spotted something she hadn't.

"Not out there, silly, with you and John?" She had to ask, it was something that had been bugging her for days.

"What do you mean?"

"Come on, I've known you long enough to figure out when you're up to something, Tony Chapman, and as your best friend I've every right to hear all the details. So talk."

"You're a nosy so-and-so, aren't you?"

"Yes, and I'm still waiting."

"Well, to be honest I'm not entirely sure I know what I'm doing, but one thing is for certain – I want children, and lots of them."

"Wasn't expecting that," Susan replied. "I thought you were all for living life to the full before thinking along those lines."

"So did I, but coming back here has sort of changed things." Tony felt her friend grab her marigold gloves.

"There's nothing wrong with that."

"I know, but …"

"But what?"

"I want John to be the father, and I know you're going to hate me but I want this farm as well. I'm horrible, aren't I?"

"Christ, Tony." Susan quickly scanned the area before she spoke again. "He's married! Are you seriously prepared to break him and Sam up just because of some dream?"

"I don't know."

"Do you love him?"

"No."

"Well that was pretty precise."

"I'm twenty-five, Susan, he's in his fifties. Don't get me wrong, I like older men, but no, I don't love him. But we do get along really well and he's not too old to father kids."

Susan gripped the marigolds even tighter. "Oh Tony, you do know what you're suggesting?"

"Yes, I think about it every day."

"You could get any rich man you like, and they might even buy you a nice place out in the country."

"What, and be someone's play thing, a mistress? No thanks, the thought of an overweight groper spending the odd dirty weekend doesn't overly appeal. This is where I belong and I've always wanted this place." She gave Susan a hard stare. "Anyway, you can talk, I've seen the way you look at Sam. I'm not daft, so you tell me, because from where I'm standing I reckon there's something going on."

Susan wasn't sure what to say next.

"As I thought," said Tony.

"Yes, okay, you're right. And if you must know, we love each other."

This wasn't the reply Tony was expecting. "Blimey, didn't think it had gone that far. Have you ..."

"Twice."

"Oh, well done, girls." Miss Goodman stood directly behind them admiring their efforts. "Ten minutes until opening, ladies."

Susan smiled and went to check the ice cream tub they'd been given as a money box. The gates opened and to the girls' surprise a mass of people swarmed the lawns with no respect for anyone but themselves as they scattered amongst the stalls. Susan stood back in horror. "Look at them all, I didn't think there were that many people in the village." Hordes of humans demanded their right to be first at whatever they could get their hands on. "God, this is like World War Three! Brace yourself, girl, this lot are after blood."

They watched as clothes flew through the air, mothers pinned this and that onto unwilling children before offering to pay no more than a pound tops, 50p for smaller items.

"I'll take this lot for a fiver, love, and I'm doing meself."

The girls' heads were now threatening to spin off their shoulders as arms shot out in all directions, haggling over 5p, 10p, 15p. These were professionals.

Tony nudged Susan in the ribs, nodding towards an old man who had clearly taken a fancy to the grim set of dentures.

"How much, gorgeous?"

"50p to you, young man."

He smiled, forcing Tony to take a step back as his gums glistened in the sunlight.

"Would you like to try them on before you buy?"

"Don't be daft, girl, they be for the dog."

Tony struggled to suppress a fit of the giggles. "You buy that," Tony shouted, "and I'll throw in the pregnancy testing kit for free."

Both watched on as he opened it and held it up in front of his squinting eyes.

"No good to me, dear. Might be handy for the dog, though, now she's got a fancy new set of teeth, them fellers will be queuing to get a sniff of her."

John basked in the glory of being Lord of the Manor, slowly wandering from one stall to another. He was occasionally stopped by locals who thought it might be good for their lowly standing in the village to be seen talking to someone of importance. He was just making his way over to purchase a cup of tea when the vicar drew alongside.

"John."

"Ah, Vicar, lovely day for it."

"Absolutely splendid, John, wonderful turnout. I must say the village will benefit greatly from the proceeds, I'm sure, and nice to see your young helper getting stuck in. He turned and looked toward Josh manning the coconut shy. "A very willing worker, I must say."

"Yes, Vicar, he's a good lad. I'm hoping to get him to farmer status before too long."

"Marvellous, we must encourage the youth of the village, must we not?"

John noticed a hesitation. "Something the matter, Vicar?"

"Oh, nothing really, but I am a little concerned about the boy's tactics towards getting trade. Please don't get me wrong, the young man is, as I'm sure when we count up the coins at the end of the day, doing rather well, but it's his method of approach that concerns me."

"Is there a problem, Vicar?"

"Not exactly a problem, but let's just say he is rather forceful with the more elderly of our community and I've had one or two complaints."

"Oh right, I didn't realise."

The vicar held up his hand. "Nothing that can't be rectified I'm sure, a quiet word perhaps?"

"Yes, of course, Vicar, I'll go over now."

"Splendid. As you say, John, lovely day, maybe see you at church very soon, and your young ladies. I'm quite certain they would enjoy the experience."

John nodded. "Yes, we'll try and make time." He wondered if the vicar would be so obliging if he knew what the girls did for a living. If he did, he may possibly withdraw his invitation.

"Josh, how's it going?"

"Fine, Mr Taylor, nothing to it once you get into it."

"Good. Josh?"

"Yes, Mr Taylor?"

"It's been brought to my attention that … how can I put this … your sales pitch may be a little demanding towards the more vulnerable of our community."

"Demanding, Mr Taylor? Wot, on the old biddies?"

"Afraid so, Josh. I'm sure you've done very well up to now but we must think of the older generation of the village. It wouldn't do having them going home traumatised; this is after all supposed to be a pleasant trip out for them."

John could see the lad thinking over the accusation. "But Mr Taylor, I've got a shitload of coconuts to get rid of."

"No, Josh, you've got a large amount of coconuts to get rid of."

The boy's head tilted to one side looking somewhat confused as to John's observation. "No, Mr Taylor, I've got a shitload, look." He stepped to one side and pointed to a large Hessian sack that lay on the floor.

"No, Josh, that's what we have on the farm."

"What, coconuts?"

"No, Josh, a load of shit."

"Oh, right, I think. Okay, Mr Taylor, I'll try a bit harder, you'll see."

"Well done, Josh, carry on the good work." Poor boy, John thought, he was clearly only trying to do his best.

John moved on hoping to purchase his cup of tea and a scone when the familiar voice of Josh wafted across the lawn. He turned to see an old lady of some considerable years staggering beneath the weight of two carrier bags. He carried on watching as her legs attempted to make it to the exit before her arms finally gave way, but regrettably she'd been spotted by the coconut mafia.

"Hey you!" Josh called again pointing his finger in her direction. "Yes, you, don't pretend you didn't hear me. That's right, you with the shopping bags, trying to sneak out without having a go for a coconut, were you?"

The woman almost stumbled as she quickened her pace, forcing the bags to hit her rapidly moving kneecaps in an attempt to get to freedom.

"I'd stop if I were you. That's right, get over here."

Looking pale and in obvious distress, she turned and dragged herself towards the open jaws of doom. "That's better. 50p a ball or two for a pound, can't say fairer than that." The poor woman fumbled through her purse, making the mistake of flashing a £5 note. "Five pounds is it, deary? I can see you're keen to get one or two to take home." She tried to stuff it back into her purse but Josh was having none of it. "Thanks." She watched helplessly as the note floated past her nose and disappear into the boy's pocket. "That'll get you ..." He desperately tried to work out how many balls she'd get but very quickly gave up. "That'll get you a shitload of balls, me dear."

Her first attempt hardly reached the end of her feet; the second whipped away and rolled out of the gate; the third veered left narrowly missing a child eating an ice cream and the fourth slipped from her hand far too soon and flew backwards over her head, landing in one of the flower beds. "Not so good at this, are you? Tell you what I'll do, you can have four coconuts for your efforts, can't say fairer than that, now can I." Josh quickly stuffed two in each bag. "That should balance you up. Now you enjoy the rest of the day, love, the gate's that way but mind the step." His last comment left her frail body dragging the bags in disgust as he turned away to focus on his next customer.

John was just about to wander over and caution him for the second time when he walked straight into Henry Satan Jones.

"Ah, John Taylor. Jolly good to see you, old boy." He sported a tweed waistcoat, bright red braces, brown corduroy trousers and a wide-brimmed shooting hat. He clearly had no idea what real country people wore.

"Henry, how are you?"

"Damned good if I do say so myself."

"Croquet lawn all sorted?"

"Excellent job, had some good chappies level the divots, hardly know your blasted cow had ever been there. All forgotten now, water under the bridge and all that. Must go, got to buy the wifey a cream tea."

John was wondering why the village had been blessed with such a pompous man and completely forgot about Josh when he noticed the girls looking slightly less busy. "Ladies, how are we both? Enjoying our little fête?"

"It's an experience," Susan replied, glancing over at Tony with a wary eye. This was awkward, she thought. After her friend's confession earlier she now felt as if she needed to get away. I think I'll have a wander, be back in a minute."

Tony quickly picked up on Susan's concern and simply nodded. "Sounds good."

John waited a moment then leant over the table. "Is she all right?"

"Yes, she's just got a bit of a headache, that's all, probably the excitement of the day."

He looked around to make sure no one was listening. "Did you mean what you said earlier?"

"I might have, but you'll have to remind me."

"You're a tease, young lady."

In truth Tony couldn't remember what she'd said, but John wasn't to know that.

"You'll see what you can arrange; I think that's what

you said."

She flashed him a flirtatious smile. "You have a good memory, John Taylor."

"I do when it comes to you."

"My offer still stands."

She saw a faint twinkle in John's eyes. "I have to go milking now, but if you're around later maybe we could walk up and check on those heifers we moved?" His grin suggested he had no intentions of looking over stock.

"I'll see how tired I am after we've finished up here."

"It's just a suggestion. So I might see you later then?"

"Maybe."

She waited until he'd gone and found herself counting the day's takings. This situation could develop a lot quicker than she'd first thought, and really needed a lot of thinking about. Damn it, her concentration wasn't there. She scanned the garden, searching for Susan, or perhaps she was looking for an excuse to push aside the possible implications of her next move. She spotted her friend at the tea stall. What she'd give to have a coffee and a slice of cake – she wasn't too keen on cream teas. She thought that wouldn't do for a prospective dairy farmer's wife, to not like cream. She ran her fingers through the money. "Mrs Taylor," she heard herself say, "Mrs Antonia Taylor." It had a certain ring to it, but like a sudden gust of wind throwing dust into her unprotected face the reality of what she was proposing almost blinded her. This could no longer be classed as some flippant game; what she did next would almost certainly affect more lives than just hers and was the inevitable heartache worth it, or should she just walk away? Her shoulders sagged with confusion.

*

The fête had finished. Tony gazed out her window at the ghostly empty marquees scattered on the lawn, desperately trying to sort out her thoughts.

John was starting to get very friendly. It would only take a click of the fingers and he would be hers. Whether sometime in the future he would come to regret his sexual urges, that was of no concern to her – she'd always been able to do what she liked to men, to make them jump when the need arose, but did she want John to jump? There would be no going back; her dreams would risk everything she already had and would she put up with a little slap and tickle on the side? Hell no. John would have to give her everything, and of course in return she was prepared to satisfy his every need – there would be no holding back as far as that side of it was concerned. John Taylor's experience in lovemaking, she was sure, would be nothing compared to what she could do to him. Oh yes, he'd be crawling at her feet, begging her to be his wife when she'd finished with him. But not just yet – his offer of checking the heifers would be far too easy for him.

A serious talk with Susan was in order; see how things were really like between her and Sam. She couldn't make any mistakes – it was frightening but also incredibly exciting to think this could all be hers. Tony tapped on Susan's bedroom door.

"Who is it?"

"It's me, Tony. Can I come in?"

"It's open."

Her hand paused over the door handle as she drew air into her lungs, for she knew this simple exchange between two friends could possibly see both their lives and those around them change forever. She entered the room and they both looked at each other. "It was fun today." Tony walked to the bed and sat down. "You owe me a fiver because I reckon about now some good-looking bitch is flashing a new set of teeth at every horny dog in the county." They tried to smile but couldn't quite get there. "We need to talk."

"I know. I should have told you about me and Sam, it's not right lying to your best friend, but things happened so fast and I had to be certain. I'm sorry."

"Forget it, you had your reasons."

"A bit like you?" Susan couldn't help her reply.

"Touché. And yes, like me. So, kiddo, what are we going to do?" Their hands met. "Seriously, I need to know what your intentions are with Sam. You don't think she's just having a little middle-aged fling? A lot of women will try it to see what same sex is like.

Susan didn't hesitate. "No, she's gay. Known it most of her life apparently, but the countryside is difficult when it comes to that sort of thing. Traditions, go against them and I'm not sure she could have handled the humiliation, but even she will admit her life's not too bad and there's a lot who would give anything for what she's got."

"What, like me, you mean?"

"I suppose so."

"Susan, I hope you don't mind me asking, but you said you made love?"

"Yes, twice. It was amazing, Tony, and not just physically, but emotionally as well, which makes all this so much harder because Sam loves this place. And now you."

Tony squeezed the girl's hand even tighter. "But what about you?"

"Me? I've come to appreciate what the countryside can offer, but I could go anywhere. I don't seem to be tied to this place emotionally like you all are."

"But you're not gay, are you?"

"No. I can take it either way so long as whoever I'm with is someone I really care for. But I do want a family like you. It doesn't have to come with a man attached, there are ways, you know."

"Of course there are, but what does Sam think about all this family stuff?"

"We haven't really discussed it in any detail but she understands. She wanted more children but that didn't happen, so perhaps I could give her that chance." Susan flopped back on the bed. "Oh Tony, why is life so complicated? We only came here to work, not potentially split up a marriage, and do we have the right to do that anyway? Let's face it, they were rubbing along just fine before we arrived."

"But were they? Just because we're out in the countryside doesn't mean to say things can't change."

Susan looked her friend in the eye. "You really want this, don't you?"

The room went deadly quite, leaving Tony the opportunity to tell the truth. "Yes, but that doesn't mean to say I've decided yet. I just need time to think."

"You can't do that forever."

"No, I know. But believe me, when I make a decision you and John will be the first to know."

Chapter 32

Sadie walked into the kitchen, her face glowing with happiness, then sat at the table.

"My, someone's looking happy today." Sam wiped her hands on a towel and came to stand next to Sadie.

"I told her," Sadie announced.

Susan stopped eating, placed the knife and fork to one side and looked at Sadie. "And?"

"She's fine with it. To be fair, she'd already guessed but just needed to hear it from me to show I cared about our relationship. Lizzie's not stupid, she knew what she was seeing and when I just happened to pop up from nowhere she smelled a rat straight away. Then circumstances took over and here we are – a couple."

Sam rested a comforting hand on the woman's shoulder. "I'm so pleased for you both. So what's next?"

"I'm off to the city for a couple of days to sort out some things and then I'm back to move in."

"Blimey, don't hang about, do you?"

"You're young, Susan, you can afford to take your time over a relationship, we can't. I know I'm not that old, but time soon slips by."

Sam sat down. "Well I think it's wonderful. Just think, we'll be neighbours. You must ask Lizzie round."

Sadie spotted a look between the two other women,

her voice dropping to a mere whisper. "How are you two getting on?"

Susan was about to answer when she was interrupted by the back door slamming open. Sam's eyes warned them to brace themselves as John appeared looking none too pleased. "Sodding bull from next door is in with the cows!" He threw his arms up in despair. "Why, if something goes wrong, does it have to be on a Sunday? Well don't just sit there, I need help. Sam, get hold of Greg and tell him to come get his ruddy bull out of my field."

Sam was sorely tempted to remind her husband that in fact it was *their* field, but looking at the steam blowing from his ears she thought better of it.

"God. This is the last thing I need," he grumbled. "Cows calving to a bloody Highland, have you seen the size of his horns? You could hang a week's washing on them!"

The women, trying not to fall into a fit of the giggles, watched John ram a whole sausage into his mouth before pointing to the others that he wanted them to follow. By the time he'd reached the back door the mouthful of sausage had dispersed sufficiently enough for him to bark at his two unwilling helpers. "Christ that was hot. Come on you two, haven't got all day, about time you did some proper work for a change, sitting around talking all day. Women, whoever invented them should be shot and as for that wife of mine, it's a job to get any sense out of her nowadays." He stomped off, leaving his reluctant team to scurry on behind.

Susan wondered if Tony really knew what she was possibly letting herself into. Dreams were one thing, but having to put up with this was something else. She could hear him ranting and
raving up ahead.

"Ruddy bull, I bet he's had more action in the last half an hour than I've seen in the past months, and where are those bloody dogs, perhaps I should load Sam up in the trailer as well and get rid of two problems at once. Damn those dogs, where are they?"

Susan found herself cursing the very ground this arrogant rude man walked on. She wasn't normally a vindictive person but this was just too much. "He's no right to talk about Sam like that," she huffed. "Certainly not in front of everyone."

Sadie wanted to reply but it was all she could do just to keep air pumping into her lungs, let alone have a decent conversation. "Hold back, girl, I'm well and truly knackered. Hell I'm out of condition. He's a man, love, that's why I gave them up, and like Sam said, we women need to stick together. If you two are serious then don't let it go. Bugger your age difference and bugger what all the rest of them say or think, you just go for it."

More abuse echoed back down the track. "Don't stand around gossiping, keep moving, he could have covered half the herd by the time you lot get there."

Without much enthusiasm the two women arrived at the gate and watched John frantically chasing a rather large hairy creature with horns the size of customised handlebars. "He doesn't think we're getting in with that, does he? Look at the size of him." Sadie prodded the girl in the ribs and pointed. "Can you imagine trying to suck those dirty great things hanging between his legs? And I'm not talking about John!"

Susan's curiosity was piqued as she gazed at a set of testicles the size of rugby balls. "I could never understand why men like that done to them."

"As I say, love, we're better off without them."

They turned to see Sam running up the track. "Come on, girl," Sadie shouted, "the fire's almost out!"

"Thanks for that!" She took a large gasp of air and looked out over the field. "How's our lord and master?" As she spoke a load of abusive language floated across the countryside while a furious John threw lumps of turf at a lumbering lump of meat.

"Oh dear, this doesn't look good." A comforting arm slipped around her waist.

"He's been very rude," Susan said. "Especially towards you, and it's not right."

"That's normal when he gets upset."

"Yes, but it's still not right."

"Don't worry yourself, Greg's on his way with his trailer, best we let him sort it out. I think by the looks of what's going on out there we'd do well to stay away."

"Don't you think we should go and help?" Sadie asked.

"No need, I think I can hear help arriving." The roar of

an engine making its way up the track could be heard, then a screech of breaks as a flash but rather unkempt Land Rover pulled up behind them. The door opened to reveal a middle-aged man in scruffy clothes and a floppy sweat-lined hat.

"Morning, ladies. Samantha." His eyes ran up and down Susan. "Reckon I should leave the bull and take this little young thing back with me." A dribble of saliva hugged the corner of his mouth as his piercing stare zeroed in on Susan's cleavage.

"Greg, you're as randy as your bull. Now go and give John a hand before he has a heart attack."

"What, the bull or your husband?"

"Both if you don't hurry."

The man openly rearranged his crotch and went to open the gate but stopped, his hand on the latch. "If you ever want to see a proper farmer at work, sweetheart, then just come round to my place, these dairy farmers don't know how to treat a woman proper like. I could even be persuaded to shake out a bit of fresh straw for you."

"Greg, behave! Now go and get your bull."

Sam pushed the gate open and pointed to the middle of the field as he deliberately brushed her side. "Don't mind handling an older cow now and again neither." With obvious pleasure he wiped away the gathering foam from his mouth then headed off swinging a large halter. "Quiet as a mouse is our Sebastian," he called back. "Don't know what all the fuss is about."

Sam shut the gate and with some relief turned back to the others. "Sorry about that, Susan, he's always the same. You were lucky – normally he's trying to pinch your bum. He even had a go at one of my breasts once."

Susan looked shocked. "That's terrible, did you tell John?"

"John was there, thought it was hilarious. You wait and see – these country men will always stick together. John will shout at us but be as nice as pie with old randy goat out there."

The young woman stamped her foot in anger. "What's wrong with everyone? Are all the men sex-starved cavemen? Has nothing changed over the centuries?"

Her outrage was met by a shake of the head. "No, it hasn't. Men can pretty much say and do what they like, within reason of course, but you'd be surprised what goes on behind closed doors."

"Well it's not right."

"Don't let them get to you, Susan. Remember we're the ones with the brains."

"Here, here, girl." Sadie stood clapping her hands. "Stick together, ladies, that's the only way forward."

*

Susan heard raised voices coming from the kitchen. John hadn't taken kindly to Sam's suggestion he take a dip in the nearest water trough to cool his temper and it hadn't helped when Greg had simply walked up to Sebastian, put the halter on, led him out of the field and straight up the trailer. This had put John in a foul mood all the way back, stating women were a waste of space and only good for three things: cooking, washing and spreading their legs. This hadn't gone down well with Sam and when he announced that as far as he was concerned his wife could only do the first two marginally well, they'd started rowing and by what Susan could hear were still at it.

Sadie had started to pack, Sam having offered to take her to catch her train in the farm's tatty old station wagon, so that left Susan who'd promised Vincent a visit but felt leaving Sam alone probably wasn't a great idea. Yet Sam had insisted she was quite able to handle anything her husband could throw at her as long as it wasn't her beloved kitchen sink.

Tony was out for the day on a helicopter trip to France and might not return until very late or even the next day. Susan wondered if this had anything to do with John's behaviour as her friend was trying to keep him at arm's length until she'd made a final decision.

Reluctantly leaving the chaos behind, she made her way out into the fresh air and filled her lungs with the breeze that brushed over the surrounding fields. She stood at her usual spot at the top of the footpath and tried to clear her mind of everything that seemed to be clogging her life. She'd needed to get away, soak up the solitude by the bucket load, cleanse her soul, and force the confusion and constant worry of doing the right thing into the back of her mind, at least for an hour or two. She gazed upon the wonder of nature as it went about its daily life then found herself crying with joy over the sudden stark realisation that there was no need to worry at all, for that dream of a loving husband lying beside her had been fundamentally wrong and in fact she had found her perfect partner. She took off and with youthful energy ran unhindered by the pressures of life, allowing every part of her body to soak up the wind of her future. She wouldn't worry about the consequences. No, she had found true love and would be damned if anyone was going to take it from her.

The rickety gate screeched as she swung it open. With hair in a tangled mess, she walked along the cobblestoned path, occasionally avoiding insect life as it scurried and darted for cover. The stems of flowering weeds wilted under the heat of the day, their bowing heads following the light until relief came from the surrounding hills.

Susan spotted Vincent in his usual place, gently rocking and gazing at nothing in particular. She waved as she strolled towards him through the tranquillity of the forgotten garden.

Vincent looked up and allowed himself that warmth he'd lost so many years ago. He knew it was Susan but just for a brief moment would dare to allow the pleasure of believing otherwise. "Susan Swan, I had wondered if you may not come today?"

"Why would you think that, Vincent? I said I would." Suddenly the old man looked as if he'd seen a ghost. "Are you all right, Vincent?" Racing to his side she grabbed a tightened fist, its cold touch filling her with concern. "You're freezing. Let me get you a blanket."

He immediately dismissed the idea as foolish to the extreme. "Nonsense, it's far too warm for such a thing. I must apologise, my dear." His eyes softened, as if he wished never to pull away from the girl standing before him. "Those words you spoke, I can see her now, my Alice. She said the exact same thing to me once in the park."

Susan could see he wanted to tell of his love for a girl he barely had the pleasure of knowing. "Go on, Vincent, I'm listening."

"It is as if it were yesterday." His mind wandered back in time. "We had not long started seeing each other and had arranged to meet by the bandstand in Regents Park, London. It had been raining, I recall, and she was late." Vincent's face crinkled with amusement. "She was never early for anything and on seeing her I commented that perhaps she had decided not to come due to the inclement weather. In fact I was convinced she wouldn't, but I can hear those exact same words that you just spoke and I can remember the look on her face, one of utter disbelief that I would ever question her commitment. It is stupid, I know, but I feel you are part of her."

Susan relished the praise but knew she mustn't encourage such thoughts.

"I apologise again." Vincent carried on. "It was wrong of me to believe in such things, you must think me a foolish old man. Please take a seat."

"Vincent." Susan looked him in the eye. "I think it's wonderful, you should never be ashamed of being in love with someone so dear to you."

"*Was*, my dear."

"No, Vincent, you still are."

He looked away, gazing across the neglected gardens. "And what of you, Susan Swan? Do you believe you have found love?"

There was no hesitation in her reply. "I have."

He pulled back his own thoughts. "Samantha is a wonderful woman."

"She is, and now I've realised I can't live without her." Susan paused. "My life, Vincent, is such a tangled mess."

A sympathetic chuckle escaped the old man's lips. "You're young, dear; everything at that age seems a problem too far."

"Now you're making fun of me."

"No, my dear. Unfortunately I tell the truth, and believe or not I was young once. Yes, it is hard to visualise, I know, but you learn a lot about this thing called life as you get older. Like manners." He sat up, rearranging his composure. "Forgive me, you've taken precious time out of your day to come and see me and not one drink has been offered." He went to get up.

"No, you stay there, Vincent, I'm quite happy to get them for you."

"No. I mean, that's very kind, my dear, but I fear you are unfamiliar with my kitchen."

Susan was a little taken aback by his abrupt tone, but this wasn't the time to push her offer.

Vincent knew he had overstepped the mark, but he had his reasons. "I'm not too old to get a lady a drink. Please, I won't be a minute."

His movements were slow and unsteady but as he lived on his own she figured he must be capable. Susan sat and waited a while, constantly glancing at the half-open door expecting him to return, uncertain of his abilities given his age. Time had a tendency to almost stop when forced to idle away the passing seconds, and eventually, deciding that a small peek would surely do no harm, she slowly made her way to the door and peered into the dimly lit room.

Vincent had his hand on a small brown teapot, his arm shaking as he poured the weak liquid into two waiting cups. With shock he turned and looked the girl in the eye. "What are you doing in here?"

She stepped back from the stark remark, her face paling as she looked at him with concern. Forcing tears back she moved closer to the door. "I'm ..." She swallowed hard and deep. "I should go, I've upset you." She went to turn and was just about to run when Vincent cried out after her.

"Stop! Please."

She froze, not knowing what to do next.

"Please, don't go, I beg of you." His tone convinced her that if he could get down on his knees and plead for her forgiveness, he surely would. She could see he wanted to say something, perhaps explain his outrage, yet the words just wouldn't pass his lips.

"What is it, Vincent?"

He cleared his throat, made his way to a small round wooden table and sat. With hands still shaking, he started to talk. "You see, Susan, you're the first woman to set foot in this room. I've not allowed another female into my life, not even Samantha. This is our home, you see, mine and Alice's. I don't need anyone else, that's until ..." He stopped.

"Until what, Vincent?"

"I think you know, my dear. But if you wish me to make a fool of myself yet again, I will gladly do so. Until you came along, Susan Swan." He clutched his head in a moment of embarrassment. "Now I have frightened you."

His hands dropped and she heard him weep as she had never heard a man weep before. Her first instinct was to go to him, but she still felt unsure. Would he turn her away? Yet the sight of that hunched figure slumped over the table convinced her that she had nothing to fear. "Oh Vincent." She went to him and reached out a reassuring arm. "I'm here."

"Alice," he cried out. "Please, please forgive me."

"It's all right, Vincent, everything's all right." Susan rested her hand upon his shoulder and without a second thought hugged the only man she really trusted.

*

Susan arrived back at the farm feeling content with her life. She knew what she had to do, where she was heading and in the short time since she had left for her visit something had convinced her to hold on to what she had. The house was eerily quiet. She walked along the hallway with a spring in her step, but suddenly paused as she passed the kitchen door. Sam was at the table looking into the distance, her eyes red with spent tears. "Are you okay?" The young woman immediately put her arm around her lover.

"Yes. He's gone milking, won't be back for another hour or so."

Susan sat down beside the woman she knew was the one she wanted to spend the rest of her life with. "He hasn't hurt you, has he?"

"Good gracious no. I'll give him that, he's not a violent man; I wouldn't stay with him if he was. No, it's just now and again he gets a little cranky, that's all – he doesn't mean it."

Susan looked at the woman's bloodshot eyes. "So why have you been crying then?"

She let out a deep heart-wrenching sigh. "Because I've realised our marriage is at risk and it's frightening. I don't think you can describe that feeling to anyone who hasn't been in the same position. You can't explain the heartache of seeing someone you've lived with all those years drifting away. Part of you is crying out to them wanting them to come back, but another part is waving goodbye, hoping perhaps to meet up again one day. It's so confusing.

Susan just wanted to tell Sam to pack her bags and they could run away together, but that was foolish, life was never that easy. She pulled away, giving Sam the space to think things through and hopefully come to the same conclusion that she had. This woman didn't need to be burdened by anything other than her own thoughts. "He said some horrible things, Sam."

"Perhaps he was right in some."

"Sam, how can you say that? He humiliated you in front of other people." To Susan's surprise there didn't seem to be any anger or spite in her voice.

"It's just his way. That's farming for you, it can get on top of you now and again, make you say things that perhaps you don't really mean."

Susan almost smashed her fist down on the table. "I don't know how you can sit there and defend him like that."

"Susan, love, he's a good man, passionate about the land, his livestock – does that not tell you something of the person I married? I think half his problem is he's missing his little play thing, and as much as I try and deny it, I think Tony is the one he'd rather be with. But I'm afraid our little Miss Muffet doesn't want to sit on his tuffet lately. I get the feeling things have cooled down somewhat. You wouldn't know anything about that, would you?"

Susan knew deep down that she had to put Sam straight, this was far too serious to carry on playing games. "Tony's not a bad person, Sam."

"I never said she was."

"No, I know, but she loves this farm and strangely enjoys helping out with the work."

"Susan, I love you dearly and don't get me wrong, I have nothing against her enthusiasm towards this place, but I'm no fool. She's playing John for what she can get, but I'm not sure what that is."

Susan wasn't sure if she should confess to Sam or not. Perhaps it wasn't a good idea just yet, although she hated keeping anything from her. Tony was at a crossroads so she really needed to tread carefully. "Does that worry you then, knowing Tony might be making up to your husband?"

Sam juggled the question in her head. "If it happens, I can't say I'm bowled over with it, but who am I to criticise? And in a bizarre way I'd be sort of pleased if it worked out. It might make my decision a lot easier."

"And what would that be?" Susan held her breath, waiting, hoping for that answer she so desperately wanted to hear.

The older woman leant back, studying the girl in front of her, someone who had quite literally turned her life upside down. But there were so many unknowns with whichever way she decided to go. "Marriage, Susan, it's such a bond between a man and a woman regardless of circumstances, it's something that can't be easily broken. You're young, free and single, and making life-changing decisions is going to be far easier for you. I'm tied to tradition; years of sharing your life with the same person forms, if nothing else, a friendship."

This wasn't what Susan wanted to hear. Sam was surely saying her commitment to their relationship could not continue. Tears started to trickle down her cheeks as she imagined life without this woman.

"Susan, you're crying."

Sam reached out to her, allowing their hands to touch, but Susan just dropped her head, fearing what Sam was about to say. "You're, you're leaving me?"

"God no, girl. You're the one I want. I was just pointing out some facts, that's all."

The girl couldn't hold the tears back as they both openly embraced. "Sam? Someone might come in."

"Really, do I look worried?"

Chapter 33

Susan met Tony on the landing as they both made their way to breakfast. "Have a good time yesterday, did we? All right for some, jet-setting off to France."

"If you must know, I hated every last minute. Randy weirdo, sticking his hands up my skirt even before we got to the helicopter. It's a long way over to France when you're constantly being groped. Horrible nasty wiry long fingers he had, and trying to poke them everywhere. I tell you, Susan, if I'd had a parachute I would have jumped, and don't even ask about last night. I'm sore in so many places it's not funny."

Susan tried to put on a sympathetic smile. "You got paid well, I bet."

"Oh yeah, he was loaded, but that's the trouble, those sort are the worst." Tony leant up against the wall reluctant to go any further. "Women shouldn't have to do things like he made me do, it's degrading." She felt a comforting arm around her waist.

"I'm sorry." Their eyes met, knowing they both wanted to talk.

Tony was first to speak out. "I've decided."

"Oh?"

"I can't go on doing this. I want a proper life, a home, a family."

Susan pulled away. "Does that mean what I think it means?"

Her friend nodded. "Yes. I've got nothing to lose."

"No, but other people have."

"You're a fine one to talk, little Miss Lovebird."

"I know, but it doesn't make it any easier."

"So are you telling me you're backing away from Sam?"

She could only shake her head.

"I thought not."

Susan stared down at the floor knowing her next confession would surely change everyone's lives forever. "I think Sam almost proposed to me yesterday."

"Well there you go, then, I'd say that pretty much opens the door for me."

"But I love Sam. You don't love John, do you?"

"No, but I could learn to."

"You can't learn to love someone, it's either there or it isn't."

"Okay, I like him a lot, he's a nice man and we all know there's not many of those about, and I'm sure we could be happy."

Susan didn't look convinced. "You're still young, there's time to fall in love, have children, a fine home."

"That's rubbish, Susan, and you know it. We've been over this before – we've both got history and frankly don't stand a hope in Hell's chance of any sort of happiness."

Susan knew deep down that Tony was right and she'd always come to same conclusion. "So we're stuffed then," she replied.

"Pretty much, unless we take this chance."

"Have you thought about what could go wrong? We could push them so far and then they might suddenly realise what they've got isn't so bad after all and we'll be out on our ear, back working the streets."

"I told you, Susan, I'm packing it in one way or the other, so like I say, we've got nothing to lose. We came here with nothing, we would leave with nothing."

"That's what I'm afraid of."

"You worry too much. Come on, we'll be fine. So what's it to be? Are we in as friends and go for it, or do we walk away?"

Susan didn't seem to have any more argument left in her. "In as friends." But no sooner had she agreed than she could hear the worry ringing in her ears. This time, though, she decided to ignore it.

"When will you start?"

"This week. I've thought about it all night and I've got an idea that will set the ball rolling. Of course it'll have to be a softly, softly approach to start with, you can't rush these things. John needs to think he can play around, have a little fun on the side, unseen behind closed doors, that sort of thing, but I'll slowly drag him in and by the end he'll be begging for it." It sounded more like a military operation, code-named 'false survival'.

Susan didn't much like what she was hearing, but she kept telling herself Tony wasn't a bad person. "You make it sound so clinical, so precise."

"Come on, Susan, it's what we do every day of the week."

"Yes, but this is for real, we're playing with people's lives."

"God, there you go worrying again. Come on, I'm starving, that French food wouldn't satisfy an English church mouse.

*

"John?" Tony brought her eyes up to meet his. They had just finished eating and were drinking the last of their tea and coffee at the kitchen table.

"Yes, Tony?"

"I've got nothing planned for today and I was thinking perhaps you might like a hand milking this afternoon? A bit of fresh air would do me good."

Sam peered out the window. "Won't get much of that in the milking parlour," she remarked pointedly as she finished washing up.

"That'll be great, Tony." The enthusiasm in his voice was almost unbearable. "Not so exciting as flying over to France for the day, hey," John jokingly replied.

"No." Her brief reply sounded weak, but only to her ears.

So, she's started already, Susan thought. Pulling up from the table she made her way to Sam's side, discreetly comforting the woman as she restlessly tried to keep busy. "Paul's coming round this afternoon," she said, trying to break the tension in the room. "He was hoping to put in an order for two caramel slices, one butterfly cake and two chocolate muffins to take away, if that's all right?"

"Yes, of course it is, and maybe I'll throw in some rhubarb crumble as well, we've got so much at the moment it's a job to keep up with the stuff."

John's ears immediately pricked up. "Rhubarb crumble? What, are we some sort of catering company now?"

His wife turned, wiping her hands on her pinny, knowing this was a good chance to subtly get her own back on her husband. "Don't think you're getting any, not after the way you behaved yesterday. Just because ..." She slowly shut her mouth as she suddenly realised what she was about to say.

"Just because what?" John asked with some curiosity.

She paused, desperately trying to cover her tracks. Clearly she couldn't tell the truth, and did he actually realise he'd missed his play thing that much? "I was about to say just because you couldn't catch that bull." It sounded lame, but at such short notice it was the best she could come up with.

"I would have if I'd had a little help from you all, but no, all you did was stand around talking."

"John, let's not start that again. Today is another day and yesterday, I hope, is all forgotten."

He crossed his arms, showing his annoyance by pouting his lips. "You started it."

Tony could only look on in puzzlement. "What's all this about?"

"Oh, we had the neighbour's bull get through the fence. A fence, I hasten to add, that should have been fixed a long time ago. Anyway, it got in with the cows, and to say he wasn't happy would be an understatement."

"What, the bull?"

"No, he couldn't have been more delighted. It was our Lordship here that got the grumps."

John felt he really needed to defend himself. "It was only because you lot wouldn't help. I bet Tony would have been far better than the lot of you put together."

Sam's hand tightened around the neck of her scrubbing brush. "Well it's a good job she's back then, isn't it, at least now I can get on with the jobs you clearly think I'm designed for." The room went dead except for the sound of a dripping tap.

Tony was suddenly hit by the stark realisation of the real world and she didn't much like it, but something deep down kept telling her to push on and reach out for her dreams no matter what the final outcome may be.

John rose from the table. "Right, I've got things to do. I'll see you at lunch." Everyone could see he only had eyes for his chosen lady; nobody else seemed to matter.

"See you later, John." God, that sounded pathetic. She had to be stronger; playing the lost puppy game wasn't her style. The afternoon milking was the first part of her plan. Get that over with then suggest milking one morning to show John she meant business, but the thought didn't appeal much. Why anyone in their right mind would want to get up at five was beyond her, but if she was going to be little Miss farmer's wife then she'd have to get used to it. Once married she'd go out two or three times a week, no more, and over time she'd stop altogether. John wouldn't dare complain, but if he did she'd just make up for it in bed – there were ways to win an argument rather than shouting at each other, but that was a long way off yet. For now all she had to do was suggest helping out for one morning, nothing more.

She had the plan worked out in her head perfectly. She'd ask John to wake her up – luckily it was still warm at night so wearing her see-through black nightie wouldn't be out of place. She'd set her alarm for 4.45 am; good God she'd never got up that early before. Her body shuddered at the thought, but that extra fifteen minutes would give her time to present herself. A casual seductive sprawl should do it. She'd need to make sure the covers were showing just enough flesh to whet his appetite, then all she'd do was pretend to be asleep. John would come in, see her half naked then do what all men naturally do, just stand and stare unashamedly before eventually waking her up. The rest she would have to make up as it developed. Yes, she allowed herself a satisfying grin, surely that would be plenty to get the hormones going, but no more – she had to drip-feed his appetite. It wouldn't do to fill his stomach too soon and she didn't want him to fall asleep on her just yet. One thing she'd learned in her profession was that men enjoyed the getting there just as much as the actual doing.

Sam washed the last of the plates as John made his way out. As soon as she heard the back door close she turned to face the two girls. She had nothing against Tony as a person – nice, yes, extremely attractive, yes, and she could see why men would fall over backwards just to be with her, but she wasn't her type. Just listen to her – wasn't her type indeed – it was still hard to believe she'd finally accepted she was gay, a word she disliked immensely. Why, she didn't know, or was she just afraid of it? Lesbian was only slightly better, but it still felt odd, or was it embarrassment? Would she ever be really ready to tell the world?

She loved Susan, no doubting that, but John? Did she ever really love him? What she now had with Susan seemed a world away from any feelings she'd ever had for her husband. The farm had given her the life she wanted to a point, but love? She dried her hands and sat at the table. "I'm sorry if I was a little sharp earlier, Tony. My dear husband and I, as you've probably guessed, had a small set-to yesterday and things haven't quite levelled out yet. Anyway, enough of that.

Tell me, what are your intentions with my husband?"

Susan unintentionally eased herself back, fearing the sparks might get in her eyes.

Sam sat patiently waiting for some sort of reply while Tony's tongue ran around rapidly drying lips, her throat tightening by the second. This wasn't part of the overall plan. Yes, she knew Sam would find out eventually, but to just come straight out and ask if she had intentions towards her husband? "I'm not sure I understand what you mean, Sam."

"Pull the other one, dear, it's got bells on it and you're far too intelligent for that. You know exactly what I mean."

The sudden realisation that she could be asked to leave if Sam didn't like what she had to say was hindering her breathing. She would have to tell the truth; anything else would be seen as deceitful.

Susan could hardly stand the silence. Why was Sam asking this question? She thought they'd accepted the situation.

"Well?" The girls jumped as the older woman pointed at Tony. "And it better be good, my girl, or you're out the door. I won't be lied to in my own kitchen."

For all the drama Susan couldn't help finding Sam's dominating nature rather a turn-on, but this wasn't the time for such thoughts.

"I ..." Tony stumbled over her words.

"Yes?" Sam demanded.

"I like your husband, a lot. I can't deny that."

"How much of a lot?" She tapped her fingers on the table impatiently.

"Perhaps more than is possibly acceptable given my position in your home."

"Don't talk riddles, young lady. Tell me straight, do you love him?"

Her answer, she was sure, would make or break her future. "I don't believe so, no." She went to rise from the chair knowing full well there was no happy ending to any of this. Her dreams felt like they had just shattered upon the tiled floor. "Maybe I should just leave."

"Tony?" Susan looked at her friend with shock at what she was suggesting.

"No, Susan. I'm sorry, Sam, and I'm sorry it's come to this, but clearly you're not happy with me staying around your husband, and I can totally understand your concerns."

"I'll be the best judge of that, young lady. Now sit down, I haven't finished with you yet. We need to clear this up once and for all because I'm fed up with all this sneaking around. Do you think you could love my husband over time?"

Finally Tony managed to swallow. "I think we could be very happy together, if that's what you're asking. I don't know about love, having never experienced it before."

Sam sat with her arms crossed, mulling over this information. "You're very tactful with your words, but really, all I want to know is that you'll look after him and your intentions are true."

It was time for Tony to lay her heart on the line, show Sam she meant no harm towards her husband. "I love this farm, Sam, the countryside it sits in and I hope to find that feeling with John. I don't know what the future holds for any of us but you can rest assured, I would never try to hurt him. I'm afraid I can't say any more than that."

The three women sat with their own thoughts, Sam's hand resting on the one person she now pinned all her hopes upon. "Very well. He's yours."

"Excuse me?" Tony almost fell off her chair.

"I said you can have him. But God help you, Tony Chapman, if I find out you have other less honourable intentions. He has his ups and downs but he doesn't deserve to be mistreated, and believe it or not I still do care for my husband. I've realised I don't love him, that affection now lies with this young lady, and I'm sure that revelation has come as no big surprise, you being best friends and all."

Tony couldn't speak; her whole body had frozen to the chair. What had just happened?

"Sam?"

"Yes, dear?"

"Am I right in thinking you have just given me

permission to take your husband?"

"That's about the sum of it, yes. Clearly I would prefer he didn't know of our arrangement, and I would hope you didn't show your affections towards one another in public. Discretion is the word, and that goes for me and Susan too. Given your capabilities I'm sure you'll keep him entertained behind closed doors, but be warned, young lady, getting involved with a dairy farmer is not something to be taken lightly." Sam assessed the girl from the other side of the table. "How are your cooking skills?"

"I can get by."

She shook her head. "Not good enough. The way to a farmer's heart is through his stomach. Bedroom activity is all very well, but it won't keep the wellies moving. We'll start tomorrow."

"Start what?"

"Cooking lessons, of course. And then there's washing techniques – you'll soon realise there's never any spare cash for luxuries in the house. The farm comes first so don't expect any newfangled machines to do the jobs; ironing is another skill to learn."

"I can iron a bit."

Sam chuckled. "What, overalls, bed sheets, work clothes? There's mountains of the stuff."

"I do my underwear."

"Really? From what I've seen, that's hardly worth getting the ironing board out for.

"Well, don't forget Mr Wren, he's very particular."

Sam shook her head. "I can see this giving up of my husband lark is going to be much harder than I thought."

Tony went to get up. "I need to go away and think; this has come as a bit of a shock."

Sam released Susan's hand. "Why don't you go with her? I'm sure you two have got a lot to talk about."

Susan would have preferred to stay, but perhaps Sam needed time alone – she knew the woman would be hurting. "Are you sure? I don't mind staying."

"No, you go with your friend; I've got things to do."

She reluctantly pushed her chair back and followed Tony, but paused in the doorway. She just wanted to run back, to comfort, to hold, to just be there, but something told her to keep moving.

Sam moved to her sink and looked out at her gardens, the gardens she so loved with the mass of late summer blooms competing for light, heads still alive with pollinators. She felt a single tear run down her cheek, her hands shaking from fear of the unknown. She was well aware of what she'd done, yet it didn't make it any easier, and to think she may well have ended their marriage. Signing her old life away seemed terrifying, but equally the thought of running headfirst into a new one, becoming who she really was, filled her with untold pleasure. There was little point bogging the mind with the consequences of what might be, of Susan tiring of her over the coming years, or finding that young handsome man who was prepared to leave the past behind. No, whatever the outcome she would deal with it.

Tony closed her bedroom door and flopped onto the bed, her head hitting the pillow. She stared up at the ceiling as she contemplated what to say next. "My God, Susan, what are we doing?"

"Surely this was what you wanted? This is your dream handed to you on a plate."

"I know, but I didn't think it would come with all this mundane stuff like cooking, washing and housework. I'm twenty-five years old – I'll be knackered before my time.

"Tony." Susan's voice carved its way through the negativity that threatened to suck the reality of the real world out of the room. "It's what we both wanted, remember? All of this could be yours – the house, the farm, the man, children, everything. And I get Sam." Her friend's mind seemed to be working overtime.

"I don't know what to do, Susan."

"Sometimes I can never make you out. He's there for the taking and you're lying there blabbing on about the finer details."

"I wouldn't call them that."

"Did you seriously think all this was going to run by itself while you play happy families? Sam's right, you have to be aware of what's involved. It's the countryside – remember most of them still live in the dark ages."

Tony rolled onto her side willing someone to give her the courage to go for her dreams. "But do you think I can do it?"

"What's changed from this morning? Then you had a plan. Now? Christ, Tony, wake up and smell the coffee. We both need this chance, you said yourself you didn't want to carry on as you were, and I certainly don't, so get off your backside and do something about it."

"You've changed your tune! But no, you're right." The girl shot up. "Oh my God, you're right!" Excitement shone from her face. "I could have it all – me, no one else." She leaped off the bed to dance around the room. "Lady of the Manor, just think about it."

"Okay, steady on. For a start it's not a manor, it's a large farmhouse, and lady of the large farmhouse you most certainly will not be. More like Lady Muck, if I know anything about farming, which is very little. You've seen how hard Sam works, and John's going to want the same out of you; nothing comes for free."

"Hells bells, Susan, are you trying to persuade me or put me off?"

"I just want you to realise what you're letting yourself in for."

She was met by a huge grin. "I don't care, I don't damn well care." Their arms met in a hug that seemed to last forever. Finally their eyes locked. "It starts this afternoon."

"That's my girl. Now go and get your man and no more of this silly talk."

Chapter 34

Tony's phone lit up like a Christmas tree, its alarm driving through her head like a rusty six-inch nail. She scrambled around in the darkness not understanding why it was going off in the middle of the night. Damn it, she must have set it wrong and yet her bleary eyes were telling her brain it was 4.45 am. She peered into the blackness just making out the shape of the window against faint light from outside. Anything other than bright sunlight at this time of year was classified as night as far as she was concerned. She looked at the time again – no, it was definitely time to get up. Cursing herself for even suggesting she'd love to come out for a morning milking, she forced her head off the pillow.

This was madness. She was tired, knackered from helping with the milking yesterday. Then they'd mended a broken fence, moved the heifers yet again and finally got in for tea at seven. She had to take her hat off to John – he did most of the work by himself every day, seven days a week, 365 days of the year. No wonder he expected his food on the table ready and waiting, but that didn't help her present situation one little bit. She suddenly realised she was supposed to be seducing John in – a quick glance – ten minutes' time. Her plan seemed so easy in the light of the day, yet in almost pitch darkness she wasn't so sure. Hell, you could hardly see, let alone look sexy in this. Her hands grappled with her less than erotic nightie, clearly never designed to accommodate a good night's sleep as it had managed to roll itself around her neck like a noose.

She fumbled, not a good start to setting the hormones racing in a man she was supposedly trying to get to the altar sometime in the future. A man who would father her ten children. Images of them joyfully playing on the lawns of her manor ... make that large farmhouse ... were rapidly being sucked into a big black hole. This part of the plan was about to come crashing down around her, causing the rumbling of a searing headache. With sheets draped in a bedraggled fashion she realised it wasn't as warm as promised. John said the temperature was just about right at five in the morning. For a penguin, maybe, but not for a scantily dressed dumb arse female who clearly had a lot to learn about farming if she wanted to become the Lady of the Ma– large farmhouse.

She caught the sound of movement and a moving light, almost certainly from a torch as it shone under her door. She had to make a decision – either stick with the half-naked sprawl but run the risk of hypothermia setting in, or pull the sheets over her head, pretend to be asleep and hope John would go away, leaving her to drift into a land of warmth and eternal sunshine. A light knocking sounded. Perhaps if she didn't answer, John would give up and go milking on his own. But no, the door slowly opened. She panicked and hurriedly pulled the sheets up just below her shoulders.

"Tony." A voice broke through the dim light. "Are you awake?"

What a stupid question, she thought. Why would

anyone in their right mind be awake at this time of the morning?

"Tony, it's me, John. It's time to get up."

Dear God, does he never give up? Her body sagged in frustration. Now she really did have a headache, and probably looked like something the cat had killed and dragged through the hedge backwards. She forced a groan to tell John she was still alive but barely conscious and dragged her eyes up to a darkened figure shining a torch directly at her. "Oh, John, is it time to get up already?" She tried to rearrange the sheets against an uncooperative tangled nightie. This wasn't how it was supposed to be – she needed to drip-feed his appetite, not chuck a bucket of water over him. The single beam of light highlighted her body, briefly exposing her silhouetted breasts. John reluctantly looked away as she surrounded herself with a jumble of covers, the nightie still attempting to strangle her neck. "I'm decent now, John."

He turned and shone his blasted torch straight at her. "You're going to need some warm clothes; I reckon there's a little nip in the air this morning."

I'll give him nip, it's ruddy freezing. "I need to get dressed, John, do you mind?" She could see him staring at her. "John, clothes."

"Oh, right." Clearly it was too cold to get up in her undressed state, so indicated where the clothes were. "Yes, of course. I'll get them, shall I?"

"That would be useful, if you don't mind."

Tony watched as he fumbled through her clothes lying neatly on a corner chair. As his hand came into contact with her delicate lace bra and matching panties he let his fingers run around the material.

"John? I need to get dressed."

"Yes, sorry."

Dawn seduction, she realised, had well and truly gone out the window. He'd just have to make do with handling her underwear instead, and by the looks of it he wasn't doing a bad job. He handed the clothes over, looking decidedly pleased with his find, and then stood back and waited.

"John, you need to turn around, I've got to get dressed."

"Right, good suggestion."

With the chill creeping into her bones, Tony quickly slipped into her clothes and stood up beside him. "Okay, I'm ready."

John peered through the darkness, his torch shining down towards the floor yet producing enough light to highlight this stunning young woman's features. How anyone could look so good this early was beyond him, but somehow she did. "Good, let's go." He waved an encouraging hand towards the door inviting her to lead the way, his light showing up any obstacles as they made their way through the house.

As they headed out into the increasing light the first thing that hit Tony was the absolute silence; just the odd distant bird rising to start another day, but little else. She noticed the light was changing and by the time they'd reached the barns her inexperienced ears were bombarded with a chorus of waking birdsong, each singing their own individual tune, something she had never in her entire life heard before. "My God, listen to it." She had stopped and was compelled to look to the sky.

John stood beside her, pointing up into the trees. "Dawn chorus. Amazing, isn't it? Something you never tire of, but make the most of it because it'll be gone soon."

The young woman swirled around, her headache gone, lungs full to the brim with chilled damp air. "It's incredible, John, I've never heard anything like it."

He couldn't help but chuckle. "That's because you women never get up early enough. Best part of the day, first thing."

Tony's smile widened. "I can see that now. Oh John, what have I been missing all these years?"

"That's just the start of it, young lady. Come on, we've got cows to get in."

They made their way up the track in search of animals Tony was sure would still be asleep, which gave her a sudden thought. Do cows actually sleep? She'd never spent any time wondering over such matters, but surely they had to rest at some point. There was so much she didn't know about the countryside. Without warning, John raised his hand and pointed towards an emerging clump of trees.

"What?" Tony struggled to see anything out of the ordinary.

"Look again," John whispered.

Then, out of the shadows of a tangled hedgerow, Tony saw a ghostly figure, its wings silently drifting upon the increasing warmth of the rising currents. They both watched as the cream-coloured bird glided along the outer boundaries of the field.

"Barn owl," John whispered. "You won't see that lying in bed in the morning."

Tony's jaw dropped, captivated by the natural beauty of something so utterly exquisite yet so simple. "It's so silent," she whispered back.

"It's hunting; picks off its prey before they even know it's about." The owl had now gone, searching the next field as the two carried on walking. "It's a good sign," explained John. "Of a healthy farm, I mean. Having owls on the place shows there's plenty of small mammals and mammals eat worms, insects, berries, it's a whole life cycle that's going on right under our noses – shows the land is in good heart. But you break that chain and everything comes crashing down. That's organic farming for you; encourages not only the crops but nature as well. It's not rocket science; just simple and effective.

The passion in John's voice took Tony by surprise. This was a side of him she hadn't experienced before – warming, caring, a man clearly dedicated to what he believed in. It was refreshing to be with a man of such character, the sort of person she could associate with. Just as well, she quietly thought, for he was the man she was determined to marry. How shallow her life was compared to his, how empty, almost meaningless if she thought about it hard enough, for this was the real world and although they'd only been out for a short time, she had unknowingly cemented her feelings for the man standing beside her.

When they reached the top of the track John opened the gate ready for the animals to walk through. "We'll scout along by the woods, push any cows back this way."

Tony saw one or two already making their way towards them; the rest were yawning, stretching their legs, arching their backs and showing a reluctance to get up so early. John led the way across damp grass and then suddenly stopped, putting a finger to his lips and pointing to a large moving mass the size of an average dog. Tony watched the dark shape waddle from side to side as if on poorly fitted wheels, its grunting echoing through the surrounding trees. She felt a hard but gentle hand wrap around hers as the creature came nearer until it finally stopped a short distance away.

John looked at Tony's concerned face and smiled, their eyes locking together as he slowly lifted a hand and clicked two fingers. The grunting stopped as a startled head rose, paused for a second and then resumed its foraging. John grinned as he let Tony's hand drop and clapped his hands twice, sending the animal scurrying off into the undergrowth.

"I've never seen a badger up close before," Tony

remarked.

"Everywhere on this farm," John replied. "Come on, we'd better get on or else we won't get the milking finished."

They followed the last stragglers out, shut the gate and made their way back towards the farm allowing Tony to move closer to John's side. Perhaps it was the feeling of being safe, protected by the man's presence that made her do this. It was, after all, his patch, his countryside that she was being given the privilege to walk upon.

Their hands brushed, leaving John wanting more. It was wrong, he knew – she was so much younger than him and there was the small fact of him being married, but something was telling him that it wasn't anything to worry about.

Tony felt his arm wrap around her waist, then hesitate before falling away. Not a word was spoken, yet each knew what the other was thinking.

Milking had finished, but for John it had felt strange, all thought of taking the girl as some sort of play thing, a mistress on the side didn't seem to add up any more. It wasn't that he couldn't take her – he was sure of that, but after this morning he'd come to respect the girl as a woman and someone who deserved to be taken seriously, a fact that had frightened him.

She'd been sent to the barn to feed the calves and as she watched them drink, she found herself thinking how early it still was and yet they'd achieved so much. For most people the day was only just starting. She imagined curtains being pulled as bleary eyes adjusted to the sudden intrusion of sunlight, their only concerns a light breakfast on the go and off to work as normal. Farming and country life, she'd come to believe, drew upon nothing remotely normal, but there was something about it that got into your very soul and she now knew it was something she needed. Some would argue otherwise – her looks and her youth would certainly have those people baffled, but surely that was her choice. But why? she could hear them say. It didn't much matter what others said because what she'd experienced today had made her realise that they were the losers.

John looked on as she made her way back. The girl was tired, he could see, but her eyes glowed with a willingness to go on and that youthful spring still remained. "You look tired."

She flicked back a stray strand of hair. "I'm fine." It was a lie, but that was of no concern.

John turned his head to one side, not wanting to seem too forward with his suggestion. "I want to show you something."

His tender tone reassured her she could accept his request without question, so she followed him out through the barns, across the orchard and up a long narrow track, its snaking potholes ending abruptly within a small clearing. He offered his hand, indicating the climb over the forgotten gate would be safe, then led the way between brambles until they finally arrived at a level grass plateau.

John stopped and gazed across a view that took Tony's breath away. "It's ..." She stopped, not wanting to break the spell as the last of the morning mist threw an eerie blanket across towering oaks hugging the banks of a trickling stream, and there in the distance the cows grazed, seemingly without a care in the world. She drew in a deep breath and then gently exhaled, not wanting to speak for fear of spoiling the magic that lay before her. The morning chill had gone, replaced by a gentle warmth that kissed her face.

"You can see a lot of the farm from here," John proudly announced. "This is my thinking place, or just somewhere to come and remind me how lucky I am."

Tony felt a sharp stab of guilt as she stared across the fields and beyond. He was still in his world of work and marriage, if only he knew of Sam's confession of their arrangement. All this around him and yet he was unaware. It just didn't seem right, but perhaps she could make it right over time. "I don't know what to say," she replied.

"There's nothing to say, I just wanted you to see it." He hesitated. "You see this is my place, I've never brought anyone else up here. You're the first."

"But surely?"

"No." John shook his head. "Not even her. It had never felt right; even after all these years, to allow Sam to share my space."

"So why me?" she asked.

"I think you know why." He turned and started to

walk away. "I've said too much. What people think and what they do are two totally different things, and I suspect you think I'm a sad old bugger chasing after impossible dreams."

She grabbed his arm. "Nothing is impossible, John." She moved closer, felt her lips brush lightly over his. Moved by a growing passion they fell into each other's arms, the kiss lasting only seconds but filling her chest with an ache she hadn't expected.

John released her and stepped back. "We'd better go, there's still a bit more work to do before breakfast."

*

Tony was first to enter the kitchen, prompting Sam to look up and smile. "You look tired."

"Well some of us have been up since five this morning."

A damp dishcloth came hurtling across the room. "Don't you start, I have enough trouble with him." John had followed on behind. "Training her good and proper I see, John."

He sat at the table and gave a look of a man who expected his food to be served right away. "Stop your whingeing, woman, and get the workers their breakfast." Without thinking he placed his arm around Tony's waist. "This one needs it and I'll tell you now she's going to make a fine farmer's wife one day."

Tony should have been embarrassed, but for everything to work out she needed to get used to this sort of behaviour. She noticed Sam was reluctant to comment, maybe for fear of saying the wrong thing.

John looked down at the steaming food with delight. "If this young lady could cook like you, she'd be perfect."

"Is that so?" Sam placed another plate on the table and gave the girl a discreet wink. "Well it just so happens I'm going to start giving her lessons, so you won't starve in your old age."

No one said a word as John pondered over what his wife had just said. He went to say something but thought better of it. Odd, he thought, but she was acting very strangely lately. "Cooking lessons, you say. You serious?"

"Very serious. Isn't that right, Tony?"

"Yes, I'm afraid so, although I'm not sure this kitchen is ready for my lack of knowledge, but if I end up being able to cook a breakfast like this I'll be a happy woman." She suddenly realised someone was missing. "Susan not up yet then?"

"No, she's got a bit of a headache, she'll be down later." As the older woman spoke she felt the touch of Susan's hands roaming her body, and was it wrong her legs felt so weak from the vision of a young woman sprawled out across the bed tempting her to take control? Her serving fork missed a waiting sausage and sent it spinning off the dish, skidding to an abrupt halt on the kitchen floor. "Blow it, all fingers and thumbs this morning." She bent down and spiked the offending article. "So, Tony," she questioned as her head popped up, "how was your first early morning milking? Had enough of dairy farming yet, or do you think you'll stick around?"

Again John wondered over another odd remark, but was too hungry to analyse the complex workings of the female brain.

Tony knew exactly what she was on about. "I have to admit when I woke up and found it was still dark the idea didn't seem too appealing, but once I got outside it was just amazing. And the dawn chorus, oh Sam, it's something else! We saw a barn owl and a badger so close I could have almost touched it, and everything's so peaceful at that time of the morning."

"Whoa, slow down, young lady, you're making my head spin. So I take it you enjoyed the experience? But I'm assuming you did do some milking, not just wildlife spotting?"

"Of course. I even know the names of one or two cows. It's funny, I never realised they could have such characters; a bit like humans really."

"I'm pleased you enjoyed it."

"Thanks, but John's a good teacher."

The man in question pointed his empty fork in his wife's direction. "See, I told you she would make a good wife."

"Yes, John, you did." The realisation of what she was doing was all too real as tears lodged, threatening to show the pain deep inside her. This wasn't going to be easy, if that's what eventually happened, but everyone had to look to the future, John included. But as yet he was unaware of his choices. "Oh, I nearly forgot, we've had a letter from our long-lost son."

The joy on the man's face told Tony there must be a strong bond between father and son.

"Good God! Is he still alive?" He was clearly trying to cover up his excitement, for it wouldn't do for a man to be seen getting all worked up over his only child.

"Don't make fun, John, you know I worry about him."

"He's a grown man, he can look after himself. So how is he then? Coming home any time soon?"

"Apparently he went walkabout in Australia, stumbled across a station and is now working there. Claims he couldn't phone or text because there's no reception, just a temperamental party landline the kangaroos keep chewing on so it's down a lot of the time. Even started riding horses, can you imagine? The best bit is he's got in with the owner's daughter!"

"Well, well." John puffed his chest out with manly pride. "The crafty young bugger, let's hope she hasn't got any brothers and he'll be in there. Just think – we might have a son who owns a big station one day."

Sam tutted at his suggestion. "Trust you to look at it like that; he's only just met her for goodness' sake."

"You know from day one when you've met the right person," said John.

Sam couldn't help noticing John's eyes quickly run over Tony. God, this was definitely going to be harder than she thought, but she needed to be strong and face up to reality. "Speaking from experience, are we?"

"I've never said a truer word." This hadn't exactly answered her question, and John knew it.

"You're going to have to take Pup to the vets pretty soon, he needs his balls cut off."

"That was a change of subject."

"Just thought I'd bring it up because I saw him humping a broom handle this morning." Sam needed to focus on something else; there was only so much she could take.

"More costs." John looked down at his remaining food. "Those vets will have the shirt off your back if you let them." He swept the last of the fried bread around his plate trying to tidy up any stray egg yolk. "Another fine meal, my dear. Well, I'd better get on. Tony, it was a pleasure to have your company and I look forward to the next time." He stuffed the last forkful into his mouth and rose from his chair.

Tony and Sam waited for the back door to close and then turned to face each other, wondering who would speak first. Their silence was broken by the appearance of Susan.

"Everything all right?" She glanced at the two women sitting at the table.

"Well I'm fine," Sam answered. "Just waiting for Tony here to elaborate on what really went on this morning."

"Oh, right." Susan let out a light chuckle. "Bet John got

his leg over and she's not telling you."

"No, he didn't. If you must know we had a very enjoyable time and as I was telling Sam earlier I learned a lot about wildlife and the cows." She could see the other two struggling not to laugh.

"Is that it?" Susan asked.

"Yes, and stop that, you're acting like children. If you must know it was a very satisfying experience."

"Satisfying? You're losing it, girl."

Tony shook a warning finger at them. "Just because you've been keeping each other warm this morning doesn't mean the rest of us have to follow. I know what you've been up to."

Susan stared straight at her friend. "You're lying, Tony Chapman. Come on out with it, tell us the truth."

Tony fell silent for a moment. God, she thought, this was going to be really odd talking about another woman's husband when she was still in the same room. "Okay, if you must know, we did hold hands." She wasn't going to tell them they'd kissed, it was hardly anything anyway, but strangely it would be something to remember for a very long time.

The other two couldn't hold their laughter in any longer, Sam finding the thought of her husband's romantic gestures hilarious.

"My husband being romantic? Wonders will never cease."

"The perfect gentleman, so there. Apart from running

his fingers over my underwear."

"Aha, I knew it." Sam wagged her finger. "That's more like the John I know."

"I wasn't wearing them at the time, he was helping me get dressed."

"Aha, even better."

"It wasn't like that. Dear God, you two are impossible. I simply asked him to get my clothes, that's all, but the fact he took rather longer than necessary is neither here nor there, and will you both stop sniggering? He was very sweet, warm and charming. Oh, I give up."

Sam eventually drew breath. "I'm so sorry, Tony, this is very rude of us. Susan, stop laughing. Naughty girl."

"Now you're mocking me."

"I really am sorry," Sam replied. "But you've got to see the funny side when a married woman gives a single twenty-five-year-old stunningly good-looking young lady permission to do what she wants to her husband. Holding hands isn't the first thing that springs to mind."

"Very funny." As Tony went to get up Sam gently grabbed her hand.

"Please, sit down, we won't joke any more." She gave Susan a dig in the ribs. "Will we?"

"No. Sorry, Tony, it'll come, give it time."

"I don't know what your expectations are," Tony answered. "Do you really what me to jump into bed with John on our first sort of date?"

"No, you're right. It's wrong of us to make fun, but nothing has changed, our agreement still stands. You tackle the situation any way you think fit; I'm only interested in his long-term happiness.

Susan moved closer and took her hand. "You still can't quite accept it, can you?"

"No, I suppose not, but I've made my decision and I'm happy to stick to it. It's not fair to everyone involved if I keep living a lie." She looked at the girl who was hoping to replace her in every possible way and saw something in her eyes that surprised her. "You're falling for him, aren't you?"

This statement caught the girl off guard. There and then it suddenly dawned on her that Sam was right.

"Are you, Tony?" Her friend gave a sympathetic glance. "Are you falling for John?"

"I don't know, and that's the honest truth. I told you I haven't experienced true love before, so I have nothing to compare my feelings against."

"Why don't you tell us what really happened?"

She fumbled with her fingers, searching for the right words. "It was nothing really; we just kissed and everything was over before I knew it, yet that touch left me floating and my heart felt like it was going to burst. But it was just a kiss – how can something so simple cause so much to happen to a person? I don't understand."

Sam was still holding hands with the one she had experienced the exact same thing with. "Oh dear." Susan nodded in agreement.

"What?" Tony demanded.

"I'm afraid you're in love, my girl, no two ways about it. Whether it lasts will remain to be seen, but right now I'd say you've got it pretty bad."

Susan let go of Sam's hand and flung her arms around her best friend. "Oh Tony, can't you see? This is wonderful, now you can move forward, this is your chance to live that dream."

Sam sat back and watched the two embrace. She was happy for her, of course, but just couldn't find it in herself to feel joy.

Chapter 35

Tony

The seasons were changing. Late summer had lost her grip, those mighty hands unable to hold the ever increasing weight of damp, chilled autumn nights. Tony watched as leaves gently fluttered to the ground. Soon it would be winter, with dark nights forcing working folk off this wonderful landscape to seek warmth and shelter beneath the rooftops of their humble dwellings.

She pulled her eyes away from the brief distraction and watched the cows as they meandered down towards the farm. Today she was alone as John had taken a rare afternoon off and had accompanied Jack to some far off farm sale, placing her in charge. Her attention drifted once again, and there in the distance she spotted a welcome sight – a barn owl in broad daylight, its majestic presence hunting effortlessly along the outer hedgerows of the farm.

A wide smile appeared on her face as she thought of that first morning milking and her first glimpse of this truly magical creature, a bird of hope that all things were as one on the land. She'd come a long way since then; that lack of knowledge concerning rural matters had blossomed into something quite gratifying and had even surprised her. She had always loved this place but only through rose-tinted glasses. The true wealth of the land and its inhabitants needed to be explained, but once shown had opened her eyes to another world.

John, too, had been seen in a different light. She was still unsure as to whether she truly loved him – it was a strong word and something not to be messed with. Perhaps over time it would become clear, but she had very quickly made up her mind he was a man to be trusted, a true companion for those dreams which she was sure would be fulfilled. The sexual side of their growing relationship was far simpler and something even she was surprised with.

Sam clearly hadn't ignited John's inner desires, but probably that wasn't her fault, more to do with what Sam herself had confessed to, and her husband's passion for everything he cared for running so deep. It had taken Tony's breath away the first time they'd made love, yet it wasn't lust that had finally driven them to share a bed – it was a genuine underlying urge to be as one and for her to allow another to enter her body purely through desire and not payment.

With relief John had insisted her life of bowing to the whimsical privilege fantasies of rich men be cut back and without complaint she'd agreed wholeheartedly. Susan, she was sure, would follow suit with little protest from Sam and finally start to plan their lives together.

The last of the cows disappeared out of sight as the track snaked its way towards the milking parlour. She looked along the sky line and noticed two figures walking slowly across a field that rose from the stream below, unashamedly holding hands while taking in the cool air of an early autumn afternoon. To Tony's knowledge, John still didn't have any idea of his wife's relationship with another woman, possibly far too concerned with his work on the farm and his growing emotions towards a certain young lady. An affair he was convinced his wife had no knowledge of. Tony had started to feel uncomfortable with the increasing pressure of keeping Sam's secret from the one person she really cared for, but they'd come to an arrangement and if nothing else it had allowed her to find the real man behind the sometimes worried face of a farmer who was only trying to make an honest living. She was convinced time would soon seek out the truth and those involved in this web of deceit may at last be allowed the chance to speak out.

She looked up at the pale sun struggling to heat the last hours of daylight. Silence, she thought, how wonderful it is. She'd left her phone indoors, a deliberate defiance against a world of troubled minds and an act of pure madness to many, but just for today it was sheer pleasure. John was sure to try and ring, convinced she wouldn't be able to cope without his guiding hands, but he had to learn to let go every now and again.

She suddenly found the gates of the yard in front of her, far too busy thinking of other things. She closed them and made her way through the barns and saw Kim stretched out enjoying the last of the warmth. The poor elderly girl was now spending more time in the comfort of loose straw, her arthritic hips telling her that life was starting to close in.

Pup had finally been to the vets and with some disgust returned somewhat sore and just a little confused as to the whereabouts of his beloved testicles. He could often be seen roaming in search for them but still managing to hump the odd stray broom handle, a habit he was unwilling to give up. Sadly he would eventually become head dog, an ambition he'd held ever since his arrival, but one he would almost certainly regret through the loss of an ever caring companion and soulmate.

Tony was starting to get ready to let the first cows in when she spotted Josh in the garden. How proud everyone was of this young man's increasing confidence to life in general, his rough nature benefiting from the ageing hands of George, a man Tony was sure knew more than he let on but a man of honourable intentions, great worth and kindness. She waved as the two went about their work, both finding peace within.

She turned and pressed a single green button, encouraging the milking machine into kick start. This was her life now. For richer, for poorer, in sickness and in health, she had committed her youth, her beauty, to serve the land, her man and her future family. Did she have any regrets? Not one.

Chapter 36

Sam

The washing seemed endless at times, but thankfully the girls' decisions to cut back on their clients had eased the workload. Sam held up one of the sheets and tutted – not before time by the looks of it. Still, they needed to be changed, if only for personal use. She felt her lips widen into a smile – personal use. There was a lot of that going on lately. Her pulse quickened as thoughts of Susan entertained her mind, but then a tinge of sadness threatened to spoil the view for she knew her husband had lain with another woman.

She climbed the stairs, confused for the future. How had it all come to this? Of course she knew, but still it didn't make it any easier. She hoped – no, she prayed – that when John finally found out about her and Susan he would accept the situation. His growing affections for Tony would, if nothing else, cushion him into realising that his wife wasn't the woman he thought she was.

She glanced down at the neatly folded bed sheets, searching for an excuse, but she knew in her own heart there was none. The door to Tony's bedroom stood before her. She gave two light knocks; the seconds passed as she waited. Why, she didn't know, because both girls were out in the garden even though the cold grip of autumn was taking hold.

Her intention was to leave the sheets just inside the door, but something was forcing her to face up to reality, to push out those last remaining demons and move on. With trepidation she found herself standing in the middle of the room. It felt strange, yet it was her room, her house, but for how much longer? She looked upon the bed her husband had made love in.

Demanding she clear her mind, she persuaded reluctant feet to move closer and face up to the truth. Hand hovering over neatly tucked-in linen, she tried to block out visions of naked bodies exploring each other's sexuality as her own body shuddered at the thought of heat rising from the bed. She suddenly pulled away. This was stupid, why was she so afraid?

With singed fingertips she gently raised them to her lips, connected with her doubts and kissed John goodbye. "No more," she whispered, then turned and headed towards Susan's room. She entered without hesitation and collapsed on the comforting mattress, her sudden weight making the four-poster creek under protest, sending pillows scattering across the floor. With fear of the unknown, she grabbed the sheets and wrapped herself within their soft folds. This is where she belonged; this was what she had secretly wanted all her life. Not the farm, not the house, not even John.

She stopped, realising what she'd just confessed. Staring up at the ceiling, she dared herself to say it out loud. "No, not even John!" she whispered. There, it had been said, but why was she now apologising to a man who wasn't in the room?

The sound of the girls interrupted her thoughts as she looked towards the open window. Their voices drew her across the room where she stood gazing out at her beloved garden, upon their youthful banter as the girls chased each other around the lawns.

"God help them," she heard herself say, for they were only children at heart. Such dance and play tugged against realism, a world that saw these young women subjected to the humiliation of men's hidden sexual desires. Anger grew within her very soul – such innocence destroyed, she thought, and yet here they were like spring lambs with seemingly not a care in the world.

Her eyes settled upon the girl she'd fallen for, a young lady who in time may tire of an older woman's affections. She would soon realise she'd been sucked in by her own inexperienced emotions and would be compelled to politely shake her hand and move on. John also ran that same risk, and perhaps the two of them would end up alone regretting their foolish desires for other company, but for her there would be no regrets, she was certain. Susan had shown her who she really was and the life she'd already missed. Country folk would shame her, she was sure. Hypocrites! What went on behind their own closed doors would have little bearing on their opinions and most would regard her as an unforgiving charlatan, a home destroyer.

John, of course, would come out as the victor, wounded but with a fancy new young bride to show off to those who wished to admire and console. Life could be cruel within the boundaries of a small village.

And of the future, she was unsure. In some ways it didn't matter, for she was a great believer in the old saying, 'things will always turn out all right in the end'.

Chapter 37

Susan

The cold bitter wind of early winter froze the breath from Susan's exhaustion. She stood gazing across the bleak open fields of farms whose people had wisely retreated within the shelter of their barns and homes. Sam had baked Vincent a Christmas gift – thick layers of chocolate hid a moist sponge that would tempt even the hardiest of slimmers, but Susan could only think of the cold. She had to thank Sam's sound advice concerning her thick wrap-around clothing with matching fancy mittens – the severe bite in the air had shocked her at first. Being well-educated she should have known better, but youth had a tendency to overlook such matters. Even now her fingers and feet felt numb.

Thank goodness she only had to go out for pleasure. Tony hadn't been so lucky, as life was getting harder on the farm with the never-ending workload of feeding, bedding and twice-a-day milking. John's constant grumbling towards frozen water pipes hadn't gone unnoticed. Tony had taken it in her stride, stuck her head down against the prevailing winds and soldiered on, seemly relishing the opportunity to work alongside her chosen partner. Nothing had been said concerning Sam's relationship; if John knew he never mentioned it and Tony had said little about her and John's ongoing affair. But to Susan's eyes their bodies seemed too exhausted to even contemplate satisfying each other's sexual needs, although she had found relief in seeing them so much in tune with each other.

Susan braced herself for the razor-sharp winds that would almost certainly cut her like a knife the moment she stepped out into the open. She left the scant shelter of the stark branches, her hands and feet frozen she forged onwards.

The sight of Vincent's gate filled her with overwhelming joy, relief sending a shot of warmth racing through her body. Although the changing seasons had stripped all life from this once nature-rich garden, it still harboured a sense of warmth to those who dared to brave the wide open landscapes. She hurried along the path and quickly knocked loudly upon a white frosted door, waiting patiently until eventually it swung open.

"Bless my soul, girl, what on earth are you doing out in this weather?"

She kissed Vincent lightly on the cheek and braved a cold smile. "It's Sunday, Vincent. I always come on a Sunday, you know that."

The old man shook his head in disbelief. "You'll catch your death, young lady. Quick, now take those damp things off and warm up next to the fire. I do believe you young people have not an ounce of common sense."

Susan couldn't help noticing his ageing bones struggling to move around the room as he retreated back to the open flames that licked up the chimney. He was slowing up – it had been noticeable over the past few months, perhaps due to the weather – it was certainly enough to slow down even the hardiest of men let alone a frail old man, but that was not all it was.

The cake tin had been unceremoniously placed upon the small wooden table and there it sat, slowly thawing out while Susan warmed her hands in front of the fire. She casually glanced towards the tin. "Sam baked you a Christmas cake and asked if you would like to come round for the farm get-together on Christmas Eve?" She knew the answer before he even replied. Sam had warned her that he rarely accepted her invitations in the past, so it was unlikely he would say yes now. As predicted, his body language showed a man not wishing to leave his home for anyone, not even her.

"It's very kind of Samantha, but my busy schedule allows little time for socialising."

"Really, Vincent, you're impossible." With just a little annoyance she kept rubbing her hands, willing the pain in her fingertips to subside while the old man stayed silent. "Isn't it lonely here at Christmas without anyone around you?" she asked.

Vincent gazed into the flames, following their erratic movements, all the while trying to think about his next words. "I'm not alone, my dear. I have Alice."

"But Vincent, she's—"

He quickly held up his hand before she could finish, then gently tapped the side of his head. "She is here, my dear, in my mind. Memories as bright as if she were sitting beside us right now. You see, Susan, my dear, the older you get the clearer those memories become; it's the only good part of this existence of mine." His lips turned up a fraction with humour. "But sometimes, I can't even remember what I did yesterday. You may smile, young lady, but in many years' time you will understand." He drew a deep sorrowful breath. "Sometimes it's as if I can almost touch her, the visions are so real. Life is strange, isn't it?" He sat and gazed into the fire, his mind clearly wandering back in time. "Forgive me, my dear, I was miles away."

"Were you thinking of her?" Susan asked.

His eyes fell upon the beauty of the girl who sat beside him. "I always think of her, even after all these years, and there is never a day that goes by that I haven't cursed those responsible for her death." His fists clenched in anger, and a long drawn-out silence hung between them.

"If I may, I want to show you something." He pushed himself out of the chair and steadied himself until he was satisfied his posture would allow him to walk unaided.

Susan stayed silent; an offer of help, she was sure, would hurt the man's pride.

"I won't be long, my dear." Making his way across the room he vanished out of sight, leaving Susan to listen to his shuffling feet as she watched the fire slowly burn down.

Minutes later Vincent returned, grasping something

in his weathered hand. It was a black and white photo of a young woman wearing a light summer dress almost identical to the one Susan had worn that first time she had walked up the garden path. The girl's hair was pinned back, showing a smile of someone who clearly loved life. Susan's hand flew to her mouth as she gasped in shock – it was as if she was gazing down at a small handheld mirror. "Vincent, I don't know what to say. She's so beautiful."

"As are you, dear."

"But the dress, I don't understand?"

The old man rested back in his chair seemingly searching for an answer, an explanation, something to offer this girl who had entered into his life. "I fear I have no answer."

Susan ran her fingers around the glass frame, hoping perhaps for a sign from the girl who stared back at her, but of course there was none. "Tell me about her, Vincent." She knew he wanted to talk and there was something that told her she had little to fear from making such a personal request.

He sat, pushing himself to speak, willing his ageing body to honour his Alice, her true nature, that spirit that woke him at night. Peering into the flickering light, he told himself not to hold back but to tell of her short but wonderful life. The glow of the fire reflected in his eyes as he felt a distinct concern for the past, nervously fumbling with his hands.

"Go on, Vincent, it's all right."

He drew a breath before speaking. "I was only fourteen at the time. Her father worked for mine, an office manager. Father had invited the more prominent of the company's employees to the house in London. I had little interest in such things, preferring to spend my hours in the garden studying the real world; nature has always fascinated me."

Susan saw his face soften slightly.

"Alice was brought along under protest, so I believe, and on arrival had been sent outside while business was discussed. She too loved the nature of a summer garden. At sixteen she was a beauty to behold and I can remember seeing her for the first time, her head bent forward taking in the scent of a single white rose. I had been watching a wasp attacking, then dissecting a fly section by section; quite fascinating. We both looked at each other and for a brief moment our eyes locked as one; something I will never forget. I'm sure we must have stood there a good minute or so before she finally wandered over and introduced herself. She was a forthright young lady, but I soon found out she also had the temperament of an angel. We talked about this and that, the time seemed to go so fast, and then she was gone, summonsed back to the house to leave with her father.

"I thought often about her as I drifted through life, rebelling against my father's wishes to join the family company. My love lay in the growing wonders of the land, not factories. It was some three years later; I had reached the grand age of seventeen. My studies had led me to believe I wanted to immerse myself into the world of nature. Father had finally relented, or just given up on me, so I was at last allowed to do what I wanted, but unrest in Europe saw people's lives and ambitions put on hold, mine included. There were now thousands of young men enlisting, willing to go to fight. For many it was a big adventure, a chance to see the world. We were told it would be over in no time, but history never lies and with the loss of so many workers I was told to buckle down and do my bit for the family business, and that is when I met Alice again. She too had been brought in, along with hundreds of other women, to work the factory floor. She was nineteen and even more beautiful than I had remembered. We started seeing each other with the occasional trip to the cinema, park walks, nothing serious.

"I remember I just couldn't believe she hadn't found herself a young man, but when asked she informed me no one had come up to her high expectations. Of course I felt honoured to be selected, if only on a friendship basis."

Susan couldn't help a light chuckle. Selected, she thought, it sounded like he was off to a cricket match.

"I see you find something amusing, my dear."

"Sorry, Vincent, it just doesn't sound a romantic way to start a relationship. Selected, I mean."

"Oh, I see. No, I suppose it doesn't, but that's how it was in those days. People had far more respect for one another. I admit I have little contact with others, but I do read the papers."

He leant forward and placed another log on the fire, allowing Susan to encourage him to go on. "Please, Vincent, I'm sorry I interrupted." The old man tried to retrace his steps, looking for a slot in his past that would allow him to pick up from where he had left off.

"Ah, yes. I was, as I have said, honoured to be 'considered', shall we say, and we spent the next year just getting to know each other while the world went mad. I was still determined not to fight, but I'm afraid the pressure upon my family and myself became too great to bear and with such heavy losses I had to join before they forced me to go, if only to save the reputation of the family.

"I was eighteen, Alice twenty. She pleaded with me not to go but it was too late, the wheels of bureaucracy had started to turn and before I knew it I was in Europe fighting a mindless senseless war that nobody wanted but no one could stop. I received letters telling me she had become close to my parents and they were very fond of her, realising perhaps that she may possibly become their future daughter-in-law. Her father had become a director so our match was very much approved, I believe. Alice had even been offered a room in my parents' home.

"I desperately wanted to see her, hold her in my arms, tell that bubbly young girl that I loved her, perhaps before it was too late. With so many dying I had to face up to reality that my chances were slim at best." He paused for a moment. "Then one day I decided to write, asking her to marry me. It was a selfish act of madness on my part, expecting someone to commit themselves to a possible corpse, but I had to have something to hold on to."

Susan could see he was hurting inside, desperate to offload the burden that had plagued him all these years.

"It was months," he continued, "before I had a reply, yet I can remember the sheer joy upon receiving that letter. Yes, she had said, with all her heart. This was the sign, I felt sure of it, that we would be together again one day." His vision wandered back to the open fire yet there was no warmth in his eyes. "But it wasn't to be. I later learnt that Alice and my parents had been killed trying to leave London for the safety of the countryside."

Susan saw the whites of his knuckles against the dim light of the room as they formed a solid mass of bone beneath the wrinkled exterior of his anger.

"Took a direct hit, you see." His voice stumbled with sorrow and loss, his breathing shallow as he struggled to control the rage against years of regret. "The three people most close to me gone in the blink of an eye, vanished as if their lives, their presence on this earth had never been. I was left with nothing, not even bodies to place in the ground, just cold empty gravestones to talk to."

His body slumped with exhaustion, prompting Susan to rise from her chair and kneel down beside him. She took hold of his limp hand and gently placed the photo frame into it. She said nothing, for this wasn't a time for words of comfort, this was Vincent's time of memories, pain and anger. She watched as the dwindling flames struggled to put out warmth, but felt no chill, just the heat from a broken heart of a man who wanted to die and finally be with the one he loved.

Chapter 38

Christmas

It was Christmas Eve and the house had been
decorated from top to bottom. The girls had insisted
that every scrap of tinsel, every dented bauble, be
ceremoniously placed upon a tree John had been sent
out to chop down. Tick still concerned him, although
he hadn't heard nor seen anything of her, and true to
her word the woman had deposited regular amounts
of cash on a weekly basis. Yet on his search for
that perfect Yuletide specimen he'd noticed the rising
smoke of a winter fire as it filtered through open
tree tops. Like a frightened deer, his overactive mind
had bombarded every nerve in his body, throwing
his brain into unnecessary chaos. The slightest rustle,
the odd snap of a branch had him leaving his own
woodland at speed, hastily dragging the first available
green specimen he could lay his hands on only to be
reprimanded over its slightly lop-sided appearance.
To John it was a tree, and surely that's all that
mattered.

He now sat at the head of the dining room table
contemplating the world. The women were all in
the kitchen helping with the washing up from the
annual farm get-together. It had gone well, with those
present revelling in the Christmas spirit. George had
brought his wife Margaret along, a large portly sort
of woman who reminded John of a rather overweight
hippopotamus, her rosy red cheeks matching a tightly
fitting dress that barely managed to conceal a pair of

breasts the size of elephant ears. George himself sat like a proper gentlemen, well turned out in a brilliant white starched shirt, tailor-made set of braces and a tartan tie to match.

Mother had dressed to impress, her fancy frock and bright burgundy lipstick positively glowing as she revelled in her role of head lady of all around her, and dear Josh had taken little persuading to accept his invitation when informed there would be as much food as he could eat providing he used a knife and fork. Sadie had come alone, Lizzie sending her apologies stating a nasty cold.

John had watched with intense interest at the closeness of his wife and Susan, their body language of two females clearly very fond of each other. It had been subtle but noticeable, given the luxury of time, to sit and observe that their hands had brushed against one another on more than a few occasions, and there was something in their eyes that got John wondering. But then what did he know about women?

He was well aware of Sam's loss now that Luke had gone travelling, so perhaps it was to be expected that she felt a need to protect, become a mother figure to the younger ones. One thing he did know about women was they were more inclined to look like more than just good friends to their own sex, yet have no hidden emotional attachment. Men were different – show such fondness to another male and instantly alarm bells would ring, being seen as a blatant act of gay tendencies. How different men and women were, he thought.

His mind drifted to the face of the girl he'd fallen for and he could remember wondering how Sam would react if she found out about his intimate relationship with another woman. His intentions to have a little play on the side like his grandfather had somehow gone seriously wrong. A mistress to satisfy his sexual needs was one thing, but this? Strangely, even right from the start, it had never been just about pure lust, the need to allow a beautiful young woman to take him to a place where his wife had never even attempted to venture, although that side of it had been quite extraordinary.

No, he had simply fallen for her charmed nature, that easy-going person who seemed to slot in so well into his way of thinking, and he'd found himself falling uncontrollably into a tangled web with a girl who not only satisfied his male needs, but filled that want for company. Her relentless drive to immerse herself into country life had taken his breath away and sent him to a place that made him want to shout out with joy. Sam had never done that, not even at the beginning; it was as if she just couldn't let him have her whole self. There was certainly no such problem with Tony, but surely this was madness. Why would someone half his age be interested in him? It just didn't make sense. Perhaps she just admired him, that's what it was all about, a passing crush for an older man. He'd heard of things like that happening but rarely did it last, there were just too many obstacles to climb to be successful. Listen to him, a middle-aged fool drooling over a pretty young thing. Such an idiot he'd become, and did he want it anyway?

He stared at the empty table, the chairs pushed out haphazardly. Yes, he did, with every bone in his body. He wanted her so much it hurt just thinking about it. Why couldn't he get her out of his head? The sight of her naked body, the way she ran her hands over his, the smell of her hair. Dear God, yes, he needed her.

"Ah, there you are, dear."

His mother's voice shook him back into the real world as he sat desperately trying to hide his hardened state. "Mother, you're back. I didn't expect to see you again this evening." The woman walked towards him and placed a wrapped parcel upon the table.

"Early Christmas present, dear. I didn't want to give it to you in front of everyone – family is one thing, but staff? Quite out of the question, as you will understand when you open it."

He looked at the neatly presented gift. "Mother, you shouldn't have. What is it?"

"Really, John, have you not learnt the art of Christmas yet? You open it, that's how these things work. It won't jump out by itself and dance upon the table unless you give it a hand."

This was exciting, he thought, his first present, and like a child studying forbidden gifts under the tree before the big day, his mind bubbled with curiosity. "I don't know, perhaps I should wait until tomorrow."

"John, open it. You're not five now, I've got things to do."

Her stern voice warned him not to argue, and with a little of the sparkle now gone from her initial friendly gesture, he slowly reached out and slid a finger beneath the festive wrapping allowing its contents to roll out. "What's this, Mother?" He watched in surprise as a bundle of fifty-pound notes security fastened by an elastic band tumbled onto the table.

"I know it's not much, dear, but it might help keep the rear leg of a cow from the knacker's yard."

John was confused. "I can't take this – the farm's doing all right now. It's a very nice thought, but seriously, we're doing okay."

His mother sat down and looked him straight in the eye. "Nonsense, John, do you honestly think I was going to let those two young ladies have all the fun? I may be old, but I can still do my bit. After all, a woman has needs, even at my age. Your father could be a very passionate man, and a woman can miss such things. There was many a time when he—"

"Mother! Please. I don't want to know, and I'm seriously having trouble understanding what you're trying to tell me."

"His name is Randy and he comes from Texas."

"Who's from Texas and who's Randy?"

"Yes, I thought I'd get this reaction." She pushed back in her chair looking irritated. "For someone who is supposed to be in charge of the farm, you're rather dim. Randy is a man."

"A man?"

"Please stop repeating me, it's awfully annoying, and if you'd let me finish I can explain. He's American, John, and quite well off as it happens, drives a very impressive BMW, you should see the leather interior."

"Mother! I'd rather not discuss another man's upholstery if you don't mind, and why has he given you all this money?"

His question was met with a look sheer disbelief. "Have you not worked it out yet? I got paid, dear boy, for favours. I think that's the best way to put it."

"Favours?"

"There you go again."

"But Mother." John sat digesting the information he'd been given and then slowly a look of utter horror formed upon his face.

"Ah, I see you've finally worked it out."

"No, Mother! You haven't!"

"I haven't what, dear?" Her expression showed a woman who was rather pleased with her efforts and no matter what her son's next words were, she had enjoyed every last minute of it.

"No, Mother, you haven't sold your body for money!"

She simply nodded. "Finally, he's cottoned on. Bravo, dear. Yes, John, I got paid for sex. Should have done it years ago, quite invigorating as it happens and it's even done my bad back the world of good."

"But ..."

"Yes, dear?"

"B ... but you're my mother! You can't do things like that!"

"And why not? You're only too happy to let those poor innocent young girls do your dirty work for you, so what's the difference with me? Anyway, you should be pleased someone's prepared to part with hard-earned cash for an older body like mine."

"But you're my mother! Oh God, what would Father have said if he knew you'd turned to prostitution."

"John, I won't have that word used, you know I find it quite vulgar."

John clutched his throbbing head as he tried to come to terms with his mother's confession. "What have I done?" he wailed. "My own mother!"

They were interrupted by the women, concerned by the raised voices. "Everything all right?" Sam asked, noting her husband's strange posture.

"It's fine, Samantha, I've just told John about Randy and I fear he's not taken it too well."

Her son lifted his head and sat, staring. "You all know?"

They all nodded, leaving Sam to try and communicate with a man who looked like his world had just exploded. "I'm sorry, John, your mother wanted to keep it a secret just in case it didn't work out. Randy is a very nice man, you should be happy for her."

"No. I can't cope with this, and what sort of name is Randy, for Christ's sake?"

His mother smiled. "Actually quite an appropriate one."

"No, Mother, please. I can't take any more." He rose from his chair. "I need some fresh air."

Sam grabbed Susan's hand and looked at Tony. "I think you'd better go and see to him."

Tony nodded gratefully at Sam's discreet acceptance of her relationship with John. "Thank you."

Sylvia could only raise an eyebrow as the young woman left the room. "Well, well! I see I'm not the only one with secrets."

Chapter 39

John

Crisp virgin snow lay thick and drifted upon frozen ground, its white overnight blanket partially shielding the countryside from the harsh bitter winds of mid-winter, so utterly perfect for those who wished to enjoy its beauty with a brisk morning walk.

John stood alone, his eyes closed, allowing his other senses to pick up every last detail of his surroundings. It never ceased to amaze him how wonderful this place he called home was, even without the ability to gaze upon its beauty. He needed to think, assess his life and those who walked beside him, to take a moment out of his busy day to clear the mind and soak up his good fortune. He wanted to force those worries and concerns into a darkened corner to be forgotten, just for a short while, leaving him the pleasure of absolute solitude.

A long ice-chilled breath filled his lungs, reminding him of the harsh winter toll, and yet he allowed himself to wander back in time to long-lost hot summer days. Of paddling as a child through crystal clear streams in search of freshwater life, of everlasting harvests and of innocent courting days watching the late evening sun dance between the pale green leaves of the beech while his head rested upon the rhythmic heartbeat of the girl he would eventually call his wife. But something was missing. A face? He searched but found nothing, only the smile of the young woman who'd now captured his very soul.

He sighed, for he knew upon opening his eyes he would be dragged back into the real world, a world of uncertainty and doubt, a world of romantic conflicts the likes he had never experienced before. There were those who would undoubtedly criticise the path he so desperately wanted to walk, but that didn't seem to matter any more.

Eyes slowly opening, he caught the bright glare of the sun as it reflected off pure white lands, making him want to retreat back into the world of uncompromising dreams, but that luxury wasn't to be. He felt overwhelming pride and gratitude towards his father and grandfather – two men to whom he owed so much, for it was mornings like this that sent a short sharp shock of contentment racing into his veins. What the future held, he was unsure.

A new farm year beckoned, but there was one thing he was certain of. This was where he belonged. This was home.